Nebula Awards 28

Nebula Awards

28

SFWA's Choices

for the Best

Science Fiction

and Fantasy

of the Year

E D I T E D   B Y

James Morrow

Harcourt Brace & Company

New York   San Diego   London

Requests for permission to make copies of any part of the work should be mailed
to: Permissions Department, Harcourt Brace & Company, 6277 Sea Harbor Drive,
Orlando, Florida 32887-6777.

The Library of Congress has cataloged this serial as follows:
The Nebula awards.—No. 18—New York [N.Y.]: Arbor House, c1983—
v.; 22cm.
Annual.
Published: San Diego, Calif.: Harcourt Brace & Company, 1984–
Published for: Science-fiction and Fantasy Writers of America, 1983–
Continues: Nebula award stories (New York, N.Y.: 1982)
ISSN 0741-5567 = The Nebula awards
1. Science fiction, American—Periodicals.
I. Science-fiction and Fantasy Writers of America.
PS648.S3N38   83-647399
813'.0876'08—dc19
AACR 2 MARC-S
Library of Congress [8709r84]rev
ISBN 0-15-100082-4
ISBN 0-15-600039-3 (Harvest: pbk.)

Designed by G. B. D. Smith
Printed in the United States of America
First edition
A B C D E

Permissions acknowledgments appear on page 329, which constitutes a continuation
of the copyright page.

In Memory of
Fritz Leiber
1910–1992

Contents

Introduction

JAMES MORROW

To the medieval troubadour, secure in his Christianity, winning a Nebula Award would not mean much. Who cares about a seven-pound block of Lucite when you're bound for the Heavenly Kingdom? But to the modern artist, not to mention the modern athlete, soldier, politician, scientist, or scholar, accolades matter terribly. The Age of Faith, in short, has been supplanted by the Age of Awards—Pulitzers, Pushcarts, Purple Hearts, Oscars, Tonys, Hugos, Edgars, Nobels, America's Cups, Super Bowl Rings—and rare is the practitioner who does not covet formal recognition by his public or his peers.

Physicist Edward Harrison discusses this shift in his marvelous history of science, *Masks of the Universe*. Writing of the Enlightenment, Harrison notes:

> Instead of Judgment and the award of treasure in Heaven, the deists believed in Posterity and the award of treasured memory on Earth. Judgment by posterity, which I shall call *the principle of pharaonic immortality*, has become one of the main driving forces in the modern world.
>
> "The king whose achievements are talked about does not die," recorded Sesostris I, and the inscribed annals of Thutmose III were placed in his sanctuary "that he might be given life for ever." The deists, like the Egyptian pharaohs of the second millennium B.C., believed that immortality lies not in another world but in the memory of generations to come.
>
> Belief in pharaonic immortality has gained widespread acceptance in modern times. The heavenly rewards of the Eternal City have become myths; in their place honors, prizes, and Emmy awards abound in the Earthly City, nourishing the need for fulfillment and serving as insignia for the attention of posterity. When distinguished persons die, glowing obituaries and biographies are written, memorials erected, and commemorative prizes instituted. Thus is their memory preserved, and they have life ever after.

It's difficult to read the above passage without feeling a little wistful. An Emmy is a pretty pathetic substitute for an Eternal City, even if Emmys are real and Eternal Cities aren't. Indeed, in many quarters the loss of the Christian consensus has proven intolerable—

so intolerable that, concomitant with the rise of science, the West has also witnessed on ongoing, robust, and passionate critique of science. The purveyors of this critique vary tremendously in their sophistication—recent decades have brought us everything from the nuanced assaults on modernity mounted by Ivan Illich, Walker Percy, and Lewis Mumford to the food for thoughtlessness served up by Jeremy Rifkin—but in each case the message is more or less the same. For science's critics, the apple that Eve devoured in Paradise enjoyed an equally notorious career several millennia later, dropping within Isaac Newton's field of vision and seeding a Second Fall: our lapse into materialistic, reductionist, "clockwork" ways of knowing the world.

The science-fiction medium, it seems to me, is particularly well equipped to engage this vital debate. An intelligent SF story can tell us more about the splendors and pitfalls of the scientific enterprise than we'll ever get from books like—to name the latest best-seller that attributes all our contemporary woes to rationality and empiricism—Bryan Appleyard's *Understanding the Present: Science and the Soul of Modern Man*. This observation of mine is not a call for action; it is a report on what is actually happening. Perusing the catalog of finalists for the twenty-eighth annual Nebula Awards, one notes a fascinating fact. The vast majority of these works implicitly or explicitly grapple with the question, Is science good or bad?

FOR NOVEL

A Million Open Doors by John Barnes (Tor)
Sarah Canary by Karen Joy Fowler (Holt)
China Mountain Zhang by Maureen F. McHugh (Tor)
A Fire Upon the Deep by Vernor Vinge (Tor)
°*Doomsday Book* by Connie Willis (Bantam)
Briar Rose by Jane Yolen (Tor)

° Indicates winner.

FOR NOVELLA

"Silver or Gold" by Emma Bull (*After the King*, Tor)
"The Territory" by Bradley Denton (*Fantasy and Science Fiction*, July 1992)
"Protection" by Maureen F. McHugh (*Isaac Asimov's Science Fiction Magazine*, April 1992)
*"City of Truth" by James Morrow (St. Martin's Press)
"Contact" by Jerry Oltion and Lee Goodloe (*Analog*, November 1991)
"Barnacle Bill the Spacer" by Lucius Shepard (*Isaac Asimov's Science Fiction Magazine*, July 1992)
"Griffin's Egg" by Michael Swanwick (St. Martin's Press; *Isaac Asimov's Science Fiction Magazine*, May 1992)

FOR NOVELETTE

"Matter's End" by Gregory Benford (*Full Spectrum 3*, Bantam)
"The July Ward" by S. N. Dyer (*Isaac Asimov's Science Fiction Magazine*, April 1991)
"The Honeycrafters" by Carolyn Gilman (*Fantasy and Science Fiction*, October/November 1991)
*"Danny Goes to Mars" by Pamela Sargent (*Isaac Asimov's Science Fiction Magazine*, October 1992)
"Suppose They Gave a Peace" by Susan Shwartz (*Alternate Presidents*, Tor)
"Prayers on the Wind" by Walter Jon Williams (*When the Music's Over*, Bantam)

FOR SHORT STORY

"Life Regarded as a Jigsaw Puzzle of Highly Lustrous Cats" by Michael Bishop (*Omni*, September 1991)
"Lennon Spex" by Paul Di Filippo (*Amazing Stories*, July 1992)
"The Mountain to Mohammed" by Nancy Kress (*Isaac Asimov's Science Fiction Magazine*, April 1992)
"Vinland the Dream" by Kim Stanley Robinson (*Isaac Asimov's Science Fiction Magazine*, November 1991)

"The Arbitrary Placement of Walls" by Martha Soukup (*Isaac Asimov's Science Fiction Magazine,* April 1992)
°"Even the Queen" by Connie Willis (*Isaac Asimov's Science Fiction Magazine,* April 1992)

When I sat down to assemble *Nebula Awards 28,* I had no particular intention of showcasing the genre's ability to analyze our Enlightenment heritage. *Understanding the Present* had not yet crossed the Atlantic, and Jeremy Rifkin had somehow lost his ability to irritate me. And yet, as it happened, each of the nominees I found most worthy of inclusion had, beyond its more immediate agenda, something provocative to say about the nature of science.

Gregory Benford's "Matter's End," for example, illuminates the scientific mind-set—its glories and also its limitations—with a knowledgeability that leaves Appleyard and Rifkin in the shadows. S. N. Dyer's "The July Ward" deals poignantly and chillingly with the issue of doctors' fallibility. In a similar vein, Kim Stanley Robinson's "Vinland the Dream" demonstrates how scientists, like everyone else, can become prey to hoaxes from without and wishful thinking from within.

Nancy Kress's "The Mountain to Mohammed" warns us of the cruel misuses to which human genome mapping might be put in the not-too-distant future. Michael Bishop's "Life Regarded as a Jigsaw Puzzle of Highly Lustrous Cats" explores the cryptic condition known as schizophrenia, steering between the romantic view of madness that informs plays like *Equus* and the neurochemical interpretation offered by medical science. In "Lennon Spex," Paul Di Filippo dramatizes a truth lamentably lost on Appleyard and his disciples: science will never tell us—and, more importantly, does not presume to tell us—anything about the soul.

The three winning works collected in this volume add their own unique voices to the discourse. Pamela Sargent's "Danny Goes to Mars" deftly satirizes the appalling scientific illiteracy of our republic's most recent ex–Vice President. Connie Willis's "Even the Queen" scores those who accuse medical intervention of being ipso facto repressive (even as they fetishize Nature's ways as intrinsically desirable). And in "City of Truth," the present writer wrestles with the fashionable but highly problematic notion of a binding reciprocity between a person's mental outlook and his physical well-being. The dangers implicit in New Age pseudoscience, I feel, are no less pernicious than those posed by Old Age fundamentalism.

This is my final performance as editor of the Nebula series, and I want to thank the people who made the job easier: my wife, Jean, who handled the correspondence; my immediate predecessors, George Zebrowski and Michael Bishop, who unselfishly offered their advice; and my editor, John Radziewicz, who never allowed me to confuse the deadline with the actual deadline. If I have made some unusual intellectual and emotional experiences available to the readers of *Nebula Awards 26*, *Nebula Awards 27*, and *Nebula Awards 28*, simultaneously giving the several dozen authors anthologized therein some measure of pharaonic immortality, then my efforts of these past three years will have been eminently worthwhile.

—*State College, Pennsylvania*
June 11, 1993

Nebula Awards 28

Is Science Fiction Out to Lunch? Some Thoughts on the Year 1992

JOHN CLUTE

Retired from service, the average hardcover book will function adequately as a doorstop. The recently published second edition of *The Encyclopedia of Science Fiction*, edited by John Clute and Peter Nicholls, could prop open the Gates of Gaza. Sheer bulk, of course, is not what makes this volume such a definitive reference. The book's true worth lies in its astonishing erudition and manifest thoroughness.

John Clute was a natural choice to coedit *The Encyclopedia of Science Fiction*. For thirty years he has been a passionate interpreter of popular literature, providing the SF field with portraits of itself that are sometimes exhilarating, sometimes exasperating, but always instructive. On more than one occasion, he has been called "the best science-fiction reviewer now active."

A founder of the most important British SF magazine, *Interzone*, Clute has also been employed as the reviews editor of the critical journal *Foundation*. His work has enlivened the pages of *Omni*, the *Times Literary Supplement*, the *New York Times*, the *Washington Post*, and many other periodicals. *Strokes*, a collection of his essays, appeared in 1988.

Writing of himself in *The Encyclopedia of Science Fiction*, Clute notes that "despite some studiously flamboyant obscurities," his criticism "remains essentially practical."

It gets easier and easier to say. Hell hell hell, lackaday, here we are in the nineties. Sliding down the scree. Ozone depletion. Global warming. What a fine mess. I mean, look at our precious science-fictional dreams, which are deserting the world as surely as the gods left Alexandria. Where can the field go, now that all its futures have become untrue? Who will buy our sick old swayback visions, beyond the million children so profoundly cynical we cannot understand their tongues, or the knives they wear on their sleeves, or the deaths they contemplate for us? So the litany goes, and who's prepared to contradict it as we continue to slide, eyes burning from the increasingly naked sun, into the clutches of the new era? Who's willing to argue

1

against our instinct that, even with the help of all the thoughts of every SF story ever written, we're simply not going to discern the light at the end of the tunnel until it's far too late to dodge the oncoming locomotive?

Though sales remain high, the genre is clearly in crisis. I, among others, have tended to think that over the past decade or so the old "agenda" SF has aged—prematurely, and at a savage rate—into a purveyor of nostalgic pabulum for consumers, and that the form of SF that Jack Williamson helped invent has become something like a poison fossil. Science fiction, born to advocate and enthuse and teach, has come by century's end, it seems, to lay a mummy's curse upon the new. Despite occasional fresh words from those who continue to write as though SF were a Door in the Wall, most of what is published is now industrial-base frozen food, portion-controlled, Sanisealed, and sharecropped, spilling like plastic hot-dogs from a million identical slots in a million vending machines.

On the other hand, might there be a whiff of redemption in all of this? Consider what happened to our green planet just after that big rock dusted off the dinosaurs (though nothing, unfortunately, has managed to stifle the remake). What happened was mammals (whom God defends), and suddenly it was a new ball game. Dinosaurs may have ruled for millions of years, employing neat metabolic-shutdown routines to maintain their huge size without burning up in June, but they were hopelessly bad at cognition and socializing. They ate, but they didn't do lunch. Mammals (I am one) are the *developers* of the animal kingdom. The difference between a dinosaur and a mammal is the difference between a mesa and Mesa Plaza. It is a distinction that might also be used to separate agenda SF from the kind of tale that should be winning prizes. The best SF being fashioned today, in other words, is like a squabble of shrews in a Mesozoic midden: it will eat anything.

In various pieces written over the past few years, I've suggested, not entirely tongue-in-cheek, that a fondness for the more ravenous varieties of SF expresses our need as readers to look for stimuli beyond the metabolic-shutdown torpor of the usual tropes; we want the genre to transcend its genome. It seemed to me that traditional SF had illuminated and given shape to the dreams of a particular historical moment, but now that moment was gone. It seemed that human beings, whose driving ambitions had earlier in this century been quite adequately articulated by the genre, were no longer likely to learn very much from the triumphalist agenda of the old SF: from the antique Future Histories we clung to like monkeys to a rotten tree; from the provincial species chauvinism that envisioned human empires replicating, throughout the galaxy, the demolition of the American West—a chauvinism that simultaneously prompted SF to ignore the very revolutions in biology that, as a genre pretending to explore the unknown, it should have conspicuously been attempting to interpret. It seemed to me, therefore, that the field needed to marry out, garnering energy and ideas from other disciplines as it taught us how to transcend our bodies, how to migrate into cyberspace like Irish immigrants fleeing a potato famine. To wit, SF needed to reconstitute itself as a series of fables of exogamy, and in fact (I've said) SF could be *defined* as fables of exogamy. This argument (I needn't be told) overstated the case and exaggerated the solutions. Today it might be better to think of exogamousness as but one strategy by which a valuable literature might survive and thrive into the next century, continually finding ways to eat its body weight daily. But right now we are famished. We have no trick of metabolic shutdown. We must reimagine the universe, or we shall soon be chewing our own vitals.

In 1992 about 700 novels were published in English in the various literatures of the fantastic—broadly science fiction, fantasy, and horror—and of these maybe 200 to 250 were strictly SF; and of that total maybe 30 to 50 books were worth reading. And of *that* total, maybe three to five will survive. Or maybe ten. Looking into 1992 was like looking into a tidal pool as the waters begin to ebb, exposing the more fragile niche species to the dry death. Singletons were particularly vulnerable; and melancholy, overspecialized, midlist creatures could be seen finning the air, brokenly. More durable were the shoal—or series—species, impossible to tell apart, each individual specimen instantly replaceable if losses were incurred. Overall there was considerable activity, without action. There was, in other words, a sense that the churned and fecund tidal pool of SF was waiting for something to happen, some direction home. It might be the Millennium: because it's soon, and we've all psyched ourselves into a state of self-fulfilling anticipation about the end of time. It might be the draining of the pool: because the recent downsizing of Bantam Books might well be contagious. It might be a new *style* of doing SF, like cyberpunk a decade earlier: to which the packagers would cling like remora, till the style sank. It might be some new writer heroine or hero: because there seemed to be a lot of talent around, though no shaping voice yet. Indeed, there were more SF writers of stature, potential or earned, capable of writing at or near their best level, than the genre had ever before harbored, perhaps. So the pool was indeed churning, but it could not be said that during 1992 it was possible to discern the shape of things to come, the demands we would have to meet as we advanced onto the steel beach, or as the steel beach—for time enters us these days—invaded our souls.

Perhaps we should remind ourselves of the brightness and confusion of the range of books published. SF novels of interest that first appeared in 1992 included Douglas Adams's *Mostly Harmless* (Heinemann); Isaac Asimov and Robert Silverberg's *The Positronic Man* (Gollancz); John Barnes's *A Million Open Doors* (Tor), a Nebula nominee; William Barton's *Dark Sky Legion: An Ahrimanic Novel* (Bantam); Greg Bear's *Anvil of Stars* (Legend); Michael Bishop's *Count Geiger's Blues* (Tor); James P. Blaylock's *Lord Kelvin's Machine* (Arkham House); Pat Cadigan's *Fools* (Bantam); Orson Scott Card's *Homecoming #1: The Memory of Earth* (Tor); two from C. J. Cherryh: *Chanur's Legacy* (DAW) and *Hellburner* (New English Library); Stephen R. Donaldson's *The Gap into Power* (Bantam); Greg Egan's *Quarantine* (Legend); Karen Joy Fowler's Nebula-nominated *Sarah Canary* (Holt, actually published in 1991); Mark S. Geston's *Mirror to the Sky* (AvoNova); Richard Grant's *Through the Heart* (Bantam); Alasdair Gray's *Poor Things* (Harcourt Brace & Company); Joe Haldeman's *Worlds Enough and Time* (Morrow); Elizabeth Hand's *Aestival Tide* (Bantam); Robert Harris's *Fatherland* (Hutchinson); Alexander Jablokov's *A Deeper Sea* (AvoNova); Ken Kesey's *Sailor Song* (Viking); Damon Knight's *Why Do Birds* (Tor); Ian MacDonald's *Hearts, Hands and Voices* (Gollancz; published in U.S.A. as *The Broken Land*, Bantam); Maureen F. McHugh's Nebula-nominated *China Mountain Zhang* (Tor); Julian May's *Jack the Bodiless* (Knopf); Judith Moffett's *Time, Like an Ever-Rolling Stream* (St. Martin's); James Morrow's *City of Truth* (Legend, 1990, but a Nebula winner after U.S. publication this year); Kim Newman's *Anno Dracula* (Simon & Schuster UK); Frederik Pohl's *Mining the Oort* (Del Rey); Tim Powers's *Last Call* (Morrow); Daniel Quinn's *Ishmael* (Bantam); Kim Stanley Robinson's *Red Mars* (HarperCollins); Richard Paul Russo's *Destroying Angel* (Headline); Charles Sheffield's *Cold as Ice* (Tor); Robert Silverberg's *Kingdoms of the Wall* (HarperCollins); two from Dan Simmons: *Children of the Night* (Putnam) and *The Hollow Man* (Bantam); Norman Spinrad's *Deus X* (Bantam); Neal Stephenson's *Snow Crash* (Bantam); two from Sheri S. Tepper: *Beauty* (Foundation Doubleday) and *Sideshow* (Bantam); Jack Vance's *Throy* (Underwood-Miller); Vernor Vinge's Nebula-nominated *A Fire Upon the Deep* (Tor); Walter Jon Williams's *Aristoi* (Tor); Jack Williamson's *Beachhead* (Tor) and Connie Willis's Nebula-winning *Doomsday Book* (Bantam).

That's almost fifty books. Some represent eccentric likings on my part, or a sense of what is SF and what is not that might offend some readers: why should I include Newman's *Anno Dracula* and leave out Anne Rice's *The Tale of the Body Thief*? I do so because one is an alternate history and the other is not, but that could easily seem perverse to a stricter eye. But let us say, for the sake of the argument, that the fifty constitute a fair and not excessively loony canon of the best SF published in 1992. The first thing that comes to mind is a sense of the almost lubricious heterogeneity of the mix: hard SF, and vampire suckers; space opera, and steampunk; agenda SF trumpeting out a final clarion call or two, and science fantasy doing a chaste riff; dystopias and planetary romances and cyberpunk runs and juveniles and time-travel and grunge. The second thing that comes to mind is how very fine some of these novels are, how lovingly constructed, how much of a gift they constitute. The third thing is the old realization that significance and worth are not synonymous, because the most significant of these novels, John Varley's *Steel Beach*, is by no means the best.

But *Steel Beach* is the one novel of 1992 that comprehensively faces every possible direction, backward and forward, agenda and mammal, cliché and thrust, known and unknown. It's set in the underground civilization humanity has established in the Moon, a century or so after our expulsion from Earth: it is, in other words, a tale out of the middle of Varley's Eight Planets Future History, though with a few postmodernist continuity glitches, so that we know we're in a real novel, not a shoal. The narrator's name is Hildy, and she/ he's a reporter (like the original Hildy in Ben Hecht and Charles MacArthur's *The Front Page* [1928]). As we experience her slow but inexorable comprehension of the true nature of the Lunar politics and economics, we find ourselves immersed in agenda SF's easy assumptions about the legibility of the universe. Moreover, this Lunar world gives off an eerie Heinleinian glow, as does Hildy himself in the cocky slang of the voice in which he tells us his tale. So *Steel Beach sounds* very backwards, from the word go. At the same time, however, something very different is being exposed. What we learn first in the understory is that Hildy feels so utterly depressed and defeated by her life that she is constantly in the throes of attempting to commit suicide. What we learn second is that the entire edifice of *Steel Beach* is a kind of prophylactic apparatus to fend off terminus: the huge odds against the survival of the human race upon the steel beach of the future. (The image comes from the beach to which the first lungfish clung, and suggests that the human race is in a similar survive-or-die position on an even harsher strand.) As a text, *Steel Beach* reads like an enchantment against suicide, a magic charm whose main claim to our attention is the author's manifest pain. It is, all in all, one of the bleakest texts in the history of genre SF, and, as the 1990s progress, it will be a vital book for us to understand.

Kim Stanley Robinson's *Red Mars* also looks like agenda SF. But unlike Varley in his terminal wrestle with melancholia, the author does not take us through his tale like Clint Eastwood killing Fords in a demolition derby. At the end of *Red Mars* there is still a world we can read: a twenty-first-century civilization that has begun to settle the next planet out. The bravery of the text lies in its departure from one of the more streamlined assumptions of the old SF: that the interval between landing on Mars and having battles there with dragon ladies will pass in the twinkling of an auctorial eye. In this book, nothing is accomplished easily on Mars, because everything that happens there continues the inextricable tangles of our own human history on planet three. *Red Mars* could plausibly be described as a "real" novel in genre clothing—except Kim Stanley Robinson would not accept the point of such a distinction, nor, on reflection, would I. In the end, what marks *Red Mars* off from most SF novels about conquering the solar system is its dynaflow enrichment of all the seams of extrapolation, so that, in the end, it reads like a chymic marriage of mainstream novel and genre tour de force.

Also told in clear was Vernor Vinge's huge and exuberant *A Fire Upon the Deep*, which rewrites the simpleminded old venues of space opera in terms of information theory and a vision of the universe as an onion, at the heart of which, like equations caught in amber, can be discerned (and dismissed) all the laws of physics that bind us to Earth. The further out you get from Galactic Center in this deeply happy structuring of reality, the faster, the brighter, the freer you get. Humans, true to postagenda assumptions, bulk small.

Stephen Donaldson's *The Gap into Power*, a long medias res section from a huge novel in progress, twists space opera into such Jacobean contortions of stress that the reader gets congested arteries from the intensity of the game, and feels pretty damned sick on finishing. In *A Million Open Doors*, John Barnes occasionally allows flashes of sophistication to infiltrate his tale of juvenile-lead protagonists who become secret agents (or something, it was hard to remember five minutes after shutting the book) of a galactic council (*could* it have been a galactic council?) and beginning (as the novel ends) to prepare themselves to monitor folk on any number of further worlds. A shoal of planetary romancelets could be in the offing; or not, given Barnes's swift intense way with a tale. But I hope he sticks to singletons, and saddens down a bit, too.

There were at least two first novels whose intensity of achievement made them read as though one were *remembering* them, out of the dream-chambers of the race. Karen Joy Fowler's *Sarah Canary*, set at the world-conquering height of the nineteenth century, traces with steely smiling delicacy the ways in which it might be possible to understand, and to misconstrue, a speechless but birdlike female creature as she drifts through the Pacific Northwest, gathering 'round her a congeries of other outcasts: a Chinese, a suffragette, an Indian, an idiot. As far as the male imperial mind of the century is concerned, they are all outside the pale, and must be coerced into being "understood." Sarah Canary herself may, in fact, be a "true" alien. As far as most SF readers are concerned, she almost certainly is. As far as the book is concerned, she is certainly "Other."

The second first novel was Maureen F. McHugh's *China Mountain Zhang*, a tale whose rich velocity had no difficulty carrying the reader through a number of sidebar narrative trips. The protagonist is a gay Chinese-American in a world where the U.S.A. (now the socialist Union of American States) is dominated by China; it is a bildungsroman, a tale of the coming to adulthood of a young human being, and it is dense with language, and rites of passage, and aperçus.

A bright, quick mammal's glitter suffuses every single character in Connie Willis's brilliant *Doomsday Book,* which won the Nebula this year (along with her "Even the Queen," whose central debate about menstruation was hilarious but *deeply* unfair to Cyclists, whose representative got about as many words in as a liberal in Heinlein Country). But *Doomsday Book,* which clearly seemed to have been written in a state of love, set up no bogey to blow over. The thirteenth-century country near Oxford to which the protagonist time-travels on a university assignment from the near future, though it has been criticized for a variety of historical inaccuracies, breathes all the same like another country of the heart. As the Black Death begins to transmogrify the culture into which she has inserted herself, the protagonist slowly becomes a figure of almost mythic density, and her rescue, in the final sentences, ends the novel like a song whose ultimate note is all we came to hear.

Each of the remaining titles could be talked about for pages, for if there was one characteristic aspect to 1992, it may be that too many discourses, too many reflections in too many mirrors, were banging together in the arena of genre. There was everywhere an air of commingled panic and empowerment: vast easy gains, feet of sand; vast easy feet of sand, hard gains. It was babel. C. J. Cherryh's *Hellburner* reads like ten jugglers leaving one room and not dropping a ball, making the first years of her rapacious ongoing Future History read like true opera. Alasdair Gray's *Poor Things* mixes Scotland riffs, Frankenstein riffs, textuality riffs, reliability riffs, while glaring at us all the while, daring us to stick our fingers into the bright dire machine. James Morrow's *City of Truth* is refreshingly unnice and sour, retelling in conte-like rhythms a Voltairean fable about a confusion of truth-saying and fact-telling, slipping at the end into a just slightly sentimentalized Death of Child. Sheri Tepper, in *Beauty,* conflates fairy tale, slick fantasy, SF, and dystopia into a savagely unremitting lament upon the thinning of our world.

It can be expected that, as the century turns, some of these stories will slip into the past tense, become further episodes in the Future Histories that never happened. Others will seem prophetic. It's hard to know which texts, in the midst of these babel days, will prove to have pointed the way, impossible to know whose voices will soar, take the tune, speak the words that hurt us till we wake.

So we read, and hope for a window, and wait.

Even the Queen

CONNIE WILLIS

Connie Willis is the sort of person who, confronted with the prospect of back surgery, arranges to have a camcorder in the operating room, subsequently intercutting the gory procedure with clips from made-for-TV movies. In the summer of 1992, while attending the Sycamore Hill Writers' Conference in North Carolina, I caught Willis's surrealistic home video, narrated in person by the patient herself, and I still don't know what to make of it. As you are about to see from the following story, Willis is both singularly eccentric and quintessentially sane, a little nutty and very wise.

She is also one of science fiction's most laureled writers. Before scoring the twofold victory celebrated in the present volume—a Best Short Story Nebula for "Even the Queen" and a Best Novel Nebula for *Doomsday Book*—Willis was honored for her novel *Lincoln's Dreams* (John W. Campbell Memorial Award); for her novella "The Last of the Winnebagos" (Nebula Award, Hugo Award); for her novelettes "At the Rialto" (Nebula) and "Fire Watch" (Nebula, Hugo); and for her story "A Letter from the Clearys" (Nebula). A heady sampling of Willis's shorter fiction, including most of the award winners, is on display in her two collections, *Fire Watch* and *Impossible Things*.

Invited to account for "Even the Queen," Willis replied:

"English teachers are always telling people to write about what they know. I did.

"Clarion instructors are always telling people to do their research. I did a *lot* of research for this story.

"Literature professors are always telling people that their stories should express their darkest fears and fondest wishes. This story does."

The phone sang as I was looking over the defense's motion to dismiss. "It's the universal ring," my law clerk Bysshe said, reaching for it. "It's probably the defendant. They don't let you use signatures from jail."

"No, it's not," I said. "It's my mother."

"Oh." Bysshe reached for the receiver. "Why isn't she using her signature?"

"Because she knows I don't want to talk to her. She must have found out what Perdita's done."

"Your daughter Perdita?" he asked, holding the receiver against his chest. "The one with the little girl?"

"No, that's Viola. Perdita's my younger daughter. The one with no sense."

"What's she done?"

"She's joined the Cyclists."

Bysshe looked inquiringly blank, but I was not in the mood to enlighten him. Or in the mood to talk to Mother. "I know exactly what Mother will say," I said. "She'll ask me why I didn't tell her, and then she'll demand to know what I'm going to do about it, and there is nothing I *can* do about it, or I obviously would have done it already."

Bysshe looked bewildered. "Do you want me to tell her you're in court?"

"No." I reached for the receiver. "I'll have to talk to her sooner or later." I took it from him. "Hello, Mother," I said.

"Traci," Mother said dramatically, "Perdita has become a Cyclist."

"I know."

"Why didn't you tell me?"

"I thought Perdita should tell you herself."

"Perdita!" She snorted. "She wouldn't tell me. She knows what I'd have to say about it. I suppose you told Karen."

"Karen's not here. She's in Iraq." The only good thing about this whole debacle was that, thanks to Iraq's eagerness to show it was a responsible world community member and to its previous penchant for self-destruction, my mother-in-law was in the one place on the planet where the phone service was bad enough that I could claim I'd tried to call her but couldn't get through, and she'd have to believe me.

The Liberation has freed us from all sorts of indignities and scourges, including Iraq's Saddams, but mothers-in-law aren't one of them, and I was almost happy with Perdita for her excellent timing. When I didn't want to kill her.

"What's Karen doing in Iraq?" Mother asked.

"Negotiating a Palestinian homeland."

"And meanwhile her granddaughter is ruining her life," she said irrelevantly. "Did you tell Viola?"

"I *told* you, Mother. I thought Perdita should tell all of you herself."

"Well, she didn't. And this morning one of my patients, Carol Chen, called me and demanded to know what I was keeping from her. I had no idea what she was talking about."

"How did Carol Chen find out?"

"From her daughter, who almost joined the Cyclists last year. *Her* family talked her out of it," she said accusingly. "Carol was convinced the medical community had discovered some terrible side effect of ammenerol and were covering it up. I cannot believe you didn't tell me, Traci."

And I cannot believe I didn't have Bysshe tell her I was in court, I thought. "I told you, Mother. I thought it was Perdita's place to tell you. After all, it's her decision."

"Oh, Traci!" Mother said. "You cannot mean that!"

In the first fine flush of freedom after the Liberation, I had entertained hopes that it would change everything—that it would somehow do away with inequality and matriarchal dominance and those humorless women determined to eliminate the word "manhole" and third-person singular pronouns from the language.

Of course it didn't. Men still make more money, "herstory" is still a blight on the semantic landscape, and my mother can still say, "Oh, *Traci!*" in a tone that reduces me to preadolescence.

"Her decision!" Mother said. "Do you mean to tell me you plan to stand idly by and allow your daughter to make the mistake of her life?"

"What can I do? She's twenty-two years old and of sound mind."

"If she were of sound mind she wouldn't be doing this. Didn't you try to talk her out of it?"

"Of course I did, Mother."

"And?"

"And I didn't succeed. She's determined to become a Cyclist."

"Well, there must be something we can do. Get an injunction or hire a deprogrammer or sue the Cyclists for brainwashing. You're a judge, there must be some law you can invoke—"

"The law is called personal sovereignty, Mother, and since it was what made the Liberation possible in the first place, it can hardly be used against Perdita. Her decision meets all the criteria for a case of personal sovereignty: it's a personal decision, it was made by a sovereign adult, it affects no one else—"

"What about my practice? Carol Chen is convinced shunts cause cancer."

"Any effect on your practice is considered an indirect effect. Like secondary smoke. It doesn't apply. Mother, whether we like it or not, Perdita has a perfect right to do this, and we don't have any right to interfere. A free society has to be based on respecting others' opinions and leaving each other alone. We have to respect Perdita's right to make her own decisions."

All of which was true. It was too bad I hadn't said any of it to Perdita when she called. What I had said, in a tone that sounded exactly like my mother's, was "Oh, Perdita!"

"This is all your fault, you know," Mother said. "I *told* you you shouldn't have let her get that tattoo over her shunt. And don't tell me it's a free society. What good is a free society when it allows my granddaughter to ruin her life?" She hung up.

I handed the receiver back to Bysshe.

"I really liked what you said about respecting your daughter's right to make her own decisions," he said. He held out my robe. "And about not interfering in her life."

"I want you to research the precedents on deprogramming for me," I said, sliding my arms into the sleeves. "And find out if the Cyclists have been charged with any free-choice violations—brainwashing, intimidation, coercion."

The phone sang, another universal. "Hello, who's calling?" Bysshe said cautiously. His voice became suddenly friendlier. "Just a minute." He put his hand over the receiver. "It's your daughter Viola."

I took the receiver. "Hello, Viola."

"I just talked to Grandma," she said. "You will not believe what Perdita's done now. She's joined the Cyclists."

"I know," I said.

"You *know?* And you didn't tell me? I can't believe this. You never tell me anything."

"I thought Perdita should tell you herself," I said tiredly.

"Are you kidding? She never tells me anything either. That time she had eyebrow implants she didn't tell me for three weeks, and when she got the laser tattoo she didn't tell me at all. *Twidge* told me. You should have called me. Did you tell Grandma Karen?"

"She's in Baghdad," I said.

"I know," Viola said. "I called her."

"Oh, Viola, you didn't!"

"Unlike you, Mom, I believe in telling members of our family about matters that concern them."

"What did she say?" I asked, a kind of numbness settling over me now that the shock had worn off.

"I couldn't get through to her. The phone service over there is terrible. I got somebody who didn't speak English, and then I got cut off, and when I tried again they said the whole city was down."

Thank you, I breathed silently. Thank you, thank you, thank you.

"Grandma Karen has a right to know, Mother. Think of the effect this could have on Twidge. She thinks Perdita's wonderful. When Perdita got the eyebrow implants, Twidge glued LEDs to hers, and I almost never got them off. What if Twidge decides to join the Cyclists, too?"

"Twidge is only nine. By the time she's supposed to get her shunt, Perdita will have long since quit." I hope, I added silently. Perdita had had the tattoo for a year and a half now and showed no signs of tiring of it. "Besides, Twidge has more sense."

"It's true. Oh, Mother, how *could* Perdita do this? Didn't you tell her about how awful it was?"

"Yes," I said. "And inconvenient. And unpleasant and unbalancing and painful. None of it made the slightest impact on her. She told me she thought it would be fun."

Bysshe was pointing to his watch and mouthing, "Time for court."

"Fun!" Viola said. "When she saw what I went through that time? Honestly, Mother, sometimes I think she's completely brain-dead. Can't you have her declared incompetent and locked up or something?"

"No," I said, trying to zip up my robe with one hand. "Viola, I have to go. I'm late for court. I'm afraid there's nothing we can do to stop her. She's a rational adult."

"Rational!" Viola said. "Her eyebrows light up, Mother. She has Custer's Last Stand lased on her arm."

I handed the phone to Bysshe. "Tell Viola I'll talk to her tomorrow." I zipped up my robe. "And then call Baghdad and see how long they expect the phones to be out." I started into the courtroom. "And if there are any more universal calls, make sure they're local before you answer."

Bysshe couldn't get through to Baghdad, which I took as a good sign, and my mother-in-law didn't call. Mother did, in the afternoon, to ask if lobotomies were legal.

She called again the next day. I was in the middle of my Personal Sovereignty class, explaining the inherent right of citizens in a free society to make complete jackasses of themselves. They weren't buying it.

"I think it's your mother," Bysshe whispered to me as he handed me the phone. "She's still using the universal. But it's local. I checked."

"Hello, Mother," I said.

"It's all arranged," Mother said. "We're having lunch with Perdita at McGregor's. It's on the corner of Twelfth Street and Larimer."

"I'm in the middle of class," I said.

"I know. I won't keep you. I just wanted to tell you not to worry. I've taken care of everything."

I didn't like the sound of that. "What have you done?"

"Invited Perdita to lunch with us. I told you. At McGregor's."

"Who is 'us,' Mother?"

"Just the family," she said innocently. "You and Viola."

Well, at least she hadn't brought in the deprogrammer. Yet. "What are you up to, Mother?"

"Perdita said the same thing. Can't a grandmother ask her granddaughters to lunch? Be there at twelve-thirty."

"Bysshe and I have a court calendar meeting at three."

"Oh, we'll be done by then. And bring Bysshe with you. He can provide a man's point of view."

She hung up.

"You'll have to go to lunch with me, Bysshe," I said. "Sorry."

"Why? What's going to happen at lunch?"

"I have no idea."

On the way over to McGregor's, Bysshe told me what he'd found out about the Cyclists. "They're not a cult. There's no religious connection. They seem to have grown out of a pre-Liberation women's group," he said, looking at his notes, "although there are also links to the pro-choice movement, the University of Wisconsin, and the Museum of Modern Art."

"What?"

"They call their group leaders 'docents.' Their philosophy seems to be a mix of pre-Liberation radical feminism and the environmental primitivism of the eighties. They're floratarians and they don't wear shoes."

"Or shunts," I said. We pulled up in front of McGregor's and got out of the car. "Any mind control convictions?" I asked hopefully.

"No. A bunch of suits against individual members, all of which they won."

"On grounds of personal sovereignty."

"Yeah. And a criminal one by a member whose family tried to deprogram her. The deprogrammer was sentenced to twenty years, and the family got twelve."

"Be sure to tell Mother about that one," I said, and opened the door to McGregor's.

It was one of those restaurants with a morning glory vine twining around the maître d's desk and garden plots between the tables.

"Perdita suggested it," Mother said, guiding Bysshe and me past the onions to our table. "She told me a lot of the Cyclists are floratarians."

"Is she here?" I asked, sidestepping a cucumber frame.

"Not yet." She pointed past a rose arbor. "There's our table."

Our table was a wicker affair under a mulberry tree. Viola and Twidge were seated on the far side next to a trellis of runner beans, looking at menus.

I turned around, half-expecting Perdita with light-up lips or a full-body tattoo, but I couldn't see through the leaves. I pushed at the branches.

"Is it Perdita?" Viola said, leaning forward.

I peered around the mulberry bush. "Oh, my God," I said.

It was my mother-in-law, wearing a black abayah and a silk yarmulke. She swept toward us through a pumpkin patch, robes billowing and eyes flashing. Mother hurried in her wake of trampled radishes, looking daggers at me.

I turned them on Viola. "It's your grandmother Karen," I said accusingly. "You told me you didn't get through to her."

"I didn't," she said. "Twidge, sit up straight. And put your slate down."

There was an ominous rustling in the rose arbor, as of leaves shrinking back in terror, and my mother-in-law arrived.

"Karen!" I said, trying to sound pleased. "What on earth are you doing here? I thought you were in Baghdad."

"I came back as soon as I got Viola's message," she said, glaring at everyone in turn. "Who's this?" she demanded, pointing at Bysshe. "Viola's new live-in?"

"No!" Bysshe said, looking horrified.

"This is my law clerk, Karen," I said. "Bysshe Adams-Hardy."

"Twidge, why aren't you in school?"

"I *am*," Twidge said. "I'm remoting." She held up her slate. "See? Math."

"I see," she said, turning to glower at me. "It's a serious enough matter to require my great-grandchild's being pulled out of school *and* the hiring of legal assistance, and yet you didn't deem it important enough to notify *me*. Of course, you *never* tell me anything, Traci."

She swirled herself into the end chair, sending leaves and sweet pea blossoms flying, and decapitating the broccoli centerpiece. "I didn't get Viola's cry for help until yesterday. Viola, you should never leave messages with Hassim. His English is virtually nonexistent. I had to get him to hum me your ring. I recognized your signature, but the phones were out, so I flew home. In the middle of negotiations, I might add."

"How *are* negotiations going, Grandma Karen?" Viola asked.

"They *were* going extremely well. The Israelis have given the Palestinians half of Jerusalem, and they've agreed to time-share the Golan Heights." She turned to glare momentarily at me. "*They* know the importance of communication." She turned back to Viola. "So why are they picking on you, Viola? Don't they like your new live-in?"

"I am *not* her live-in," Bysshe protested.

I have often wondered how on earth my mother-in-law became

a mediator and what she does in all those negotiation sessions with Serbs and Catholics and North and South Koreans and Protestants and Croats. She takes sides, jumps to conclusions, misinterprets everything you say, refuses to listen. And yet she talked South Africa into a Mandelan government and would probably get the Palestinians to observe Yom Kippur. Maybe she just bullies everyone into submission. Or maybe they have to band together to protect themselves against her.

Bysshe was still protesting. "I never even met Viola till today. I've only talked to her on the phone a couple of times."

"You must have done something," Karen said to Viola. "They're obviously out for your blood."

"Not mine," Viola said. "Perdita's. She's joined the Cyclists."

"The Cyclists? I left the West Bank negotiations because you don't approve of Perdita joining a biking club? How am I supposed to explain this to the president of Iraq? She will *not* understand, and neither do I. A biking club!"

"The Cyclists do not ride bicycles," Mother said.

"They menstruate," Twidge said.

There was a dead silence of at least a minute, and I thought, it's finally happened. My mother-in-law and I are actually going to be on the same side of a family argument.

"All this fuss is over Perdita's having her shunt removed?" Karen said finally. "She's of age, isn't she? And this is obviously a case where personal sovereignty applies. You should know that, Traci. After all, you're a judge."

I should have known it was too good to be true.

"You mean you approve of her setting back the Liberation twenty years?" Mother said.

"I hardly think it's that serious," Karen said. "There are antishunt groups in the Middle East, too, you know, but no one takes them seriously. Not even the Iraqis, and they still wear the veil."

"Perdita is taking them seriously."

Karen dismissed Perdita with a wave of her black sleeve. "They're a trend, a fad. Like microskirts. Or those dreadful electronic eyebrows. A few women wear silly fashions like that for a little while, but you don't see women as a whole giving up pants or going back to wearing hats."

"But Perdita. . . ." Viola said.

"If Perdita wants to have her period, I say let her. Women functioned perfectly well without shunts for thousands of years."

Mother brought her fist down on the table. "Women also functioned *perfectly well* with concubinage, cholera, and corsets," she said, emphasizing each word with her fist. "But that is no reason to take them on voluntarily, and I have no intention of allowing Perdita—"

"Speaking of Perdita, where is the poor child?" Karen said.

"She'll be here any minute," Mother said. "I invited her to lunch so we could discuss this with her."

"Ha!" Karen said. "So you could browbeat her into changing her mind, you mean. Well, I have no intention of collaborating with you. *I* intend to listen to the poor thing's point of view with interest and an open mind. Respect, that's the key word, and one you all seem to have forgotten. Respect and common courtesy."

A barefoot young woman wearing a flowered smock and a red scarf tied around her left arm came up to the table with a sheaf of pink folders.

"It's about time," Karen said, snatching one of the folders away from her. "Your service here is dreadful. I've been sitting here ten minutes." She snapped the folder open. "I don't suppose you have Scotch."

"My name is Evangeline," the young woman said. "I'm Perdita's docent." She took the folder away from Karen. "She wasn't able to join you for lunch, but she asked me to come in her place and explain the Cyclist philosophy to you."

She sat down in the wicker chair next to me.

"The Cyclists are dedicated to freedom," she said. "Freedom from artificiality, freedom from body-controlling drugs and hormones, freedom from the male patriarchy that attempts to impose them on us. As you probably already know, we do not wear shunts."

She pointed to the red scarf around her arm. "Instead, we wear this as a badge of our freedom and our femaleness. I'm wearing it today to announce that my time of fertility has come."

"We had that, too," Mother said, "only we wore it on the back of our skirts."

I laughed.

The docent glared at me. "Male domination of women's bodies began long before the so-called 'Liberation,' with government regulation of abortion and fetal rights, scientific control of fertility, and finally the development of ammenerol, which eliminated the reproductive cycle altogether. This was all part of a carefully planned takeover of women's bodies, and by extension, their identities, by the male patriarchal regime."

"What an interesting point of view!" Karen said enthusiastically.

It certainly was. In point of fact, ammenerol hadn't been invented to eliminate menstruation at all. It had been developed for shrinking malignant tumors, and its uterine lining–absorbing properties had only been discovered by accident.

"Are you trying to tell us," Mother said, "that men *forced* shunts on women?! We had to *fight* everyone to get it approved by the FDA!"

It was true. What surrogate mothers and antiabortionists and the fetal rights issue had failed to do in uniting women, the prospect of not having to menstruate did. Women had organized rallies, petitioned, elected senators, passed amendments, been excommunicated, and gone to jail, all in the name of Liberation.

"Men were *against* it," Mother said, getting rather red in the face. "And the religious right and the maxipad manufacturers and the Catholic church—"

"They knew they'd have to allow women priests," Viola said.

"Which they did," I said.

"The Liberation hasn't freed you," the docent said loudly. "Except from the natural rhythms of your life, the very wellspring of your femaleness."

She leaned over and picked a daisy that was growing under the table. "We in the Cyclists celebrate the onset of our menses and rejoice in our bodies," she said, holding the daisy up. "Whenever a Cyclist comes into blossom, as we call it, she is honored with flowers and poems and songs. Then we join hands and tell what we like best about our menses."

"Water retention," I said.

"Or lying in bed with a heating pad for three days a month," Mother said.

"*I* think I like the anxiety attacks best," Viola said. "When I went off the ammenerol, so I could have Twidge, I'd have these days where I was convinced the space station was going to fall on me."

A middle-aged woman in overalls and a straw hat had come over while Viola was talking and was standing next to Mother's chair. "I had these mood swings," she said. "One minute I'd feel cheerful and the next like Lizzie Borden."

"Who's Lizzie Borden?" Twidge asked.

"She killed her parents," Bysshe said. "With an ax."

Karen and the docent glared at both of them. "Aren't you supposed to be working on your math, Twidge?" Karen said.

"I've always wondered if Lizzie Borden had PMS," Viola said, "and that was why—"

"No," Mother said. "It was having to live before tampons and ibuprofen. An obvious case of justifiable homicide."

"I hardly think this sort of levity is helpful," Karen said, glowering at everyone.

"Are you our waitress?" I asked the straw-hatted woman hastily.

"Yes," she said, producing a slate from her overalls pocket.

"Do you serve wine?" I asked.

"Yes. Dandelion, cowslip, and primrose."

"We'll take them all," I said.

"A bottle of each?"

"For now. Unless you have them in kegs."

"Our specials today are watermelon salad and *chou-fleur grati-née*," she said, smiling at everyone. Karen and the docent did not smile back. "You handpick your own cauliflower from the patch up front. The floratarian special is sautéed lily buds with marigold butter."

There was a temporary truce while everyone ordered. "I'll have the sweet peas," the docent said, "and a glass of rose water."

Bysshe leaned over to Viola. "I'm sorry I sounded so horrified when your grandmother asked if I was your live-in," he said.

"That's okay," Viola said. "Grandma Karen can be pretty scary."

"I just didn't want you to think I didn't like you. I do. Like you, I mean."

"Don't they have soyburgers?" Twidge asked.

As soon as the waitress left, the docent began passing out the pink folders she'd brought with her. "These will explain the working philosophy of the Cyclists," she said, handing me one, "along with practical information on the menstrual cycle." She handed Twidge one.

"It looks just like those books we used to get in junior high," Mother said, looking at hers. " 'A Special Gift,' they were called, and they had all these pictures of girls with pink ribbons in their hair, playing tennis and smiling. Blatant misrepresentation."

She was right. There was even the same drawing of the fallopian tubes I remembered from my middle school movie, a drawing that had always reminded me of *Alien* in the early stages.

"Oh, yuck," Twidge said. "This is disgusting."

"Do your math," Karen said.

Bysshe looked sick. "Did women really *do* this stuff?"

The wine arrived, and I poured everyone a large glass. The docent pursed her lips disapprovingly and shook her head. "The Cyclists do not use the artificial stimulants or hormones that the male patriarchy has forced on women to render them docile and subservient."

"How long do you menstruate?" Twidge asked.

"Forever," Mother said.

"Four to six days," the docent said. "It's there in the booklet."

"No, I mean, your whole life or what?"

"A woman has her menarche at twelve years old on the average and ceases menstruating at age fifty-five."

"I had my first period at eleven," the waitress said, setting a bouquet down in front of me. "At school."

"I had my last one on the day the FDA approved ammenerol," Mother said.

"Three hundred and sixty-five divided by twenty-eight," Twidge said, writing on her slate. "Times forty-three years." She looked up. "That's five hundred and fifty-nine periods."

"That can't be right," Mother said, taking the slate away from her. "It's at least five thousand."

"And they all start on the day you leave on a trip," Viola said.

"Or get married," the waitress said.

Mother began writing on the slate.

I took advantage of the cease-fire to pour everyone some more dandelion wine.

Mother looked up from the slate. "Do you realize with a period of five days, you'd be menstruating for nearly three thousand days? That's over eight solid years."

"And in between there's PMS," the waitress said, delivering flowers.

"What's PMS?" Twidge asked.

"Premenstrual syndrome was the name the male medical establishment fabricated for the natural variation in hormonal levels that signal the onset of menstruation," the docent said. "This mild and entirely normal fluctuation was exaggerated by men into a debility." She looked at Karen for confirmation.

"I used to cut my hair," Karen said.

The docent looked uneasy.

"Once I chopped off one whole side," Karen went on. "Bob had to hide the scissors every month. And the car keys. I'd start to cry every time I hit a red light."

"Did you swell up?" Mother asked, pouring Karen another glass of dandelion wine.

"I looked just like Orson Welles."

"Who's Orson Welles?" Twidge asked.

"Your comments reflect the self-loathing thrust on you by the patriarchy," the docent said. "Men have brainwashed women into thinking menstruation is evil and unclean. Women even called their menses 'the curse' because they accepted men's judgment."

"I called it the curse because I thought a witch must have laid a curse on me," Viola said. "Like in 'Sleeping Beauty.'"

Everyone looked at her.

"Well, I did," she said. "It was the only reason I could think of for such an awful thing happening to me." She handed the folder back to the docent. "It still is."

"I think you were awfully brave," Bysshe said to Viola, "going off the ammenerol to have Twidge."

"It was awful," Viola said. "You can't imagine."

Mother sighed. "When I got my period, I asked my mother if Annette had it, too."

"Who's Annette?" Twidge said.

"A Mouseketeer," Mother said and added, at Twidge's uncomprehending look, "On TV."

"High-rez," Viola said.

"The Mickey Mouse Club," Mother said.

"There was a high-rezzer called the Mickey Mouse Club?" Twidge said incredulously.

"They were days of dark oppression in many ways," I said.

Mother glared at me. "Annette was every young girl's ideal," she said to Twidge. "Her hair was curly, she had actual breasts, her pleated skirt was always pressed, and I could not imagine that she could have anything so *messy* and undignified. Mr. Disney would never have allowed it. And if Annette didn't have one, I wasn't going to have one either. So I asked my mother—"

"What did she say?" Twidge cut in.

"She said every woman had periods," Mother said. "So I asked her, 'Even the Queen of England?' and she said, 'Even the Queen.' "

"Really?" Twidge said. "But she's so *old!*"

"She isn't having it now," the docent said irritatedly. "I told you, menopause occurs at age fifty-five."

"And then you have hot flashes," Karen said, "and osteoporosis and so much hair on your upper lip you look like Mark Twain."

"Who's—" Twidge said.

"You are simply reiterating negative male propaganda," the docent interrupted, looking very red in the face.

"You know what I've always wondered?" Karen said, leaning conspiratorially close to Mother. "If Maggie Thatcher's menopause was responsible for the Falklands War."

"Who's Maggie Thatcher?" Twidge said.

The docent, who was now as red in the face as her scarf, stood up. "It is clear there is no point in trying to talk to you. You've all been completely brainwashed by the male patriarchy." She began grabbing up her folders. "You're blind, all of you! You don't even see that you're victims of a male conspiracy to deprive you of your biological identity, of your very womanhood. The Liberation wasn't a liberation at all. It was only another kind of slavery!"

"Even if that were true," I said, "even if it had been a conspiracy to bring us under male domination, it would have been worth it."

"She's right, you know," Karen said to Mother. "Traci's absolutely right. There are some things worth giving up anything for, even your freedom, and getting rid of your period is definitely one of them."

"Victims!" the docent shouted. "You've been stripped of your femininity, and you don't even care!" She stomped out, destroying several squash and a row of gladiolas in the process.

"You know what I hated most before the Liberation?" Karen said, pouring the last of the dandelion wine into her glass. "Sanitary belts."

"And those cardboard tampon applicators," Mother said.

"I'm never going to join the Cyclists," Twidge said.

"Good," I said.

"Can I have dessert?"

I called the waitress over, and Twidge ordered sugared violets. "Anyone else want dessert?" I asked. "Or more primrose wine?"

"I think it's wonderful the way you're trying to help your sister," Bysshe said, leaning close to Viola.

"And those Modess ads," Mother said. "You remember, with those glamorous women in satin brocade evening dresses and long white gloves, and below the picture was written, 'Modess, because. . . .' I thought Modess was a perfume."

Karen giggled. "I thought it was a brand of *champagne!*"

"I don't think we'd better have any more wine," I said.

The phone started singing the minute I got to my chambers the next morning, the universal ring.

"Karen went back to Iraq, didn't she?" I asked Bysshe.

"Yeah," he said. "Viola said there was some snag over whether to put Disneyland on the West Bank or not."

"When did Viola call?"

Bysshe looked sheepish. "I had breakfast with her and Twidge this morning."

"Oh." I picked up the phone. "It's probably Mother with a plan to kidnap Perdita. Hello?"

"This is Evangeline, Perdita's docent," the voice on the phone said. "I hope you're happy. You've bullied Perdita into surrendering to the enslaving male patriarchy."

"I have?" I said.

"You've obviously employed mind control, and I want you to know we intend to file charges." She hung up. The phone sang again immediately, another universal.

"What is the good of signatures when no one ever uses them?" I said and picked up the phone.

"Hi, Mom," Perdita said. "I thought you'd want to know I've changed my mind about joining the Cyclists."

"Really?" I said, trying not to sound jubilant.

"I found out they wear this red scarf thing on their arm. It covers up Sitting Bull's horse."

"That is a problem," I said.

"Well, that's not all. My docent told me about your lunch. Did Grandma Karen really tell you you were right?"

"Yes."

"Gosh! I didn't believe that part. Well, anyway, my docent said you wouldn't listen to her about how great menstruating is, that you all kept talking about the negative aspects of it, like bloating and cramps and crabbiness, and I said, 'What are cramps?' and she said, 'Menstrual bleeding frequently causes headaches and discomfort,' and I said, 'Bleeding?!? Nobody ever said anything about bleeding!' Why didn't you tell me there was blood involved, Mother?"

I had, but I felt it wiser to keep silent.

"And you didn't say a word about its being painful. And all the hormone fluctuations! Anybody'd have to be crazy to want to go through that when they didn't have to! How did you stand it before the Liberation?"

"They were days of dark oppression," I said.

"I *guess!* Well, anyway, I quit and now my docent is really mad. But I told her it was a case of personal sovereignty, and she has to respect my decision. I'm still going to become a floratarian, though, and I *don't* want you to try to talk me out of it."

"I wouldn't dream of it," I said.

"You know, this whole thing is really your fault, Mom! If you'd told me about the pain part in the first place, none of this would have happened. Viola's right! You never tell us *anything!*"

Danny Goes to Mars

PAMELA SARGENT

Let me seize this opportunity to announce that Pamela Sargent will be editing the next three books in the Nebula Awards series. She is a most felicitous choice. Even before Sargent published her first novel, *Cloned Lives* (1976), she had made a name for herself as an anthologist, celebrating the growing subgenre of feminist SF with *Women of Wonder* (1975), a volume so popular it quickly spawned two sequels: *More Women of Wonder* (1976) and *The New Women of Wonder* (1978).

Over the years, Sargent has enriched the field with dozens of stories, a cluster of young-adult books, and such acclaimed full-length novels as *The Golden Space* and *The Shore of Women*. Fans of her short fiction will find it collected in *Starshadows* and *The Best of Pamela Sargent*. Sargent's most ambitious SF work to date is a trilogy about the terraforming of our system's second planet, beginning with *Venus of Dreams*, proceeding through *Venus of Shadows*, and climaxing with the soon-to-be-released *Child of Venus*. Her epic mainstream novel about Genghis Khan, *Ruler of the Sky*, recently appeared from Crown Books.

"I couldn't help myself," Sargent informs us concerning her Nebula-winning novelette. "Once Dan Quayle emerged as George Bush's running mate, I became an avid collector of Quayle lore.

"To reporters in Hawaii in 1989, the Vice President submitted the following wisdom: 'Hawaii has always been a very pivotal role in the Pacific. It is in the Pacific. It is part of the United States that is an island that is right there.' Then there was Quayle's immortal statement to the United Negro College Fund: 'What a waste it is to lose one's mind, or not to have a mind is being very wasteful. How true that is.' There was also my personal favorite, the statement about Mars that prefaces my story.

"It was for people like me that *The Quayle Quarterly* was created. But it's possible to overdose on this sort of thing. When I reached the point of knowing what fraternity Quayle joined as an undergraduate at DePauw (Delta Kappa Epsilon)—and that his high school crowd in Huntington, Indiana, included three guys named Taylor Cope, Dave Roush, and Robert Steele (upon hearing that Quayle had received the Republican nomination for Vice President, Steele reportedly called an old buddy and said, 'Jesus Christ, let's leave the country')—I had to find a way to justify my mastery of all this trivia.

"So I wrote a story about him."

*Mars is essentially in the same orbit [as Earth]. Mars is somewhat
the same distance from the sun, which is very important. We have
seen pictures where there are canals, we believe, and water. If there
is water, that means there is oxygen. If oxygen, that means we can
breathe.*

—J. Danforth Quayle, Vice President of the United States,
as quoted in *Mother Jones*, January 1990

The Vice President had known that this White House lunch would
be different. For one thing, the President's voice kept shifting from
his Mr. Rogers pitch to his John Wayne tone, and that always made
Dan nervous. For another, the former Chief of Staff was there as a
guest, and that bothered him.

John Sununu might have mouthed off in public about how much
Dan had learned on the job, but away from the cameras, his big MIT
brain couldn't be bothered with even saying hello to the Vice President. Not that it really mattered, since Nunu, as most of the White
House staff called him behind his back, had pretty much treated
everybody that way, except when he was having a temper tantrum.
Almost everyone had been relieved when the former Chief of Staff
had been eased out of that position.

Now, here he was in the White House again, sitting around at
this intimate lunch as if he still had the President's full confidence.
Maybe the President needed Big John's help on some scientific deal
or other; Dan hoped it was that, and not something political. He
squinted slightly, thinking of Robert Stack. That was the ticket, putting
on that Robert Stack I'm-a-nice-guy-but-don't-mess-with-me kind of
expression.

"A squeaker," the President said, "a real squeaker. Almost didn't
pull it out. The Democrats—bad. Attack from the right—even worse.
Got something up our sleeve, though—they'll say, Never saw *that*
coming."

The Vice President tried to look attentive. Sometimes he couldn't
figure out what the President was talking about. Once he had worried
about that, before discovering that many members of the White House
staff had the same problem.

"Council on Competitiveness, and, uh, the space thing, too—
you're our man there," the President was saying now. Marilyn had

guessed that the President might be toying with the idea of a space spectacular, and Big John, whatever his lacks in the political arena, was one of the few advisers who could understand the scientific ins and outs. It made sense, what with that big breakthrough in developing an engine for space travel. Dan didn't know exactly how it worked, but it could get a ship to the Moon almost overnight—if there was an "overnight" in space.

"Mars," the President said. "About time."

"Mars?" Dan sat up. That was an even better idea than going to the Moon.

"We're sending out feelers." The former Chief of Staff adjusted his glasses, looking as if this project was his idea. Maybe it was; maybe that was how he had gotten back into the President's good graces. "The Japanese have hinted they might foot most of the bill if one of their people is among the astronauts. The Saudis'll pick up the rest if we get one of their men on board. The Russians would do almost anything to take their people's minds off the mess over there, and we can use one of those long-term habitat modules they've developed for the crew's quarters. Putting a cosmonaut on the crew in return for that would be a hell of a lot cheaper than sending more aid down that rathole."

"Impressive," the President said. "Won't cost us."

"We can get this going before the midterm elections," Big John muttered. "America's reaching for the stars again—that should play pretty goddamned well, and you can use the brotherhood angle, too." He shifted his stocky body in his chair. "A crash program for building the ship will create jobs. The crew can be trained, and the ship ready to go, by the summer of ninety-five. Two weeks or less to Mars, depending on where it is in relation to Earth's orbit, and back in plenty of time for the presidential primaries."

"With the new nuclear fission–to-fusion pulse engine," Dan said, "that's possible." He'd picked up a few things during his meetings with the Space Council. He was a little annoyed that no one had even hinted at the possibility of a Mars trip, but then he was usually the last guy to find anything out. "With that kind of engine, we could cross from, say, Mercury to Jupiter in less than a hundred days." He had heard one of the NASA boys say that. Or had it been less than thirty days? Not that it made that much difference, at least to him.

The former Chief of Staff lifted his brows in surprise. Sununu had a habit of looking at him like that sometimes, the way Dan's high school teachers and college professors had looked at him when he actually managed to come up with a correct answer.

"But you know," the Vice President continued, "you could take longer to train the crew, and have this whole Mars deal going on during the primary season. That might actually help me more, having it happen right while I'm running."

"Two terms," the President said, sounding a lot more like John Wayne than Mr. Rogers this time. "Straight line from nineteen-eighty. I want a Republican in the White House in two-thousand-and-one. Maybe the Navy band could play that music at the inauguration, you know, the piece in that movie—"

" 'Also Sprach Zarathustra,' " the former Chief of Staff said, then turned toward the Vice President. "The theme from *2001.*" He had that funny smile on his face, the one that made his eyes seem even colder.

"What I was thinking, though," Dan said, "is that people have short memories." That was a piece of political wisdom he had picked up, partly because his own memory wasn't so great. "So it might make more sense to have a ship on Mars right in the middle of the primaries. It'd sure be a help to be able to make speeches about that, and—"

"Unless something goes wrong. That could really fuck up the campaign, a big space disaster." Big John folded his arms over his broad chest. "But we'll just have to see that doesn't happen. Besides, that sucker has to be back before the primaries." His smile faded. "See, the thing is—"

"On the crew, Dan," the President interrupted. "Still young, and you're in good shape—think it'll work."

The Vice President set down his fork. "What would work?"

The former Chief of Staff unfolded his arms. "The President is saying that he'd like you to go to Mars."

Dan was too stunned to speak.

"If you'll volunteer, that is," the President said.

The Vice President steadied himself, hoping his eyes had not widened into his Bambi-caught-in-the-headlights look. Big John might be willing to shove him aboard a ship heading for Mars just to get back in the good graces of the White House, but the President, for a guy without a whole lot of principles, was a gentleman. A man who never forgot to write thank-you notes wasn't the kind of person to force his Veep on a risky space mission.

"Well." Dan frowned. "Do I really have to do this?"

Big John said, "It may be the only way we can get you elected. It sure as hell would give you an edge, and you're going to need one. The President was getting it from the right, but you're going to be getting it from the moderate Republicans." He sneered. "We're only talking a two- or three-week trip, hardly more than a space shuttle flight. Come back from Mars, and you wouldn't just be the Vice President—you'd be a hero." He said the words as if he didn't quite believe them.

"Hard to run against a hero," the President said. He pressed his hands together, then flung them out to his sides. "Moderates— trouble. But it's up to you, Dan. Think you can handle this Mars thing—make sure there's good people on the crew with you—but you gotta decide."

The Vice President swallowed, trying for his Robert Stack look once more. He was about to say he would have to talk it over with Marilyn, but Big John would give him one of his funny looks if he said that.

"I'll consider it very seriously," he said. If Marilyn thought this was a good idea, he might have to go along with it.

"You do that," the former Chief of Staff said quietly.

He explained it all to his wife after dinner. There would be the months of training, but a house would be provided for him, and the family could visit him in Houston. They could even move there temporarily, but Dan wasn't about to insist on that. His son Tucker was in college, so it wouldn't much matter to him where they lived, but the move might be disruptive for Corinne and Ben.

"I can see it, in a way," he said. "If I do this, I might be unbeatable. On the other hand, it didn't work for John Glenn."

"But this is *Mars*, honey," Marilyn said. "John Glenn didn't go to Mars." She brushed back a lock of brown hair, then frowned. Dan had the sinking feeling that this whole business had already been decided. Whatever his fears about the journey, he was more afraid of facing the President and telling him he had decided not to volunteer. Besides, this space stuff might finally put an end to all the mockery. Maybe there wouldn't be any more jokes about his lousy grades and his golf trips and being on beer duty during his stint in the National Guard. Maybe that bastard Garry Trudeau would finally stop depicting him as a feather in his *Doonesbury* comic strip.

"I'd miss you a lot," Marilyn said.

"I'd miss you, too." He slipped an arm over her shoulders. "But it isn't like it's going to be one of those three-year-round-trip deals. If that's what it was, I would have said no right on the spot. They said it would be safe."

She rested her head against his chest. "Nobody could top this, you know. I doubt you'd have any challengers in the primaries afterwards, and the Democrats won't have the easy time they expected against you. Even then—"

He owed it to Marilyn. He wouldn't have gotten this far without her; in a way, it was too bad she couldn't go to Mars with him. She'd had to give up her law practice in Indiana when he was first elected to Congress, and later, her hopes of finding a job when he was running for Vice President. She had wised him up after his election to the Senate, after the story about his colleague Tom Evans and that Parkinson babe broke; if he had listened to Marilyn in the first place, he wouldn't have been in Palm Beach with them that weekend. She had given him good advice and sacrificed plenty for him. The least he could do was make her First Lady. "What should I do?" he asked.

Marilyn drew away from him and sat up. "There's only one thing to do," she murmured. "This is too big for us to decide by ourselves, so we have to put it in God's hands. He'll show us what's right."

He folded his hands, bowed his head, and tried to summon up a prayer. He definitely needed the Lord's help on this one, but had the feeling that God was likely to agree with the President.

When Dan agreed to become an astronaut, it seemed that a great weight was lifted from his shoulders. The announcement brought the expected press and television coverage, along with varying reactions from stunned commentators, but the conventional wisdom was that he could probably handle his Vice Presidential duties as well in Houston or on Mars as he could anywhere else.

There was a press conference to endure with his four fellow crew members, and the interviews, but he got through them all without any major gaffes, except for calling the moons of Mars Photos and Zenith. That snotty nerd George Will had tried to get him on some old remarks he had made about the Red Planet having canals, but Dan had muddied the waters with a bunch of memorized statistics he had mastered in the years since, along with a comment about having been under the spell of some Ray Bradbury stories. It was smart of his staff to feed him that stuff about Bradbury's *Martian Chronicles* along with the other information. Dan had not only made Will look like a bully, but had also given viewers the impression that the Vice President actually read books.

In Houston, at least, he would not have to do many interviews, on the grounds that they might interfere with his training. This did not keep some reporters from trying to get leaked information about his progress.

There was little for them to discover. Surprisingly, the training was not nearly as rigorous as he had expected. The other American on the crew, Ashana Washington, was both a physicist and an experienced pilot; she would technically be in command of the expedition. Prince Ahmed was also a pilot, although the ship itself would be piloted automatically during the voyage. Sergei Vavilov and Kiichi Taranaga each had a string of degrees in various subjects requiring big brains, and since they, like Prince Ahmed, spoke fluent English, the Vice President, to his great relief, would not have to try to learn a foreign language.

Basically, Dan knew, he would be little more than a passenger. Learning about the Mars vessel and its capacities was more interesting than Cabinet meetings, and messing around with the NASA computers was a little like those video games he had sometimes played with Tucker and Ben. The crew had to be in good shape, but he had always jogged and played a fair amount of tennis. He often missed Marilyn and the kids, but they had been apart for extended periods during political campaigns in the past, and their weekends together more than made up for it. He didn't have to talk to reporters, although occasionally he didn't mind posing for photographers in his NASA garb with a Robert Redford grin on his face. Once a week, some of his staffers and the President's would fly down to brief him on various matters, but Washington often seemed far away.

He had wondered if his fellow astronauts would take to him, since they would have to spend at least a couple of weeks in isolation with him—longer if NASA decided they should remain in a Martian base camp for a while, which they might have to do if they found anything really interesting. Within three weeks after his arrival in Houston, however, he was golfing twice a week with Kiichi, jogging in the mornings with Prince Ahmed after the Saudi's morning prayers, and playing tennis with Sergei, who, despite his small size, had one hell of a backhand.

Only Ashana had intimidated him just a little. The tall, good-looking black woman was too damned brainy and formal for him to regard her as a real babe—not that he, as a married man and a future Presidential candidate, was inclined to dwell on her apparent babe qualities anyway. Maybe Ashana thought that she was commanding this expedition for the same reason Clarence Thomas was on the Supreme Court. That was another reason to keep his distance. It wouldn't help his chances for the White House if Ashana turned into another Anita Hill.

He might have gone on being distantly polite to her, if, a month and a half into his training, he hadn't been drawn into a pickup basketball game with a few of the NASA officers. Ashana came by, and before he knew it, she was giving him some good advice on how to improve his jump shots.

Basketball was the glue that sealed their friendship, but Dan had nearly blown it when Ashana had come to his house one weekend to meet his family and watch a game. "I should have known," he said as he settled into his chair, "that you'd be a hoop fan."

Ashana's face suddenly got very stiff. Next to her on the sofa, Marilyn was rolling her eyes and giving him her I-don't-believe-you-just-said-that look.

"Exactly why should you have known?" Ashana asked in a small but kind of scary voice.

"In your official biography—I mean, you grew up in Indiana, didn't you? Everybody's a fan there."

Ashana relaxed, but he didn't quite understand why she had laughed so hard afterward.

———

He admitted it to himself; if he had to be a hero to win the election, this was the way to do it. His crewmates were the real experts, so he could leave all the major decisions to them. He would, of course, do his best to be helpful. Sergei would use him as a subject in some medical experiments, and he could also help Kiichi sort his soil samples. That would be great, if they actually found life on Mars, even if it was only something like the mildew that sometimes showed up in the Vice Presidential residence.

People were really getting psyched about this mission. After all the economic bad news of recent years, putting people to work on the ship, now called the *Edgar Rice Burroughs,* and its systems, as well as expanding the size of the Russian and American space stations to house those who had to work on the *Burroughs* in orbit, had given the economy a boost. Part of that was the new jobs, but most of it was simply that the country was regaining its confidence. This Mars thing would propel him into the White House on a wave of good feeling, and he would lead the country into the next century during his second term. By then, the economy would be booming under the impetus of a revived space program. Dan wasn't exactly sure how this would happen, but would let his advisers figure that out when it was time for them to write his speeches.

It was, when he thought about it, amazing that the Mars mission had won such widespread support. There were, of course, some people who had to bitch, like those protestors who showed up at the Johnson Space Center or Cape Canaveral to protest the ship's technology, but they were the kind who panicked whenever they saw the word "fission," especially if "fusion" was sitting right next to it. A comedian on David Letterman's show had said something about how a dopehead must have thought of putting the Vice President aboard, and so maybe they should have called the ship the *William S. Burroughs.* Dan didn't see what was so funny about that, but it didn't really matter. Most of the clippings Marilyn brought to him on her visits had optimistic words about the mission and comments from various people about his bravery and increasing maturity.

Almost before he knew it, he and his fellow astronauts were being flown to Florida, where they would spend their final days before liftoff; a space shuttle would carry them to the *Burroughs.* The President

would be there, along with several ambassadors and any other dignitaries who had managed to wangle an invitation. A whole contingent
of family and friends were coming in from Indiana to view the launch,
which would be covered by camera teams and reporters from just
about everywhere. Everything had gone basically without a hitch so
far, although they were going to be late taking off for the *Burroughs;*
the shuttle launch had been postponed until October, what with a
few small delays on construction and testing. Still, the Mars ship and
its systems had passed every test with flying colors, and this had
inspired a number of articles contending, basically, that American
workers had finally gotten their shit together again. More kids were
deciding to take science and math courses in school. There was a
rumor that *Time* magazine had decided early that Dan would have
to be their Man of the Year.

Only one dark spot marred his impending triumph. That creep
Garry Trudeau was now depicting him as a feather floating inside a
space helmet and referring to him as "the candidate from Mars."

The *Burroughs* wasn't exactly the kind of sleek ship Dan had seen in
movies about space. Its frame held two heavily shielded habitat modules, the lander, and the Mars base assembly. The large metallic bowl
that housed the pulse engine was attached to the end of the frame.
The whole thing reminded him a little of a giant Tootsie Roll with a
big dish at one end, but he felt confident as he floated into the crew's
quarters through an open lock. The President and Barbara had wished
him well, and Marilyn and the kids had looked so proud of him. If
he had known that being courageous was this simple, maybe he would
have tried it sooner.

Inside the large barrel of this habitat, five seats near wall screens
had been bolted to what would be the floor during acceleration. He
propelled himself toward a seat and strapped himself in without a
qualm. The *Burroughs* circled the Earth, then took off like a dream;
Dan, pressed against his seat, watched in awe as the globe on the
screen shrank to the size of a marble.

The ship would take a little while to reach one g, at which point
the crew could get up and move around. The *Burroughs* would continue to accelerate until they were halfway to Mars, at which point
it would begin to decelerate. The faster the ship boosted, the more

gravity it would have; at least that was how Dan understood the matter. Even though it might have been kind of fun to float around the *Burroughs*, he had been a bit queasy during the shuttle flight, and was just as happy that they wouldn't have to endure weightlessness during the voyage. He had heard too many stories about space sickness and the effects of weightlessness on gas; he didn't want to puke and fart all the way to Mars.

Dan had little time to glance at the viewscreens when he finally rose from his seat. The others were already messing around with the computers and setting up experiments and generally doing whatever they were supposed to do; his job now was to monitor any transmissions from Earth.

He sent back greetings, having rehearsed the words during the last few days. He didn't have anything really eloquent to say about actually being out in space at last, but a lot of astronauts weren't great talkers. When he was about to sign off, the NASA CapCom patched him through to Marilyn.

She had cut out James J. Kilpatrick's latest column to read to him. The columnist had written: "Lloyd Bentsen once said of the Vice President, 'You're no Jack Kennedy.' This has been verified in a way Senator Bentsen could never have predicted. This man is no Jack Kennedy. Instead, he has donned the mantle of Columbus and the other great explorers of the past."

That was the kind of thing that could really make a guy feel great.

There was little privacy on the *Burroughs*. What with the shielding, the engine, the Mars lander they would use when they reached their destination, and the base camp assembly that would be sent to the Martian surface if NASA deemed a longer stay worthwhile, there wasn't exactly an abundance of space for the crew in the habitat modules. The next ship, which was already being built, would have the additional luxuries of a recreational module, along with separate sleeping compartments, but NASA had cut a few corners on this one.

The bathroom, toilet and shower included, was the size of a small closet; their beds, which had to be pulled out from the walls, were in the adjoining module, with no partitions. The whole place smelled like a locker room, maybe because the modules had been part of the Russian space station before being recycled for use in this mission.

The food tasted even worse than some of the stuff Dan had eaten in the Deke house at DePauw.

But their comfort was not entirely overlooked; the *Burroughs* had a small library of CDs, videodiscs, and books stored on microdot. Within twenty-four hours, Dan and his companions had worked out a schedule so that each of them would have some time alone in the bed compartment to read, listen to music, or take a nap. There was no sense getting on one another's nerves during this voyage, and some solitude would ease any tensions.

Dan went to the sleeping quarters during his scheduled time on the third day out, meaning to watch one of his favorite movies, *Ferris Bueller's Day Off*. He could stretch out on one of the beds and still see the screen on the wall in the back. He nodded off just as Ferris Bueller, played by Matthew Broderick, was calling up his friend Cameron on the phone; he woke up to the sounds of "Twist and Shout." Matthew Broderick was gyrating on a float in the middle of a Chicago parade.

Dan had missed most of the movie. He must have been more tired than he realized, even though he didn't have as much to do as the rest of the crew. Sergei had said something about doing some medical tests on him. He looked at his watch, set on Eastern Standard Time, which they were keeping aboard ship, and noticed that it was past 8:00 P.M. He stared at the screen, not understanding why the movie was still on until he realized that the player had gone back to the beginning of the disk and started running the film again. It was Ahmed's time to use the compartment now, so why wasn't the Prince here bugging him about it? On top of that, nobody had come to get him for dinner.

He sat up slowly. A weird feeling came over him, a little like the nervousness he had felt before calling his father about trying to get into the Guard. He got to his feet and climbed the ladder through the passageway that connected this module to the next.

The hatch at the end of the short passage was open as he came up. His shipmates were slumped over the table where they usually ate, their faces in their trays. Dan crept toward them, wondering if this was some kind of joke. "Okay, guys," he said, "you can cut it out now." They were awfully still, and Sergei had written something on the table in Cyrillic letters with his fingers and some gravy. "Okay, you faked me out. Come on." Dan stopped behind Kiichi and nudged him, then saw that the Japanese had stopped breathing. Very slowly, he moved around the table, taking each person's pulse in turn. The arms were flaccid, the bodies cold.

"Oh, my God," he said. "Oh, my God." He sank to the floor, covered his face with his hands, and sat there for a long time until a voice called out to him from the com.

"Houston to *Burroughs*. Houston to *Burroughs*." He got up and stumbled toward the com. "Come in, *Burroughs*." He sat down and turned on the com screen.

Sallie Werfel, the CapCom, stared out at him from the screen.

"They're dead," he blurted out. "They're all dead." Not until after he had said it did he remember that NASA had planned a live broadcast for that evening. "Oh, my God."

Sallie gazed back at him with a big smile on her face; it would take a while for his words to reach her, since signals had to work harder to get through all that space. Then her smile disappeared, and she was suddenly shouting to somebody else before turning to the screen once more.

"We're off the air," she said. "All right, what the hell do you mean about—"

"They're all dead," he replied. "At the table. Turn on the cameras and take a look. Sergei wrote something next to his tray, but it's in Russian."

Sallie was whispering to a man near her. Some more time passed. "All right, Dan," she said very quietly. "I want you to stay right where you are for the moment. We've got the cameras on the others now. You're absolutely sure they're, uh, gone?"

"Yeah."

A few more minutes passed. "We're looking at Sergei's message. A couple of our people here know Russian, so we should have a translation in just a little bit. While we're waiting, I want to know exactly what you were doing during the last few hours."

"Not much," he said. "I mean, it was my turn for some private time—we had, like, a schedule for times to be alone, you know? So I went to the other module thinking I'd catch a movie." He was about to say he had been watching *Ferris Bueller's Day Off*, but thought better of it. "What I remember is that Ashana was on the treadmill working out, and Sergei and Ahmed were checking some numbers or something. Kiichi was in the can—er, bathroom. I fell asleep, and when I woke up and looked at the time, it was past dinner. Then I came out and—" He swallowed hard. "Oh, my God." He waited.

"Take it easy, Dan," she said finally. "We're opening up a line to the White House right now."

An alien, he thought. Some creepy blob thing, the kind of creature they showed in old sci-fi movies, had somehow found its way aboard the ship. He imagined it oozing out to kill his companions during dinner, then concealing itself somewhere aboard the *Burroughs* to wait for him. Except that it wouldn't find too many places it could hide in the crew's quarters. Maybe the alien was concealed in the Mars lander by now, waiting for him. He shuddered. It couldn't be an alien. There wasn't any way for one to get aboard.

"We've got a translation," Sallie was saying. Dan forced his attention back to the screen. "We know what Sergei wrote." Her eyes glistened; he held his breath. "Not the food. Fever. Feels like flu."

"What?" He waited.

"Flu. Influenza." She lifted a hand to her temples. "He's telling us it wasn't anything in the food, that it felt as if they were coming down with something."

Everything had happened awfully fast. The whole business might be some sort of weird assassination attempt; maybe someone had figured out a way to poison the main module's air system. It was pure chance that he had not been sitting there with the others. But why would anyone want to assassinate him? Only the Democrats had anything to gain from that, and they had so many loose cannons that somebody would have leaked such a plot by now.

He didn't know whether to be relieved or not when Sallie contacted him an hour later and gave him NASA's hypothesis. They suspected that his comrades had been the victims of an extremely virulent but short-lived virus—virulent because the others had died so quickly, and short-lived because Dan, in the same module breathing the same air, was still alive. They had come up with this explanation after consulting with the Russians, who had admitted that milder viruses had occasionally afflicted their cosmonauts. The closed ecologies of their modules had never been perfect. What that meant was that things could get kind of scuzzy in there.

The next order of business was to dispose of the bodies. Dan put on his spacesuit and tried not to look at the food-stained faces of his dead comrades as he dragged them one by one into the airlock.

They deserved a prayer. The only ones he knew were Christian prayers, but maybe Kiichi and Ahmed wouldn't mind, and he suspected Sergei was more religious than he let on. He whispered the Lord's Prayer, and then another he had often used at prayer breakfasts. Too late, he realized that a prayer said at meals might not be the most appropriate thing, given that his companions had died over their chow.

He looked up from the bodies as the outside door slid slowly open to reveal the blackness of space. His comrades deserved a few more words before he consigned them to the darkness.

"You guys," he whispered, "you were some of the best friends I ever had. You were definitely the smartest."

It took a while to get the bodies outside. As he watched them drift away from the ship, tears rose to his eyes. He was really going to miss them.

Sallie contacted Dan an hour before the President was to address the nation and the world. The most important thing now was for Dan to seem in control of himself when it was time for his own broadcast. The NASA scientists were fairly certain that Dan wouldn't suffer the fate of the others; there was only a slight chance that the mysterious virus would reappear to infect him. He didn't find this very consoling, since there had been only a slight chance of such a thing happening in the first place.

"Do me a favor, Sallie," Dan said. "If I do kick off, don't let the media have tapes of it or anything. I mean, I don't want Marilyn and my kids watching that stuff on CNN or something." He waited. The time for round-trip signals was growing longer.

"You got it, Dano."

The President made his announcement, and Dan went on an hour later to show that he was still able to function. He had no prepared speech, but the most important thing was to look calm and not hysterical. He succeeded in that, mostly because he felt too stunned and empty to crack up in front of the hundreds of millions who would be viewing him from Earth.

Sallie spoke to him after his appearance. Ashana Washington's parents and brother had already retained counsel, and there was talk of massive lawsuits. He might have known that the lawyers would get in on this immediately.

"The most important thing now," Sallie said, "is to bring you home as fast as possible. You'll reach your destination four days from now." She narrowed her eyes. "The *Burroughs* is already programmed to orbit Mars automatically, so all we have to do is let it swing around and head back to Earth. You can get back in—"

"I'm not going to land?" he asked, and waited even longer.

Sallie sat up. "Land?"

"I want to land, Sallie. Don't you understand? I have to now. The others would have expected me to—I've got to do it for them." He searched for another phrase. "It means they won't have died in vain. I can do it—you can program the lander, and I can go down to the surface. Maybe I can't do the experiments and stuff they were going to, but I can set up the cameras and bring back soil samples. It wouldn't be right not to try. And if I'm going to die, I might as well die doing something."

He waited for his words to reach her. "Dan," she said at last, "you surprise me."

It would probably surprise the hell out of the President, too. "I've got to do it, Sallie." He frowned, struggling with the effort of all this thinking. "Look, if I land, it'll inspire the world to bigger and better space triumphs. We'll get that bigger space station built and the more advanced ships, too. But if you just bring me back, all the nuts will start whining again about what a waste all this was and how four people died for nothing." He waited.

"I'll do what I can, Dan." She shook her head. "I don't have much to say about this, but I can speak up for you. In the end, though, it's probably going to be up to the President."

"Then put me through to him now."

He hashed it out with the President in the slow motion of radio delay, listened to the objections, and replied by invoking the memory of his dead comrades. When the President, looking tense and even more hyper than usual, signed off by saying he would have to consult with his advisers, Dan was certain he had won. He felt no surprise when word came twelve hours later that he would be allowed to undertake the landing.

After all, if the President didn't let him go ahead, it was like admitting publicly that he had put an incompetent without adequate training aboard the *Burroughs*. The President, having finally salvaged his place in history, wasn't about to go down in the record books as a doofus.

David Bowie was singing about Major Tom and Ground Control. Kiichi had been a David Bowie fan, so a lot of Bowie's music, everything from his Ziggy Stardust phase up through Tin Machine, was in the *Burroughs's* music collection. Dan had never been into David Bowie, who struck him as being kind of fruity, but now he felt as if he understood this particular song.

Sometimes, during his work with the President's Council on Space, Dan had wondered why some early astronauts had gotten kind of flaky after returning to Earth. These were macho test pilot guys, not the kind of men anyone would expect to get mystical or weirded out. But as he moved around the ship, which was usually silent except for the low throbbing hum of the engine and an occasional beep from the consoles, he was beginning to feel a bit odd himself, as if his mind had somehow moved outside of his body.

He had never thought all that much about God. He had, of course, never doubted that God was out there going about His business; he had simply never thought about the Lord that much, except when he was in church or saying a prayer. When he was a boy, he had imagined a God something like his grandfather Pulliam, an angry old man ready to smite all those liberal Democrats, Communists, and other forces of darkness. Later on, when he was older and more mature, God had seemed more like a sort of basketball coach or golf pro.

Now, when he gazed at the image of Mars on his screen, a rust-red dot surrounded by blackness, he had the strangest feeling that he had never really understood the Lord at all. God had created all this, the planets and the space between them and the stars that were so far away he could not even comprehend the distance. God, in some ways, was a lot like the NASA computers, but there was even more to Him than that. Dan wasn't quite sure how to put it; things like that were hard to explain. He supposed that was what it meant to be mystical—having weird feelings you couldn't quite put into words. And faith was believing what no one in his right mind would believe even though it was true.

NASA kept him busy during his waking hours programming the Mars lander and checking out its systems. After supper, he usually worked on his speech, with some suggestions NASA was passing along from his speechwriters. They had given him another speech earlier, but he couldn't use that one now. With what had happened, this one would have to be really inspiring.

Yet he still had his moments of solitude, the times when he felt, for the first time in his life, what it was like to be utterly alone. He couldn't actually be alone, he supposed, since God had to be somewhere in the vicinity, but there were times when it seemed that the emptiness of space had seeped into him.

Mars swelled until it filled the screen, and then his ship was falling around the planet. There was no way to avoid weightlessness now; the *Burroughs* had begun to decelerate after the halfway point of the journey, and its engine had finally shut down. Dan put on his spacesuit and floated through the tunnel that connected the crew's quarters with the module holding the base assembly. He wouldn't be setting up a Mars base, though, since NASA didn't want him fooling around down there for very long. He entered the last module, which held the lander.

He pressed his hand against the lander's door; it slid open. The lander had food, a small lavatory, and equipment for experiments. There was even a Mars rover on board so that he could ride around on the surface. He wouldn't be doing much, though, except for shooting a bunch of stuff with the cameras and gathering soil samples. The important thing was to land, make his speech, mess around for a little while, catch some shut-eye, and then get back to the *Burroughs*.

He strapped himself into one of the chairs. The four empty seats made him feel as if the ghosts of the others were with him. NASA had allowed each of the astronauts to bring along a small personal possession to take down to the Martian surface, and Dan had his companions' choices with him in the lander. Ahmed had brought a

Koran, Kiichi a vintage Louisville Slugger with Joe DiMaggio's signature engraved on it, Sergei a set of nested Russian dolls, and Ashana a pair of Nikes personally autographed by Michael Jordan. A lump rose in his throat.

The doors to the outside were opening; he tensed. The President had spoken to him just a couple of hours ago, telling him that everyone in the world would be waiting for his first transmission from the surface. In spite of the tragedy, Dan's determination to carry out the landing had inspired everybody in the country. Having come so far, humankind would not be discouraged by this setback; the Vice President had shown the way. Construction of the next ship was moving along; it would probably be spaceworthy by spring, and a follow-up Mars mission would give an even bigger boost to Dan's candidacy. At this point, he would probably carry all the states, and even D.C., in the general election.

"Asteroids," the President had said. "Lotta resources there. Just get one of those things in Earth orbit, where we can go into, uh, a mining mode, and supply-side economics can work." It was nice for Dan to think that, when he finally became President, things might be moving along so well that he'd have plenty of time for golf, the way Eisenhower had.

The lander glided forward toward the new world below.

Mars filled his screen. Dan, pressed against his seat, braced himself. He had known what to expect; his training had included maneuvers with a model of the Mars rover in areas much like the Martian surface. Yet actually seeing it this close up still awed him. It looked, he thought, like the biggest sand trap in the universe.

His chair trembled under him as he landed. Dan waited, wanting to make sure everything was all right before he got up. Time to contact Earth, but in the excitement of actually being on Mars, he had forgotten what he was supposed to say.

He cleared his throat. "Guys," he said, "I'm down." That ought to do the job.

Over four minutes passed before he heard what sounded like cheers at the other end. Sallie was saying something, but he couldn't make out the words. By then, he was rummaging through the compartments of his spacesuit looking for the cards that held his speech.

"—all ecstatic," Sallie's voice said. "Congratulations, and God bless you—you don't know how much—"

He sighed, realizing at last that he had forgotten the cards. He might have known that, during the most important moment of his life, he would have to ad-lib.

Dan waited in the small airlock until the door slid open. Above him was the pinkish red sky of an alien world. A rust-colored barren landscape stretched to the horizon, which, he noticed, seemed closer than it should be, then he remembered that Mars was smaller than Earth. He felt a lot lighter, too, since Mars, being a smaller place, didn't have as much gravity.

He made his way down the ladder to the surface, then inhaled slowly. "Whoa," he said aloud, overcome with awe at the immensity of this accomplishment and sorrow that his dead comrades could not share the moment with him. "Jeez." He pressed his lips together, suddenly realizing that history would record man's first words on the surface of Mars as "Whoa" and "Jeez."

"Well, here I am," he said, knowing he would have to wing it. "I almost can't believe I'm here. Man, if anybody had told me when I was a kid that I'd go to Mars, I would have thought—" He paused. "Anyway, the thing is, I wish the others were here with me, because they're the ones who really deserved to make this trip. What I mean is, I'm really going to miss them, but I can tell you all I'm not ever going to forget them. It's why I'm here, because of them. In other words, I figured I had to come down and stand here for them." He remembered that he was supposed to plant the United Nations flag about now, and took the pole out from under his arm. "Now we'll go forward." The words he had planned to say at this point were something like that. "And someday, other people will come here and turn into Martians." Dan cleared his throat. "Guess I'll show you around a little now."

He scanned the landscape with a camera, then went back to the lander. By then, the President had given him his congratulations, and Marilyn had gotten on to talk to him after that. He was happy to hear his wife's voice, even though, what with having to wait a few minutes until she heard him and could reply, it wasn't actually possible to have what he would call a real conversation. This far from Earth, the signals had to work even harder to reach him.

The rover had been lowered from another side of the lander on a platform. Since about all he could do was take pictures and gather soil samples, NASA wanted him to drive around and take them in different places. They didn't want him to go too far or take any unnecessary risks, and maybe, now that he'd given a speech of sorts, he could let the images of the Martian surface speak for themselves.

He rode around, careful not to drive too fast since there were some nasty-looking rocks and rims of small craters nearby, until the orange sky grew darker. By the time he got back to the lander with his samples, the sky was nearly black and the sun a bright swirl on the horizon.

I actually got here, he thought, then remembered the others with a pang.

He slept well, then got up to say his farewells to the Red Planet— although Rusty Planet might be a better name for it. Another ride, some more pictures and samples, and he was ready to go. He hoped the NASA scientists weren't too unhappy with his answers to their questions about what unusual things he might have observed. Hell, *everything* seemed pretty unusual here, when he stopped to think about it.

He went inside, then strapped in. "Ready to go," he said. There were just a couple of buttons to push, and he had practiced a lot during the last days aboard the *Burroughs* to be sure he didn't make a mistake. He pressed one, waited for it to light up, then hit the next. For a few moments, he wondered why he couldn't feel the lander taking off, then realized that it wasn't moving.

"Uh, Mars to Houston," he said, then waited until he heard Sallie's voice respond. "I hate to say this, but I'm not going anywhere. Should I hit those whosits again, or what?"

Nearly ten minutes later, he heard Sallie's reply. Her first word was "Shit."

No matter how many times he activated the controls, nothing happened. Mission Control had various theories about what might be wrong, none of which were doing him any good. Gradually it dawned on him that he might be stranded. Twenty-four hours after he reached that conclusion, Sallie confirmed it. They could not pinpoint the problem at that distance. They did not want to take any risks with the lander. He was reminded of which buttons to push in order to bring down the Mars base assembly.

It could have been worse, he told himself. There were enough provisions in the lander alone to last him more than a month, since his companions weren't there to share them. With the supplies the base assembly had, he could survive until a rescue mission arrived.

There would be such a mission. The President assured him of that, as did Sallie. Another ship would be on its way to him within a few months. The wonderful thing was that his mission, despite the tragedy, was in its own way a success, even if he wasn't in the best position to appreciate that fact. A man had made it to Mars and was now on its surface, and the fate of his fellow astronauts had only temporarily stemmed the rising tide of optimism and hope. Humankind would return to the Moon and reach out to the other planets. Dan, who had insisted on landing instead of turning back, would be remembered by future generations of space explorers.

How his present predicament might affect the elections was not discussed. The President had said something vague about getting him back there in time for the convention. Now that Dan was a true hero, it didn't look as though there would be any opposition in the Republican primaries anyway.

Dan tried to feel comforted by this, but the campaign, and everything else, seemed awfully far away.

A distant object shaped like a shuttlecock dropped toward the cratered plain. Its engines fired; the object landed two kilometers away.

Dan sighed with relief at the sight of the base assembly. He had been worrying that something might go wrong at this point; one disadvantage of being a hero was that sometimes it required you to be dead. Now he would be safe, and could keep busy making observations, watching movies, working out, and in general keeping himself together until the rescue mission arrived. It was sort of depressing to know he'd miss Thanksgiving and Christmas, although fortunately there were some turkey dinners among the provisions, and Mission Control had promised to sing carols for him.

He climbed into the rover and started toward the barrels of the base assembly; he'd check it out first, then come back another time to load up whatever he might need from the lander. His staff had promised to transmit the text for the official announcement of his candidacy in a few days, and he supposed they would want him to make some speeches from Mars later, during the primaries. Maybe being on Mars, whatever the disadvantages, was better than having to trudge through New Hampshire.

He had to admit it; life in the somewhat more spacious quarters of the Mars base wasn't too bad in some ways. He was getting used to the desolate orange landscape and the way the sun set so suddenly. There were movies and records enough to keep him occupied, although he was beginning to see that there were limits to how many times he could watch some movies, even ones as great as *Ferris Bueller's Day Off*.

But there were times when the solitude, even with all the messages NASA was relaying from Earth, really got to him. There wasn't a whole lot a guy could do all alone, except for stuff it was better not to think about too much. He had spoken to Marilyn and the kids a couple of times, but having to speak and then wait long minutes for the response made him realize how far he was from everything he knew.

Maybe things would pick up when he really got into his campaign. There was plenty he could do, even out here. His staff was already trying to set him up for a "Nightline" appearance, which would probably have to be taped so that the delay between Ted Koppel's questions and his answers could be deleted. His staff should be transmitting the text for the official announcement of his candidacy any day now.

Dan had finished struggling into his spacesuit and was about to put on his helmet when the com started beeping at him. Maybe his speechwriters had finally gotten their act together. He sat down and turned on the screen.

The President's face stared out at him. "Uh, hello, Mr. President," Dan said. "I was just about to take a drive over to the lander—there's some stuff I want to move here."

"I don't know how to tell you this, Dan," the President said. "Something's gone, well, a bit awry. Might have known the Democrats would think of some devious—see, we're going to have to postpone your announcement for a while."

"But why?"

He waited a long time for the President's answer. "The Democrats—they're saying you have to be on Earth to make your announcement. Somebody found some loophole or other in the law, and they're arguing that you can't declare and run for president while you're on Mars. Got our guys working on it—think they can beat those bastards in court—but by the time they do, it may be too late to file and get you on primary ballots. Could try to get write-ins, but the rules are, uh, different in every state."

Dan tried to recall if there was something in the law the Democrats could use to pull a stunt like this. He couldn't think of anything, but then he hadn't been exactly the biggest brain in law school. Maybe the Democrats would drag out John Glenn, however old he was, to run this time. They'd probably use Ashana's family in the campaign, too; they had plenty of reason to be pissed off at the Administration.

"You said I could get back by the convention," Dan murmured. "I mean, aren't the delegates free to switch their votes if they want?"

The minutes passed. "Well, you're right on the money there, and no question they'd turn to you, but—see, NASA's got sort of a little problem with the new ship. Nothing for you to worry about, just some bitty technical thing they can definitely iron out, but they're certain they can have you back here next fall."

Dan was beginning to see more problems. The Democrats might use his predicament against the Republicans. They would say he wouldn't be stranded there if the Administration had thought more about real science and space exploration and less about politics and publicity stunts, if they hadn't been rushing to put him on another planet. He wouldn't be on the campaign trail to inspire people and to invoke the names of his comrades; he would be only a distant voice and grainy image from Mars. The whole business might turn into as big a bummer as the end of the Gulf War.

"What are we going to do?" Dan asked.

When the President replied, he said, "Well, there's a lotta sentiment here to make Marilyn our candidate."

That figured. The idea was so perfect that Dan was surprised he hadn't thought of it himself. The Democrats would look mean-spirited slinging mud at a hero's wife, one waiting and praying for her husband to return safely.

"All I can say," Dan said quietly, "is that she has my full support."

Dan finished loading the rover, climbed in, and drove slowly toward the scattered Tootsie Rolls of his base. He had not had to talk to Marilyn very long to convince her to run; in fact, he had expected her to object a lot more to the idea. She would make a pretty good president, though—maybe a better one than he would have been.

He had packed up the personal items of his comrades—Ashana's Nikes, Ahmed's Koran, Kiichi's bat, and Sergei's dolls—feeling that he wanted his dead friends' things with him. He had also brought his golf balls and his favorite wood. The club, which had a persimmon head, had cost him a pretty penny, but he liked a driver with a solid hardwood head.

An inspiration came to him. He stopped the rover, climbed down, then took out one of his balls and the wood. Stepping over a small crater, he set down the ball, then gripped his club. Getting in a smooth swing was going to be rough with his spacesuit on, but he thought he could manage it. Alan Shepard might be the first guy to tee off on the Moon, but Dan would be the first to do so on another planet.

He swung his club and knew the head's sweet spot had met the ball. The small white orb arched above the orange cratered landscape and soared toward the distant pink sky.

Matter's End

GREGORY BENFORD

Twenty years ago, while working as an instructional-materials specialist in Massachusetts, I conceived a dystopian novel about the problem of human aggression. Because the story took place on an imaginary planet, I began to suspect it was science fiction, an instinct confirmed when the manuscript was ultimately published as such. Soon afterward, I found myself having a few beers in a roach-ridden Cambridge apartment with the noted SF scholar Jeffrey M. Elliot—never mind the details—and, having resolved to learn something about the field into which I'd stumbled, I asked, "Hey, Jeff, what novels should I read?"

Without hesitation, Elliot replied, "*Macrolife* by George Zebrowski and *In the Ocean of Night* by Gregory Benford."

I hadn't heard of either novel or either author, but I followed Elliot's advice, and I'm glad I did. Zebrowski's book impressed me with its sweep, Benford's with its style—a subtle, elegant voice relating a "hard SF" story of scientists on the trail of an alien intelligence.

In 1974 Benford received the Nebula Award for "If the Stars Are Gods," a novelette written in collaboration with Gordon Eklund. The 1980 Nebula for Best Novel went to Benford's *Timescape*, which also won the John W. Campbell Memorial Award. His other books include *Across the Sea of Suns*, *Against Infinity*, *Artifact*, *Heart of the Comet* (with David Brin), *Great Sky River*, and *Tides of Light*. *In Alien Flesh* offers up a smorgasbord of Benford's shorter works.

" 'Matter's End' is another of my looks at the lives of physicists, with every scientific detail taken directly from the world," Benford informs us about his Nebula-nominated novelette. "The moist mysteries of its besieged India are from life, too—a long visit I paid there to attend an International Astronomical Society meeting—but augmented by some thoughts on how biotech will affect the developing world. The story's philosophical basis is a mixture of the 'implicate order' theories of quantum mechanics and Platonist ideas about the nature of knowing. These are not my views, mind you, as a working physicist—but they do serve the cause of the story, so I used them."

When Dr. Samuel Johnson felt himself getting tied up in an argument over Bishop Berkeley's ingenious sophistry to prove the nonexistence of matter, and that everything in the universe is merely ideal, he kicked a large stone and answered, "I refute it thus." Just what that action assured him of is not very obvious, but apparently he found it comforting.

—Sir Arthur Eddington

India came to him first as a breeze like soured buttermilk, rich yet tainted. A door banged somewhere, sending gusts sweeping through the Bangalore airport, slicing through the 4 A.M. silences.

Since the Free State of Bombay had left India, Bangalore had become an international airport. Yet the damp caress seemed to erase the sterile signatures that made all big airports alike, even giving a stippled texture to the cool enamel glow of the fluorescents.

The moist air clasped Robert Clay like a stranger's sweaty palm. The ripe, fleshy aroma of a continent enfolded him, swarming up his nostrils and soaking his lungs with sullen spice. He put down his carry-on bag and showed the immigration clerk his passport. The man gave him a piercing, ferocious stare—then mutely slammed a rubber stamp onto the pages and handed it back.

A hand snagged him as he headed toward baggage claim.

"Professor Clay?" The face was dark olive with intelligent eyes riding above sharp cheekbones. A sudden white grin flashed as Clay nodded. "Ah, *good*. I am Dr. Sudarshan Patil. Please come this way."

Dr. Patil's tone was polite, but his hands impatiently pulled Clay away from the sluggish lines, through a battered wooden side door. The heavy-lidded immigration guards were carefully looking in other directions, hands held behind their backs. Apparently they had been paid off and would ignore this odd exit. Clay was still groggy from trying to sleep on the flight from London. He shook his head as Patil led him into the gloom of a baggage storeroom.

"Your clothes," Patil said abruptly.

"What?"

"They mark you as a Westerner. Quickly!"

Patil's hands, light as birds in the quilted soft light, were already plucking at his coat, his shirt. Clay was taken aback at this abruptness. He hesitated, then struggled out of the dirty garments, pulling his loose slacks down over his shoes. He handed his bundled clothes to Patil, who snatched them away without a word.

"You're welcome," Clay said. Patil took no notice, just thrust a wad of tan cotton at him. The man's eyes jumped at each distant sound in the storage room, darting, suspecting every pile of dusty bags.

Clay struggled into the pants and rough shirt. They looked dingy in the wan yellow glow of a single distant fluorescent tube.

"Not the reception I'd expected," Clay said, straightening the baggy pants and pulling at the rough drawstring.

"These are not good times for scientists in my country, Dr. Clay," Patil said bitingly. His voice carried that odd lilt that echoed both the Raj and Cambridge.

"Who're you afraid of?"

"Those who hate Westerners and their science."

"They said in Washington—"

"We are about great matters, Professor Clay. Please cooperate, please."

Patil's lean face showed its bones starkly, as though energies pressed outward. Promontories of bunched muscle stretched a mottled canvas skin. He started toward a far door without another word, carrying Clay's overnight bag and jacket.

"Say, where're we—"

Patil swung open a sheet-metal door and beckoned. Clay slipped through it and into the moist wealth of night. His feet scraped on a dirty sidewalk beside a black tar road. The door hinge squealed behind them, attracting the attention of a knot of men beneath a vibrant yellow streetlight nearby.

The bleached fluorescence of the airport terminal was now a continent away. Beneath a line of quarter-ton trucks, huddled figures slept. In the astringent street-lamp glow he saw a decrepit green Korean Tochat van parked at the curb.

"In!" Patil whispered.

The men under the streetlight started walking toward them, calling out hoarse questions.

Clay yanked open the van's sliding door and crawled into the second row of seats. A fog of unknown pungent smells engulfed him. The driver, a short man, hunched over the wheel. Patil sprang into the front seat and the van ground away, its low gear whining.

Shouts. A stone thumped against the van roof. Pebbles rattled at the back.

They accelerated, the engine clattering. A figure loomed up from the shifting shadows and flung muck against the window near Clay's face. He jerked back at the slap of it. "Damn!"

They plowed through a wide puddle of dirty rainwater. The engine sputtered and for a moment Clay was sure it would die. He looked out the rear window and saw vague forms running after them. Then the engine surged again and they shot away.

They went two blocks through hectic traffic. Clay tried to get a clear look at India outside, but all he could see in the starkly shadowed street were the crisscrossings of three-wheeled taxis and human-drawn rickshaws. He got an impression of incessant activity, even in this desolate hour. Vehicles leaped out of the murk as headlights swept across them and then vanished utterly into the moist shadows again.

They suddenly swerved around a corner beneath spreading, gloomy trees. The van jolted into deep potholes and jerked to a stop. "Out!" Patil called.

Clay could barely make out a second van at the curb ahead. It was blue and caked with mud, but even in the dim light would not be confused with their green one. A rotting fetid reek filled his nose as he got out the side door, as if masses of overripe vegetation loomed in the shadows. Patil tugged him into the second van. In a few seconds they went surging out through a narrow, brick-lined alley.

"Look, what—"

"Please, quiet," Patil said primly. "I am watching carefully now to be certain that we are not being followed."

They wound through a shantytown warren for several minutes. Their headlights picked up startled eyes that blinked from what Clay at first had taken to be bundles of rags lying against the shacks. They seemed impossibly small even to be children. Huddled against decaying tin lean-tos, the dim forms often did not stir even as the van splashed dirty water on them from potholes.

Clay began, "Look, I understand the need for—"

"I apologize for our rude methods, Dr. Clay," Patil said. He gestured at the driver. "May I introduce Dr. Singh?"

Singh was similarly gaunt and intent, but with bushy hair and a thin, pointed nose. He jerked his head aside to peer at Clay, nodded twice like a puppet on strings, and then quickly stared back at the narrow lane ahead. Singh kept the van at a steady growl, abruptly yanking it around corners. A wooden cart lurched out of their way, its driver swearing in a strident singsong. "Welcome to India," Singh said with reedy solemnity. "I am afraid circumstances are not the best."

"Uh, right. You two are heads of the project, they told me at the NSF."

"Yes," Patil said archly, "the project that officially no longer exists and unofficially is a brilliant success. It is amusing!"

"Yeah," Clay said cautiously, "we'll see."

"Oh, you will see," Singh said excitedly. "We have the events! More all the time."

Patil said precisely, "We would not have suggested that your National Science Foundation send an observer to confirm our findings unless we believed them to be of the highest importance."

"You've seen proton decay?"

Patil beamed. "Without doubt."

"Damn."

"Exactly."

"What mode?"

"The straightforward pion and positron decay products."

Clay smiled, reserving judgment. Something about Patil's almost prissy precision made him wonder if this small, beleaguered team of Indian physicists might actually have brought it off. An immense long shot, of course, but possible. There were much bigger groups of particle physicists in Europe and the U.S. who had tried to detect proton decay using underground swimming pools of pure water. Those experiments had enjoyed all the benefits of the latest electronics. Clay had worked on the big American project in a Utah salt mine, before lean budgets and lack of results closed it down. It would be galling if this lone, underfunded Indian scheme had finally done it. Nobody at the NSF believed the story coming out of India.

Patil smiled at Clay's silence, a brilliant slash of white in the murk. Their headlights picked out small panes of glass stuck seemingly at random in nearby hovels, reflecting quick glints of yellow back into the van. The night seemed misty; their headlights forked ahead. Clay thought a soft rain had started outside, but then he saw that thousands of tiny insects darted into their headlights. Occasionally big ones smacked against the windshield.

Patil carefully changed the subject. "I . . . believe you will pass unnoticed, for the most part."

"I look Indian?"

"I hope you will not take offense if I remark that you do not. We requested an Indian, but your NSF said they did not have anyone qualified."

"Right. Nobody who could hop on a plane, anyway." *Or would,* he added to himself.

"I understand. You are a compromise. If you will put this on . . ." Patil handed Clay a floppy khaki hat. "It will cover your curly hair. Luckily, your nose is rather more narrow than I had expected when the NSF cable announced they were sending a Negro."

"Got a lot of white genes in it, this nose," Clay said evenly.

"Please, do not think I am being racist. I simply wished to diminish the chances of you being recognized as a Westerner in the countryside."

"Think I can pass?"

"At a distance, yes."

"Be tougher at the site?"

"Yes. There are 'celebrants,' as they term themselves, at the mine."

"How'll we get in?"

"A ruse we have devised."

"Like that getaway back there? That was pretty slick."

Singh sent them jouncing along a rutted lane. Withered trees leaned against the pale stucco two-story buildings that lined the lane like children's blocks lined up not quite correctly. "Men in customs, they would give word to people outside. If you had gone through with the others, a different reception party would have been waiting for you."

"I see. But what about my bags?"

Patil had been peering forward at the gloomy jumble of buildings. His head jerked around to glare at Clay. "You were not to bring more than your carry-on bag!"

"Look, I can't get by on that. Chrissake, that'd give me just one change of clothes—"

"You left bags there?"

"Well, yeah, I had just one—"

Clay stopped when he saw the look on the two men's faces.

Patil said with strained clarity, "Your bags, they had identification tags?"

"Sure, airlines make you—"

"They will bring attention to you. There will be inquiries. The devotees will hear of it, inevitably, and know you have entered the country."

Clay licked his lips. "Hell, I didn't think it was so important."

The two lean Indians glanced at each other, their faces taking on a narrowing, leaden cast. "Dr. Clay," Patil said stiffly, "the 'celebrants' believe, as do many, that Westerners deliberately destroyed our crops with their biotechnology."

"Japanese companies' biologists did that, I thought," Clay said diplomatically.

"Perhaps. Those who disturb us at the Kolar gold mine make no fine distinctions between biologists and physicists. They believe that we are disturbing the very bowels of the earth, helping to further the destruction, bringing on the very end of the world itself. Surely you can see that in India, the mother country of religious philosophy, such matters are important."

"But your work, hell, it's not a matter of life or death or anything."

"On the contrary, the decay of the proton is precisely an issue of death."

Clay settled back in his seat, puzzled, watching the silky night stream by, cloaking vague forms in its shadowed mysteries.

2

Clay insisted on the telephone call. A wan winter sun had already crawled partway up the sky before he awoke, and the two Indian physicists wanted to leave immediately. They had stopped while still in Bangalore, holing up in the cramped apartment of one of Patil's graduate students. As Clay took his first sip of tea, two other students had turned up with his bag, retrieved at a cost he never knew.

Clay said, "I promised I'd call home. Look, my family's worried. They read the papers, they know the trouble here."

Shaking his head slowly, Patil finished a scrap of curled brown bread that appeared to be his only breakfast. His movements had a smooth liquid inertia, as if the sultry morning air oozed like jelly around him. They were sitting at a low table that had one leg too short; the already rickety table kept lurching, slopping tea into their saucers. Clay had looked for something to prop up the leg, but the apartment was bare, as though no one lived here. They had slept on pallets beneath a single bare bulb. Through the open windows, bare of frames or glass, Clay had gotten fleeting glimpses of the neighborhood—rooms of random clutter, plaster peeling off slumped walls, revealing the thin steel cross-ribs of the buildings, stained windows adorned with gaudy pictures of many-armed gods, already sunbleached and frayed. Children yelped and cried below, their voices reflected among the odd angles and apertures of the tangled streets, while carts rattled by and bare feet slapped the stones. Students had apparently stood guard last night, though Clay had never seen more than a quick motion in the shadows below as they arrived.

"You ask much of us," Patil said. By morning light his walnut-brown face seemed gullied and worn. Lines radiated from his mouth toward intense eyes.

Clay sipped his tea before answering. A soft, strangely sweet smell wafted through the open window. They sat well back in the room so nobody could see in from the nearby buildings. He heard Singh tinkering downstairs with the van's engine.

"Okay, it's maybe slightly risky. But I want my people to know I got here all right."

"There are few telephones here."

"I only need one."

"The system, often it does not work at all."

"Gotta try."

"Perhaps you do not understand—"

"I understand damn well that if I can't even reach my people, I'm not going to hang out here for long. And if I don't see that your experiment works right, nobody'll believe you."

"And your opinion depends upon . . . ?"

Clay ticked off points on his fingers. "On seeing the apparatus.

Checking your raw data. Running a trial case to see your system response. Then a null experiment—to verify your threshold level on each detector." He held up five fingers. "The works."

Patil said gravely, "Very good. We relish the opportunity to prove ourselves."

"You'll get it." Clay hoped to himself that they were wrong, but he suppressed that. He represented the faltering forefront of particle physics, and it would be embarrassing if a backwater research team had beaten the world. Still, either way, he would end up being the expert on the Kolar program, and that was a smart career move in itself.

"Very well. I must make arrangements for the call, then. But I truly—"

"Just do it. Then we get down to business."

The telephone was behind two counters and three doors at a Ministry for Controls office. Patil did the bribing and cajoling inside and then brought Clay in from the back of the van. He had been lying down on the backseat so he could not be seen easily from the street.

The telephone itself was a heavy black plastic thing with a rotary dial that clicked like a sluggish insect as it whirled. Patil had been on it twice already, clearing international lines through Bombay. Clay got two false rings and a dead line. On the fourth try he heard a faint, somehow familiar buzzing. Then a hollow, distant click.

"Angy?"

"Daddy, is that you?" Faint rock music in the background.

"Sure, I just wanted to let you know I got to India okay."

"Oh, Mommy will be so glad! We heard on the TV last night that there's trouble over there."

Startled, Clay asked, "What? Where's your mother?"

"Getting groceries. She'll be *so* mad she missed your call!"

"You tell her I'm fine, okay? But what trouble?"

"Something about a state leaving India. Lots of fighting, John Trimble said on the news."

Clay never remembered the names of news announcers; he regarded them as faceless nobodies reading prepared scripts, but for his daughter they were the voice of authority. "Where?"

"Uh, the lower part."

"There's nothing like that happening here, honey. I'm safe. Tell Mommy."

"People have ice cream there?"

"Yeah, but I haven't seen any. You tell your mother what I said, remember? About being safe?"

"Yes, she's been worried."

"Don't worry, Angy. Look, I got to go." The line popped and hissed ominously.

"I miss you, Daddy."

"I miss you double that. No, squared."

She laughed merrily. "I skinned my knee today at recess. It bled so much I had to go to the nurse."

"Keep it clean, honey. And give your mother my love."

"She'll be *so* mad."

"I'll be home soon."

She giggled and ended with the joke she had been using lately. "G'bye, Daddy. It's been real."

Her light laugh trickled into the static, a grace note from a bright land worlds away. Clay chuckled as he replaced the receiver. She cut the last word of "real nice" to make her good-byes hip and sardonic, a mannerism she had heard on television somewhere. An old joke; he had heard that even "groovy" was coming back in.

Clay smiled and pulled his hat down further and went quickly out into the street where Patil was waiting. India flickered at the edge of his vision, the crowds a hovering presence.

3

They left Bangalore in two vans. Graduate students drove the green Tochat from the previous night. He and Patil and Singh took the blue one, Clay again keeping out of sight by lying on the backseat. The day's raw heat rose around them like a shimmering lake of light.

They passed through lands leached of color. Only gray stubble grew in the fields. Trees hung limply, their limbs bowing as though exhausted. Figures in rags huddled for shade. A few stirred, eyes white in the shadows, as the vans ground past. Clay saw that large boles sat on the branches like gnarled knots with brown sheaths wrapped around the underside.

"Those some of the plant diseases I heard about?" he asked.

Singh pursed his lips. "I fear those are the pouches like those of wasps, as reported in the press." His watery eyes regarded the withered, graying trees as Patil slowed the car.

"Are they dangerous?" Clay could see yellow sap dripping from the underside of each.

"Not until they ripen," Singh said. "Then the assassins emerge."

"They look pretty big already."

"They are said to be large creatures, but of course there is little experience."

Patil downshifted and they accelerated away with an occasional sputtering misfire. Clay wondered whether they had any spare spark plugs along. The fields on each side of the road took on a dissolute and shredded look. "Did the genetech experiments cause this?" he asked.

Singh nodded. "I believe this emerged from the European programs. First we had their designed plants, but then pests found vulnerability. They sought strains that could protect crops from the new pests. So we got these wasps. I gather that now some error or mutation has made them equally excellent at preying on people and even cows."

Clay frowned. "The wasps came from the Japanese aid, didn't they?"

Patil smiled mysteriously. "You know a good deal about our troubles, sir."

Neither said anything more. Clay was acutely conscious that his briefing in Washington had been detailed technical assessments, without the slightest mention of how the Indians themselves saw their problems. Singh and Patil seemed either resigned or unconcerned; he could not tell which. Their sentences refracted from some unseen nugget, like seismic waves warping around the earth's core.

"I would not worry greatly about these pouches," Singh said after they had ridden in silence for a while. "They should not ripen before we are done with our task. In any case, the Kolar fields are quite barren, and afford few sites where the pouches can grow."

Clay pointed out the front window. "Those round things on the walls—more pouches?"

To his surprise, both men burst into merry laughter. Gasping,

Patil said, "Examine them closely, Dr. Clay. Notice the marks of the species which made them."

Patil slowed the car and Clay studied the round, circular pads on the whitewashed vertical walls along the road. They were brown and matted and marked in a pattern of radial lines. Clay frowned and then felt enormously stupid: the thick lines were handprints.

"Drying cakes, they are," Patil said, still chuckling.

"Of what?"

"Dung, my colleague. We use the cow here, not merely slaughter it."

"What for?"

"Fuel. After the cakes dry, we stack them—see?" They passed a plastic-wrapped tower. A woman was adding a circular, annular tier of thick dung disks to the top, then carefully folding the plastic over it. "In winter they burn nicely."

"For heating?"

"And cooking, yes."

Seeing the look on Clay's face, Singh's eyes narrowed and his lips drew back so that his teeth were bright stubs. His eyebrows were long brush strokes that met the deep furrows of his frown. "Old ways are still often preferable to the new."

Sure, Clay thought, the past of cholera, plague, infanticide. But he asked with neutral politeness, "Such as?"

"Some large fish from the Amazon were introduced into our principal river three years ago to improve fishing yields."

"The Ganges? I thought it was holy."

"What is more holy than to feed the hungry?"

"True enough. Did it work?"

"The big fish, yes. They are delicious. A great delicacy."

"I'll have to try some," Clay said, remembering the thin vegetarian curry he had eaten at breakfast.

Singh said, "But the Amazon sample contained some minute eggs that none of the proper procedures eliminated. They were of a small species—the candiru, is that not the name?" he inquired politely of Patil.

"Yes," Patil said, "a little being who thrives mostly on the urine of larger fish. Specialists now believe that perhaps the eggs were inside the larger species, and so escaped detection."

Patil's voice remained calm and factual, although while he spoke he abruptly swerved to avoid a goat that spontaneously ambled onto the rough road. Clay rocked hard against the van's door, and Patil then corrected further to stay out of a gratuitous mudhole that seemed to leap at them from the rushing foreground. They bumped noisily over ruts at the road's edge and bounced back onto the tarmac without losing speed. Patil sat ramrod straight, hands turning the steering wheel lightly, oblivious to the wrenching effects of his driving.

"Suppose, Professor Clay, that you are a devotee," Singh said. "You have saved to come to the Ganges for a decade, for two. Perhaps you even plan to die there."

"Yeah, okay." Clay could not see where this was leading.

"You are enthused as you enter the river to bathe. You are perhaps profoundly affected. An intense spiritual moment. It is not uncommon to merge with the river, to inadvertently urinate into it."

Singh spread his hands as if to say that such things went without saying.

"Then the candiru will be attracted by the smell. It mistakes this great bountiful largesse, the food it needs, as coming from a very great fish indeed. It excitedly swims up the stream of uric acid. Coming to your urethra, it swims like a snake into its burrow, as far up as it can go. You will see that the uric flow velocity will increase as the candiru makes its way upstream, inside you. When this tiny fish can make no further progress, some trick of evolution tells it to protrude a set of sidewise spines. So intricate!"

Singh paused a moment in smiling tribute to this intriguing facet of nature. Clay nodded, his mouth dry.

"These embed deeply in the walls and keep the candiru close to the source of what it so desires." Singh made short, delicate movements, his fingers jutting in the air. Clay opened his mouth, but said nothing.

Patil took them around a team of bullocks towing a wooden wagon and put in, "The pain is intense. Apparently there is no good treatment. Women—forgive this indelicacy—must be opened to get at the offending tiny fish before it swells and blocks the passage completely, having gorged itself insensate. Some men have an even worse choice. Their bladders are already engorged, having typically not been much emptied by the time the candiru enters. They must decide whether to attempt the slow procedure of poisoning the small thing and waiting for it to shrivel and withdraw its spines. However, their bladders might burst before that, flooding their abdomens with urine and of course killing them. If there is not sufficient time . . ."

"Yes?" Clay asked tensely.

"Then the penis must be chopped off," Singh said, "with the candiru inside."

Through a long silence Clay rode, swaying as the car wove through limitless flat spaces of parched fields and ruined brick walls and slumped whitewashed huts. Finally he said hoarsely, "I . . . don't blame you for resenting the . . . well, the people who brought all this on you. The devotees—"

"They believe this apocalyptic evil comes from the philosophy which gave us modern science."

"Well, look, whoever brought over those fish—"

Singh's eyes widened with surprise. A startled grin lit his face like a sunrise. "Oh no, Professor Clay! We do not blame the errors, or else we would have to blame equally the successes!"

To Clay's consternation, Patil nodded sagely.

He decided to say nothing more. Washington had warned him to stay out of political discussions, and though he was not sure if this was such, or if the lighthearted way Singh and Patil had related their story told their true attitude, it seemed best to just shut up. Again Clay had the odd sensation that here the cool certainties of Western biology had become diffused, blunted, crisp distinctions rendered into something beyond the constraints of the world outside, all blurred by the swarming, dissolving currents of India. The tin-gray sky loomed over a plain of ripe rot. The urgency of decay here was far more powerful than the abstractions that so often filled his head, the digitized iconography of sputtering, splitting protons.

4

The Kolar gold fields were a long, dusty drive from Bangalore. The sway of the van made Clay sleepy in the back, jet lag pulling him down into fitful, shallow dreams of muted voices, shadowy faces, and obscure purpose. He awoke frequently amid the dry smells, lurched up to see dry farmland stretching to the horizon, and collapsed again to bury his face in the pillow he had made by wadding up a shirt.

They passed through innumerable villages that, after the first few, all seemed alike with their scrawny children, ramshackle sheds, tin roofs, and general air of sleepy dilapidation. Once, in a narrow town, they stopped as rickshaws and carts backed up. An emaciated cow with pink paper tassels on its horns stood square in the middle of the road, trembling. Shouts and honks failed to move it, but no one ahead made the slightest effort to prod it aside.

Clay got out of the van to stretch his legs, ignoring Patil's warning to stay hidden, and watched. A crowd collected, shouting and chanting at the cow but not touching it. The cow shook its head, peering at the road as if searching for grass, and urinated powerfully. A woman in a red sari rushed into the road, knelt, and thrust her hand into the full stream. She made a formal motion with her other hand and splashed some urine on her forehead and cheeks. Three other women had already lined up behind her, and each did the same. Disturbed, the cow waggled its head and shakily walked away. Traffic started up, and Clay climbed back into the van. As they ground out of the dusty town, Singh explained that holy bovine urine was widely held to have positive health effects.

"Many believe it settles stomach troubles, banishes headaches, even improves fertility," Singh said.

"Yeah, you could sure use more fertility." Clay gestured at the throngs that filled the narrow clay sidewalks.

"I am not so Indian that I cannot find it within myself to agree with you, Professor Clay," Singh said.

"Sorry for the sarcasm. I'm tired."

"Patil and I are already under a cloud simply because we are scientists, and therefore polluted with Western ideas."

"Can't blame Indians for being down on us. Things're getting rough."

"But you are a black man. You yourself were persecuted by Western societies."

"That was a while back."

"And despite it you have risen to a professorship."

"You do the work, you get the job." Clay took off his hat and wiped his brow. The midday heat pressed sweat from him.

"Then you do not feel alienated from Western ideals?" Patil put in.

"Hell no. Look, I'm not some sharecropper who pulled himself up from poverty. I grew up in Falls Church, Virginia. Father's a federal bureaucrat. Middle class all the way."

"I see," Patil said, eyes never leaving the rutted road. "Your race bespeaks an entirely different culture, but you subscribe to the program of modern rationalism."

Clay looked at them quizzically. "Don't you?"

"As scientists, of course. But that is not all of life."

"Um," Clay said.

A thousand times before he had endured the affably condescending attention of whites, their curious eyes searching his face. No matter what the topic, they somehow found a way to inquire indirectly after his *true* feelings, his *natural* emotions. And if he waved away these intrusions, there remained in their heavy-lidded eyes a subtle skepticism, doubts about his authenticity. Few gave him space to simply be a suburban man with darker skin, a man whose interior landscape was populated with the same icons of Middle America as their own. Hell, his family name came from slaves, given as a tribute to Henry Clay, a nineteenth-century legislator. He had never expected to run into stereotyping in India, for chrissakes.

Still, he was savvy enough to lard his talk with some homey touches, jimmy things up with collard greens and black-eyed peas and street jive. It might put them at ease.

"I believe a li'l rationality could help," he said.

"Um." Singh's thin mouth twisted doubtfully. "Perhaps you should regard India as the great chessboard of our times, Professor. Here we have arisen from the great primordial agrarian times, fashioned our gods from our soil and age. Then we had orderly thinking, with all its assumptions, thrust upon us by the British. Now they are all gone, and we are suspended between the miasmic truths of the past and the failed strictures of the present."

Clay looked out the dirty window and suppressed a smile. Even the physicists here spouted mumbo jumbo. They even appeared solemnly respectful of the devotees, who were just crazies like the women by the cow. How could anything solid come out of such a swamp?

The chances that their experiment was right dwindled with each lurching, damp mile.

They climbed into the long range of hills before the Kolar fields. Burned-tan grass shimmered in the prickly heat. Sugarcane fields and rice paddies stood bone dry. In the villages, thin figures shaded beneath awnings, canvas tents, lean-tos, watched them pass. Lean faces betrayed only dim, momentary interest, and Clay wondered if his uncomfortable disguise was necessary outside Bangalore.

Without stopping they ate their lunch of dried fruit and thin, brown bread. In a high hill town, Patil stopped to refill his water bottle at a well. Clay peered out and saw down an alley a gang of stick-figure boys chasing a dog. They hemmed it in, and the bedraggled hound fled yapping from one side of their circle to the other. The animal whined at each rebuff and twice lost its footing on the cobblestones, sprawling, only to scramble up again and rush on. It was a cruel game, and the boys were strangely silent, playing without laughter. The dog was tiring; they drew in their circle.

A harsh edge to the boys' shouts made Clay slide open the van door. Several men were standing beneath a rust-scabbed sheet-metal awning nearby, and their eyes widened when they saw his face. They talked rapidly among themselves. Clay hesitated. The boys down the alley rushed the dog. They grabbed it as it yapped futilely and tried to bite them. They slipped twine around its jaws and silenced it. Shouting, they hoisted it into the air and marched off.

Clay gave up and slammed the door. The men came from under the awning. One rapped on the window. Clay just stared at them. One thumped on the door. Gestures, loud talk.

Patil and Singh came running, shouted something. Singh pushed the men away, chattering at them while Patil got the van started. Singh slammed the door in the face of a man with wild eyes. Patil gunned the engine and they ground away.

"They saw me and—"

"Distrust of outsiders is great here," Singh said. "They may be connected with the devotees, too."

"Guess I better keep my hat on."

"It would be advisable."

"I don't know, those boys—I was going to stop them pestering that dog. Stupid, I guess, but—"

"You will have to avoid being sentimental about such matters," Patil said severely.

"Uh—sentimental?"

"The boys were not playing."

"I don't—"

"They will devour it," Singh said.

Clay blinked. "Hindus eating meat?"

"Hard times. I am really quite surprised that such an animal has survived this long," Patil said judiciously. "Dogs are uncommon. I imagine it was wild, living in the countryside, and ventured into town in search of garbage scraps."

The land rose as Clay watched the shimmering heat bend and flex the seemingly solid hills.

5

They pulled another dodge at the mine. The lead green van veered off toward the main entrance, a cluster of concrete buildings and conveyer assemblies. From a distance, the physicists in the blue van watched a ragtag group envelop the van before it had fully stopped.

"Devotees," Singh said abstractedly. "They search each vehicle for evidence of our research."

"Your graduate students, the mob'll let them pass?"

Patil peered through binoculars. "The crowd is administering a bit of a pushing about," he said in his oddly cadenced accent, combining lofty British diction with a singsong lilt.

"Damn, won't the mine people get rid—"

"Some mine workers are among the crowd, I should imagine," Patil said. "They are beating the students."

"Well, can't we—"

"No time to waste." Singh waved them back into the blue van. "Let us make use of this diversion."

"But we could—"

"The students made their sacrifice for you. Do not devalue it, please."

Clay did not take his eyes from the nasty knot of confusion until they lurched over the ridgeline. Patil explained that they had been making regular runs to the main entrance for months now, to establish a pattern that drew devotees away from the secondary entrance.

"All this was necessary, and insured that we could bring in a foreign inspector," Patil concluded. Clay awkwardly thanked him for the attention to detail. He wanted to voice his embarrassment at having students roughed up simply to provide him cover, but something in the offhand manner of the two Indians made him hold his tongue.

The secondary entrance to the Kolar mine was a wide, tin-roofed shed like a low aircraft hangar. Girders crisscrossed it at angles that seemed to Clay dictated less by the constraints of mechanics than by the whims of the construction team. Cables looped among the already rusting steel struts and sang low notes in the rot-tinged wind that brushed his hair.

Monkeys chattered and scampered high in the struts. The three men walked into the shed, carrying cases. The cables began humming softly. The weave above their heads tightened with pops and sharp cracks. Clay realized that the seemingly random array was a complicated hoist that had started to pull the elevator up from miles beneath their feet. The steel lattice groaned as if it already knew how much work it had to do.

When it arrived, he saw that the elevator was a huge rattling box that reeked of machine oil. Clay lugged his cases in. The walls were broad wooden slats covered with chicken wire. Heat radiated from them. Patil stabbed a button on the big control board and they dropped quickly. The numbers of the levels zipped by on an amber digital display. A single dim yellow bulb cast shadows onto the wire. At the fifty-third level the bulb went out. The elevator did not stop.

In the enveloping blackness Clay felt himself lighten, as if the elevator was speeding up.

"Do not be alarmed," Patil called. "This frequently occurs."

Clay wondered if he meant the faster fall or the lightbulb. In the complete dark, he began to see blue phantoms leaping out from nowhere.

Abruptly he became heavy—and thought of Einstein's *Gedanken* experiment, which equated a man in an accelerating elevator to one standing on a planet. Unless Clay could see outside, check that the massive earth raced by beyond as it clasped him further into its depths, in principle he could be in either situation. He tried to recall how Einstein had reasoned from an imaginary elevator to deduce that matter curved space-time, and could not.

Einstein's elegant proof was impossibly far from the pressing truth of *this* elevator. Here Clay plunged in thick murk, a weight of tortured air prickling his nose, making sweat pop from his face. Oily, moist heat climbed into Clay's sinuses.

And he was not being carried aloft by this elevator, but allowed to plunge into heavy, primordial darkness—Einstein's vision in reverse. No classical coolness separated him from the press of a raw, random world. That European mindscape—Galileo's crisp cylinders rolling obediently down inclined planes, Einstein's dispassionate observers surveying their smooth geometries like scrupulous bank clerks—evaporated here like yesterday's stale champagne. Sudden anxiety filled his throat. His stomach tightened and he tasted acrid gorge. He opened his mouth to shout, and as if to stop him, his own knees sagged with suddenly returning weight, physics regained.

A rattling thump—and they stopped. He felt Patil slam aside the rattling gate. A sullen glow beyond bathed an ornate brass shrine to a Hindu god. They came out into a steepled room of carved rock. Clay felt a breath of slightly cooler air from a cardboard-mouthed conduit nearby.

"We must force the air down from above." Patil gestured. "Otherwise this would read well over a hundred and ten Fahrenheit." He proudly pointed to an ancient battered British thermometer, whose mercury stood at ninety-eight.

They trudged through several tunnels, descended another few hundred feet on a ramp, and then followed gleaming railroad tracks. A white bulb every ten meters threw everything into exaggerated relief, shadows stabbing everywhere. A brown cardboard sign proclaimed from the ceiling:

FIRST EVER COSMIC RAY NEUTRINO INTERACTION
RECORDED HERE IN APRIL 1965

For over forty years, teams of devoted Indian physicists had labored patiently inside the Kolar gold fields. For half a century, India's high mountains and deep mines had made important cosmic-ray experiments possible with inexpensive instruments. Clay recalled how a joint Anglo-Indian-Japanese team had detected that first neutrino, scooped it from the unending cosmic sleet that penetrated even to this depth. He thought of unsung Indian physicists sweating here, tending the instruments and tracing the myriad sources of background error. Yet they themselves were background for the original purpose of the deep holes: Two narrow cars clunked past, full of chopped stone.

"Some still work this portion," Patil's clear voice cut through the muffled air. "Though I suspect they harvest little."

Pushing the rusty cars were four wiry men, so sweaty that the glaring bulbs gave their sliding muscles a hard sheen like living stone. They wore filthy cloths wrapped around their heads, as if they needed protection against the low ceiling rather than the heat. As Clay stumbled on, he felt that there might be truth to this, because he sensed the mass above as a precarious judgment over them all, a sullen presence. Einstein's crisp distinctions, the clean certainty of the *Gedanken* experiments, meant nothing in this blurred air.

They rounded an irregular curve and met a niche neatly cut off by a chain-link fence.

PROTON STABILITY EXPERIMENT
TATA INSTITUTE OF FUNDAMENTAL RESEARCH, BOMBAY
80th Level Heathcote Shaft, KFG
2,300 meters depth

These preliminaries done, the experiment itself began abruptly. Clay had expected some assembly rooms, an office, refrigerated 'scope cages. Instead, a few meters ahead the tunnel opened in all directions. They stood before a huge bay roughly cleaved from the brown rock.

And filling the vast volume was what seemed to be a wall as substantial as the rock itself. It was an iron grid of rusted pipe. The pipes were square, not round, and dwindled into the distance. Each had a dusty seal, a pressure dial, and a number painted in white. Clay estimated them to be at least a hundred feet long. They were stacked Lincoln Log fashion. He walked to the edge of the bay and looked down. Layers of pipe tapered away below to a distant floodlit floor and soared to meet the gray ceiling above.

"Enormous," he said.

"We expended great effort in scaling up our earlier apparatus," Singh said enthusiastically.

"As big as a house."

Patil said merrily, "An American house, perhaps. Ours are smaller."

A woman's voice nearby said, "And nothing lives in this iron house, Professor Clay."

Clay turned to see a willowy Indian woman regarding him with a wry smile. She seemed to have come out of the shadows, a brown apparition in shorts and a scrupulously white blouse, appearing full-blown where a moment before there had been nothing. Her heavy eyebrows rose in amusement.

"Ah, this is Mrs. Buli," Patil said.

"I keep matters running here, while my colleagues venture into the world," she said.

Clay accepted her coolly offered hand. She gave him one quick, well-defined shake and stepped back. "I can assist your assessment, perhaps."

"I'll need all your help," he said sincerely. The skimpy surroundings already made him wonder if he could do his job at all.

"Labor we have," she said. "Equipment, little."

"I brought some cross-check programs with me," he said.

"Excellent," Mrs. Buli said. "I shall have several of my graduate students assist you, and of course I offer my full devotion as well."

Clay smiled at her antique formality. She led him down a passage into the soft fluorescent glow of a large data-taking room. It was crammed with terminals and a bank of disk drives, all meshed by the usual cable spaghetti. "We keep our computers cooler than our staff, you see," Mrs. Buli said with a small smile.

They went down a ramp, and Clay could feel the rock's steady heat. They came out onto the floor of the cavern. Thick I beams roofed the stone box.

"Over a dozen lives, that was the cost of this excavation," Singh said.

"That many?"

"They attempted to save on the cost of explosives," Patil said with a stern look.

"Not that such will matter in the long run," Singh said mildly. Clay chose not to pursue the point.

Protective bolts studded the sheer rock, anchoring cross-beams that stabilized the tower of pipes. Scaffolding covered some sections of the blocky, rusty pile. Blasts of compressed air from the surface a mile above swept down on them from the ceiling, flapping Clay's shirt.

Mrs. Buli had to shout, the effort contorting her smooth face. "We obtained the pipes from a government program that attempted to improve the quality of plumbing in the cities. A failure, I fear. But a godsend for us."

Patil was pointing out electrical details when the air conduits wheezed into silence. "Hope that's temporary," Clay said in the sudden quiet.

"A minor repair, I am sure," Patil said.

"These occur often," Singh agreed earnestly.

Clay could already feel prickly sweat oozing from him. He wondered how often they had glitches in the circuitry down here, awash in pressing heat, and how much that could screw up even the best diagnostics.

Mrs. Buli went on in a lecturer's singsong. "We hired engineering students—there are many such, an oversupply—to thread a single wire down the bore of each pipe. We sealed each, then welded them together to make lengths of a hundred feet. Then we filled them with argon and linked them with a high-voltage line. We have found that a voltage of 280 keV . . ."

Clay nodded, filing away details, noting where her description differed from that of the NSF. The Kolar group had continuously modified their experiment for decades, and this latest enormous expansion was badly documented. Still, the principle was simple. Each pipe was held at high voltage, so that when a charged particle passed through, a spark leaped. A particle's path was followed by counting the segments of triggered pipes. This mammoth stack of iron was a huge Geiger counter.

He leaned back, nodding at Mrs. Buli's lecture, watching a team of men at the very top. A loud clang rang through the chasm. Sparks showered, burnt orange and blue. The garish plumes silhouetted the welders and sent cascades of sparks down through the lattice of pipes.

For an instant Clay imagined he was witnessing cosmic rays sleeting down through the towering house of iron, illuminating it with their short, sputtering lives.

"—and I am confident that we have seen well over fifty true events," Mrs. Buli concluded with a jaunty upward tilt of her chin.

"What?" Clay struggled back from his daydreaming. "That many?"

She laughed, a high tinkling. "You do not believe!"

"Well, that is a lot."

"Our detecting mass is now larger," Mrs. Buli said.

"Last we heard it was five hundred tons," Clay said carefully. The claims wired to the NSF and the Royal Society had been skimpy on details.

"That was years ago," Patil said. "We have redoubled our efforts, as you can see."

"Well, to see that many decays, you'd have to have a hell of a lot of observing volume," Clay said doubtfully.

"We can boast of five *thousand* tons, Professor Clay," Mrs. Buli said.

"Looks it," Clay said laconically to cover his surprise. It would not do to let them think they could overwhelm him with magnitudes. Question was, did they have the telltale events?

The cooling air came on with a thump and *whoosh*. Clay breathed it in deeply, face turned up to the iron house where protons might be dying, and sucked in swarming scents of the parched countryside miles above.

6

He knew from the start that there would be no eureka moment. Certainty was the child of tedium.

He traced the tangled circuitry for two days before he trusted it. "You got to open the sack 'fore I'll believe there's a cat in there," he told Mrs. Buli, and then had to explain that he was joking.

Then came a three-day trial run, measuring the exact sputter of decay from a known radioactive source. System response was surprisingly good. He found their techniques needlessly Byzantine, but workable. His null checks of the detectors inside the pipes came up goose-egg clean.

Care was essential. Proton decay was rare. The Grand Unified Theories that had enjoyed such success in predicting new particles had also sounded a somber note through all of physics. Matter was mortal. But not very mortal, compared with the passing flicker of a human lifetime.

The human body had about 10^{29} neutrons and protons in it. If only a tiny fraction of them decayed in a human lifetime, the radiation from the disintegration would quickly kill everyone of cancer. The survival of even small life-forms implied that the protons inside each nucleus had to survive an average of nearly a billion billion years.

So even before the Grand Unified Theories, physicists knew that protons lived long. The acronym for the theories was GUTs, and a decade earlier graduate students like Clay had won T-shirts with insider jokes like IT TAKES GUTS TO DO PARTICLE PHYSICS. But proving that there was some truth to the lame nerd jests took enormous effort.

The simplest of the GUTs predicted a proton lifetime of about 10^{31} years, immensely greater than the limit set by the existence of life. In fact, it was far longer even than the age of the universe, which was only a paltry 2×10^{10} years old.

One could check this lifetime by taking one proton and watching it for 10^{31} years. Given the short attention span of humans, it was better to assemble 10^{31} protons and watch them for a year, hoping one would fizzle.

Physicists in the United States, Japan, Italy, and India had done that all through the 1980s and 1990s. And no protons had died.

Well, the theorists had said, the mathematics must be more complicated. They discarded certain symmetry groups and thrust others forward. The lifetime might be 10^{32} years, then.

The favored method of gathering protons was to use those in water. Western physicists carved swimming pools six stories deep in salt mines and eagerly watched for the characteristic blue pulse of dying matter. Detecting longer lifetimes meant waiting longer, which nobody liked, or adding more protons. Digging bigger swimming pools was easy, so attention had turned to the United States and Japan . . . but still, no protons died. The lifetime exceeded 10^{32} years.

The austerity of the 1990s had shut down the ambitious experiments in the West. Few remembered this forlorn experiment in Kolar, wedded to watching the cores of iron rods for the quick spurt of decay. When political difficulties cut off contact, the already beleaguered physicists in the West assumed the Kolar effort had ceased.

But Kolar was the deepest experiment, less troubled by the hail of cosmic rays that polluted the Western data. Clay came to appreciate that as he scrolled through the myriad event-plots in the Kolar computer cubes.

There were 9×10^9 recorded decays of all types. The system rejected obvious garbage events, but there were many subtle enigmas. Theory said that protons died because the quarks that composed them could change their identities. A seemingly capricious alteration of quarky states sent the proton asunder, spitting forth a zoo of fragments. Neutrons were untroubled by this, for in free space they decayed anyway, into a proton and electron. Matter's end hinged, finally, on the stability of the proton alone.

Clay saw immediately that the Kolar group had invested years in their software. They had already filtered out thousands of phantom events that imitated true proton decay. There were eighteen ways a proton could die, each with a different signature of spraying light and particle debris.

The delicate traceries of particle paths were recorded as flashes and sparkles in the house of iron outside. Clay searched through endless graphic printouts, filigrees woven from digital cloth.

"You will find we have pondered each candidate event," Mrs. Buli said mildly on the sixth day of Clay's labors.

"Yeah, the analysis is sharp," he said cautiously. He was surprised at the high level of the work but did not want to concede anything yet.

"If any ambiguity arose, we discarded the case."

"I can see that."

"Some pions were not detected in the right energy range, so of course we omitted those."

"Good."

Mrs. Buli leaned over to show him a detail of the cross-checking program, and he caught a heady trace of wildflowers. Her perfume reminded him abruptly that her sari wrapped over warm, ample swells. She had no sagging softness, no self-indulgent bulgings. The long oval of her face and her ample lips conveyed a fragile sensuality . . .

He wrenched his attention back to physics and stared hard at the screen.

Event vertices were like time-lapse photos of traffic accidents, intersections exploding, screaming into shards. The crystalline mathematical order of physics led to riots of incandescence. And Clay was judge, weighing testimony after the chaos.

7

He had insisted on analyzing the several thousand preliminary candidates himself, as a double blind against the Kolar group's software. After nine days, he had isolated sixty-seven events that looked like the genuine article.

Sixty-five of his agreed with Mrs. Buli's analysis. The two holdouts were close, Clay had to admit.

"Nearly on the money," he said reflectively as he stared at the Kolar software's array.

"You express such values," Mrs. Buli said. "Always a financial analogy."

"Just a way of speaking."

"Still, let us discard the two offending events."

"Well, I'd be willing—"

"No, no, we consider only the sixty-five." Her almond eyes gave no hint of slyness.

"They're pretty good bets, I'd say." Her eyebrows arched. "Only a manner of speech."

"Then you feel they fit the needs of theory."

Her carefully balanced way of phrasing made him lean forward, as if to compensate for his judge's role. "I'll have to consider all the other decay modes in detail. Look for really obscure processes that might mimic the real thing."

She nodded. "True, there is need to study such."

Protons could die from outside causes, too. Wraithlike neutrinos spewed forth by the sun penetrated even here, shattering protons.

Murderous muons lumbered through as cosmic rays, plowing furrows of exploding nuclei.

Still, things looked good. He was surprised at their success, earned by great labor. "I'll be as quick about it as I can."

"We have prepared a radio link that we can use, should the desire come."

"Huh? What?"

"In case you need to reach your colleagues in America."

"Ah, yes."

To announce the result, he saw. To get the word out. But why the rush?

It occurred to him that they might doubt whether he himself would get out at all.

8

They slept each night in a clutch of tin lean-tos that cowered down a raw ravine. Laborers from the mine had slept there in better days, and the physicists had gotten the plumbing to work for an hour each night. The men slept in a long shed, but gave Clay a small wooden shack. He ate thin, mealy gruel with them each evening, carefully dropping purification tablets in his water, and was rewarded with untroubled bowels. He lost weight in the heat of the mine, but the nights were cool and the breezes that came then were soft with moisture.

The fifth evening, as they sat around a potbellied iron stove in the men's shed, Patil pointed to a distant corrugated metal hut and said, "There we have concealed a satellite dish. We can knock away the roof and transmit, if you like."

Clay brightened. "Can I call home?"

"If need be."

Something in Patil's tone told him a frivolous purpose was not going to receive their cooperation.

"Maybe tomorrow?"

"Perhaps. We must be sure that the devotees do not see us reveal it."

"They think we're laborers?"

"So we have convinced them, I believe."

"And me?"

"You would do well to stay inside."

"Um. Look, got anything to drink?"

Patil frowned. "Has the water pipe stopped giving?"

"No, I mean, you know—a drink. Gin and tonic, wasn't that what the Brits preferred?"

"Alcohol is the devil's urine," Patil said precisely.

"It won't scramble my brains."

"Who can be sure? The mind is a tentative instrument."

"You don't want any suspicion that I'm unreliable, that it?"

"No, of course not," Singh broke in anxiously.

"Needn't worry," Clay muttered. The heat below and the long hours of tedious work were wearing him down. "I'll be gone soon's I can get things wrapped up."

"You agree that we are seeing the decays?"

"Let's say things're looking better."

Clay had been holding back even tentative approval. He had expected some show of jubilation. Patil and Singh simply sat and stared into the flickering coals of the stove's half-open door.

Slowly Patil said, "Word will spread quickly."

"Soon as you transmit it on that dish, sure."

Singh murmured, "Much shall change."

"Look, you might want to get out of here, go present a pa-per—"

"Oh no, we shall remain," Singh said quickly.

"Those devotees could give you trouble if they find—"

"We expect that this discovery, once understood, shall have great effects," Patil said solemnly. "I much prefer to witness them from my home country."

The cadence and mood of this conversation struck Clay as odd, but he put it down to the working conditions. Certainly they had sacrificed a great deal to build and run this experiment amid crippling desolation.

"This result will begin the final renunciation of the materialistic worldview," Singh said matter-of-factly.

"Huh?"

"In peering at the individual lives of mere particles, we employ the reductionist hammer," Patil explained. "But nature is not like a salamander, cut into fragments."

"Or if it were," Singh added, "once the salamander is so sliced, try to make it do its salamander walk again." A broad white grin split the gloom of nightfall.

"The world is an implicate order, Dr. Clay. All parts are hinged to each other."

Clay frowned. He vaguely remembered a theory of quantum mechanics that used that term—"implicate order," meaning that a deeper realm of physical theory lay beneath the uncertainties of wave mechanics. Waves that took it into their heads to behave like particles, and the reverse—these were supposed to be illusions arising from our ignorance of a more profound theory. But there was no observable consequence of such notions, and to Clay such mumbo jumbo from theorists who never got their hands dirty was empty rhapsodizing. Still, he was supposed to be the diplomat here.

He gave a judicial nod. "Yeah, sure—but when the particles die, it'll all be gone, right?"

"Yes, in about 10^{34} years," Patil said. "But the *knowledge* of matter's mortality will spread as swiftly as light, on the wind of our transmitter."

"So?"

"You are an experimentalist, Dr. Clay, and thus—if you will forgive my putting it so—addicted to cutting the salamander." Patil made a steeple of his fingers, sending spindly shadows rippling across his face. "The world we study is conditioned by our perceptions of it. The implied order is partially from our own design."

"Sure, quantum measurement, uncertainty principle, all that." Clay had sat through all the usual lectures about this stuff and didn't feel like doing so again. Not in a dusty shed with his stomach growling from hunger. He sipped at his cup of weak Darjeeling and yawned.

"Difficulties of measurement reflect underlying problems," Patil said. "Even the Westerner Plato saw that we perceive only imperfect modes of the true, deeper world."

"What deeper world?" Clay sighed despite himself.

"We do not know. We *cannot* know."

"Look, we make our measurements, we report. Period."

Amused, Singh said, "And that is where matters end?"

Patil said, "Consensual reality, that is your 'real' world, Professor Clay. But our news may cause that bland, unthinking consensus to falter."

Clay shrugged. This sounded like late-night college bullshit sessions among boozed-up science nerds. Patty-cake pantheism, quantum razzle-dazzle, garbage philosophy. It was one thing to be open-minded and another to let your brains fall out. Was *every*body on this wrecked continent a booga-booga type? He had to get out.

"Look, I don't see what difference—"

"Until the curtain of seeming surety is swept away," Singh put in.

"Surety?"

"This world—this universe!—has labored long under the illusion of its own permanence." Singh spread his hands, animated in the flickering yellow glow. "We might die, yes, the sun might even perish—but the universe went on. Now we prove otherwise. There cannot help but be profound reactions."

He thought he saw what they were driving at. "A Nobel Prize, even."

To his surprise, both men laughed merrily. "Oh no," Patil said, arching his eyebrows. "No such trifles are expected!"

9

The boxy meeting room beside the data bay was packed. From it came a subdued mutter, a fretwork of talk laced with anticipation.

Outside, someone had placed a small chalky statue of a grinning elephant. Clay hesitated, stroked it. Despite the heat of the mine, the elephant was cool.

"The workers just brought it down," Mrs. Buli explained with a smile. "Our Hindu god of auspicious beginnings."

"Or endings," Patil said behind her. "Equally."

Clay nodded and walked into the trapped, moist heat of the room. Everyone was jammed in, graduate students and laborers alike, their dhotis already showing sweaty crescents. Clay saw the three students the devotees had beaten and exchanged respectful bows with them.

Perceiving some need for ceremony, he opened with lengthy

praise for the endless hours they had labored, exclaiming over how startled the world would be to learn of such a facility. Then he plunged into consideration of each candidate event, his checks and counter-checks, vertex corrections, digital-array flaws, mean free paths, ion-ization rates, the artful programming that deflected the myriad possible sources of error. He could feel tension rising in the room as he cast the events on the inch-thick wall screen, calling them forth from the files in his cubes. Some he threw into 3-D, to show the full path through the cage of iron that had captured the death rattle of infinity.

And at the end, all cases reviewed, he said quietly, "You have found it. The proton lifetime is very nearly 10^{34} years."

The room burst into applause, wide grins and wild shouts as everyone pressed forward to shake his hand.

10

Singh handled the message to the NSF. Clay also constructed a terse though detailed summary and sent it to the International Astronomi-cal Union for release to the worldwide system of observatories and universities.

Clay knew this would give a vital assist to his career. With the Kolar team staying here, he would be their only spokesman. And this was very big, media-mesmerizing news indeed.

The result was important to physicists and astronomers alike, for the destiny of all their searches ultimately would be sealed by the faint failures of particles no eye would ever see. In 10^{34} years, far in the depths of space, the great celestial cities, the galaxies, would be ebbing. The last red stars would flicker, belch, and gutter out. Perhaps life would have clung to them and found a way to persist against the growing cold. Cluttered with the memorabilia of the ages, the islands of mute matter would turn at last to their final conqueror—not en-tropy's still hand, but this silent sputter of protons.

Clay thought of the headlines: UNIVERSE TO END. What would *that* do to harried commuters on their way to work?

He watched Singh send the stuttering messages via the big sat-ellite dish, the corrugated tin roof of the shed pulled aside, allowing him to watch burnt-gold twilight seep across the sky. Clay felt no elation, as blank as a drained capacitor. He had gone into physics because of the sense it gave of grasping deep mysteries. He could look at bridges and trace the vectored stability that ruled them. When his daughter asked why the sky was blue, he actually knew, and could sketch out a simple answer. It had never occurred to him to fear flying, because he knew the Bernoulli equation for the pressure that held up the plane.

But this result . . .

Even the celebratory party that evening left him unmoved. Graduate students turned out in their best khaki. Sitar music swarmed through the scented air, ragas thumping and weaving. He found his body swaying to the refractions of tone and scale.

"It is a pity you cannot learn more of our country," Mrs. Buli remarked, watching him closely.

"Right now I'm mostly interested in sleep."

"Sleep is not always kind." She seemed wry and distant in the night's smudged humidity. "One of our ancient gods, Brahma, is said to sleep—and we are what he dreams."

"In that case, for you folks maybe he's been having a nightmare lately."

"Ah yes, our troubles. But do not let them mislead you about India. They pass."

"I'm sure they will," Clay replied, dutifully diplomatic.

"You were surprised, were you not, at the outcome?" she said piercingly.

"Uh, well, I had to be skeptical."

"Yes, for a scientist certainty is built on deep layers of doubt."

"Like my daddy said, in the retail business deal with everybody, but count your change."

She laughed. "We have given you a bargain, perhaps!"

He was acutely aware that his initial doubts must have been obvious. And what unsettled him now was not just the hard-won success here, but their strange attitude toward it.

The graduate students came then and tried to teach him a dance. He did a passable job, and a student named Venkatraman slipped him a glass of beer, forbidden vice. It struck Clay as comic that the Indian government spent much energy to suppress alcohol but did little about the population explosion. The students all laughed when he made a complicated joke about booze, but he could not be sure whether they meant it. The music seemed to quicken, his heart thumping to keep up with it. They addressed him as Clay*ji*, a term of respect, and asked his opinion of what they might do next with the experiment. He shrugged, thinking '*Nother job, sahib?* and suggested using it as a detector for neutrinos from supernovas. That had paid off when the earlier generation of neutrino detectors picked up the 1987 supernova.

The atom bomb, the 1987 event, now this—particle physics, he realized uncomfortably, was steeped in death. The sitar slid and rang, and Mrs. Buli made arch jokes to go with the spicy salad. Still, he turned in early.

11

To be awakened by a soft breeze. A brushing presence, sliding cloth . . . He sensed her sari as a luminous fog. Moonlight streaming through a lopsided window cast shimmering auras through the cloth as she loomed above him. Reached for him. Lightly flung away his sticky bedclothes.

"I—"

A soft hand covered his mouth, bringing a heady savor of ripe earth. His senses ran out of him and into the surrounding dark, coiling in air as he took her weight. She was surprisingly light, though thick-waisted, her breasts like teacups compared with the full curves of her hips. His hands slid and pressed, finding a delightful slithering moisture all over her, a sheen of vibrancy. Her sari evaporated. The high planes of her face caught vagrant blades of moonlight, and he saw a curious tentative, expectant expression there as she wrapped him in soft pressures. Her mouth did not so much kiss his as enclose it, formulating an argument of sweet rivulets that trickled into his porous self. She slipped into place atop him, a slick clasp that melted him up into her, a perfect fit, slick with dark insistence. He closed his eyes, but the glow diffused through his eyelids, and he could see her hair fanning through the air like motion underwater, her luxuriant weight bucking, trembling as her nails scratched his shoulders, musk rising smoky from them both. A silky muscle milked him at each heart-thump. Her velvet mass orbited above their fulcrum, bearing down with feathery demands, and he remembered brass icons, gaudy Indian posters, and felt above him Kali strumming in fevered darkness. She locked legs around him, squeezing him up into her surprisingly hard muscles, grinding, drawing forth, pushing back. She cried out with great heaves and lungfuls of the thickening air, mouth going slack beneath hooded eyes, and he shot sharply up into her, a convulsion that poured out all the knotted aches in him, delivering them into the tumbled steamy earth—

12

—and next, with no memories between, he was stumbling with her . . . down a gully . . . beneath slanting silvery moonlight.

"What—what's—"

"Quiet!" She shushed him like a schoolmarm.

He recognized the rolling countryside near the mine. Vague forms flitted in the distance. Wracked cries cut the night.

"The devotees," Mrs. Buli whispered as they stumbled on. "They have assaulted the mine entrance."

"How'd we—"

"You were difficult to rouse," she said with a sidelong glance.

Was she trying to be amusing? The sudden change from mysterious supercharged sensuality back to this clipped, formal professionalism disoriented him.

"Apparently some of our laborers had a grand party. It alerted the devotees to our presence, some say. I spoke to a laborer while you slept, however, who said that the devotees knew of your presence. They asked for you."

"Why me?"

"Something about your luggage and a telephone call home."

Clay gritted his teeth and followed her along a path that led among the slumped hills, away from their lodgings. Soon the mine entrance was visible below. Running figures swarmed about it like black gnats. Ragged chants erupted from them. A *waarrk waarrk* sound came from the hangar, and it was some moments until Clay saw long chains of human bodies hanging from the rafters, swinging themselves in unison.

"They're pulling down the hangar," he whispered.

"I despair for what they have done inside."

He instinctively reached for her and felt the supple warmth he had embraced seemingly only moments before. She turned and gave him her mouth again.

"We—back there—why'd you come to me?"

"It was time. Even we feel the joy of release from order, Professor Clay."

"Well, sure . . ." Clay felt illogically embarrassed, embracing a woman who still had the musk of the bed about her, yet who used his title. "But . . . how'd I get here? Seems like—"

"You were immersed. Taken out of yourself."

"Well, yeah, it was good, fine, but I can't remember anything."

She smiled. "The best moments leave no trace. That is a signature of the implicate order."

Clay breathed in the waxy air to help clear his head. More mumbo jumbo, he thought, delivered by her with an open, expectant expression. In the darkness it took a moment to register that she had fled down another path.

"Where'll we go?" he gasped when he caught up.

"We must get to the vans. They are parked some kilometers away."

"My gear—"

"Leave it."

He hesitated a moment, then followed her. There was nothing irreplaceable. It certainly wasn't worth braving the mob below for the stuff.

They wound down through bare hillsides dominated by boulders. The sky rippled with heat lightning. Puffy clouds scudded quickly in from the west, great ivory flashes working among them. The ground surged slightly.

"Earthquake?" he asked.

"There were some earlier, yes. Perhaps that has excited the devotees further tonight, put their feet to running."

There was no sign of the physics team. Pebbles squirted from beneath his boots—he wondered how he had managed to get them on without remembering it—and recalled again her hypnotic sensuality. Stones rattled away down into narrow dry washes on each side. Clouds blotted out the moonglow, and they had to pick their way along the trail.

Clay's mind spun with plans, speculations, jittery anxiety. Mrs. Buli was now his only link to the Western fragment of India, and he could scarcely see her in the shadows. She moved with liquid grace, her sari trailing, sandals slapping. Suddenly she crouched down. "More."

Along the path came figures bearing lanterns. They moved silently in the fitful silvery moonlight. There was no place to hide, and the party had already seen them.

"Stand still," she said. Again the crisp Western diction, yet her ample hips swayed slightly, reminding him of her deeper self.

Clay wished he had a club, a knife, anything. He made himself stand beside her, hands clenched. For once his blackness might be an advantage.

The devotees passed, eyes rapt. Clay had expected them to be singing or chanting mantras or rubbing beads—but not shambling forward as if to their doom. The column barely glanced at him. In his baggy cotton trousers and formless shirt, he hoped he was un-remarkable. A woman passed nearby, apparently carrying something across her back. Clay blinked. Her hands were nailed to the ends of a beam, and she carried it proudly, palms bloody, half crucified. Her face was serene, eyes focused on the roiling sky. Behind her was a man bearing a plate. Clay thought the shambling figure carried marbles on the dish until he peered closer and saw an iris, and realized the entire plate was packed with eyeballs. He gasped and faces turned toward him. Then the man was gone along the path, and Clay waited, holding his breath against a gamy stench he could not name. Some muttered to themselves, some carried religious artifacts, beads and statuettes and drapery, but none had the fervor of the devotees he had seen before. The ground trembled again.

And out of the dark air came a humming. Something struck a man in the line and he clutched at his throat, crying hoarsely. Clay leaped forward without thinking. He pulled the man's hands away. Lodged in the narrow of the throat was something like an enormous cockroach with fluttering wings. It had already embedded its head in the man. Spiky legs furiously scrabbled against the soiled skin to dig deeper. The man coughed and shouted weakly, as though the thing was already blocking his throat.

Clay grabbed its hind legs and pulled. The insect wriggled with surprising strength. He saw the hind stinger too late. The sharp point struck a hot jolt of pain into his thumb. Anger boiled in him. He held on despite the pain and yanked the thing free. It made a sucking sound coming out. He hissed with revulsion and violently threw it down the hillside.

The man stumbled, gasping, and then ran back down the path, never even looking at them. Mrs. Buli grabbed Clay, who was staggering around in a circle, shaking his hand. "I will cut it!" she cried.

He held still while she made a precise cross cut and drained the blood. "What . . . what *was* that?"

"A wasp-thing from the pouches that hang on our trees."

"Oh, yeah. One of those bio tricks."

"They are still overhead."

Clay listened to the drone hanging over them. Another devotee shrieked and slapped the back of his neck. Clay numbly watched the man run away. His hand throbbed, but he could feel the effects ebbing. Mrs. Buli tore a strip from her sari and wrapped his thumb to quell the bleeding.

All this time, devotees streamed past them in the gloom. None took the slightest notice of Clay. Some spoke to themselves.

"Western science doesn't seem to bother 'em much now," Clay whispered wryly.

Mrs. Buli nodded. The last figure to pass was a woman who limped, sporting an arm that ended not in a hand but in a spoon, nailed to a stub of cork.

He followed Mrs. Buli into enveloping darkness. "Who were they?"

"I do not know. They spoke seldom and repeated the same words. Dharma and samsara, terms of destiny."

"They don't care about us?"

"They appear to sense a turning, a resolution." In the fitful moonglow her eyes were liquid puzzles.

"But they destroyed the experiment."

"I gather that knowledge of your Western presence was like the wasp-things. Irritating, but only a catalyst, not the cause."

"What *did* make them—"

"No time. Come."

They hurriedly entered a thin copse of spindly trees that lined a streambed. Dust stifled his nose and he breathed through his mouth. The clouds raced toward the horizon with unnatural speed, seeming to flee from the west. Trees swayed before an unfelt wind, twisting and reaching for the shifting sky.

"Weather," Mrs. Buli answered his questions. "Bad weather."

They came upon a small crackling fire. Figures crouched around it, and Clay made to go around, but Mrs. Buli walked straight toward it. Women squatted, poking sticks into the flames. Clay saw that something moved on the sticks. A momentary shaft of moonlight showed the oily skin of snakes, tiny eyes crisp as crystals, the shafts poking from yawning white mouths that still moved. The women's faces of stretched yellow skin anxiously watched the blackening, sizzling snakes, turning them. The fire hissed as though raindrops fell upon it, but Clay felt nothing wet, just the dry rub of a fresh abrading wind. Smoke wrapped the women in gray wreaths, and Mrs. Buli hurried on.

So much, so fast. Clay felt rising in him a leaden conviction born of all he had seen in this land. So many people, so much pain— how could it matter? The West assumed that the individual was important, the bedrock of all. That was why the obliterating events of the West's own history, like the Nazi Holocaust, by erasing humans in such numbing numbers, cast grave doubt on the significance of any one. India did something like that for him. Could a universe that produced so many bodies, so many minds in shadowed torment, care a whit about humanity? Endless, meaningless duplication of grinding pain . . .

A low mutter came on the wind, like a bass theme sounding up from the depths of a dusty well.

Mrs. Buli called out something he could not understand. She began running, and Clay hastened to follow. If he lost her in these shadows, he could lose all connection.

Quickly they left the trees and crossed a grassy field rutted by ancient agriculture and prickly with weeds. On this flat plain he could see that the whole sky worked with twisted light, a colossal electrical discharge feathering into more branches than a gnarled tree. The anxious clouds caught blue and burnt-yellow pulses and seemed to relay them, like the countless transformers and capacitors and voltage drops that made a worldwide communications net, carrying staccato messages laced with crackling punctuations.

"The vans," she panted.

Three brown vans crouched beneath a canopy of thin trees, further concealed beneath khaki tents that blended in with the dusty fields. Mrs. Buli yanked open the door of the first one. Her fingers fumbled at the ignition.

"The key must be concealed," she said quickly.

"Why?" he gasped, throat raw.

"They are to be always with the vans."

"Uh-huh. Check the others."

She hurried away. Clay got down on his knees, feeling the lip of the van's undercarriage. The ground seemed to heave with inner heat, dry and rasping, the pulse of the planet. He finished one side of the van and crawled under, feeling along the rear axle. He heard a distant plaintive cry, as eerie and forlorn as the call of a bird lost in fog.

"Clayji? None in the others."

His hand touched a small slick box high up on the axle. He plucked it from its magnetic grip and rolled out from under.

"If we drive toward the mine," she said, "we can perhaps find others."

"Others, hell. Most likely we'll run into devotees."

"Well, I—"

Figures in the trees. Flitting, silent, quick.

"Get in."

"But—"

He pushed her in and tried to start the van. Running shapes in the field. He got the engine started on the third try and gunned it. They growled away. Something hard shattered the back window into a spiderweb, but then Clay swerved several times and nothing more hit them.

After a few minutes his heart-thumps slowed, and he turned on the headlights to make out the road. The curves were sandy and he did not want to get stuck. He stamped on the gas.

Suddenly great washes of amber light streamed across the sky, pale lances cutting the clouds. "My God, what's happening?"

"It is more than weather."

Her calm, abstracted voice made him glance across the seat. "No kidding."

"No earthquake could have collateral effects of this order."

He saw by the dashboard lights that she wore a lapis lazuli necklace. He had felt it when she came to him, and now its deep blues seemed like the only note of color in the deepening folds of night.

"It must be something far more profound."

"What?"

The road now arrowed straight through a tangled terrain of warped trees and oddly shaped boulders. Something rattled against the windshield like hail, but Clay could see nothing.

"We have always argued, some of us, that the central dictate of quantum mechanics is the interconnected nature of the observer and the observed."

The precise, detached lecturer style again drew his eyes to her. Shadowed, her face gave away no secrets.

"We always filter the world," she said with dreamy momentum, "and yet are linked to it. How much of what we see is in fact taught us, by our bodies, or by the consensus reality that society trains us to see, even before we can speak for ourselves?"

"Look, that sky isn't some problem with my eyes. It's *real*. Hear that?" Something big and soft had struck the door of the van, rocking it.

"And we here have finished the program of materialistic science, have we not? We flattered the West by taking it seriously. As did the devotees."

Clay grinned despite himself. It was hard to feel flattered when you were fleeing for your life.

Mrs. Buli stretched lazily, as though relaxing into the clasp of the moist night. "So we have proven the passing nature of matter. What fresh forces does that bring into play?"

"Huh!" Clay spat back angrily. "Look here, we just sent word out, reported the result. How—"

"So that by now millions, perhaps billions of people know that the very stones that support them must pass."

"So what? Just some theoretical point about subnuclear physics, how's that going to—"

"Who is to say? What avatar? The point is that we were believed. Certain knowledge, universally correlated, surely has some impact—"

The van lurched. Suddenly they jounced and slammed along the smooth roadway. A bright plume of sparks shot up behind them, brimming firefly yellow in the night.

"Axle's busted!" Clay cried. He got the van stopped. In the sudden silence, it registered that the motor had gone dead.

They climbed out. Insects buzzed and hummed in the hazy gloom.

The roadway was still straight and sure, but on all sides great blobs of iridescent water swelled up from the ground, making colossal drops. The trembling half-spheres wobbled in the frayed moonlight. Silently, softly, the bulbs began to detach from the foggy ground and gently loft upward. Feathery luminescent clouds above gathered on swift winds that sheared their edges. These billowing, luxuriant banks snagged the huge teardrop shapes as they plunged skyward.

"I . . . I don't . . ."

Mrs. Buli turned and embraced him. Her moist mouth opened a redolent interior continent to him, teeming and blackly bountiful, and he had to resist falling inward, a tumbling silvery bubble in a dark chasm.

"The category of perfect roundness is fading," she said calmly.

Clay looked at the van. The wheels had become ellipses. At each revolution they had slammed the axles into the roadway, leaving behind long scratches of rough tar.

He took a step.

She said, "Since we can walk, the principle of pivot and lever, of muscles pulling bones, survives."

"How . . . this doesn't . . ."

"But do our bodies depend on roundness? I wonder." She carefully lay down on the blacktop.

The road straightened precisely, like joints in an aged spine popping as they realigned.

Angles cut their spaces razor-sharp, like axioms from Euclid.

Clouds merged, forming copious tinkling hexagons.

"It is good to see that some features remain. Perhaps these are indeed the underlying Platonic beauties."

"What?" Clay cried.

"The undying forms," Mrs. Buli said abstractly. "Perhaps that one Western idea was correct after all."

Clay desperately grasped the van. He jerked his arm back when the metal skin began flexing and reshaping itself.

Smooth glistening forms began to emerge from the rough, coarse earth. Above the riotous, heaving land the moon was now a brassy cube. Across its face played enormous black cracks like mad lightning.

Somewhere far away his wife and daughter were in this, too. *G'bye, Daddy. It's been real.*

Quietly the land began to rain upward. Globs dripped toward the pewter, filmy continent swarming freshly above. Eons measured out the evaporation of ancient sluggish seas.

His throat struggled against torpid air. "Is . . . Brahma . . . ?"

"Awakening?" came her hollow voice, like an echo from a distant gorge.

"What happens . . . to . . . us?"

His words diffracted away from him. He could now see acoustic waves, wedges of compressed, mute atoms crowding in the exuberant air. Luxuriant, inexhaustible riches burst from beneath the ceramic certainties he had known.

"Come." Her voice seeped through the churning ruby air.

Centuries melted between them as he turned. A being he recognized without conscious thought spun in liquid air.

Femina, she was now, and she drifted on the new wafting currents. He and she were made of shifting geometric elements, molecular units of shape and firm thrust. A wan joy spread through him.

Time that was no time did not pass, and he and she and the impacted forces between them were pinned to the forever moment that cascaded through them, all of them, the billions of atomized elements that made them, all, forever.

In Memoriam: Fritz Leiber

POUL ANDERSON
DAVID HARTWELL
STEPHEN KING

Beyond the mundane pressures involved in assembling a Nebula Awards anthology—tracking down permissions, staying within the prescribed page count—a singular sadness looms. During his or her three-year tenure, a Nebula editor will almost inevitably be called upon to document the death of a colleague. In *Nebula Awards 26*, I was obliged to publish a tribute to the late Donald A. Wollheim. In *Nebula Awards 27*, I presented a cluster of Isaac Asimov obituaries. And now we have lost Fritz Leiber.

The first of the Leiber eulogizers I have selected, Poul Anderson, has been called "the enduring explosion" by his fellow writer James Blish, a sobriquet that evokes not only the sheer volume of Anderson's output—upwards of fifty novels and two hundred short stories—but also its audacity and breadth. Accolades attest to the quality of Anderson's work: seven Hugos, three Nebulas, and a Gandalf. As something of a parvenu in the field of speculative literature, I remain eternally grateful that among the novels pressed upon me by my SF-addicted college roommate was Anderson's *Tau Zero*, which Blish has called "the ultimate hard science-fiction novel." Twenty years later, *Tau Zero* still resonates within me.

After Anderson's reminiscences comes an epitaph by science-fiction editor David Hartwell. Hearing the term "science-fiction editor," one normally thinks of either a harried paperback impresario struggling to fill the next month's list or an apoplectic former fan frantically assembling the upcoming issue of his magazine. But Hartwell's formidable reputation traces almost exclusively to his efforts within the more staid domain of SF hardcovers. Besides being the guiding light behind Simon & Schuster's acclaimed Timescape program of the late seventies and early eighties, he has more recently acquired and shaped a score of major books for Arbor House, William Morrow, and Tor. Hartwell's anthologies include *The Dark Descent, Masterpieces of Fantasy and Enchantment, Masterpieces of Fantasy and Wonder,* and the definitive *World Treasury of Science Fiction*.

Leiber exerted a lasting influence not only on the science-fiction community but also on the horror field, a truth made vivid by Stephen King's poignant tribute. For those of you who've been living on the back of the moon during the past twenty years, King's novels include *Carrie, Salem's Lot, The Shining, The Stand, The Dead Zone, Firestarter, Cujo, Pet Sematary, Christine, Misery, It, The Tommyknockers, The Dark Half, Needful Things, Gerald's Game*, and (with Peter Straub) *The Talisman*. His shorter works are collected in *Night Shift, Creepshow, Different Seasons, Skeleton Crew, Four Past Midnight*, and *Nightmares and Dreamscapes*. In 1982 King's *Danse Macabre* won the Hugo Award for Best Nonfiction Work. At last count, he had 175 million books in print.

GENTLEMAN FRITZ

Poul Anderson

> *When half-Gods go*
> *The Gods arrive.*

Yes, but what do you do when the Gods themselves depart?

Ever more of late the great ones have been leaving us, the creators who in the Golden Age made science fiction and fantasy what they are today and who continued their greatness until the end. Now Fritz Leiber is gone.

Memories follow him like shadows cast by his tall figure—no, not only memories, but works that endure, from such dazzling early originalities as *Conjure Wife* and *Gather, Darkness!* on through the years to his very last. He was never content to repeat himself but was always moving toward new frontiers, always delighting us not only with his style and wit but with his wellspring freshness.

This, though, is not the place to discuss the writings. Literary historians will be doing that for a long time. So will his colleagues, who owe him so much, and countless enchanted readers. Here I would just like to share a few recollections of the man himself.

I first saw him at the 1949 World Science Fiction Convention in Cincinnati. Back then, such affairs were small and friendly; you could actually meet people, relax, and get acquainted. Towering, classically handsome, Fritz came across as impressively in person as he did in his writings. Yet he was soft-spoken, modest, amiable, lovable. The opinion I formed of him then I expressed much later when it became my honor to do an introduction to *The Best of Fritz Leiber:* "It is etymologically wrong but psychologically right to define a gentleman as one who is gentle, yet very much a man." I went on to say something about his having been at various times a championship fencer, a chess player (rated expert), an actor, a lay preacher, a drama instructor, a staff writer for various periodicals, and much else. "And, of course," I observed, "in his writing he has stared down—or laughed down— death, horror, human absurdity, with guts worthy of a Jeffers, Kafka, or Cervantes."

However, this is not the place for a biography either. Fritz wrote about himself with rare candor and objectivity, while a number of his stories contain a strong autobiographical element. If the academic establishment ever appropriates him, it will find it has on its hands another Montaigne, Pepys, or Boswell.

We didn't have much more contact until the mid-fifties, when he and his wife, Jonquil, moved to southern California from the Midwest. From time to time they visited my wife, Karen, and me in our home, and we visited them in theirs, and we'd also meet now and then at SF conventions and parties. It's not betraying any secrets to reveal that Fritz and Jonquil had something of an alcohol problem. But it never lessened his courtesy or, something deeper, his graciousness. Rather, occasionally when he'd had a few he'd recite G. K. Chesterton's flamboyant ballad "Lepanto" in that wonderful stage voice— what an experience!

Eventually Jonquil's health failed, and she died. Fritz's elegy to her, in a booklet of his poems, is among the most touching things I have ever read. He moved to San Francisco, overcame his alcoholism, and burst as an author into a novalike brilliance that never faded.

Nor did his lively interest in everything around him. He grew intimate with his adopted city, discovering treasures that most of the natives never suspected were there. In his regular *Locus* column he discussed not only his hobby of astronomy but practically every other subject that fascinated him. Even at the last, as physical infirmities closed in, he was attending conventions as one of their liveliest participants. Meanwhile he became a great-grandfather and married a longtime close friend, Margo Skinner.

In my introduction to *The Best of Fritz Leiber* I told how on 13 July 1973 my wife "gave an elaborate dinner to honor the memory of E. R. Eddison, upon the date of Lessingham's translation into Zimiamvia. Only those who would understand what that means were invited, and they were expected to come in costume. Fritz graced the party as the oldest, most sharply humorous, and best-dressed man present." What I shall now add is that, as he and I sat on the lawn of my suburban house, waiting for the food to be ready, a hummingbird came a-hovering, and we watched it for a while. He remarked that it's all wrong that these creatures are New World; something so exquisite ought to be Japanese. The thought lives on in me because of its being so very Fritz Leiber.

DOING IT RIGHT

David Hartwell

Looking back, I'm struck by the fact that Fritz Leiber was a great writer from the very start, beginning with the fantasy stories he published in *Weird Tales, Unknown Worlds,* and *Astounding.* His ability to take on big ideas, to present mature characters enmeshed in the real complexities of life, and to think intelligently about religion, politics, and sex was always there—as was the impressively high level of stylistic sophistication. Early in his career, he stole a march on Philip K. Dick, Martin Amis, and Poul Anderson all at once by writing "The Man Who Never Grew Young," about the only ordinary man to have eternal life—forced to live it, however, in reverse time. "I envy those who grow young. I yearn for the sloughing off of wisdom and responsibility, the plunge into a period of love-making and breathless excitement, the carefree years before the end."

That's how good he got, and stayed.

I remember reading Fritz Leiber's stories in the 1950s (my golden age) and, intrigued and impressed, looking for his byline in back-issue magazines and hunting out the hardcovers in bookstores. I was particularly fond of the Leiber stories reprinted by Judy Merril in her Year's Best volumes, but my two favorites were "Space-Time for Springers," and *The Big Time.* He was one of the big names in SF, but most of his books were hard to find.

It wasn't till 1962 that I obtained a copy of *Gather, Darkness!* and wrote my first SF review. By that time I had been reading for a decade and knew the standard things we all thought were the true history of the field. I knew he was "of the Lovecraft circle," that he'd been a headliner for *Unknown Worlds* and *Astounding* in the forties, that he had started writing again in the fifties but was not, basically, a novelist. And that true SF types found him a little suspect because of his major commitment to fantasy and horror (then firmly ranked lower on the evolutionary ladder than SF). I used my spiffy new college education to discuss *Gather, Darkness!* in terms of Jacobean drama. Fritz was kind enough to write an interested reply. His response helped make me the review junkie I am today.

I saw him for the first time at Discon I in 1963. It was my first Worldcon, and I was constantly excited by glimpses of legendary heroes, from Doc Smith to James Blish. I don't remember the context, but I remember the man, the image. Fritz was impressive; he stood out in a crowd the way you might hope a major literary figure would.

Fritz Leiber stood six feet, four inches tall (same height as Terry Carr, Terry told me humorously, proudly) and was a giant of fantasy, science-fiction, and horror literature in the twentieth century. In his final decade he was stooped with age, and feeble enough to require a wheelchair at conventions. His famous, ringing, orator's voice, the voice of a trained actor and trained clergyman, typically came as a surprise, issuing as it did from the mild old man of recent World Fantasy conventions. I hope fans and readers appreciate just how lucky they were to meet and talk to him in his last few years.

I am proud that the science-fiction field treated Fritz rather well before his death, when he was no longer the handsome, charismatic figure of the thirties, forties, fifties, sixties, and even the seventies. Like his mentor, H. P. Lovecraft (and his other role model, Robert E. Howard), he was an outsider (as theater people often are). Early on, he chose the fantasy fiction field as his home, and proceeded to transform it, first, by inventing a new form of sword and sorcery fiction; second, by helping to create contemporary urban horror fiction; and third, by writing pivotal stories during the SF revolution in the early fifties, deconstructing the superheroes of the forties and paving the way for new styles: hip, alienated, erotic. There is real justification for backdating the lineage of cyberpunk (cyberbeat?) to Fritz's visions of the future from the fifties.

All this he accomplished before he wrote the Change War stories, started winning Hugos, Nebulas, and World Fantasy Awards, and got named Grand Master by every organization that gives such a title in our associated genres. He was never paid a lot of money, certainly not what he deserved, for *Conjure Wife,* or Fafhrd and the Gray Mouser, or any of his brilliantly atmospheric stories. His writing had slowed to a thin stream of gems by the time bestsellerdom became a reality for fantasy, horror, and science fiction.

On the other hand, he liked his apartment in a bad neighborhood in San Francisco; he chose to stay there when he could have moved because he was at home in bohemian surroundings, with the down-and-out, the poets, the poor, the alienated. At some periods in his life he drank too much, like many other authors. He writes poignantly about his love of fantasy, of San Francisco, of alcohol, and of many other things in *Our Lady of Darkness,* in which Franz Weston, his central character, is a fictionalized self-portrait.

This book marked the first occasion we worked together as author and editor, and I found it stimulating and pleasant to be at last among Fritz's real supporters. My final such experience will be overseeing the publication of "The Doings of Daniel Kesserich," a fine Love-craftian novella that was lost for years. It's a mature Leiber work from the forties, rejected at the time apparently for its length. "Oh, yes," said Fritz, when I called him about the manuscript I had found. "I had wondered what happened to that one."

We occupy a field in which glimpses of wonder, awe, and fear are often prized more highly than craft and execution. Fritz was one of the few who always took the trouble to write well, to do it right. Consequently, he became a model for his peers and for many younger authors, especially in recent decades, when, for the first time since the thirties, fantasy and horror have moved out from beneath science fiction's umbrella of hospitality. Fritz's ultimate value is more obvious in retrospect than it was during his career, when in any given year there was likely to be some hot new SF writer who seemed more important and influential than Fritz, someone without half his craft or imagination, someone who often didn't last. Fritz lasted. His body of writings looks more significant today than it did ten or twenty years ago.

Now is the age of the passing of SF's giants, and Fritz Leiber has died. Our memories, and the works, remain.

A WORLD WITHOUT FRITZ

Stephen King

The sense of shock at Fritz Leiber's death will be, I think, mercifully short lived. He had not been in the best of health in recent years (although you could not tell that from reading his work; it remained as witty, as interesting, and as idiosyncratic as ever), and he was eighty-one years old. Yet shock is not really what the loss of our old comrades and colleagues is about, I think—it's about sorrow and that sense of displacement that comes with consideration of a world where that person's living influence no longer exists. Yes, we can be grateful that Fritz was not cut down in mid-flight, as was Charles Beaumont or Henry Kuttner or H. P. Lovecraft, but that's not apt to lessen our sense of loss, and it certainly will not fill the empty place in our ranks that was once filled with Fritz's long-shouldered form and intelligent, civilized face.

Never mind "dark fantasy" or "magical reality" or "literature of the underside" or whichever fancy buzzword for what we do happens to be in vogue this week; Fritz was a damned good horror writer, a damned good science-fiction writer, a damned good satirist, and a damned good fantasist—at the last he was so good that he was occasionally able to bind all these genres together, as he did in novels like *A Specter Is Haunting Texas*, in stories like "A Deskful of Girls" and "The Girl with the Hungry Eyes," and in his fascinating and often hilarious cycle of tales about Fafhrd and the Gray Mouser.

As far as I'm concerned (and the reader will take my prejudices into account when forming his or her own judgment), Fritz's best work was in the horror genre. His novel *Conjure Wife,* coupled with the publication of Richard Matheson's seminal story "Born of Man and Woman," formed the womb in which the fabulously vital—and fabulously profitable—creature we call "modern horror" was nurtured. Certainly without *Conjure Wife* there is no *Rosemary's Baby* or *The Stepford Wives*, and probably without *Night's Black Agents* there is no *Books of Blood* or *Night Shift*. Along with Matheson and Robert Bloch, Fritz Leiber kept the flame of popular horror alive, husbanding it carefully in the materialistic fifties, when the horrors of Cthulhu and Nyarlahotep had been supplanted by the more mundane thermonuclear visions of such writers as Pat Frank, the Mc-Carthy-era version of Tom Clancy. Fritz and his colleagues did not do this by accident or magic; they did it by wrapping the bone of ancient evil within the flesh of modern life as it came to be lived in post–World War II America, the banal Age of Lucy and Desi.

Yet the most remarkable thing about Fritz's work may have been his refusal to lapse into either silence or self-imitation. He was not content to be simply a curator but continued to be an innovator, influencing the course of the horror genre well after the field had become a supermarket and chain-bookstore mainstay. His novel *Our Lady of Darkness* (an expansion of the mind-blowing novella "The Pale Brown Thing"), published in 1977, virtually redefined the field for those of us who were interested in using it to mirror our very real, very rational fears about our culture, lives, and future. In *Our Lady of Darkness,* Fritz Leiber posited the ability of a city to actually *become alive,* and by doing so he created a kind of sublime rainbow with Jorge Luis Borges at one end and H. P. Lovecraft at the other. It was a bravura performance by a man who was then pushing seventy . . . and in a field where writers have often done their most vital work by the age of thirty.

I met Fritz at a convention in the late seventies, but as anyone who has ever attended a con as GoH (even back in those relatively sedate days) will tell you, developing a dialogue under such conditions is laughable. I had a more satisfying meeting with him about three years later, in his beloved San Francisco. I was on a book tour, staying the night at the Mark Hopkins Hotel. I got Fritz's number from Kirby McCauley, rang him, and caught him in (I believe Fritz was living on Geary at that time—almost literally right around the corner). I asked him if he'd like to come over to the hotel for a drink, and he agreed at once.

I clearly remember seeing him enter the doorway of the bar and stand there for a moment, looking around—that amazingly tall, amazingly spare figure seen in silhouette, somehow reminiscent of Boris Karloff. He saw me, raised one gnarled hand in greeting, and came over. We had a wonderful chat that afternoon, and what I remember particularly are the man's kindness and his insatiable curiosity . . . a writer's curiosity, yes, but most particularly a *fantasy* writer's curiosity, as wide-ranging and impartial as a child's.

I remember something else, as well. I was drinking beer (while I usually wouldn't have one until after five, this had been a particularly trying day), but Fritz refused to take anything except a glass of tonic water with a slice of lemon in it. He raised it with a hand that trembled slightly and clinked it against my glass before drinking. When I asked if he'd like something a little stronger, he shook his head with the sweet, slightly down-tilted smile one sees in so many photographs of Fritz. "No," he said, "I am not currently drinking alcohol. I've reached the age when I must take care of myself. I believe, if I take care of myself, I may be good for another seven years. Perhaps ten."

That conversation in the bar of the Mark Hopkins Hotel took place in 1982, and it occurred to me as I sat down to write this little remembrance that he got the whole ten . . . and *used* them.

Good-bye, Fritz. If there is another side, I hope you'll let me buy you a drink or two, alcoholic or otherwise, when I get there. In the meantime, all your old comrades and colleagues miss you. There was never a writer like you, and never will be.

Let There Be Fandom

FREDERIK POHL

In 1992 the officers of the Science-fiction and Fantasy Writers of America voted to accord Grand Master status to Frederik Pohl. This particular variety of Nebula Award is a rare and hard-won honor, recognizing a lifetime of achievement in the field. According to SFWA's bylaws, the accolade may be bestowed no more than six times in a decade.

It would be difficult to imagine a more appropriate or satisfying choice for Grand Master than Fred Pohl. Born in New York City on November 26, 1919, Pohl grew up during SF's Golden Age and went on to wear the full array of science-fiction hats: fan, agent, magazine editor, short-story writer, novelist. In 1977 he received the Nebula Award for his novel *Man Plus*, and the following year he won a Nebula, a Hugo, and the John W. Campbell Memorial Award for *Gateway*. As Robert H. Wilcox put it in *Twentieth Century Science-Fiction Writers*, "Frederik Pohl is a star among stars. He has shaped and seasoned the literature of science fiction as almost no one else has."

The opening pages of *The Way the Future Was*—Pohl's delightfully modest 1979 autobiography—accomplished something remarkable: he took the particulars of his own nostalgia and made them universal, as if each of us somehow harbored an abiding fondness for Depression-era SF. Pohl's childhood became all our childhoods, his sentiments all our sentiments. The piece that follows, "Let There Be Fandom," represents my attempt to condense the second and third chapters of *The Way the Future Was* into a concise but plenary memoir chronicling the birth of American science fiction. If the seams show, I'm the one to blame. If the joy and excitement of SF's early days shine through, give the credit to Grand Master Pohl.

In the Beginning there was Hugo Gernsback, and he begat *Amazing Stories*.

In the fullness of time, about three years' worth, a Depression smote the land, and *Amazing* was riven from him in a stock shuffle; whereupon he begat *Air Wonder Stories* and *Science Wonder Stories*, looked upon them and found them incomplete, and joined them each unto the other to be one flesh, named *Wonder Stories*. And Hugo looked upon the sales figures of *Wonder Stories* and pondered mightily that they were so low. Whereupon a Voice spake unto him, saying, "Hugo, nail those readers down," so that he begat the Science Fiction League, and thus was Fandom born.

If there had not been a Science Fiction League, it would have been necessary to invent one. The time was ripe. In the early thirties, to be a science-fiction reader was a sad and lonely thing. There weren't many of us, and we hadn't found each other to talk to. A few activists had tried to get something going, digging addresses out of the letter columns of the science-fiction magazines and starting tiny correspondence clubs, but the largest of them had maybe a dozen members, and for the rest of us there was the permanent consciousness of being alone in a hostile world. The hordes of the unblessed weren't merely disinterested in science fiction, they ridiculed it.

From Gernsback's point of view, what he had to sell was a commodity that a few people wanted very much indeed but most people wouldn't accept if it were given away free. He couldn't do a lot about recruiting new readers, but he was aware that there were a great many in-and-outers, people who would buy an issue of *Wonder Stories* now and then, and thus were obviously prime prospects, but had not formed the every-month addiction that he sought. Well, sir. The arithmetic of that situation was pretty easy to figure. If the seventy percent of his readers who averaged three issues a year could be persuaded to buy every issue, he would *triple* his sales. What Hugo hoped for from the Science Fiction League was a plain buck-hustle, a way of keeping readers loyal.

What we fans hoped for from it was Paradise. As soon as the notice appeared I rushed to join, but my membership number was 490, even so. I didn't mind. I was thrilled to think that there were 489 others like me, when I had in my whole life seen only one or two. The announcement promised that chapters would be chartered in all major cities; club news would be published in every issue of the magazine, members would be encouraged to become each other's pen pals—what fun! Hugo promised that some of the members would be foreign—imagine discussing *Spacehounds of IPC* or *The Man Who Awoke* with someone who lived in England or Australia! Imagine joining a chapter, sitting in a room filled with people who knew what you meant when you used terms like "time machines" or "ray guns," and didn't laugh! Imagine just knowing people who did not think science fiction was junk.

Sadly, the Science Fiction League did not in the long run do much for *Wonder Stories*. The readers joined up, but they did not recruit new ones; and the ones who joined were unanimously the ones who had been reading every issue, anyway. The magazine limped along for a few more years, stalling its creditors and underpaying its writers when it paid them at all, and before the end of the decade was sold to the knacking shop of the Thrilling Group.

But whatever the SFL did for Gernsback, it did an awful lot for us practitioners of the solitary vice of science fiction. It got us out of the closet and into Fandom, leading directly to such group orgies as the worldcons of today, with casts of thousands openly engaged in the celebration of SF.

I had, as it happened, met one or two fellow fans before that.

One was a boy in my eighth-grade class in Public School 9 in Brooklyn. That was a close-knit class to begin with, because we were all united in a bond of common terror. Our teacher, Maude Mary Mahlman, was nine feet tall, ferocious of mien, and possessed of compound eyes, like a fly, so that even when she seemed to be looking at the blackboard or a student across the room, at least one facet was always and unwinkingly fixed on *me*. She told us that herself, and I believed every word she said. For a time. Then my courage came back. By the end of the term I had learned to look industrious when daydreaming, and I actually wrote a short science-fiction story, my very first, under her eyes on a drowsy May morning in English class. (The story had something to do with Atlantis. That's all I remember, except that it was awful.)

In the same class, Owen Jordan sat nearby, and lived close to my house. We would walk home together and sometimes stop off at his place or mine to play chess, and he was the one who tuned me in to the existence of a magazine I had not previously known existed, *Astounding*. The first issue he loaned me had a cover illustrating the story "Manape the Mighty," and so naive (or despairing) was I that I read only that story and returned it to him before he pointed out that all the other stories in the issue were science fiction. But we lost touch shortly after that. We graduated from grammar school, and I went off to Brooklyn Tech.

There was no high school specializing in science fiction, which is what really interested me. There was not yet even a high school of science, and perhaps that's a pity, because I think I might have liked being a physicist or an astronomer. What there was, was Brooklyn Technical High School. It was said to give many courses in science, which I recognized as being some part of science fiction, and besides, it was an honor school, requiring a special examination for entrance, which appealed to my twelve-year-old snob soul.

Brooklyn Tech was a revolutionary concept in high schools, dedicated to the quick manufacture of technologists. In 1932 its own building was still under construction, and it was housed temporarily in a sprawl of out-of-date schools and one abandoned factory, at the Brooklyn end of the Manhattan Bridge, where the laboratories and workshops could be accommodated.

In my second term, my home room was in Annex 1, identified as Brooklyn PS 1 when it was built, probably around the time of the Civil War (or the Punic). It was by all odds the dingiest structure I have ever spent much time in. The toilets were plugged and foul. Leaking pipes overhead left white nacre on the walls. The heating system was a mockery, and the time was February of 1933, cold as hell. Fortunately, only a few of my classes were in Annex 1. In mid-morning I shifted to Annex 5, a much newer, nicer school next to a playground, six or seven face-frozen blocks away. Then in the afternoon I had classes in the Main Building, the whilom factory, just on the other side of the constant truck rumble of Flatbush Avenue. After the first few days I noticed that I was dodging the trucks in the company of the same tall, skinny guy with glasses—he looked quite a lot like me, or actually quite a lot handsomer than me—and he turned out to be a science-fiction fan. His name was Joseph Harold Dockweiler, but he wasn't terribly pleased with it, and a few years later he changed it to Dirk Wylie.

Dirk was the sort of best friend every young person should have. Our interests were similar, but not identical. We were much of the same age, and almost identically of the same stage of growth, so that we discovered the same things about the world at the same time: girls, smoking, drinking, reading, science fiction. If you mapped a schematic diagram of Dirk onto one of me, nearly all the points at the centers of our personalities would match exactly. Off to one side was my growing interest in politics and society, which Dirk found unexciting; off to another, his in weapons and cars, which I shared at most tepidly.

Dirk lived in Queens Village, an hour from Tech by subway and bus. Like me, he was an only child. Like me, he had no close ties with the kids next door. Like me, he had a tolerant home environment, willing to let him grow on his own. Like me, he had a Collection.

The possession of a Collection is one of the diagnostic signs of Fandom. Another is Trying to Write, and Dirk shared that symptom with me, too. We found out these things about each other within the first week following our meeting, after which there was no question that, at least until further notice, we two loners were going to be Best Friends.

In our sophomore year at Brooklyn Tech, the New Building at last was completed and we moved in. How modern and grand it seemed! Five or six stories tall, with an athletic field on the roof, shiny, clean laboratories instead of the jagged zinc of the old factory, an auditorium with air-conditioning and the fullest projection facilities; the thing even had a radio station of its own. Pretty Fort Greene Park was just across the street, and the concentrated heart of Brooklyn's downtown only a five-minute walk away. The magnetism was too powerful to resist; Dirk and I walked there every afternoon, to go to a burlesque theater, or a movie, or just to explore.

Let me tell you about Brooklyn. For the first part of Brooklyn's life it was not a conquered province of New York City, it was a competitor. Even after the consolidation it still competed. Brooklyn had its own baseball team (the Dodgers), its own library system (better than New York's in every respect, except for, maybe, the Fifth Avenue reference facility), its own parks (after Frederick Law Olmsted designed Central Park in Manhattan, he took what he had learned to Brooklyn and laid out the even more spectacular Prospect Park), its own museums, its own zoo. Downtown Brooklyn had its own department stores—Namm's, Loeser's, A & S—and I still think they were nicer than, and almost as big as, Macy's or Gimbels. Downtown Brooklyn had four or five first-run movie houses, including the Brooklyn Paramount, as lavish a marble-staired temple as any in the world, at least until the Radio City Music Hall came along. On Fulton Street it even had legitimate theaters, with the same sorts of bills as theaters in Boston or Chicago. Road companies of Broadway shows played there after the New York runs had closed, and sometimes Broadway shows opened there for tryouts before risking the metropolis across the river. And all these marvels, stores and shows, bookshops and burlesques, parks and playgrounds, were within our grasp. If Brooklyn palled, New York was just over the bridge; often enough we walked across the East River and up Broadway as far as Union Square to check out the secondhand book and magazine stores on Fourth Avenue. School could not compete. Outside it we were learning the world.

Which was changing.

The Depression had settled in, but Franklin Delano Roosevelt was inaugurated a week or two after Dirk and I met, and there was talk of a New Deal. Society seemed to be evolving into something new before our eyes. So was science. We heard about things like relativity and the expanding universe—not just in the SF magazines, but even on the radio. The world seemed to be into science fiction almost as much as Dirk and I were, at least in a nuts-and-bolts way. Airplanes were practically common in the sky, whereas a few years earlier a plane's appearance had been reason enough for housewives to leave the dishes in the sink and run outside to gawk. There were dirigibles, and the new Empire State Building, almost a quarter mile of masonry stretching up to scrape the sky, was topped with a mooring mast for blimps (or for King Kong to cling to). There was a kid in our classes at Brooklyn Tech who actually *flew*—yes, had a real pilot's license, spun the prop, took off, landed, was full of stories about how you could walk into an unseen spinning propeller and be chopped into ground round before you knew it, about hairy landings in the fog and storms aloft. I had fantasies about getting a plane of my own, preferably one of the swallow-tailed or heart-shaped or magnetically driven jobs out of *Wonder Stories,* then challenging my friend to a race and beating his ass off. I knew that that was fantasy. But what else except fantasy was he doing, every Saturday at Floyd Bennett Field?

In a way that had never happened before in the history of the human race, the world was looking into the future. Most especially Dirk and I. Most particularly through science fiction. When the Science Fiction League came along, we both sent our applications off at once, and almost by return mail I got a postcard from a man who identified himself as one George Gordon Clark. He was, he announced, Member 1 of the Science Fiction League. Not only that, he had been authorized to form Chapter 1, and I was invited to attend Meeting 1.

It was at night, and most of an hour away by subway, but I would not have missed it for rubies.

When G. G. Clark started the Brooklyn Science Fiction League, I do not think he knew what he was getting into.

Clark was a grown-up adult human being, in his late twenties or thereabouts. He had a job, and he had a Collection that made even Dirk's look sick. Clark not only had every copy of every science-fiction magazine ever published, but they had that fresh-from-the-mint look of having been bought new from the corner candy store, rather than being picked up secondhand. He even had a few variorum editions, such as a copy of *Amazing Stories* on which one plate of the three-color cover had failed to print, so that it was all ghostly blues and greens. He also had more SF books than I had ever seen in one place before, and he even had science-fiction fan magazines, of which I had never previously even heard.

I think Clark must have been less than delighted with the scruffy adolescents who turned up in response to his postcard. Not one of us was within ten years of his age. At least one—Arthur Selikowitz, a tall, skinny polymath who entered Rensselaer Polytechnic Institute not long after at the age of thirteen—could not then have been quite eleven. At our organizational meeting the first thing we did was to elect Clark chairman. There was no alternative. Not only did he outrank us all (Member 1), but it was his hall. We met some of the time in his cellar library (allowed to touch The Collection only one at a time, and with Clark hovering vigilantly by), sometimes in a rented classroom of a nearby public school. The term "nearby," of course, refers to its proximity to Clark. All the rest of us had to travel miles.

It is hard for me to remember what we did at these meetings, and I think the probable reason is that we did very little. There was a certain amount of reading the minutes and passing amendments to the bylaws, and not much else. After a while we decided to publish a mimeographed fan magazine of our own. I became its editor (largely, I think, because I had my own typewriter), and it may have been the first place in which words of mine were actually published. I haven't seen a copy of *The Brooklyn Reporter* in many years and doubt that there was much in it worth reading, but it was marvelously exciting to me then. My words were going out to readers all over the country! (Not very *many* readers, no. But quite geographically dispersed.) People I had never seen were writing letters to comment on my articles!

What we science-fiction fans mostly wanted to do with each other's company was to talk—about science fiction, and about the world. Robert's Rules of Order didn't seem to provide for much of that, so we formed the habit of The Meeting After the Meeting. After enduring an hour or so of parliamentary rules, we troops would bid farewell to our leader and walk in a body to the nearest station of the El. On the way we would stop off at a soda fountain. This had three very good features: it gave us an informal atmosphere for talk, it supplied us with ice-cream sodas, and it got rid of G. G. Clark, so that we kids could be ourselves. The only bad part of it was that we had to adjourn the regular meetings pretty early, since none of us were old enough to stay out very late. But, considering what was happening at the regular meetings, that was no sacrifice.

All it takes to publish a fanzine is the will to make it happen, and maybe access to somebody else's mimeograph machine, and in a pinch you can get by without the latter. (There have been carbon-copied fanzines, limited to as many sheets of paper as you can roll into a typewriter.) Consequently there is a lot that is not very interesting to read even by the standards of the fellow who wrote it ("Gosh, friends, this is lousy, isn't it?"), and even a hostile reception does not necessarily keep a fanzine from continuing ("Wow, gang, you really slammed the lastish, but wotthehell, we'll keep plugging").

No matter how deficient in redeeming social virtues a fanzine may seem to you and me, it always has one: it is educating the person who puts it out. Ray Bradbury got his start in fanzines. So did a couple dozen of the other best science-fiction writers around.

When I got my hands on the levers of power in *The Brooklyn Reporter*, I didn't think of it as a training program. I thought of it as fun, scary fun in a way, because I perceived that I could make a fool of myself in a more public fashion than I had ever been able to before. But pleasure apart from that.

What we printed was confined to the things that interested us, and although we did not consciously think out the probability that such material would also interest those people just like us who would, we hoped, be our readers, that's still a good way of being an editor. We printed news of what was going on in our club ("Eight members present at the last meeting, and Joseph Harry Dockweiler joined"), reviews of the professional science-fiction magazines ("The newest Van Manderpootz story is about a professor who has spectacles that can see into the future. It's a hack idea, but Weinbaum's comic treatment saves it"), gossip about the pros ("Doc Smith has just completed the mathematical calculations for his next Skylark novel, which runs to one hundred thousand words, or longer than the serial will be"), and letters. Oh, yes, letters, lots of letters, and probably they were the most interesting things in many of the magazines. Some fanzines, like the long-lasting West Coast *Voice of the Imagi-Nation,* printed nothing else.

We also published amateur stories and poems. Usually they had been rejected by all the pros, for good reason. Sometimes they were a kind of writing for which professional markets did not seem to exist. My favorite of the fanzines I edited was a tiny quarter-size mimeographed job named *Mind of Man,* and what it was mostly about was playing with words. *MoM* was tiny, infrequent, and died at an early age, but I loved it. The contents owed something to Lewis Carroll and quite a lot to James Joyce (whose "work in progress," later called *Finnegans Wake,* was running in batches in a strange little magazine called *transition*). There was also a little science fiction in *Mind of Man* now and then, but you had to look pretty close to find it; then, as now, there was no rule that the contents of an SF fanzine had to have anything to do with SF. I wrote nearly everything published in it, including a lot of, ah, poetry? Call it that—

Necroptic life, in Thursday bliss,
Exploits the winnowed worker's brawn,
While taurine canines gently kiss
With urine the aurescid lawn.

I would guess that the total circulation of *Mind of Man* ran well into two figures, and that counts the pass-arounds; but there were those who liked it. Even years later, people sometimes quoted *MoM* poems to me from memory, and I was always immensely flattered.

While we were staining our fingers with mimeograph ink, our eyes were still firmly fixed on the professional magazines. They looked like Heaven.

To their editors and writers, I am sure they looked a lot less than heavenly; the Depression was still with us, sparing no man nor magazine. But *figurez-vous*, even at half a cent a word, a 5,000-word story would fetch twenty-five dollars. Twenty-five dollars happened to be what my mother earned every week, a sum on which she supported us both. But, of course, the money was not the point.

So I wrote my stories, and I sent them out. I didn't actually finish very many of them; I was given to beginning a story, reading what I had written, deciding it was awful, and throwing it away. In such judgments I was no doubt right, but if I had known then what I know now, I would have forced myself to finish these stories anyway, for the practice and the discipline. Of the hundreds upon hundreds of sheets of paper I covered with typing in the mid-1930s, only a few dozen wound up as "finished" stories, mostly very short, and with them I assaulted the professional editors.

The conventional and best way to submit stories, then as now, was to mail them in. That cost money, maybe a dime each way for each submission. I quickly realized that for half that much I could take the subway to the editors' offices and hand the stories over myself, at the negligible expense of a few hours of my own time.

Astounding had gone down the tube as a member of the Clayton pulp chain, but Street & Smith had bought into the wreckage, and the magazine was back in business. Its editor was a man named F. Orlin Tremaine, and it was housed in a dilapidated old slum on Seventh Avenue, a block below Barneys clothing store. I have no idea when the building was new, probably sometime in the Middle Jurassic. The lower floors were filled with printing presses, shaking the whole structure as they rolled. The building had a hydraulic elevator. To make it go up or down, the operator had to tug on a rope outside the car itself. The building had long since been declared a hazard by the fire marshal, and so smoking was prohibited everywhere in it. (That didn't actually stop anybody, it only inconvenienced them a little. When John Campbell became editor a little later on, he kept a copper ashtray on his desk, copper because of its high thermal conductivity, and whisked it into a drawer when the early-warning system announced the presence of a fire warden.) To get from the reception room to any editor's office involved going up and down staircases, squeezing past rolls of paper stored to feed the ground-floor presses, and reveling in the fascinating smells of printer's ink and rotting wood.

I didn't get past the reception room the first couple of times. On my initial attempt I was met at the desk by a diffident young male assistant to Tremaine; he took the manuscript from my grubby young hands, flipped through it, and announced that I didn't have my name and address typed in the upper right-hand corner of the first page. It was on the last page, I told him. Well enough, he said, but it's *supposed* to be on the first one. He also pointed out that standard typing paper was 8½ × 11 inches and plain white, while what I was using was several inches longer than that and had narrow blue lines down the left-hand margin. Sorry about that, I said. (I didn't tell him the reason. My mother worked in a law office at that time, and legal cap was what she filched to bring home to me.) But he allowed me to leave the story with him, and a week or two later I got a penny postcard from Street & Smith, announcing that it was "ready for pickup." The card was a printed form, from which I deduced that I was not the only writer who had more time than postage stamps.

I came to see a great many of those cards over the years. Tremaine never bought a word from me, or even came close. But he was nice about it. After the first couple of submissions he began inviting me down to his office to chat, and toward the end of his tenure even took me out to lunch now and then.

I cannot tell you how much this inflated me, not only in my own ego but in the estimation of my fellow fans. Heaven knows what he got out of it. Since I was editing several fanzines at the time, it is possible that he mistook me for some kind of power figure among the readers, but I don't really believe so. I think Tremaine was just a good guy.

He was also a good editor. John Campbell is the worshipped god in the pantheon of *Astounding,* but Tremaine did some smart things. It was not his fault that he knew nothing at all about science fiction when he took the job on; Street & Smith bought the magazine and handed it to him as a chore, and that was that. He did his best to learn, and he succeeded. He published some incredible rot. He even wrote some of the sappiest of it, or at least so gossip says: "Warner Van Lorne," one of the most frequent bylines in his magazine, was supposed to be Tremaine himself. But he made a few wise moves, including hiring John Campbell to succeed him when he was moved upstairs. I liked Tremaine, respected him, missed him when he left, and wondered if this young punk Campbell would ever measure up to his predecessor's standards.

Tremaine was no scientist, and so *Astounding* during his tenure was likely to contain some galumphing horrors, but the virtue of that defect was that he published some pretty fascinating stuff that any scientifically trained person would never touch. Not just stories. *Astounding* ran nearly the complete works of Charles Fort in interminable serial form: compendia of curious and inexplicable happenings —minnows falling from a clear sky, strange lights of airships seen before airships were invented. The towering flights of fantasy in the Tremaine *Astounding* were an attractive change from the nuts-and-bolts gadgetry of Gernsback's *Wonder* or the stilted stodge of T. O'Conor Sloane's *Amazing.*

Nevertheless, as *Astounding* didn't seem to want to buy what I had to sell, I took my wares to the others, too. *Wonder Stories* was a grubby kind of magazine, full of self-glorifying little digs at the competition, such as long lists of titles of stories published in other magazines under the heading "Stories We Reject Appear Elsewhere." (Don Wollheim once remarked it should have read "Stories We Don't Pay For Appear Elsewhere.") Yet it had two things going for it. One was that the major find of the mid-thirties, a new writer named Stanley G. Weinbaum, turned up there long before he was seen in any other magazines. Weinbaum was great; his first story, "A Martian Odyssey," still appears on most lists of all-time best science fiction. Well it should. Weinbaum invented in it a character of a sort no one had thought to create before, an ostrich-shaped alien creature named Tweel who didn't think, talk, act, or look like a human, but was nevertheless a *person*. All other writers in the field, once the egg had been demonstrated to stand on its end, immediately began to invent personalized-alien creatures of their own, and have continued to do so ever since.

The other thing that made *Wonder* attractive was that they had mighty nice rejection slips. From *Astounding* I never even saw a slip, just the penny postcard that told me to come and carry away another corpse, but most magazines printed up little three-by-five or so forms, along the general lines of

> We regret that your submitted material is not suitable for our needs at this time, but thank you for letting us see it.
>
> THE EDITORS

Wonder's were nothing like that. I usually wrote very short stories, rarely having the confidence to attempt anything much over 2,000 words, and so it sometimes seemed to me that *Wonder's* rejections were longer than the stories concerned. There was a form letter signed by Hugo himself, benignly explaining how strict his standards were. There was a printed check-off sheet, listing thirty or so reasons for rejection:

( ) Plot stale
( ) Errors in science
( ) Material offensive to moral standards

and lots more. And, to take the sting out of it, there was a jolly little "translation" of a "Chinese rejection slip." ("Your honorable contribution is so breathtakingly excellent that we do not dare publish it, since it would set a standard no other writer would be able to reach.") It was almost fun to be rejected by *Wonder*. Impersonal fun, though. Hugo Gernsback was by no means as gregarious a personality as F. Orlin Tremaine.

Their offices were on Hudson Street in lower Manhattan, and Dirk and I hiked over there from Brooklyn Tech a time or two. We milled around in the anteroom, under the original oil paintings of covers from Gernsback's gadget and radio magazines, but we never got past the reception desk. After about two visits the girl made it clear to us that we never would, and so for submissions to *Wonder* I scraped up stamp money.

I never got past the reception desk at *Amazing*, either, but

T. O'Conor Sloane, Ph.D., did something for me no other editor had done. He made me a pro. Sloane was quite an old man, white-bearded and infirm of gait. He was a marvel to me just on account of his age—my own grandfather, who died around that time, was only in his sixties, and Sloane was at least a decade or two past that. But he was amiable and cordial enough; he would totter out to meet me, chat for a moment, and retire with that week's offering in his hand.

His talent as a science-fiction editor was not, I am sorry to say, marked. His scientific attitudes had been fixed somewhere around the rosy twilight of his career, say 1910, and anything since then he dismissed as fantasy. He put himself firmly on record as denying that any human being would ever leave the surface of the Earth in a spaceship, and to us Skylark addicts that was diagnostically treason. What he published was a queer mix of flamboyant space adventure and barely imaginative stories of exploration, all heavily weighted with his interminably balanced blurbs, editorials, and comments on letters.

I cannot resist describing one set of the space adventures for you. They began with a story called "The Jameson Satellite," written by Neil R. Jones. "The Jameson Satellite" was about a very rich university professor who had nothing much to do with his money and nobody to leave it to. He decided to use it to make himself the dandiest tomb a fellow could have, and so he built in his backyard a rocket ship, big and powerful enough to take his body into orbit, where it would circle Earth, preserved by the absolute zero of space, until the end of time. After a while, it all came about as he planned. He died. His executor had his unembalmed corpse loaded into the rocket, they lit the fuse, and *zap,* there went all that was mortal of Professor Jameson right into orbit.

But there was more. The Earth rolled along. Time passed. The human race became extinct, the sun itself grew cold—and yet Jameson was still there in the deep freeze. And then, in the fullness of time, strangers came poking around. They were machine-men called Zoromes. They had once had fleshly bodies and looked more or less like you and me (except that they had tentacles and a few other peculiarities of anatomy), and when they discovered the Jameson satellite with its cargo of still-fresh meat, they had no trouble doing with the human corpse what they had done with their own bodies long and long ago: they built him an artificial body, took out his brain, thawed it, and stuck it into the machine. And so thereafter, for endless adventures, Professor Jameson lived once again, as the Zorome called 21MM392.

The Zorome stories were among the most popular series of the 1930s, and not just with me. There was another reader, a youngster named Bob Ettinger, who liked them as much as I did. A few decades later, when Ettinger was grown up and a scientist on the faculty of a Midwest university, he remembered old Professor Jameson's deep freeze and wondered just how much science was in that science fiction. So he dug into the biochemistry and the physics, checked out what was known about the effects of liquid-gas temperatures on animal tissue, even checked the current cost quotations for liquid helium and triply insulated containers big enough to hold you and me . . . and evolved the proposal described in his book, *The Prospects of Immortality*, for freezing everyone who dies until such time as medical science figures out how to thaw him out and repair him. Right now there are a couple of dozen corpsicles in the United States (Walt Disney is supposed to be one of them) waiting for that great thawing-out day.

In my personal scale of priorities, the fact that Sloane gave the world the freezing program is somewhat overshadowed by the fact that he gave me my first paid publication ever. It wasn't a story, it was a poem (called "Elegy to a Dead Planet: Luna," and if you feel for any reason that you must read it—I don't know why that would be so—you can find it in a book called *The Early Pohl*). People ask me from time to time when I made my first sale. For me, that's hard to answer. I wrote the poem in 1935. Sloane accepted it in 1936. It was published in 1937. And I was paid for it in 1938.

Funny thing. I never had another line in *Amazing*, from that day to this. Sloane actually accepted another poem, and I had bright hopes of laying stories on him as well, but before anything could be published, much less paid for, *Amazing* too was sold to the knackers, and Sloane disappeared from the science-fiction scene. The new owners made it sell better than it ever had, but by publishing fairly simple-minded stories—or so I judged them; the objective facts are that I didn't care much for what they published, and they didn't care much for what I wrote, and after a while I stopped even trying them. By then I had found more hospitable markets, anyway. But there's a certain nostalgia. You never forget your first sale.

The thirties were the great years of the film—for everyone, not just science-fiction fans. Every hamlet had its own million-dollar Palace of the Movies, plush carpets and tinkling fountains, architecturally a bastard son of the Bolshoi out of the Baths of Caracalla. Most were left over from the manic expansion of the twenties, but nerve was seeping back into the builders. The Radio City Music Hall opened when I was around thirteen. The Music Hall didn't care much for science fiction on its screen, but the hall itself was a kind of science fiction, ultramodern of 1932, and I must have visited it fifty times to see whatever was there to see: my first color film (*Becky Sharp*); Will Rogers comedies; my first, and to this day almost only, 3-D picture (a short subject; you wore red and green celluloid goggles to make it work); above all, the Fred Astaire and Ginger Rogers musicals, on which I doted. The Music Hall gave you more than a film. There was a stage show with the Rockettes and the Corps de Ballet, and a symphonic overture and an organ interlude, intended to empty out the house between shows. I had a fixed itinerary at the Music Hall. Up in one of the balconies for the film itself, so I could smoke. Down in the front rows, far left, to watch Jesse Crawford at microscopically close range as he played the organ. Middle aisles of the orchestra, two-thirds of the way back, to see the Rockettes.

But there was a growing amount of science fiction, too, if not in the Music Hall, then at some other theater, even the "nabes." The original *King Kong* (only film I have ever seen that gave me nightmares). Claude Rains in *The Invisible Man*. Boris Karloff in *Frankenstein*. The very first SF film I saw was *Just Imagine*, produced in 1930, about the incredibly distant future world of 1980 (autogyro traffic cops, Martians, babies out of a slot machine): it was a slapstick comedy starring El Brendel, notable now mostly because it was the first American film featuring lovely Maureen O'Sullivan, later Tarzan's favorite Jane. There were gadgety future-adventure movies like *F P 1 Does Not Reply* (floating airport in the middle of the Atlantic, where planes refueled en route to Europe) and *Transatlantic Tunnel* (marvelous zappy machines boring through the undersea rock). There were semisatirical spoofs like *It's Great to Be Alive*. What was great about it, for the hero, was that some pestilence had killed every male in the world but him, and he was therefore the object of every girl's affections. It was a musical, and the way the girls courted him was through song and dance numbers.°

Not all of the science-fiction and fantasy films were really much good (as you maybe have already figured out!), but among them there were two that turned me on to a degree no subsequent film has matched.

One of them was *Death Takes a Holiday*. It starred Fredric March. Its theme music was Sibelius's *Valse Triste,* which stayed in my mind for months on end. (After a while I wrote words to it, so I could sing it in the shower.) March played the part of Death, proud anthropomorphic Prince of Darkness, sulkily curious about why mortal beings bother living their brief, tatty little lives. He takes time off to visit a house party in Nice or Graustark (villagers tossing rosebuds into an open car, pergolas, drawing rooms, reflecting pools). His intention is to satisfy his curiosity, but he falls in love. While he is on vacation no one dies. Suffering is prolonged. His fellow guests figure out his identity and beg him to get back on the job, but he won't go without the girl. . . . Well, the plot does not bear rational examination, but I loved it. What I love I love a lot. I saw it twenty-three times.

The other film that blew my mind was *Things to Come*. I still think it is the finest science-fiction film ever made, greater than *Metropolis*, more meaningful than *2001*. I concede that it looks pretty quaint now, but so will *Star Wars* in another forty years. I saw *Things to Come* thirty-three times before I stopped counting. Quite recently I saw it again—in fact, took on the chore of organizing a college science-fiction film festival just to give myself the chance to see it. It is still *grand*.

Things to Come was the first major film for Ralph Richardson and Raymond Massey, and I have had an immense liking for both of them ever since. It wasn't exactly a story. It was almost a documentary, and financially speaking it was a bomb. But every frame is engraved

---

°E.g., a troupe of Eastern European lady wrestlers singing:
We are the girls from Czechoslovakia.
We are strong, and how we can sock-y-ya.

on my mind. So is Arthur Bliss's score. For years I had the 78-rpm album of the music, until the winter I unwisely left the wax discs on a radiator. Now I have an illicit tape dubbed off the radio, and I still think it's fine. The film was real science fiction, not papier-mâché Godzillas or carrot-shaped Martians. It was written by a real science-fiction writer, in fact the father of us all, old H. G. Wells himself. And it was handsomely filmed with actors who knew what they were about.

Let me confess to something. I think a great deal of *Death Takes a Holiday* and *Things to Come* rubbed off in the deep-down core of my brain. I have no particular fear of dying, and I think that part of the reason for my tranquillity lies in some subliminal feeling that when it happens it will be old Fredric March who takes me by the hand and says, "Hey, Fred, long time no see." And in spite of all the evidence, I am optimistic about the future of the world. I have a conviction that bad times and good all pass, and all are endurable, and that is what *Things to Come* had to say. You can blow up the world as often as you like, but there is a future, there is always a future, and while some of it will be bad, some of it will be better than anyone has ever known.

For the opening of *Things to Come* we fans got up a real theater party—not a very big one (I think about six of us could afford tickets), but there we were, en masse, going to taste this great new experience together. James Blish, kid fan from far-off East Orange, New Jersey, came in to join us. Like all of us, he wanted to be a writer. Like all of us, he was learning how in the fanzines, publishing one of his own and writing for others. And like a lot of us, he got his heart's desire, with books like *Cities in Flight* and *A Case of Conscience* among the long list of first-rate work that only ended with his death.

Jim Blish from New Jersey, Bob Lowndes from Connecticut—we were becoming quite cosmopolitan. Evidently there were specimens of our own breed in other parts of the world. We had linked up with them through fanzine and letter, but we hungered for personal contact. And so, one Sunday in 1936, half a dozen of us got on the train for Philadelphia and were met by half a dozen Philadelphia fans, and so the world's very first science-fiction convention took place. Considering the historical significance of the event, it is astonishing how little I remember about what happened there. It's no good looking for the official minutes, either: I was the secretary who took them, and I have no idea where I put them. Philly fan John V. Baltadonis's father owned a bar, and we met in one corner of it for the business part of the session. Robert A. Madle and Oswald Train were part of the Philadelphia contingent, and I still see them pretty regularly at SF conventions; so was Milton A. Rothman, who published a few stories (some of them with me) under the name of Lee Gregor before deciding to devote his time to nuclear physics. From New York were Johnny Michel, Don Wollheim, Will Sykora, Dave Kyle, and myself.

The last convention I went to had 4,000 people in attendance, and it was by no means the biggest SF convention ever. There must be a hundred of them a year in the United States, and maybe another hundred here and there in the rest of the world.

But that was the first.

The July Ward

S. N. DYER

The most amusing photograph in the June 1993 *Locus*—the issue covering the twenty-eighth annual Nebula Awards banquet—shows a female author holding up an article of clothing she'd evidently received shortly after the results were announced. I WAS ON THE NEBULA BALLOT, the garment reads, AND ALL I GOT WAS THIS STUPID T-SHIRT.

Now S. N. Dyer has got something else: a reprint of her striking story, "The July Ward," in *Nebula Awards 28.*

The fiction of S. N. Dyer has appeared under various pseudonyms in *Asimov's, Amazing, Omni,* and the anthologies *Universe* and *Blood Is Not Enough.* Describing herself as "a San Francisco native in exile," Dyer goes on to explain that she lives with a six-toed calico cat, Bigfoot, who is fond of "prancing around on the computer keyboard when I'm not in the room, thereby rewriting my manuscripts."

As you might infer from "The July Ward," Dyer is also a practicing physician. Asked to comment on her nominated story, she responded, simply, "At 3 A.M., when you've been working twenty hours straight, a bright, silent hospital corridor can be damn spooky."

There is a place of which all doctors know, but none will speak.

It is 6:30 in the morning, and hardly worth anyone's while to try for sleep. The medical student has just finished writing admission orders for the new patient, and the night nurse is studying the page with a mixture of annoyance and disdain.

Watson ignores them, ignoring also the CT scan she has been admiring, with its textbook-perfect depiction of a brain demolished by a bullet. She closes her eyes and, in the process of rubbing them, experiences the intensive care unit anew.

There is the breathing of the ancient man with Cheyne-Stokes respirations: shallow, deep, deeper, loud gasp and shudder, shallow, shallower, pause for a long time. An old ventilator is breathing for the newest patient: *whoosh clunk sssshh,* over and over, twenty times a minute. As counterpoint, the unit's sole heart monitor beeps an out-of-sync 80/minute, with the occasional interposed beat of an extra systole, or the brief syncopation of a bigeminal rhythm.

Next, Watson becomes aware of the early morning smells, of blood and decay, tube-feeding and feces, cheap wine and vomitus. Soon, someone will mop the floor and someone else deliver trays, and the odors of ammonia and hospital food will merge into the unsavory whole.

She opens her eyes, taking in the cracked plaster, six beds, shelves piled haphazardly with a random selection of unneeded equipment; sighing, she begins moving towards the door. As she passes the man in bed four, his bandaged head swivels to follow her.

"Waitress!" he calls. "Waitress, I want a tuna fish sandwich!"

The medical student—Watson has just spent twenty-two straight hours in his company and cannot remember his first name, just the inhumanly neat way he signs it—comes to her defense.

"Excuse me, Mr. Johnson," he says. "You're not in a restaurant."

Watson grimaces. The pushy kid is going to try to orient the patient. Had she ever been so naive and idealistic, even on her own second day of the wards? *T*. His name starts with a *T*.

"Mr. Johnson, you're in the neurology/neurosurgery intensive care unit of Warren G. Harding Industrial County Hospital."

The patient ignores him, repeating angrily, "Waitress, I want a tuna fish sandwich."

Watson says, "Here, let me show you how it's done." She approaches the patient, standing at the foot of his hospital bed.

"Waitress . . ." he begins.

"I'm sorry, sir. This is not my table."

Grabbing her student by the elbow, she leads him out of the unit. The benches outside are mercifully empty, so they need not be polite to hovering families. "Now what?" he asks.

"Huh?" She is trying to remember if he's named Tony or Tom or Ted.

"What do we do now?" He has never been on call before, and he's riding an adrenaline high. Twenty-two hours, and he's gung ho for more.

She pauses to think about it. A considerate resident might tell him to go work on his presentation, but who needs to prepare to talk about a simple gunshot wound? Or, up at University Hospital, she might tell him to clean up, change, eat breakfast. But here at Harding the showers in the doctors' call rooms have no curtains and no water. Besides, it's accepted that the team coming off call will continue to wear wrinkled, blood-spattered scrubsuits, as a visual reminder to everyone else that they are tired, and short-tempered, and not likely to look charitably upon any attempts at denigration or one-upmanship. And the cafeteria will not open for another half-hour.

Gazing out the window, Watson can see the sky growing pink behind the silhouettes of the hospital complex. There are half a dozen towers of varying height and architecture, monuments to half a dozen periods of relative affluence. The majority of buildings are now silent and dark.

"It's kind of like an old castle," she says. "You know, built with no plan, every generation adding something."

"With secret passages and haunted dungeons?" asks the kid, playing along. This cheers her. She tried this routine on another student once, eleven long months ago, only to discover he was a cheap knockoff robot with missing humor circuits. Attempt to tell that kind of medical student a joke, and he'll reply, "Will this be on the test?"

She points to the buildings in turn, starting with the ruins of the nursing dorm. "The original Norman donjon." Then the infectious disease wing, a gift of the New Deal. "The fenestrated keep, built by the Mad Duke in 1485." Next, she aims at the New Tower, the last addition, built during the nationwide hospital expansion of the sixties, and where most of the patients are now housed. "The Georgian wing."

Getting even further into the spirit of it all, Tom—she has noticed the nametag on his short white jacket with its pockets crammed full of instruments and manuals—cackles. "Look, that light. Could it be . . . the la-bor-a-try of Doctor Frankenstein?"

She decides that she likes him after all, and decides what they will do next. Checking her watch—it is now twenty to seven—she nods down the half-lit hall. "Come on."

They go down the stairwell to the basement, the same basement they have traversed all night, bringing patients from the emergency room to radiology and then to ICU. As they stride, cockroaches scurry angrily from their path. Tom flinches once.

"Jeez!" he says. "It must be two inches long."

Watson feels momentarily sorry for him. His origins are written all over him: a neat, lawned half-acre in some well-kept suburb. The medical school has charged her with his education, and what has she done for him so far? Shown him drunks puking up blood and wine; a battered woman who attempts to steal his stethoscope when he leaves the room to get her a pain shot; children with needle tracks; and his final wonder, six-legged vermin that he has previously known only from the jokes on TV. But now she will show him something to make up for it all. Veering from the yellow line painted on the floor, the line that brings them home through the maze of corridors, she pries open a door that has been painted closed.

"There is a dimension beyond time and space . . ." she says, in her best Rod Serling voice, and leads him up dust-caked stairs illuminated only by their penlights. Two flights up, they lean hard against another door, and emerge into a large room.

"This is part of the original hospital," she says, her voice echoing against high ceilings. Her breath forms mist in the air—many windows are broken—and Tom tries to button his jacket, but the bulging pockets prevent it. "They built the new parts over and around the old foundation. But these are the first wards. They were still used up until the late seventies."

They prowl the empty ward, which is hesitantly brightening with sunrise. As the shadows diminish, they begin to make out cobwebs and cracked plaster. Pigeons, nesting in the rafters, glare at the intruders.

"There'd be patients down both sides, and in the summer when it got full, they'd run a row of beds down the middle. You'd move screens to examine a patient, or if someone was terminal."

"Look at this!" Tom has found a wooden wheelchair, not that much more antique or decrepit than those they have been using all night to transport patients, and sits on the hard, uncomfortable seat. Watson pushes him past the nursing desk in the hall, and into the adjoining ward. "They built them long and thin like this to maximize fresh air. The Florence Nightingale approach. This would be the women's ward." One of the tires is flat, and the student bounces regularly as they progress. The chair leaves thin tracks in the dirt.

Tom leaps from the chair and runs to an incredibly tall floor fan, reaching to his breast pocket. "Great!" His footsteps raise clouds of dust that smell like guano.

"When it got hot, they'd put a tub of ice at the front of a ward, and aim a fan over it." A patient had told her that, an old, old woman who'd been a nurse at this very hospital during the Depression. When Watson had met her, she'd been in her nineties, bony and pale, identical in appearance to all other patients in their nineties, as if those final ten years erase the distinguishing characteristics that make up the individual. But she had been surprisingly aware, and when she had died. . . .

"Where's this go?" asks Tom, waving at a heavy dark wood door on the outside wall, a door that should, by rights, lead nowhere.

"Don't open that! It's not time to open that—we'd better get back," snaps Watson, turning abruptly. Her footsteps blend into street noises that are only now growing audible. Tom looks briefly about the ward, allows his gaze to linger upon the door, then runs to follow his resident.

At breakfast, their table is invaded by the surgery housestaff. They are in street clothes, and even the ones who have been up all night wear ties and neatly pressed short white coats. It is barely seven, but they have already completed an hour of rounding, and soon will be in the operating room. Tom stares in disbelief at their trays, piled high with pancakes, sausage, bacon, pints of chocolate milk, and large Styrofoam cups of coffee. Surgeons are very serious about breakfast. They usually don't get a second meal.

The surgeons glance in Watson's general direction. "Hey," says the tallest one. He must be their chief resident; his white coat is knee-length. Also, years of work and abuse and sleep deprivation have worn away what little tact or courtesy he might ever have possessed. "Hey, you neuro?"

"Uh-huh."

"You got that gunshot?"

Watson takes a long sip of coffee before replying. "John Doe number three." It has been a busy night for the unidentified.

Tom has been told that the gentleman in question is *his* patient, so he volunteers further information. "Thirty-eight caliber. The entrance is right occipital, and the exit left fronto-parietal." Saying this makes him feel very professional.

"Condition?" asks the surgeon, looking at Watson instead. She does not appreciate his snubbing her medical student, and knows also that if her own chief were here, he would be ignoring her as well. He has an arrogant manner that makes her uncertain if she feels furious or worthless.

"Bullet turned the brain to Jell-O. He's herniated."

"Brain-dead?"

"Not yet. But soon."

"Suicide?"

"No. Met the Dude Brothers."

Tom asks, "Huh?"

She looks away from the surgery chief to explain, a carefully calculated breach of etiquette. "You ask someone in the E.R. who beat them up, it's always 'some dudes.' No one will ever tell you who did it, or admit that it was only one guy."

"The Dude Brothers," Tom repeats, pleased, as if every new bit of slang makes him that much closer to being a doctor.

"Homicide," the surgeon is saying. "That's a little tougher, but the coroner's usually cooperative. He a druggie?"

She shakes her head. There is a drug war going on, and the wound pattern is that favored in street executions. But, like the previous victims in the current conflict, her patient appears to have been an enforcer, not an addict. "No tracks. He's a great specimen."

The surgeon smiles. Finally. She knows exactly what he is thinking. *One heart. One liver. Two kidneys.*

"And a partridge in a pear tree," she adds aloud, confirming the surgeons' opinion that you gotta be crazy to go into neurology. "Just one problem. He's a John Doe. No organ donor card. No family. And even if we found them . . ."

The surgeon gives her that look, like he's Bonaparte, Caesar, Patton, and she's some worthless foot soldier assigned to hold the ridge.

"Let me worry about that. You just keep him going 'til we get permission to harvest the organs."

They straggle in to morning rounds, clutching Styrofoam lifelines. Breakfast and caffeine have worked paradoxically; the now off-call team is starting to crash. Watson is shivering as she tells the group (her fellow junior resident, the chief resident, two internal medicine interns, two nameless third-year medical students) about the new admissions. Tom is leaning against the wall, yawning, occasionally pinching himself, and in no way following the rules of medical decorum that he so carefully memorized a few days ago. For a second he actually drifts off to sleep, and sees the ghost of Osler coming through the ICU door, shouting "You will never be a doctor!" But then one of his classmates takes pity on him, and nudges him awake.

The residents are looking at him with bemused expressions. The years have almost numbed them to the pain of sleep deprivation, though they vaguely remember a time when they were still aware of their suffering. But the memories are dreamlike and uncertain, like a view into a prior incarnation.

"You get used to it," Watson says encouragingly.

The other resident grins at his students, who have not yet experienced an on-call night, and asks Tom, "So how's it feel, now that you're not a virgin anymore?"

"Rounds," the chief reminds them.

They move to the bedside of the gunshot victim, and Tom begins a formal and totally disorganized presentation. The chief cuts him short after less than a minute. "Save it for the attending," he suggests. "Make it quick and dirty for work rounds."

Tom looks at Watson, who nods. He says, "John Doe number three. Met the Dude Brothers." The other medical students look puzzled, and their resident whispers, "Later."

They retire to the view box, where the chief resident makes funny humming noises while reviewing the CAT scan, briefly pimps the students (who cannot yet tell a bullet fragment from a calcified pineal gland), and then they return to the man on the bed. A fly has landed on the patient's half-open right eye.

"Shit," says Watson. "I told the nurse to lacrilube them shut." She has respect for corneas, even though John Doe number three will never need his again.

The chief demonstrates the way that the lids no longer spring closed, then shines a light in each eye. The pupils do not react.

"Midposition, fixed," he says. "What's that mean?"

The students stare blankly.

"What's with you guys? Don't you know any neuro?"

The other resident whispers to the chief. The medical student year is not quite in sync with the housestaff's; their students last week had been at the end of third year, almost seniors—knowledgeable, canny, battle hardened. Now they have raw recruits again.

"Okay," the chief says. "I'll show you how to examine a comatose patient. First thing, you see if he can breathe on his own." So he disconnects the tube that connects the ventilator to John Doe's endotracheal tube, and they watch to see if any breaths occur. The respirator alarm begins to blare. Unfortunately, as it is an old machine, the alarm can't be switched off. Watson puts fingers in her ears to block out the raucous noise.

"Tell me if he starts," the chief directs, and runs through the rest of the exam, squeezing fingers and toes to cause pain, sticking Q-Tips in the eyes, tongue blades down the throat, ice water in the ears. The patient makes no response to any of these noxious stimuli, and after three breathless minutes, Watson reattaches the respirator. The alarm stops.

"Papilledema. Take a look," directs the chief, handing his ophthalmoscope to a student. She bends in close to an eye, trying to focus through the pupil to the retina behind, like trying to look through one keyhole into another keyhole. It is a technique that requires skill the student does not yet possess, and is made even more difficult by corneas clouded by exposure and neglect.

Watson notices that the medical student is holding her breath, and grins sympathetically. No one ever says anything about it, but the brain-dead smell different. Not a particularly unpleasant odor, like gangrene or enteric bacteria, but a faint, cold, wet, indefinable smell that Watson associates with patients with liquefied cortex.

"Okay, enough, you can come back later," the chief says, changing his mind. Each student attempting fundoscopy will run through what little rounding time is left. "Three minutes without any respiratory effort? Okay, so he's brain-dead. What now?"

"Surgery wants him."

The other resident snickers. "Hey buddy, they want your body." The interns laugh, and the students look at them distastefully, except for Tom. He's starting to grasp the housestaff's grim humor.

"Fine with me," says the chief. "Get an EEG to confirm it, and they can have him whenever they want."

Watson points to the name on the wristband. *John Doe.*

"Oh. That's a problem." He looks around the unit. There is still one empty bed. "He can stay while they work that out. But if we need the bed. . . ."

An intern—he trained at one of those small Caribbean schools, looks a little like Dennis the Menace grown up, and is always a bit slow on the uptake—says, "Hey, wait a minute. Organ donation? Don't we need permission from next-of-kin?"

Watson lets her mouth drop open. "Holy shit, you're right! Quick, Fred, go call the Doe family and ask them!"

The intern is halfway to the phone before he realizes that he's been had.

They are barely finishing rounding on the ward when the other resident is beeped to the E.R. He calls down, then gathers up his students and starts out. "Gunshot," he calls to Watson and the chief. He jabs his female student right about the midthoracic spine.

"The Dude Brothers have been busy little boys today," says the chief. "Take a 'tern; the studs should stay for attending rounds." The students look disappointed, worried they'll miss something exciting.

The team files into the conference room, a grimy place with mismatched chairs, windows nailed shut to prevent patient suicides, and a single window air conditioner that barely works. A few textbooks—the most recent at least ten years out of date—and dozens of X-ray folders litter the counters, near a primitive monocular microscope, bottles of outdated stain reagents, and a hemocytometer box labeled STEAL THIS AND DIE! The box is empty.

On the wall is an X-ray view box that looks old enough that, in a rare whimsical mood brought on by acute and chronic exhaustion, Watson tries to visualize when it was new, hanging in a room where the wood paneling and marble are as yet unplastered. She imagines a conference of doctors, in high collars and starched white coats. On the view box, a visiting Dr. Dandy is showing off his first pneumoencephalogram.

She returns to the present and her own conference. A professor has come down from the University to hear the new cases and offer advice. Unfortunately, their current attending is junior faculty, newly arrived from one of the more civilized programs. If they presented to him complex, obscure, and abstruse cases, perhaps something caused by an enzyme deficiency isolated only last week, or a rare cranial nerve syndrome first described in 1925, he might be informative and invaluable. Instead, they confront him daily with the same and the mundane: alcohol withdrawal seizures, delirium tremens, head trauma, alcohol withdrawal seizures. Tom presents his case and shows him John Doe's brain scan, and after the professor has pimped the students on which is bullet and which is calcified pineal, he has little else to add.

Later, back in the ICU, Watson sees the surgical chief resident going through John Doe's chart. She strides over quickly. As she passes bed four, the patient with the bandage starts up again.

"Waitress, I want . . ."

"It's not her table," snaps Tom.

Watson says, in her most unctuous voice, "May I help you?"

The alien chief wants blood and histocompatibility typing, cultures, more frequent vital signs, stat syphilis and AIDS serologies. He wants the intravenous fluids changed to the surgeons' favorite, lactated Ringers. He wants everything to be thoroughly buffed when he triumphantly delivers the still-beating heart, the gleaming red liver, the happily perfusing kidneys, and the extraneous shell of body that surrounds them, to the transplant team up at the University Hospital.

The neurology chief steps in. "Look, I know this is important to you, and we'll help all we can. But there isn't any family to give permission yet, and the man's brain-dead." He decides to elaborate. General surgery residents are notorious for their incomprehension of neurologic principles.

"Everything upstairs is gone, including the autonomic centers in the medulla. His heart and blood pressure and kidneys are on autopilot now, and pretty soon they'll just get out of control, like an untuned engine that idles faster and faster and then goes haywire. You can keep a brain-stem preparation going for months, but this guy's brain-dead; he won't last three days, and that's if we work hard."

"Then work hard. Or is that too much for you guys?"

Watson's chief gives him his *if you had one more neuron you'd have a synapse* smile, and answers sweetly, "We'll keep him as long as we can, or until we need a unit bed. And we're full now."

"You've got one empty!" protests the surgeon.

At that minute the ICU doors swing open and the other resident and Fred the intern roll in a new patient.

"Besides," says the chief, "even if you find the family, I'll bet a beer you don't get the parts. I've been here a long time and I've never . . ."

The surgeon nods, stalking out. "A beer." No one ever pays off on these bets.

The chief notices Tom standing there, mouth agape, and decides to finish his sentence. ". . . I've never had anyone donate organs. Face it, the families of people who live and die by violence don't tend to be altruistic."

Tom frowns, trying to absorb and properly file away that bit of information.

As the new patient is being lifted off the gurney, he gazes across at John Doe and laughs. "Hey! Johnny! Hey, they got you too? Serves you right, you son of a bitch."

At noon, bored policemen descend upon the unit. They question the new patient, who won't tell them anything—his occupation, his assailants' identities, John Doe's real name. The police don't seem to care much. "It's not like they're shooting innocent kids or housewives or something," one of them remarks to the chief. Life might even improve if every drug dealer in the city shot every other.

Tom hovers about the periphery, wearing an expression of intense fascination that he tries unsuccessfully to hide. He has not been this close to an actual policeman since Mister Traffic Safety reminded his first-grade class to look both ways before crossing.

"What about our John Doe?" asks Watson.

"Is he gonna die?" the cop replies.

"He *is* dead. Technically brain-dead. I could turn off the ventilator now, only surgery's dying to use his parts for transplant. For that, we need family permission."

"We're running his prints."

"He's bound to have priors," the other policeman says.

Watson nods. "We'll keep him alive until you give us a name. Right, Tom?"

Pleased to be included, the student nods. "Right."

The new admission has a bullet lodged in his vertebral canal at T-10. In a way, he's lucky. If the bullet had not stopped there, it would have continued on through lung, diaphragm, and liver, leaving an awful mess. However, the man is now permanently paralyzed below the umbilicus, never again to feel his legs, walk, fornicate, or control his bowels and bladder. He does not have a great appreciation for his good luck, or for the medical care that he is receiving, and everyone is secretly pleased when the consulting neurosurgeon decides that the wound needs to be debrided operatively. General anesthesia will give everyone a temporary break from his complaints.

Before leaving for the day, Tom and Watson look in on John Doe #3 one last time. He lies quietly, no movements except the periodic rise and fall of his chest as the respirator cycles. His body temperature is starting to climb and, though Watson expects this is just due to hypothalamic dysfunction, she orders chest X ray, blood and urine cultures, puts him on a cooling blanket and Tylenol suppositories, and covers potential infection with a broad-spectrum antibiotic.

"Say good night, John Doe," she says as she exits.

"Good night, John Doe," replies Tom, in a high-pitched voice.

The next morning they find out their patient's real name; it is not as memorable as John Doe, so they continue to refer to him as such. No one is surprised to find that he has more arrests than their attending has publications. He even has an outstanding warrant for murder, so the police put a shackle around the irreversibly comatose man's ankle to chain him to the bedframe, and assign three shifts of deputies to sit at the foot of the bed and make sure he does not escape.

"Great use of our tax dollars, huh?" asks Watson. She hauls Doe's knee into the air and tries for a reflex, knowing well that he has none, but enjoying the way the shackles clink as she does it.

The deputy is ready for retirement, and looks about as dangerous as any fat, elderly, napping man, but the presence of a uniform and a gun gives the chief resident some comfort. Their paraplegic patient is contemplating singing to the police, giving them details of the drug war, its strategies, finances, and generals. The chief is convinced that any moment now, Uzi-wielding dope dealers will enter the ICU and spray it with bullets, taking out their erstwhile colleague and any unlucky witnesses. Whenever the doors swing open, the chief flinches and starts to duck, and finally he decides that it's time to visit the lab where he'll be working next month.

His paranoia infects the rest of the team. The other resident and an intern remember that they really ought to be in outpatient clinic; the students decamp to the library; Fred actually volunteers to scrub with a bad-tempered neurosurgeon on a routine back surgery.

Watson manages to reach John Doe's mother, in another state. The woman has the usual reaction to bad news. "How could this happen?" Watson avoids the response on the tip of her tongue—"Because he's a murderer, and this time someone got him first"—and tries to be kind and supportive. She explains how they've done everything medically possible, but the damage from the bullet is just too great. She expresses condolences, and finally broaches the subject of organ donation.

"It's so unfortunate," she says. A life cut short at only twenty-eight. Family and children—none of them legitimate—bereaved. But there's an opportunity for some good to come from this tragedy. His kidneys, liver, and heart can give life and hope to some other women's sons, some other children's fathers.

"Are you crazy?" replies John Doe's mother. "That stuff's his. We're not giving nothing away."

"Fine," says Watson. She has given up arguing with selfishness—all it's ever accomplished is to increase her aggravation. Senseless tragedy is senseless tragedy, and it won't be redeemed.

Tom is checking John Doe's pressure. "It's going down."

"No shit," replies Watson, nudging the Foley collection bag with her foot. It is topping off with dilute urine. "When was this changed?"

"Half an hour ago. I think."

"He's pissing out pure water. So, what's that mean?"

The student looks at her blankly.

"Diabetes insipidus," she explains. "Posterior pituitary's gone."

He looks at her with surprise. Despite all the lectures and exam questions on renal physiology and sodium homeostasis, he has not until this moment realized that the facts he learned might apply to actual patients. "What do we do?"

She considers. If she follows the logical path, now that the next-of-kin has refused organ donation, and simply turns off the ventilator, she will have to notify the family, declare the patient legally dead, and go through all the other bureaucratic nonsense that such a case entails. There just isn't time for this; she has patients waiting in the emergency room.

"Vasopressin, and chase the fluids," she says, pointing at the as yet uncreased *Manual of Medical Therapeutics* in Tom's right coat pocket. "Read about D. I. Hey, what a learning experience!"

Hearing her voice, the bandaged patient across the aisle wakes. "Waitress, I want a tuna fish sandwich."

It is almost five before she finishes in the emergency room, having seen a succession of head injuries, hysterics, seizures (alcohol withdrawal, and patients with epilepsy who neglected to take their pills), and finally a brain hemorrhage stroke (a hypertensive who did not take his pills).

She calls the unit. Fred the intern comes on the line. "Got a big bleed, needs a bed in the unit. I'll be right up, and disconnect John Doe."

"Too late," replies Fred. "He crashed and Tom couldn't handle it. I just declared him."

"Great." That will save her some time. Then she hears yelling in the background. "What's up?"

"That surgeon. He came in just when Doe transferred to the Eternal Care Unit, and he's pitching a fit."

"Doesn't he know the family refused?"

A phrase comes through, barely comprehensible. "You killed him! Now you've killed four other people too!"

"Shit," Watson cries. "Get him off of Tom. I'll be right there." She drops the receiver back onto the hook, tells a nurse "Hold him here in the E.R. till we clear the bed," and strides the yellow line in the basement to the stairway. Bounding up the stairs, she almost collides with the surgery chief.

"Where the hell do you get the right to yell at my student?"

"You stupid shits let him die!"

"He was *already* dead, goddamn it."

She pushes past him, not hearing his reply in its entirety. It just doesn't pay to fight with people who are taller and more powerful. Heading into the unit, she sees the nurse and her aide already fussing over the body. The room is quieter now that the respirator has stopped its cycling. The deputy is awake, and talking softly into the telephone.

"Tom? Hey, Fred, where's Tom?"

The intern is writing the death note. Not looking up, he points out the doors.

"Where'd he go?"

The nurse smiles as she replies. She hates her dead-end, thankless, underpaid job in this awful excuse for a hospital. The distress of young doctors in training is one of the few things in her life that gives her any pleasure. "That doctor kept calling him a murderer, and he looked like he was going to cry, and he left."

"Oh, God," Watson whispers. She knows where he has gone. She knows she has to stop him.

There is a place of which all doctors know, though none are told. It may be reached by many paths. Watson runs to the stairwell in the basement, and then up to the old ward. She can see fresh footprints in the dust, leading to the door that should not be there. It opens with a wrench, and she takes the dark and twisted stairs cautiously. Reaching the bottom, she finds herself in the basement again, unlit save by small, high windows half-blocked by debris. The air is still and musty, and the only sounds are her breathing, and the rustle of something that she hopes is a mouse.

"Tom?" she calls, then heads off down the corridor. Further down it is lined with cabinets filled with pathology slides. They spill out of the drawers and a few lie upon the floor. Stopping as the basement becomes a tunnel, she leans briefly against a cabinet. A slide falls to the ground, shattering. Watson bends over, glancing at the remnants.

A slice of cervical spinal cord lies embedded for eternity between glass and coverslip. The stain has faded over the years, but the dorsal and lateral columns are clearly paler. This is the autopsy relic of some man or woman born years before Watson, or even Watson's parents; born to die of a disease that now Watson can recognize with an offhand glance, and could treat easily with B-12 injections. Is life fair? she muses. Not hardly.

She stands and sprints down the tunnel. A veritable catacomb lies beneath the hospital. There are tunnels between buildings; dank tunnels to the mental hospital a block away (said to be more safe than crossing the street in the middle of the night, but nonetheless to be avoided); unknown tunnels to unknown places. Every few years a drunk will wander out of the emergency room and get lost in the tunnels, to be found weeks later by horrified engineers. And then there is this tunnel, which intersects none of the others.

A single window is set into the wall. Watson pauses, wipes clear a circle on the glass, and finds herself looking into the hospital's pathology suite from an unexpected view. She is down low, near the antique autopsy table with its grooves and pails. Across from her is the door into the morgue, and to the left she can see the steep, hard rows of the amphitheater.

She runs on. It is close now. If she stops, holds her breath, concentrates, she might hear a variety of sounds. Sobs. Moans. Agonal respirations. The lamentations of the living and the final exhalations of the dying. The screams of the delirious and the shrieks of the unanesthetized.

Ahead is a halo of light, coming around the edges of a door in the wall at the end of the tunnel. It is a wooden door, dark, ponderous, smooth and pale about the handle, and the brass embossed sign, in square letters with serifs, bears the name. THE JULY WARD.

Tom has his hand upon the knob, and is preparing to enter. "No!" shouts Watson, managing to reach him and slam shut the door, while spinning him away from it. "No, it's not your time yet. . . ."

He looks at her with reddened eyes. Where does the light come from, now that the door is closed? She only knows that she can see the tears, welling in the inner canthi of his eyes.

"It's not your time yet," she repeats. "You're not a doctor, you can't go in there. Or you'll never come out."

"But I killed him . . . the surgery chief said . . ."

"The surgery chief is an asshole. You didn't kill John Doe. He was already dead!"

She leads him back down the hall. "You can't go in there yet. Not yet.

"In two years, on July first, you'll become an intern. Someday you'll have a patient. You won't know what's wrong—you're young, inexperienced, you can't know everything, and ultimately no one else can help you. It's inevitable. Someday—maybe it'll be in July, maybe it won't—someday, someone will die because you don't know something, or you made a wrong decision. And you're a doctor. Then, you can come here. You may be in another hospital entirely, but you'll come here, and you'll find your patient. . . ."

He looks back. The door seems indistinct now. "Did you . . ."

"Do you know how many pages there are in *Harrison's Textbook of Internal Medicine?*" she asks. "At least 1,200, big pages, with little print. You know how much mention rhabdomyolysis gets in *Harrison's?* One line. One line about a fairly frequent, potentially fatal condition. I've read a sixty-page paper on it. But that was a little late."

They find themselves, strangely, in the basement of the hospital near the yellow line, which they follow towards the ICU. A gurney passes by, pushed by an orderly. Something large and wrapped in plastic lies on the gurney, its identity undisguised by a sheet.

Watson and Tom stand to the side, letting the gurney pass. She waves. "Good-bye, John Doe number three."

"Now what?"

She shrugs. "Now you go home and get a good night's sleep. We're on call again tomorrow." She stops a moment, frowning. "I imagine it'll be a tough day, too. The chief won't stay around much, now that we've lost our deputy."

Tomorrow is indeed a bad day. They miss lunch, they miss dinner. The Dude Brothers have been busy. The unit is full of head trauma cases, with more on the ward, making do with less careful observation. The paraplegic patient, still in the unit because of a mysterious fever, has gone beyond anger and is depressed now, speaking to no one. To either side of him, semiconscious men moan and occasionally retch. As Watson passes the bandaged man in bed four, he sits bolt upright, stares at her, and shouts, "I want a tuna fish sandwich!"

"Stand in line," she replies.

Tom has been futilely sticking a syringe over and over into one of the new admissions, trying to start an intravenous line. Watson comes over to watch him.

"You're getting the hang of it," she remarks. "Only you'll never get this one."

He shakes his head. "These are great veins. They're standing right up, you can see them . . . it must be my technique."

"Your technique's fine, the fault's his. He's a junkie. Those veins are thrombosed." She takes away the arm, and hunts. There's some-thing on the right thumb that she may be able to thread with a twenty-two-gauge butterfly needle. It's that, or a central line.

"Make you a deal," she says. "You go for burgers, and I'll get the IV."

"Fries and a shake?"

"Diet cola."

He laughs, hunts his many pockets for car keys, and leaves. She sits down and reapplies the tourniquet, slapping the man's forearm to bring up the veins. They're all shot, literally. Maybe she should go on TV, as a public service announcement. Don't shoot dope, kids. You'll ruin your veins. Then, when the doctors need to put in an IV, they'll have to stick a big old needle right into the major veins in your chest, with the chance of bleeding, or infection, or a collapsed lung.

"Aha." She decides she can get that sucker on the thumb after all, maybe even with a twenty-gauge. Having survived an internship, Watson has the hubris to believe that she could draw blood from a turnip. She tears off strips of tape, opens the betadine ointment, has everything ready, then wipes alcohol on the vein and stops.

"Damn." She'll need an armboard. "Hey," she calls. No one answers. The night nurse must be busy, or asleep somewhere. She drops the arm back on the bed, tourniquet still on. Were he conscious, the man would be writhing in pain. She goes into the stockroom in front, hunting angrily. Don't they have anything? And if so, why isn't it where it should be?

She hears the doors to the unit open.

"Good," she mutters. It's past visiting hours, so it can only be the nurse returning. She'll know where the armboards are. Unless, of course, it's Tom, coming back to see if she prefers Burger King or McDonald's. She heads out of the supply room, and freezes.

"What do you guys want?" says the voice of the paraplegic drug dealer.

"We don't want you to talk," a voice replies.

"Oh, shit," Watson starts to say, and shrinks back into the door-way. *Oh, shit.* The chief resident's paranoia was on target.

She can hear the sound of a gun, of silenced bullets going into soft flesh and the mattress behind. *Thock thock thock.* Just like on TV. She holds her breath, afraid to breathe. They'll be looking around the unit now, anyone else they need to waste? They are going from bed to bed, now they are at the back end of the unit. Two of them. Pistols, not Uzis. The chief resident was wrong. If they'll just go in to check the nursing lounge, maybe she can duck out.

She is almost to the front door when the patient in bed four sees her. "Waitress!"

The men with guns bolt out of the lounge, and she abandons silence and begins to run. A bullet passes by her head. Pistols must be hard to aim. No wonder the bullets always seem to wind up in unexpected places in her patients.

Ducking into the stairwell, she wishes she'd stayed in better shape. She can work thirty-six hours straight, but running is beyond her. Already, as she heads down the basement, hearing the stairwell door slam and then open again behind her, already she is winded.

Where to go? The pharmacy? Locked. The emergency room? They do have a guard there. But by the time he figures out what's going on, figures out how to draw his gun, the place will be an abbatoir. Where to go?

She knows.

She cuts off into a tunnel. Why did they have to build the morgue so far away, so cut off even from the original hospital? Was it to contain germs? Or as some kind of symbolic gesture?

"Stop, motherfucker!" a man's voice yells at her. The shot that follows makes compliance unlikely. Goddamn, which way? She's only been to one autopsy here. Go ahead, they tell the docs. Keep Dad or Grampa or little Joey alive long after he should be allowed to die. So we keep his heart going and his lungs working and keep him in agony because his body can't survive, but they won't let us let him go. And when he finally dies, days or weeks or months after he should have—You want an autopsy? What, are you crazy? Hasn't he suffered enough?

The morgue. This is the way. She tries the door, then hits it angrily with her palm. Locked. Okay. Up the tunnel. It's slanting uphill. If you lost your grip on a gurney carrying a corpse, it would careen downhill until it ran into a wall, or came to rest near the outpatient pharmacy, where the clinic patients wait to have their prescriptions filled. Wouldn't that be a cheerful sight?

The door to the amphitheater is unlocked. It's dark inside, except for a light someone's left on down in front, by the display cases. Did doctors ever trip on these precipitous stairs, interrupting some learned professor's discourse as they toppled to their deaths? She has to take them slowly, watched by the ancient dissections below. Here are skeletons and bottled fetuses and hands, palms flayed open to show their inner workings, reaching out as on the Sistine Chapel. Here is the preserved torso of a young man who lived and died before motorcars or radio, and when he was struck down by a horsedrawn trolley, astonished doctors found that his organs were all on the wrong side. Here is the face of an infant with a single eye, and a trunklike nose above it. Here are legs poised forever to step, hearts waiting to beat. Here are the heads of unsuspecting paupers who have been made into demonstrations of normal anatomy, and wear expressions that seem vaguely surprised.

She gets to the door with the window, alongside the guttered table with its century of knife marks. The door is barely noticeable, dark wood faded into dark wood. She grabs the handle and twists. It is not locked. Who would want to try it? But it is stuck, and she takes it with both hands and braces her foot and pulls. The men are coming in the door now, about to take aim but momentarily shocked by the grisly displays.

"Sheeeit," a man says. The other whistles.

Watson snatches up the nearest object, a breadloafed slice of brain embeddened in a block of glass. It is very old; the definition between gray and white matter has faded, and the sloshing liquid inside has a froth at the top, yellow cholesterol leached out over the years. She throws the specimen, then another, and finally the entire cerebellum for good measure. None come close, but the sounds of smashing and the smell of ancient fixative give her a feeling of accomplishment.

The nearest thug raises his pistol. Watson falls back against the door—and it opens outward.

"I'll be damned," she says, and begins to run down the hall, past the rows of cabinets, too heavy to topple. Behind her, she can hear curses, as her foes try to get down the steep steps, now slick with lipid-rich alcohol and bits of brain.

They aren't even trying to shoot anymore, just running after her, closing the lead. She doesn't want to think about what's going to happen when they catch her. And then she sees it. The dark door and the brass sign.

She pulls it open, and she is inside. Inside the July Ward.

It is an old-fashioned ward, beds down either side, but some are barely pallets, others old-fashioned hospital beds, still others are high-tech automatic beds, one even with a ventilator at its side. Patients stare at her from each bed, recognize that she is not the one for whom they wait, and look away. Ghostly orderlies—she cannot make out their details—approach, recognize her as a doctor, and step aside deferentially.

She stops running, smooths her white coat and straightens her scrubsuit, then goes down the row of beds, walking purposefully but sedately, the way a doctor should, glancing at the nametags and the bedside vitals charts. Many of the patients in the newer beds are in their nineties, and all patients in their nineties look alike.

Behind her, she can hear her enemies enter, hears a gunshot that seems to hit the ceiling, hears polite but firm voices (whispery, unreal).

"You cannot be here."

"Leggo, man. Shit, what *is* this?"

"This is the July Ward," comes the answer. "In this ward we admit only special patients: the first patient that a doctor lets die too soon; that a doctor kills. You cannot be here."

Watson has found the bed she is looking for. There is an old woman on it, frail and edematous, fluids running into an arm marked with bruises and swelling from ancient veins that cannot long support a line. The bag at the end of her catheter shows scant urine, with the faint pink tinge that Watson now knows might mean rhabdomyolysis, muscle breakdown products that, left untreated—or even despite treatment—may kill the kidneys. And the patient.

The woman in the bed looks up. "Yes, dear?" she asks. You can hear the fluid in her lungs as she speaks.

"I came to . . . say I'm sorry."

"You've already apologized," the woman replies, very kindly. "You'll have to stop coming here. It just isn't healthy." Watson turns away, and the old woman calls after her, softening the hard advice. "But thank you for visiting, dear. It was very kind."

Behind her, she can hear the woman address the patient in the next bed. "My doctor. Such a nice girl."

Watson strides back between the rows of patients, past the two gunmen, subdued now by orderlies. She sees the men, faces blanched with fear, unable to speak as they twist in the grip of arms that will not come into focus. Their eyes are wide with terror and pleading, and she finds it hard to not stop and order their release. But she does have some common sense.

"You keep this ward very well," Watson says. The orderlies nod. It is always good for a doctor to compliment the staff on a job well done. "I won't be back."

She closes the door behind her. What will become of the gunmen? She has no idea. But she knows this: only two kinds of people may enter the July Ward—doctors, and the dead. And only the doctors may leave.

But not completely. Never completely.

There is a place of which all doctors know, but none will speak.

Lennon Spex

PAUL DI FILIPPO

Paul Di Filippo is no stranger to this series. Readers of *Nebula Awards 24* were treated to an original essay, "My Alphabet Starts Where Your Alphabet Ends," a tongue-in-cheek but oddly persuasive indictment of the SF field for not heaping Hugos, Nebulas, Gandalfs, a Grand Master Award, and other honors upon Theodor Geisel, a.k.a. Dr. Seuss. (The title alludes to Seuss's *On Beyond Zebra*.) Then, exploiting that delightful literary form pioneered by Jorge Luis Borges and Stanislaw Lem, Di Filippo graced *Nebula Awards 25* with a review of a nonexistent book—*Mega-Awesome SF: The True Story Behind "Forever Plus!"*, an account of how a computer-written tale, appearing in various lengths throughout a single year, swept the Nebula Awards in all four categories.

Di Filippo's fiction has been published in *Fantasy and Science Fiction, New Pathways, Amazing Stories, Twilight Zone, Night Cry, Synergy,* and *Mirrorshades: The Cyberpunk Anthology.* His short story "Kid Charlemagne" was a Nebula finalist for 1987.

Invited to comment on "Lennon Spex," Di Filippo replied:

"One day, legend has it, John said to Paul, 'I've got a bloody song here I can't finish.'

" 'Me too, mate,' replied Paul.

"One of them flashed first, and the other intuited and flashed back.

" 'Well, why don't we try—'

" '—putting them together!'

"And thus was born 'A Day in the Life,' one of the Beatles' most memorable songs.

"Since I first heard this story, this technique has proven invaluable to me more than once, and was indeed the furnace in which 'Lennon Spex' was forged. For years I had had two separate story ideas: the visualization of emotional 'tendrils' and the notion of a magic pair of glasses once worn by John Lennon. How the tendrils would be made manifest, or what the spectacles would show, were both a mystery to me. Until one day the two seemingly unconnected ideas fused.

"I think the magnificent Reese's Peanut Butter Cups were also invented this way, so there's really no disputing the power of this trick.

"Aside from matters of technique, I'd like to use this forum to reiterate the debt I—we—all owe to John Lennon, for his life and his art. If the eighties were a nasty decade, it was at least partly attributable to their starting with Lennon's assassination. One less bodhisattva in this sorrow-drenched world. As for the recent spate of publicity given to Mark David Chapman—can you tell me now, fifty years afterwards, the name of Gandhi's killer?

"See you later, John. Somewhere across the universe, man."

I am walking down lower Broadway, not far from Canal Jeans, when I see the weirdest peddler dude.

Now, when you consider that the wide sidewalk is jammed with enterprising urban riffraff—Africans with their carved monkeywood animals; Farrakhanized Black Muslims with their oils and incense; young white punks with their hand-screened semi-obscene T-shirts; sleazy old white guys with their weasel-skin Gucci bags and smeary Hermès scarves; Vietnamese with their earrings and panty hose and pirated tapes—and when you also realize that I, Zildjian, am totally inured to this spectacle through long habituation, then you realize that this guy must be incredibly weird.

Except he isn't. Weird, that is. Not bizarre. I guess it's more that he's incongruous, like.

He appears to be a Zen monk. Japanese or Chinese, Korean or Vietnamese, it's hard to figure. His head is shaven, he wears a golden robe and straw sandals, and he looks more serene than a Park Avenue matron after her first Valium of the day. His age could be anywhere from a year short of a legal drink to a year beyond early retirement.

The monk is apparently selling secondhand prescription eyeglasses. He has a TV tray with a meager selection neatly arrayed thereon. I see no handy-dandy lens-grinding equipment, so I assume there is no customizing. This gives new meaning to the term "cut-rate rip-off."

I stop in front of the monk. He bows. I am forced to bow back. Uncomfortable, I fall to examining his stock.

Tucked away behind the assorted cat's-eye, filigreed, tortoise-shell old-lady spex lies one special pair of glasses, their stems neatly folded like ballerina legs, as incongruous among their companions as the monk among his.

I pick these glasses up and examine them.

They are a pair of simple gold wire-rims with transparent, perfectly circular lenses. The stems extend from the middle of the outer circumference on each lens; the bridge is higher, about two-thirds of the way up along the inside. The spectacles have no adornments.

Suddenly, I realize that these are what we would have called, more years ago than I care to ponder, "Lennon glasses." First popularized by Beatle John in the *Sgt. Pepper* album photos, later shown shattered on a posthumous jacket, they remain forever associated with his image, though he was to switch in later years to various aviator-style frames, undoubtedly seeking to harmonize his face with Yoko's in marital solidarity.

I do not suffer from either near- or farsightedness; I have no intention of buying the frames and replacing the lenses with polarized ones, since I believe in the utility of unmediated sunlight. Yet something compels me to ask if I can try them on.

"Can I, uh, try these on?" I ask the monk.

He smiles. (A smile from one of his disciples was how the Buddha knew his message was getting through.) "You bet."

I unfold the stems. I notice a blot of what appears to be fresh blood on one stem. Maybe it's ketchup from some strolling patron's chili dog. Never squeamish, I lick my thumb and attempt to wipe it off. The blot temporarily disappears under my rubbing, then rematerializes.

The monk has noticed my actions. "Not to worry," he says. "Just a small stain from the shooting. Will most definitely not affect utility of the glasses. Please, try."

So I slip them on.

The rowboat is painted in psychedelic Day-Glo swirls of color; the wide rippled water that cradles it is purple. I am sitting on the middle bench, drifting downstream without oars.

On either shore, tangerine trees are interspersed with cellophane flowers of yellow and green that grow so incredibly high. The sky—you guessed it—is marmalade. With actual flecks of orange peel and English-muffin clouds. A complete nutritious breakfast.

"Holy Salvador Dali," I whimper. I dip my hands into the purple water, stirring a scent of grape juice, and frantically try to divert the boat to shore.

"Zildjian," calls someone above me.

I answer quite slowly: "Yuh . . . yeah?"

"Stop paddling and look up."

The floating girl has kaleidoscope eyes and wears a lot of shiny gems, but not much else.

"You're being given a gift, Zildjian. There's no need to panic."

"Oh, man, I'm not sure—"

The boat is rocking. No, it's not. I'm sitting astride a centaur. Only instead of hooves, he's got bentwood rockers. He's propelling himself across a field, while eating a Scooter pie.

Lucy is beside me on another rocking-horse person. "Calm down, Zildjian. We don't invite many people here. You're the first in years and years. Trust me."

"What happened to the last guy who trusted you?"

Lucy pouts. "That was humanity's fault, not ours."

She opens the door of a taxi for me. It's made of old issues of the *Washington Post* and the *New York Times* with headlines about Vietnam. When I climb inside, my head goes through the newspaper roof and into the clouds. Lucy's too. As we cut through the moist vapor like wheeled giraffes, I find myself mesmerized by the sun reflected in Lucy's eyes.

She's leading me into the train station. "Just try them for a while. What have you got to lose? Here, see how good they look on you."

She summons over a porter made of modeling clay who resembles Gumby. His tie is formed of mirror shards pressed into his chest. I study my reflection in the looking-glass tie. The glasses don't look half bad. . . .

The turnstile bumps my crotch and squeaks, "Sorry!"

"Have fun," says Lucy, and pushes me through.

I am clutching a streetlight on Broadway. I recognize it because it is the one that still bears a tattered remnant of a poster protesting the most recent war, on which someone has scrawled a particularly clever slogan: "Real eyes realize real lies."

Looking up, I anticipate the worst.

But no. The world—seen through what surely must be nonprescription lenses—is normal.

Except for the people.

Every last person is crowned, like Medusa, with a nest of tendrils.

From the skull of each person exit innumerable organic-looking extrusions that terminate about eighteen inches away from their heads.

The tendrils are all colors, thicknesses, and textures. Their ends are sheared off flat, and they do not droop. It is as if they enter another dimension a foot and a half away from the individual.

The people look rather like rainbow dandelions gone to seed.

A dog stops to pee on my pole. Its head, too, is studded with worms, but not as many as the humans'.

A nasty thought occurs to me. I release my grip on the pole and slowly raise my hands to my own head.

I too am wearing a snaky turban. I can feel the velvety/rubbery/slimy/scratchy hoses rooted to my cranium.

I rip off the Lennon glasses.

Everyone's head-snakes are gone. Mine too, I can tell by touch.

With trepidation, I put the glasses back on. The snakes come back.

I sense someone by my side. It's the peddler monk.

He alone of everyone in my sight has but one tendril coming from his head. It's golden like his robe and, emerging from the exact center of his crown, rises vertically.

The monk smiles again and lifts one hand to his golden carousel-horse pole.

"Goes straight to Buddha," he says, and laughs. "Use glasses wisely. Good-bye."

He vanishes into the mass of pedestrians.

Still wearing the glasses, I wearily sit myself down on a stoop.

Man, how can all these people be oblivious of the spaghetti coming out of their heads? Why don't they feel its weight? Come to think of it, why don't I feel the weight of mine? I reach up and find the offending objects still tangible. How can something be perceptible to the touch yet weigh nothing? Or is it that we're just used to the weight . . . ?

The mutt that nearly peed on my foot comes over to keep me company. I offer my hand and it starts to lick it. As it slobbers, I watch its doggy head in horror.

A new tendril is emerging from its skull! And it is questing like a cobra toward me!

Suddenly into my field of vision from above a matching tendril of my own pokes, heading toward the canine feeler!

I jerk my hand away. The dog snarls, and its tentative tendril changes color and texture, as does mine. But now they seem less eager to meet.

Nobody ever called me Carl Sagan. But I am a fairly quick study. And you would have to be as dumb as a Georgia senator not to figure out what is going on with these worms.

These tendrils coming out of everyone's head represent emotional attachments, bonds, links of feeling and karma. All the connections we pick up in life. Strings of love and hate, just like some bad pop song.

The dog has stopped snarling and is licking itself. As an experiment I extend my hand again. The dog sniffs tentatively, then gently strops my fingers.

This time, I let our feelers connect and fuse.

I love this dog! Good dog! It's practically in my lap, giving my face a tongue-bath. It loves me too. Aw, poor street-critter. I'm really ashamed of what I'm going to do next.

I grab hold of the seamless cable connecting our heads and yank it out of the dog's skull. Better to experiment with his head than mine. There's a slight resistance, then the connection comes away with a subliminal *pop!*

The dog yelps, then apathetically climbs off me and goes to sleep.

The cable in my hand, now anchored only at my end, is squirming, trying to reattach itself to the dog. I don't let it, and within seconds it just sort of withers up and vanishes like a naked hard-on in a blizzard. I can feel a ghostly patch fading on my skull. The cable, I realize, wasn't that strong to begin with, pink and thin as a pencil, and didn't put up much of a fight to survive.

Armed with this new insight into the nature of the head-spaghetti, I watch the people around me more closely.

Everyone, I now notice, is continually extruding new feelers every few seconds. In fact, if I focus my vision through the Lennon glasses in some nameless way, I see close to people's scalps a haze of movement rather like the waving of polyps and coral in some undersea forest.

The vast majority of these embryonic attachments are transient, dying as fast as they are born. F'rinstance:

A woman pauses before the window of a clothing store. She casts a line out like a fly fisherman toward an outfit on a mannequin. Passing right through the plate glass, it connects for a moment, and then she reels it back in and strides off.

Of course. You can have serious attachments to nonliving things too.

And as if to repeat the lesson, a guy pulls his Jaguar up to a miraculously empty space, parks, and gets out. The cable connecting him and the car is as thick as your wrist. But that doesn't stop him from flicking out a feeler toward a passing Mercedes. Your cheatin' heart . . . Or head, as the case may be.

A delivery guy sends out a probe aimed at a classy babe in furs, which, needless to say, is not reciprocated.

An old woman with a walker whips out a feeler toward a young doctor-type.

A girl whom I half know, an architecture student at NYU, shoots out an extension just like one of Spiderman's webs to an elaborately carved cornice that catches her eye.

A dude and his babe stop at a corner, kiss and part. The connection between them is thick and strong. As they get further apart, beyond the combined three-foot extension of their bond, it hazes out at its midpoint, entering whatever extradimensional continuum allows individuals to remain connected to distant people and things.

I've seen enough.

It's time for me to go home and learn more.

Standing in front of my bathroom mirror, I begin to pull the cables out of my head, one at a time.

Out comes this gnarly gray vine. What resistance . . . Whoops, suddenly I don't feel anything for my folks! Mom, Dad, what are parents good for anyhow? It's spooky. There's just a big blank spot where there used to be filial fondness. I don't like this. Better plug this one back in. . . .

What's this thin slick red-white-and-blue-striped one? Yank it. Patriotism? Who'd'a thought I had one of those? Wonder what it connects to on the other end? The White House? The Lincoln Memorial? Plymouth Rock? Different for everyone, maybe . . .

Here's a little slippery green eel of a thing. Tweak it out. Holy shit, that game-show hostess! I never even knew on a conscious level that I had the hots for her! Mega-gross. Man, I'm killing this one. I hold it to one side till it crumbles away. Can't be too careful about where you put your feelings.

Like a mad, old-time switchboard operator, I spend the next couple of hours pulling cables, memorizing which ones channel what feelings. (Once I yank too many simultaneously and get kind of spacey feeling, as if adrift in the cosmos, spinning aimlessly across the universe.) I soon learn how to tell the difference between one-way connections, such as those to inanimate objects or unresponsive fellow humans (Sherry Gottlieb, a high-school crush), and two-way ones, such as those to another person who feels for you too. There's a different kind of pulse in each; a unidirectional flow in the former, an alternating current in the latter.

Since I basically like myself as I am, I plug nearly all of my attachments back in, although I do eliminate the ones for Twinkies and cigarettes.

A sudden inspiration dawns on me like sunrise on Mercury. I could get rich from these glasses! All I have to do is open an aversion-therapy center. I'll practice some mumbo jumbo, yank people's addictive connections—assuming, and I think it's a safe bet, that everyone's cables resemble mine—and presto, you're looking at the next prebankruptcy Donald Trump (only without the bad taste).

But then I remember the parting words of the monk who gave me the glasses: "Use them wisely." And how about that single connection he had? "Goes straight to Buddha" . . . ?

I take off the glasses and look at the ineradicable spot of blood on the frames. I think about John Lennon. What did he do with these glasses?

I imagine a little devil popping into being on my left shoulder. He's leaning on a pitchfork, wearing a derby, and smoking a cigar. He blows smoke into my ear and says, "He got rich, you schmuck!"

An angel appears on my right shoulder. Wings emerging from his black leather jacket, he's holding an electric guitar in place of a harp. "But that's not all he did, Zildjian. He made a lot of people happy. He contributed to progress. He improved the culture."

"He laid a lot of dames," says the devil.

"Yes, but always sought to express a philosophy of life, to illuminate people."

"Nothing gets a babe illuminated hotter than a dose of philosophy."

The angel flies over my head and lands next to the devil. "You cynical philistine!"

"Hey, back off!" The devil brandishes his pitchfork, puffing on his cigar till the coal glows. The angel hefts his guitar like a club and takes a swipe at his opponent. They both tumble off my shoulder, locked in that eternal pro-wrestling match of the spirit.

Their arguments have helped me make up my mind. I will use the glasses to feather my personal nest a little. But I will also do something very good for humanity with them.

But while the personal options are quite clear to me, the larger ones persist in staying somewhat hazy.

I let them remain so. The first thing I want to do is head over to Cynthia's apartment.

Cynthia and I broke up for what we both correctly surmised was the last time just a week ago. The cause was my telling her that this hunky actor she admired reminded me of an ambulatory roast beef, and probably had as many brains. From the nature of this tiff, you can probably gather that our relationship was not all that deep.

But I am still attached to her. I know, because I found the tendril. But it turns out to be strictly a one-way hookup, all the emotion flowing out of me and hitting a barrier on her end like a sperm hitting a diaphragm.

Now I am going to change that.

Cynthia is home. She is getting ready for her waitress job. I find her very attractive in the cowgirl boots and short skirt with tail feathers featured on the help at Drumsticks 'n' Hot Licks, the fried-chicken country-western club, and I tell her so.

"Yeah, great," Cynthia replies rather coldly. She keeps her back to me, adjusting her strawberry-blonde coiffure in the mirror. I am amazed that she can get her brush through all the karma-cords, which apparently offer no resistance.

Cynthia eyes me in the looking glass, and I am briefly reminded of the plasticine porter's tie. It's hard to believe that she cannot see all my tendrils, including the one leading to her, but it is true. Then she notices my spectacles.

"Since when did you start wearing glasses?"

"Since I met a Buddhist street vendor who sent me on a trip to another dimension."

"Yeah, right. You'll never change, Zil. What do you want? I assume you didn't come over here just to compliment me. Come on, out with it. No mind games, either. And make it fast, 'cause I've got to get to work."

"Cynthia, we need to talk," I begin, laying down some sensitive-type patter just to distract her. She has turned away from the mirror and is bent forward, rummaging through her purse. Meanwhile, I am inching closer, within reach of her personal emotional attachments.

I zero in on one that is a livid purple and resembles in some strange indefinable way my own connection to the game-show hostess. I deftly grab it and unplug it from Cynthia's head.

She twitches and says, "Hey, what are you doing?"

"Just admiring the scent of your hair."

"Well, quit it. You're creeping me out."

I push the connection into my own head. Just as I thought! It goes straight to that hambone actor who was the cause of our breakup. I am suddenly overwhelmed with impure thoughts about his bod. Yuck! This is not for me. I pop the tendril out and jack it into Cynthia again.

Then I do something I haven't attempted before.

I pull on the cable in the other direction, trying to yank it out of the actor, where I doubt it's heavily anchored. My physical effort is apparently transmitted successfully along the cable through the extraspatial dimension it traverses, for it suddenly comes loose.

I swiftly fuse the end of Cynthia's one-way cable for the actor with my one-way cable for her, which I have just unplugged at her end.

She straightens up as if goosed by Godzilla and wheels around to face me.

"Zildjian, you're—you're different somehow. . . ."

Even knowing what's going on, I am overwhelmed by the synergy of the new connection, which is full and taut as a firehose under pressure. "Cynthia, I—you—"

"Oh, come play in my strawberry field!"

After that, it's our own private Beatlemania.

The next few days proceed swimmingly.

I get a new car and a line of credit without even putting on a necktie. It's only a small matter of establishing the proper connections. At the car dealer's up near the Plaza Hotel, I borrow the owner's hookup to his elderly grandmother.

"No money down, no payments till next year, and no finance charges? Why not? I'm sure you're good for it."

At the bank, I utilize the loan officer's feelings toward his mistress to secure a large sum of cash, a Gold Card, and no-charge checking with $50,000 overdraft protection. The only complication is his hand on my knee.

I maintain both these links for a few days to insure that the dupes do not come to their senses and renege on the deals before they are solid. (I am a little troubled about the cold shoulders that are no doubt being received by Granny and Lolita, but reassure myself that things will soon be back to normal for them.) Finally, I gratefully sever the adopted links, watching them retract through their trans-dimensional wormholes. Hopefully, they will reestablish themselves with their natural objects.

What a relief, I can tell you. It has always been my philosophy that you've gotta go through this world as free as you can, and these extra bonds drag me down.

I think from time to time of the monk and his single golden cord. . . .

Cynthia and I spend the next couple of weeks having some major fun, she having turned in her tail feathers. We eat at the best tables in the best restaurants, gain immediate entrance into the smartest clubs, receive front-row concert tickets for the hottest acts gratis, and in general carve a path through the city like Henry Moore through a block of granite.

One day Cynthia asks me to accompany her to the hospital, where her sister has just had a baby.

At the maternity-ward window, I stare in disbelief at all the squalling or sleeping infants.

Each one has a single golden cord, just like the monk's. A few of the older ones have tentative parental connections, but basically it's just that one heavenly stalk going straight up to who-knows-where.

After that, I start examining kids everywhere more intently.

Most of them seem to maintain their heavenly birthright pretty much intact up till about age three. After that, it starts to dwindle and dim, getting thinner and paler until it finally vanishes around age ten, tops.

In all of New York, I fail to find an adult other than the missing monk who still has what he or she was born with. And that includes, natch, me.

Of course, I am not exactly hanging in the places where such a person might necessarily be found.

And although several times I almost take the opportunity to unplug a kid's golden cord and sample the current flowing down it, I never quite dare.

I realize I'm afraid it might reveal how shallow what I'm doing is. . . .

One day about a month after getting the Lennon spectacles, just when I am starting to get bored with how easy life is, I am driving alone down First Avenue when I encounter an enormous flock of cars being herded by a squad of sheepdog cops. Poking my head out the window, I politely inquire of a policeman as to what's going on.

"It's the President," replies the cop. "He's speaking to the UN before the war starts."

"The war? I thought the war was over. . . ."

"That was the last one. This is a new one."

"Well, who are we against this time?"

"Whatsamatta, doncha watch TV? The enemy is South Arabiraniopistan. Their leader's here too. He'll be lucky if he don't get lynched."

I am not sure I have gotten the name of the country right; I never was one for following politics much. But this war-thing is definitely bad news of at least the magnitude of the incarceration of James Brown.

Suddenly I recall my vow to do something good for all humanity.

I get out of the car and hand my keys to the cop.

"Here, park this, willya?"

He starts to open his mouth to utter some typical cop thing, but I deftly make use of his obedience cable to his superiors (a slimy thing I always hate to touch), and secure his complete cooperation.

The UN is crawling with security. I watch for a few minutes until I ascertain who the head honcho is. Then I approach him.

This is not a time to cut corners, so I indulge in a little overkill. Not only do I quickly yank and plug into my skull his obedience connection to his distant boss, but I also take over his links with his wife, dog, son, and what appears to be his riding lawnmower. (I always said these G-men were sickos.)

"Would you mind escorting me in?" I ask sweetly.

"Of course, sir. Right this way."

Issuing orders over his walkie-talkie, the Secret Service agent soon conducts me backstage in the Assembly chamber.

I now face a minor problem: how to get close enough to the President for what I need to do. My outfit is certainly not going to help, as I am wearing a Hawaiian shirt, green scrub pants a friend stole from Bellevue, and huaraches.

Improvise, improvise. "Loan me your suit coat."

"Certainly."

Thus somewhat more suitably accoutered, clutching a shopping list from my pocket as if it were a classified memo I must deliver, I step out onto the dais, my captive agent dutifully running interference for me.

The platform is full of seated dignitaries. The Secretary General is speaking at a podium. Television cameras are focused on us. I have always wanted to appear on television, but not in this fashion. . . .

Using the narrow space behind the rank of chairs, I sidle up inch by inch to where the President and his counterpart are seated. The Prez's prep-school Puritan face is puckered into a mask of righteous indignation. The leader of our enemy wears a smug duplicitous puss like what you might see on a drug dealer who just successfully tossed his stash out the car window and down a sewer before the narcs closed in.

No one is paying any attention to me.

Yet.

A thick orange scaly hawser of hate runs between the two leaders. I've never seen anything so malignant-looking. I truly believe for the first time in the reality of war.

I am now within reach of the emotional linkages of these geopolitical megalomaniacs. Unfortunately, people are starting to take notice of me, and not in a kindly way.

Before they decide to do something, I act.

Gripping the hate-cord with both hands, I attempt to yank its ends out of the leaders' heads. The resistance is immense. I strain—to the audience, both at home and in the Assembly, it must look, I am sure, as if I am gripping an imaginary barbell with the leaders' heads as weights and trying to press it for an Olympic record.

Finally, the hate-cord pops out. Both leaders jerk like gaffed barracudas.

I can't resist leaning forward and whispering in their ears.

"Imagine there's no countries, boys, it's easy if you try. And war is over, if you want it. . . ."

In the next instant, I pop the Prez's patriotism link and plug it into the head of the South Arabiraniopistan guy. Then I swiftly jack the other guy's loyalty into the Prez.

All the hoodoo movements this involves over the heads of the two leaders is apparently too much for the unseduced security people, who now pile on me as if I were the football in a Super Bowl game.

My Lennon glasses shoot off my face and fly through the air. I think I hear them crack. But I could be wrong. Sounds are rather muffled through a layer of human flesh atop me.

I black out.

During this more than usually unconscious state, Lucy appears to me, naked and resplendently begemmed.

"A fine job, Zildjian. You are welcome to visit us anytime." She starts to fade.

"Wait, hold on, how do I get back to where I once belonged . . . ?"

But there is no answer.

I am in prison for only six months. The pants from Bellevue helped my insanity defense. I don't mind. Even if no one else realizes what I've done, I can relish being a working-class hero. Much to my amazement, Cynthia visits me three times a week. I had somehow thought that all the relationships I had rigged would vanish with the glasses.

During my imprisonment, I am proud to report, our President and the leader of South Arab-etc., after their stunning reconciliation in front of the entire world, are photographed playing miniature golf together at Disney World, and America agrees to purchase its new ally's entire output of camel-dung fertilizer, or some such similar commodity.

One day thereafter, I am walking down Broadway when I see the weirdest peddler dude.

I cautiously approach the monk. He smiles broadly and points to the top of my head.

"Nice-looking lotus blossom you got there."

I don't let on that I am pleased. "Hunh. Whatcha got for sale today?"

The monk holds up a pair of clunky black retro plastic frames. They look vaguely familiar. . . .

"The name 'Peggy Sue' mean anything to you?"

The Mountain to Mohammed

NANCY KRESS

"There seem to be few subjects that Nancy Kress, in an already fascinating career, will be unable to assimilate," writes John Clute in *The Encyclopedia of Science Fiction*. The emotional and intellectual sweep of Kress's last three novels testifies to the accuracy of Clute's remark. In *An Alien Light*, a race called the Ged undertakes a study of a *Homo sapiens sapiens*, seeking to understand this species's bizarre penchant for aggressiveness. In *Brain Rose*, the victims of a memory-stealing disease attempt to recover their former incarnations through a dubious medical procedure known as Previous Life Access Surgery. *Beggars in Spain*—an expansion of Kress's Nebula- and Hugo-winning novella of the same name—takes place in a brave new world of children genetically engineered to go without sleep.

Equally ambitious themes animate Kress's shorter works, the best of which are collected in *Trinity and Other Stories* and *The Aliens of Earth*. In 1985 she won a Best Short Story Nebula for "Out of All Them Bright Stars."

" 'The Mountain to Mohammed' concerns a future that is almost our present, which is why I wrote the story," Kress informs us. "Insurance companies are already starting to look at genetic inheritance as they go about deciding who gets health coverage and who does not. As human genome mapping progresses, the situation can only get more acute. Usually I write about technology in a positive way; this is the darker side of our rage to understand our biological selves. And of our rage when we do."

> *A person gives money to the physician.*
> *Maybe he will be healed.*
> *Maybe he will not be healed.*
>
> —The Talmud

When the security buzzer sounded, Dr. Jesse Randall was playing *go* against his computer. Haruo Kaneko, his roommate at Downstate Medical, had taught him the game. So far nineteen shiny black and white stones lay on the grid under the scanner field. Jesse frowned; the computer had a clear shot at surrounding an empty space in two moves, and he couldn't see how to stop it. The buzzer made him jump.

Anne? But she was on duty at the hospital until one. Or maybe he remembered her rotation wrong. . . .

Eagerly he crossed the small living room to the security screen. It wasn't Anne. Three stories below a man stood on the street, staring into the monitor. He was slight and fair, dressed in jeans and frayed jacket with a knit cap pulled low on his head. The bottoms of his ears were red with cold.

"Yes?" Jesse said.

"Dr. Randall?" The voice was low and rough.

"Yes."

"Could you come down here a minute to talk to me?"

"About what?"

"Something that needs talkin' about. It's personal. Mike sent me."

A thrill ran through Jesse. This was it, then. He kept his voice neutral. "I'll be right down."

He turned off the monitor system, removed the memory disk, and carried it into the bedroom, where he passed it several times over a magnet. In a gym bag he packed his medical equipment: antiseptics, antibiotics, sutures, clamps, syringes, electromed scanner, as much equipment as would fit. Once, shoving it all in, he laughed. He dressed in a warm peacoat bought secondhand at the Army-Navy store and put the gun, also bought secondhand, in the coat pocket. Although, of course, the other man would be carrying. But Jesse liked the feel of it, a slightly heavy drag on his right side. He replaced the disk in the security system and locked the door. The computer was still pretending to consider its move for *go,* although, of course, it had near-instantaneous decision capacity.

"Where to?"

The slight man didn't answer. He strode purposefully away from the building, and Jesse realized he shouldn't have said anything. He followed the man down the street, carrying the gym bag in his left hand.

Fog had drifted in from the harbor. Boston smelled wet and gray, of rotting piers and dead fish and garbage. Even here, in the Morningside Security Enclave, where part of the apartment maintenance fees left over from security went to keep the streets clean. Yellow lights gleamed through the gloom, stacked twelve stories high but crammed close together; even insurables couldn't afford to heat much space.

Where they were going, there wouldn't be any heat at all.

Jesse followed the slight man down the subway steps. The guy paid for both of them, a piece of quixotic dignity that made Jesse smile. Under the lights he got a better look: the man was older than he'd thought, with webbed lines around the eyes and long, thin lips over very bad teeth. Probably hadn't ever had dental coverage in his life. What had been in his genescan? God, what a system.

"What do I call you?" he said as they waited on the platform. He kept his voice low, just in case.

"Kenny."

"All right, Kenny," Jesse said, and smiled. Kenny didn't smile back. Jesse told himself it was ridiculous to feel hurt; this wasn't a social visit. He stared at the tracks until the subway came.

At this hour the only other riders were three hard-looking men, two black and one white, and an even harder-looking Hispanic girl in a low-cut red dress. After a minute Jesse realized she was under the control of one of the black men sitting at the other end of the car. Jesse was careful not to look at her again. He couldn't help being curious, though. She looked healthy. All four of them looked healthy, as did Kenny, except for his teeth. Maybe none of them were uninsurable; maybe they just couldn't find a job. Or didn't want one. It wasn't his place to judge.

That was the whole point of doing this, wasn't it?

The other two times had gone as easy as Mike said they would. A deltoid suture on a young girl wounded in a knife fight, and burn treatment for a baby scalded by a pot of boiling water knocked off a stove. Both times the families had been so grateful, so respectful. They knew the risk Jesse was taking. After he'd treated the baby and left antibiotics and analgesics on the pathetic excuse for a kitchen counter, a board laid across the nonfunctional radiator, the young Hispanic mother had grabbed his hand and covered it with kisses. Embarrassed, he'd turned to smile at her husband, wanting to say something, wanting to make clear he wasn't just another sporadic do-gooder who happened to have a medical degree.

"I think the system stinks. The insurance companies should never have been allowed to deny health coverage on the basis of genescans for potential disease, and employers should never have been allowed to keep costs down by health-based hiring. If this were a civilized country, we'd have national health care by now!"

The Hispanic had stared back at him, blank-faced.

"Some of us are trying to do better," Jesse said.

It was the same thing Mike—Dr. Michael Cassidy—had said to Jesse and Anne at the end of a long drunken evening celebrating the halfway point in all their residencies. Although, in retrospect, it seemed to Jesse that Mike hadn't drunk very much. Nor had he actually said very much outright. It was all implication, probing masked as casual philosophy. But Anne had understood, and refused instantly. "God, Mike, you could be dismissed from the hospital! The regulations forbid residents from exposing the hospital to the threat of an uninsured malpractice suit. There's no money."

Mike had smiled and twirled his glasses between fingers as long as a pianist's. "Doctors are free to treat whomever they wish, at their own risk, even uninsurables. *Carter v. Sunderland.*"

"Not while a hospital is paying their malpractice insurance as residents, if the hospital exercises its right to so forbid. *Janisson v. Lechchevko.*"

Mike laughed easily. "Then forget it, both of you. It's just conversation."

Anne said, "But do you personally risk—"

"It's not right," Jesse cut in—couldn't she see that Mike wouldn't want to incriminate himself on a thing like this?—"that so much of the population can't get insurance. Every year they add more genescan pretendency barriers, and the poor slobs haven't even got the diseases yet!"

His voice had risen. Anne glanced nervously around the bar. Her profile was lovely, a serene curving line that reminded Jesse of those Korean screens in the expensive shops on Commonwealth Avenue. And she had lovely legs, lovely breasts, lovely everything. Maybe, he'd thought, now that they were neighbors in the Morningside Enclave. . . .

"Another round," Mike had answered.

Unlike the father of the burned baby, who never had answered

Jesse at all. To cover his slight embarrassment—the mother had been so effusive—Jesse gazed around the cramped apartment. On the wall were photographs in cheap plastic frames of people with masses of black hair, all lying in bed. Jesse had read about this: it was a sort of mute, powerless protest. The subjects had all been photographed on their deathbeds. One of them was a beautiful girl, her eyes closed and her hand flung lightly over her head, as if asleep. The Hispanic followed Jesse's gaze and lowered his eyes.

"Nice," Jesse said. "Good photos. I didn't know you people were so good with a camera."

Still nothing.

Later, it occurred to Jesse that maybe the guy hadn't understood English.

The subway stopped with a long screech of equipment too old, too poorly maintained. There was no money. Boston, like the rest of the country, was broke. For a second Jesse thought the brakes weren't going to catch at all and his heart skipped, but Kenny showed no emotion and so Jesse tried not to either. The car finally stopped. Kenny rose and Jesse followed him.

They were somewhere in Dorchester. Three men walked quickly toward them, and Jesse's right hand crept toward his pocket. "This him?" one said to Kenny.

"Yeah," Kenny said. "Dr. Randall," and Jesse relaxed.

It made sense, really. Two men walking through this neighborhood probably wasn't a good idea. Five was better. Mike's organization must know what it was doing.

The men walked quickly. The neighborhood was better than Jesse had imagined: small row houses, every third or fourth one with a bit of frozen lawn in the front. A few even had flower boxes. But the windows were barred, and over all hung the gray fog, the dank cold, the pervasive smell of garbage.

The house they entered had no flower box. The steel front door, triple-locked, opened directly into a living room furnished with a sagging sofa, a TV, and an ancient daybed whose foam-cast headboard flaked like dandruff. On the daybed lay a child, her eyes bright with fever.

Sofa, TV, headboard vanished. Jesse felt his professional self take over, a sensation as clean and fresh as plunging into cool water. He knelt by the bed and smiled. The girl, who looked about nine or ten, didn't smile back. She had a long, sallow, sullen face, but the long brown hair on the pillow was beautiful: clean, lustrous, and well-tended.

"It's her belly," said one of the men who had met them at the subway. Jesse glanced up at the note in his voice, and realized that he must be the child's father. The man's hand trembled as he pulled the sheet from the girl's lower body. Her abdomen was swollen and tender.

"How long has she been this way?"

"Since yesterday," Kenny said, when the father didn't answer.

"Nausea? Vomiting?"

"Yeah. She can't keep nothing down."

Jesse's hands palpated gently. The girl screamed.

Appendicitis. He just hoped to hell peritonitis hadn't set in. He didn't want to deal with peritonitis. Not here.

"Bring in all the lamps you have, with the brightest watt bulbs. Boil water—" He looked up. The room was very cold. "Does the stove work?"

The father nodded. He looked pale. Jesse smiled and said, "I don't think it's anything we can't cure, with a little luck here." The man didn't answer.

Jesse opened his bag, his mind racing. Laser knife, sterile clamps, scaramine—he could do it even without nursing assistance, provided there was no peritonitis. But only if . . . the girl moaned and turned her face away. There were tears in her eyes. Jesse looked at the man with the same long, sallow face and brown hair. "You her father?"

The man nodded.

"I need to see her genescan."

The man clenched both fists at his side. Oh, God, if he didn't *have* the official printout . . . sometimes, Jesse had read, uninsurables burned them. One woman, furious at the paper that would forever keep her out of the middle class, had mailed hers, smeared with feces and packaged with a plasticine explosive, to the President. There had been headlines, columns, petitions . . . and nothing had changed. A country fighting for its very economic survival didn't hesitate to expend frontline troops. If there was no genescan for this child, Jesse couldn't use scaramine, that miracle immune-system booster, to which about 15 percent of the population had a fatal reaction. Without scaramine, under these operating conditions, the chances of postoperative infection were considerably higher. If she couldn't take scaramine . . .

The father handed Jesse the laminated printout, with the deeply embossed seal in the upper corner. Jesse scanned it quickly. The necessary RB antioncogene on the eleventh chromosome was present. The girl was not potentially allergic to scaramine. Her name was Rosamund.

"Okay, Rose," Jesse said gently. "I'm going to help you. In just a little while you're going to feel so much better. . . ." He slipped the needle with anesthetic into her arm. She jumped and screamed, but within a minute she was out.

Jesse stripped away the bedclothes, despite the cold, and told the men how to boil them. He spread betadine over her distended abdomen and poised the laser knife to cut.

The hallmark of his parents' life had been caution. *Don't fall, now! Drive carefully! Don't talk to strangers!* Born during the Depression—the other one—they invested only in Treasury bonds and their own one-sixth acre of suburban real estate. When the marching in Selma and Washington had turned to killing in Detroit and Kent State, they shook their heads sagely: *See? We said so. No good comes of getting involved in things that don't concern you.* Jesse's father had held the same job for thirty years; his mother considered it immoral to buy anything not on sale. They waited until she was over forty to have Jesse, their only child.

At sixteen, Jesse had despised them; at twenty-four, pitied them; at twenty-eight, his present age, loved them with a despairing gratitude not completely free of contempt. They had missed so much, dared so little. They lived now in Florida, retired and happy and smug. "The pension"—they called it that, as if it were a famous diamond or a well-loved estate—was inflated by Collapse prices into providing a one-bedroom bungalow with beige carpets and a pool. In the pool's placid, artificially blue waters, the Randalls beheld chlorined visions of triumph. "Even after we retired," Jesse's mother told him proudly, "we didn't have to go backward."

"That's what comes from thrift, son," his father always added.

"And hard work. No reason these deadbeats today couldn't do the same thing."

Jesse looked around their tiny yard at the plastic ducks lined up like headstones, the fanatically trimmed hedge, the blue-and-white striped awning, and his arms made curious beating motions, as if they were lashed to his side. "Nice, Mom. Nice."

"You know it," she said, and winked roguishly. Jesse had looked away before she could see his embarrassment. Boston had loomed large in his mind, compelling and vivid and hectic as an exotic disease.

There was no peritonitis. Jesse sliced free the spoiled bit of tissue that had been Rosamund's appendix. As he closed with quick, sure movements, he heard a click. A camera. He couldn't look away, but out of a sudden rush of euphoria he said to whoever was taking the picture, "Not one for the gallery this time. This one's going to *live*."

When the incision was closed, Jesse administered a massive dose of scaramine. Carefully he instructed Kenny and the girl's father about the medication, the little girl's diet, the procedures to maintain asepsis that, since they were bound to be inadequate, made the scaramine so necessary. "I'm on duty the next thirty-six hours at the hospital. I'll return Wednesday night, you'll either have to come get me or give me the address, I'll take a taxi and—"

The father drew in a quick, shaky breath like a sob. Jesse turned to him. "She's got a strong fighting chance, this procedure isn't—" A woman exploded from a back room, shrieking.

"No, no, nooooo. . . ." She tried to throw herself on the patient. Jesse lunged for her, but Kenny was quicker. He grabbed her around the waist, pinning her arms to her sides. She fought him, wailing and screaming, as he dragged her back through the door. "Murderer, baby killer, nooooooo—"

"My wife," the father finally said. "She doesn't . . . doesn't understand."

Probably doctors were devils to her, Jesse thought. Gods who denied people the healing they could have offered. Poor bastards. He felt a surge of quiet pride that he could teach them different.

The father went on looking at Rosamund, now sleeping peacefully. Jesse couldn't see the other man's eyes.

Back home at the apartment, he popped open a beer. He felt fine. Was it too late to call Anne?

It was—the computer clock said 2:00 A.M. She'd already be sacked out. In seven more hours his own thirty-six-hour rotation started, but he couldn't sleep.

He sat down at the computer. The machine hadn't moved to surround his empty square after all. It must have something else in mind. Smiling, sipping at his beer, Jesse sat down to match wits with the Korean computer in the ancient Japanese game in the waning Boston night.

Two days later he went back to check on Rosamund. The rowhouse was deserted, boards nailed diagonally across the window. Jesse's heart began to pound. He was afraid to ask information of the neighbors; men in dark clothes kept going in and out of the house next door, their eyes cold. Jesse went back to the hospital and waited. He couldn't think what else to do.

Four rotations later the deputy sheriff waited for him outside the building, unable to pass the security monitors until Jesse came home.

COMMONWEALTH
OF MASSACHUSETTS

Suffolk County   *Superior Court*

To Jesse Robert Randall of Morningside Security Enclave, Building 16, Apartment 3C, Boston, within our County of Suffolk. Whereas Steven & Rose Gocek of Boston within our County of Suffolk have begun an action of Tort against you returnable in the Superior Court holden at Boston within our County of Suffolk on October 18, 2004, in which action damages are claimed in the sum of $2,000,000 as follows:

TORT AND/OR CONTRACT
FOR MALPRACTICE

as will more fully appear from the declaration to be filed in said Court when and if said action is entered therein:

WE COMMAND YOU, if you intend to make any defense of said action, that on said date or within such further time as the law allows you cause your written appearance to be entered and your written answer or other lawful pleadings to be filed in the office of the Clerk of the Court to which said writ is returnable, and that you defend against said action according to law.

Hereof fail not at your peril, as otherwise said judgment may be entered against you in said action without further notice.

Witness, Lawrence F. Monastersky, Esquire, at <u>Boston</u>, the <u>fourth</u> day of <u>March</u> in the year of our Lord two thousand <u>four</u>.

Alice P. McCarren
Clerk

Jesse looked up from the paper. The deputy sheriff, a soft-bodied man with small, light eyes, looked steadily back.

"But what . . . what happened?"

The deputy looked out over Jesse's left shoulder, a gesture meaning he wasn't officially saying what he was saying. "The kid died. The one they say you treated."

"Died? Of what? But I went back . . ." He stopped, filled with sudden sickening uncertainty about how much he was admitting.

The deputy went on staring over his shoulder. "You want my advice, Doc? Get yourself a lawyer."

Doctor, lawyer, Indian chief, Jesse thought suddenly, inanely. The inanity somehow brought it all home. He was being sued. For malpractice. By an uninsurable. Now. Here. Him, Jesse Randall. Who had been only trying to help.

"Cold for this time of year," the deputy remarked. "They're dying of cold and malnutrition down there, in Roxbury and Dorchester and Southie. Even the goddamn weather can't give us a break."

Jesse couldn't answer. A wind off the harbor fluttered the paper in his hand.

"These are the facts," the lawyer said. He looked tired, a small man in a dusty office lined with secondhand law books. "The hospital purchased malpractice coverage for its staff, including residents. In doing so, it entered into a contract with certain obligations and exclusions for each side. If a specific incident falls under these exclusions, the contract is not in force with regard to that incident. One such exclusion is that residents will not be covered if they treat un-

insured persons unless such treatment occurs within the hospital setting or the resident has reasonable grounds to assume that such a
person is insured. Those are not the circumstances you described
to me."

"No," Jesse said. He had the sensation that the law books were
falling off the top shelves, slowly but inexorably, like small green and
brown glaciers. Outside, he had the same sensation about the tops of
buildings.

"Therefore, you are not covered by any malpractice insurance.
Another set of facts: over the last five years jury decisions in malpractice cases have averaged 85 percent in favor of plaintiffs. Insurance companies and legislatures are made up of insurables, Dr.
Randall. However, juries are still drawn by lot from the general citizenry. Most of the educated general citizenry finds ways to get out
of jury duty. They always did. Juries are likely to be 65 percent or
more uninsurables. It's the last place the have-nots still wield much
real power, and they use it."

"You're saying I'm dead," Jesse said numbly. "They'll find me
guilty."

The little lawyer looked pained. "Not 'dead,' Doctor. Convicted—most probably. But conviction isn't death. Not even professional
death. The hospital may or may not dismiss you—they have that
right—but you can still finish your training elsewhere. And malpractice suits, however they go, are not of themselves grounds for denial
of a medical license. You can still be a doctor."

"Treating who?" Jesse cried. He threw up his hands. The books
fell slightly faster. "If I'm convicted I'll have to declare bankrupt-
cy—there's no way I could pay a jury settlement like that! And even
if I found another residency at some third-rate hospital in Podunk,
no decent practitioner would ever accept me as a partner. I'd have
to practice alone, without money to set up more than a hole-in-the-
corner office among God-knows-*who* . . . and even that's assuming I
can find a hospital that will let me finish. All because I wanted to
help people who are getting shit on!"

The lawyer took off his glasses and rubbed the lenses thoughtfully
with a tissue. "Maybe," he said, "they're shitting back."

"What?"

"You haven't asked about the specific charges, Doctor."

"Malpractice! The brat died!"

The lawyer said, "Of massive scaramine allergic reaction."

The anger leached out of Jesse. He went very quiet.

"She was allergic to scaramine," the lawyer said. "You failed to ascertain that. A basic medical question."

"I—" The words wouldn't come out. He saw again the laminated genescan chart, the detailed analysis of chromosome 11. A camera clicking, recording that he was there. The hysterical woman, the mother, exploding from the back room: *noooooooooo. . . .* The father standing frozen, his eyes downcast.

It wasn't possible.

Nobody would kill their own child. Not to discredit one of the fortunate ones, the haves, the insurables, the employables. . . . No one would do that.

The lawyer was watching him carefully, glasses in hand.

Jesse said, "Dr. Michael Cassidy—" and stopped.

"Dr. Cassidy what?" the lawyer said.

But all Jesse could see, suddenly, was the row of plastic ducks in his parents' Florida yard, lined up as precisely as headstones, garish hideous yellow as they marched undeviatingly wherever it was they were going.

"No," Mike Cassidy said. "I didn't send him."

They stood in the hospital parking lot. Snow blew from the east. Cassidy wrapped both arms around himself and rocked back and forth.

"He didn't come from us."

"He said he did!"

"I know. But he didn't. His group must have heard we were helping illegally, gotten your name from somebody—"

"But why?" Jesse shouted. "Why frame me? Why kill a child just to frame *me*? I'm nothing!"

Cassidy's face spasmed. Jesse saw that his horror at Jesse's position was real, his sympathy genuine, and both useless. There was nothing Cassidy could do.

"I don't know," Cassidy whispered. And then, "Are you going to name me at your malpractice trial?"

Jesse turned away without answering, into the wind.

———

Chief of Surgery Jonathan Eberhart called him into his office just before Jesse started his rotation. Before, not after. That was enough to tell him everything. He was getting very good at discovering the whole from a single clue.

"Sit down, Doctor," Eberhart said. His voice, normally austere, held unwilling compassion. Jesse heard it, and forced himself not to shudder.

"I'll stand."

"This is very difficult," Eberhart said, "but I think you already see our position. It's not one any of us would have chosen, but it's what we have. This hospital operates at a staggering deficit. Most patients cannot begin to cover the costs of modern technological health care. State and federal governments are both strapped with enormous debt. Without insurance companies and the private philanthropical support of a few rich families, we would not be able to open our doors to anyone at all. If we lose our insurance rating we—"

"I'm out on my ass," Jesse said. "Right?"

Eberhart looked out the window. It was snowing. Once Jesse, driving through Oceanview Security Enclave to pick up a date, had seen Eberhart building a snowman with two small children, probably his grandchildren. Even rolling lopsided globes of cold, Eberhart had had dignity.

"Yes, Doctor. I'm sorry. As I understand it, the facts of your case are not in legal dispute. Your residency here is terminated."

"Thank you," Jesse said, an odd formality suddenly replacing his crudeness. "For everything."

Eberhart neither answered nor turned around. His shoulders, framed in the gray window, slumped forward. He might, Jesse thought, have had a sudden advanced case of osteoporosis. For which, of course, he would be fully insured.

He packed the computer last, fitting each piece carefully into its original packing. Maybe that would raise the price that Second Thoughts was willing to give him: *look, almost new, still in the original box*. At the last minute he decided to keep the playing pieces for *go*, shoving them into the suitcase with his clothes and medical equipment. Only this suitcase would go with him.

When the packing was done, he walked up two flights and rang Anne's bell. Her rotation ended a half hour ago. Maybe she wouldn't be asleep yet.

She answered the door in a loose blue robe, toothbrush in hand. "Jesse, hi, I'm afraid I'm really beat—"

He no longer believed in indirection. "Would you have dinner with me tomorrow night?"

"Oh, I'm sorry, I can't," Anne said. She shifted her weight so one bare foot stood on top of the other, a gesture so childish it had to be embarrassment. Her toenails were shiny and smooth.

"After your next rotation?" Jesse said. He didn't smile.

"I don't know when I—"

"The one after that?"

Anne was silent. She looked down at her toothbrush. A thin pristine line of toothpaste snaked over the bristles.

"Okay," Jesse said, without expression. "I just wanted to be sure."

"Jesse—" Anne called after him, but he didn't turn around. He could already tell from her voice that she didn't really have anything more to say. If he had turned it would have been only for the sake of a last look at her toes, polished and shiny as *go* stones, and there really didn't seem to be any point in looking.

He moved into a cheap hotel on Boylston Street, into a room the size of a supply closet with triple locks on the door and bars on the window, where his money would go far. Every morning he took the subway to the Copley Square library, rented a computer cubicle, and wrote letters to hospitals across the country. He also answered classified ads in the *New England Journal of Medicine,* those that offered practice out-of-country where a license was not crucial, or low-paying medical research positions not too many people might want, or supervised assistantships. In the afternoons he walked the grubby streets of Dorchester, looking for Kenny. The lawyer representing Mr. and Mrs. Steven Gocek, parents of the dead Rosamund, would give him no addresses. Neither would his own lawyer, he of the collapsing books and desperate clientele, in whom Jesse had already lost all faith.

He never saw Kenny on the cold streets.

The last week of March, an unseasonable warm wind blew from the south, and kept up. Crocuses and daffodils pushed up between the sagging buildings. Children appeared, chasing each other across the garbage-laden streets, crying raucously. Rejections came from hospitals, employers. Jesse had still not told his parents what had happened. Twice in April he picked up a public phone, and twice he saw again the plastic ducks marching across the artificial lawn, and something inside him slammed shut so hard not even the phone number could escape.

One sunny day in May he walked in the Public Garden. The city still maintained it fairly well; foreign tourist traffic made it profitable. Jesse counted the number of well-dressed foreigners versus the number of ragged street Bostonians. The ratio equaled the survival rate for uninsured diabetics.

"Hey, mister, help me! Please!"

A terrified boy, ten or eleven, grabbed Jesse's hand and pointed. At the bottom of a grassy knoll an elderly man lay crumpled on the ground, his face twisted.

"My grandpa! He just grabbed his chest and fell down! Do something! Please!"

Jesse could smell the boy's fear, a stink like rich loam. He walked over to the old man. Breathing stopped, no pulse, color still pink . . .

No.

This man was an uninsured. Like Kenny, like Steven Gocek. Like Rosamund.

"Grandpa!" the child wailed. "Grandpa!"

Jesse knelt. He started mouth-to-mouth. The old man smelled of sweat, of old flesh. No blood moved through the body. "Breathe, dammit, breathe," Jesse heard someone say, and then realized it was he. "*Breathe,* you old fart, you uninsured deadbeat, you stinking ingrate, breathe—"

The old man breathed.

He sent the boy for more adults. The child took off at a dead run, returning twenty minutes later with uncles, father, cousins, aunts, most of whom spoke some language Jesse couldn't identify. In that twenty minutes none of the well-dressed tourists in the Garden approached Jesse, standing guard beside the old man, who breathed carefully and moaned softly, stretched full-length on the grass. The tourists glanced at him and then away, their faces tightening.

The tribe of family carried the old man away on a homemade stretcher. Jesse put his hand on the arm of one of the young men. "Insurance? Hospital?"

The man spat onto the grass.

Jesse walked beside the stretcher, monitoring the old man until he was in his own bed. He told the child what to do for him, since no one else seemed to understand. Later that day he went back, carrying his medical bag, and gave them the last of his hospital supply of nitroglycerin. The oldest woman, who had been too busy issuing orders about the stretcher to pay Jesse any attention before, stopped dead and jabbered in her own tongue.

"You a doctor?" the child translated. The tip of his ear, Jesse noticed, was missing. Congenital? Accident? Ritual mutilation? The ear had healed clean.

"Yeah," Jesse said. "A doctor."

The old woman chattered some more and disappeared behind a door. Jesse gazed at the walls. There were no deathbed photos. As he was leaving, the woman returned with ten incredibly dirty dollar bills.

"Doctor," she said, her accent harsh, and when she smiled Jesse saw that all her top teeth and most of her bottom ones were missing, the gum swollen with what might have been early signs of scurvy.

"Doctor," she said again.

He moved out of the hotel just as the last of his money ran out. The old man's wife, Androula Malakassas, found him a room in somebody else's rambling, dilapidated boardinghouse. The house was noisy at all hours, but the room was clean and large. Androula's cousin brought home an old, multi-positional dentist chair, probably stolen, and Jesse used that for both an examining and an operating table. Medical substances—antibiotics, chemotherapy, IV drugs—which he had thought of as the hardest need to fill outside of controlled channels, turned out to be the easiest. On reflection, he realized this shouldn't have surprised him.

In July he delivered his first breech birth, a primapara whose labor was so long and painful and bloody he thought at one point he'd lose both mother and baby. He lost neither, although the new mother cursed him in Spanish and spat at him. She was too weak for the saliva to go far. Holding the warm-assed, nine-pound baby boy, Jesse had heard a camera click. He cursed too, but feebly; the sharp thrill of pleasure that pierced from throat to bowels was too strong.

In August he lost three patients in a row, all to conditions that would have needed elaborate, costly equipment and procedures: renal failure, aortic aneurysm, narcotic overdose. He went to all three funerals. At each one the family and friends cleared a little space for him, in which he stood surrounded by respect and resentment. When a knife fight broke out at the funeral of the aneurysm, the family hustled Jesse away from the danger, but not so far away that he couldn't treat the loser.

In September a Chinese family, recent immigrants, moved into Androula's sprawling boardinghouse. The woman wept all day. The man roamed Boston, looking for work. There was a grandfather who spoke a little English, having learned it in Peking during the brief period of American industrial expansion into the Pacific Rim before the Chinese government convulsed and the American economy collapsed. The grandfather played *go*. On evenings when no one wanted Jesse, he sat with Lin Shujen and moved the polished white and black stones over the grid, seeking to enclose empty spaces without losing any pieces. Mr. Lin took a long time to consider each move.

In October, a week before Jesse's trial, his mother died. Jesse's father sent him money to fly home for the funeral, the first money Jesse had accepted from his family since he'd finally told them he had left the hospital. After the funeral Jesse sat in the living room of his father's Florida house and listened to the elderly mourners recall their youths in the vanished prosperity of the fifties and sixties.

"Plenty of jobs then for people who're willing to work."

"Still plenty of jobs. Just nobody's willing any more."

"Want everything handed to them. If you ask me, this collapse'll prove to be a good thing in the long run. Weed out the weaklings and the lazy."

"It was the sixties we got off on the wrong track, with Lyndon Johnson and all the welfare programs—"

They didn't look at Jesse. He had no idea what his father had said to them about him.

Back in Boston, stinking under Indian summer heat, people

thronged his room. Fractures, cancers, allergies, pregnancies, punctures, deficiencies, imbalances. They were resentful that he'd gone away for five days. He should be here; they needed him. He was the doctor.

The first day of his trial, Jesse saw Kenny standing on the courthouse steps. Kenny wore a cheap blue suit with loafers and white socks. Jesse stood very still, then walked over to the other man. Kenny tensed.

"I'm not going to hit you," Jesse said.

Kenny watched him, chin lowered, slight body balanced on the balls of his feet. A fighter's stance.

"I want to ask something," Jesse said. "It won't affect the trial. I just want to know. Why'd you do it? Why did *they?* I know the little girl's true genescan showed 98 percent risk of leukemia death within three years, but even so—how could you?"

Kenny scrutinized him carefully. Jesse saw that Kenny thought Jesse might be wired. Even before Kenny answered, Jesse knew what he'd hear. "I don't know what you're talking about, man."

"You couldn't get inside the system. Any of you. So you brought me out. If Mohammed won't go to the mountain—"

"You don't make no sense," Kenny said.

"Was it worth it? To you? To them? Was it?"

Kenny walked away, up the courthouse steps. At the top waited the Goceks, who were suing Jesse for two million dollars he didn't have and wasn't insured for, and that they knew damn well they wouldn't collect. On the wall of their house, wherever it was, probably hung Rosamund's deathbed picture, a little girl with a plain, sallow face and beautiful hair.

Jesse saw his lawyer trudge up the courthouse steps, carrying his briefcase. Another lawyer, with an equally shabby briefcase, climbed in parallel several feet away. Between the two men the courthouse steps made a white empty space.

Jesse climbed, too, hoping to hell this wouldn't take too long. He had an infected compound femoral fracture, a birth with potential erythroblastosis fetalis, and an elderly phlebitis, all waiting. He was especially concerned about the infected fracture, which needed careful monitoring because the man's genescan showed a tendency toward weak T-cell production. The guy was a day laborer, foul-mouthed and ignorant and brave, with a wife and two kids. He'd broken his leg working illegal construction. Jesse was determined to give him at least a fighting chance.

Hopeful Monsters: The SF and Fantasy Films of 1992

NICK LOWE

"Throughout the history of science fiction it has been an article of faith among its readers that filmed SF was an abomination," states film historian John Baxter in his valuable little book, *Science Fiction in the Cinema*, "that it degraded the field and provided nothing of interest to the serious mind." The problem with this assertion—to paraphrase Henry Fielding—is that it isn't true. Show me a fan of SF literature, and I'll show you someone who takes a conspicuous interest in science-fiction movies, if not as a cheerful devotee of the genre per se then as someone who actively laments that it so rarely rises to the heights of *Blade Runner*, *Close Encounters of the Third Kind*, *2001: A Space Odyssey*, *Forbidden Planet*, *The Day the Earth Stood Still*, or—reaching back to the era covered by Frederik Pohl elsewhere in this volume—*Things to Come* and *Metropolis*.

Among the genre's authors and editors, too, there has always been a feeling that "filmed SF" matters. During the last decade, a tradition has emerged whereby each Nebula anthology includes a survey of the year's science-fiction and fantasy movies. For *Nebula Awards 28*, I was fortunate enough to obtain the services of a gentleman named Nick Lowe.

Lowe is known primarily within the SF community for "Mutant Popcorn," the witty and incisive film column he's been contributing to *Interzone* since 1985. "In real life," he informs me, "I'm a London University classics lecturer, so I spend my days banging ancient Greek verbs into the resistant heads of grunge-clad youth, before slipping away into phone booths to emerge by moonlight as a briefly glimpsed shadow in the preview theaters of Soho's media underworld. I've no explanation for my lifelong simultaneous passions for ancient literature and twentieth-century SF, except that for me they're self-evidently one and the same thing.

"The reason I enjoy writing about film for SF readers—indeed, I couldn't imagine writing about it for any other audience—is the wonderful sense of a shared culture, community, and vantage. We all know the stuff we see on screen is decades behind what we read, but that fact doesn't inhibit our pleasure mechanism in the least. At the moment, the *Interzone* gig is about all the extramural writing I do, what with the treadmill of academic publications, the lure of backpack travel, and my continuing struggle to be the hottest palm-wine guitarist in Hampstead."

The big hits of 1992 were *Batman Returns, Aladdin,* and *Bram Stoker's Dracula,* with *Alien³, Death Becomes Her, Forever Young, The Lawnmower Man,* and *Universal Soldier* performing well; the disasters were *Radio Flyer, Freejack, Cool World,* and *Toys;* and the overwhelming impression was of a cinema desperately trying to reinvent itself. After fifteen years as a key commercial genre, Hollywood SF has played out the easy options. None of the old formulas seem to work any more, except as vehicles for dispiriting camp satire. Space opera, time travel, and future earths have all regressed to the small screen, with nothing obvious emerging in their place. Film critics from our own future will no doubt glibly diagnose the nineties as suffering from a weird millennial psychosis that took the form of a tunnel-visioned refusal to confront, imagine, or even discuss the immensities of time and space that frame us. But the real, mundane truth is probably just that audiences have grown too sophisticated to accept the outdated, simplistic Hollywood notions of classical SF visions and themes, and that the film industry is thumping every button in reach, trying to find a switch that works.

Whatever its cause, this identity crisis has pushed SF and fantasy movies into the paradoxical position of taking bigger creative risks in an ever-more conservative and safe-playing general Hollywood climate. Thus, for example, 1992 saw a small but significant rise in the studios' willingness to give maverick *auteurs* unprecedented slack on very large, expensive productions in the hope of something new and profitable emerging. Interestingly, and perhaps encouragingly, two of these (Tim Burton's *Batman Returns* and Coppola's *Dracula*) paid back the gamble generously, with only Barry Levinson's *Toys* closing the year with a blast of frosty air. By contrast, the big pictures like *Alien³* and *Death Becomes Her* that were largely assembled and packaged by the studios fell distinctly short of expectation, with a visible feeling of dissipated energy and purpose.

One symptom of the crisis was a significant delve into the back catalog, with both *Blade Runner* and *The Abyss* rereleased in "Director's Cut" form—presumably as promos for laser and video versions, though as it turned out the restored *Blade Runner* in particular did very good business, playing uninterrupted for over eight months in London. This edition lost the hated happy ending and voice-over narration, resurrected an embarrassing and meaningless unicorn dream, and tweaked numerous other scenes in unobtrusive ways. But since it's never been any secret how Ridley Scott's original cut was supposed to end, or that the voice-overs were a studio-enforced afterthought, its significance was less in the restoration than in the chance for public reappraisal of *the* seminal SF movie of the eighties ten years later. The script, lead performances, and shoot-outs don't always hold up, the atmosphere is diluted by familiarity with innumerable pastiches, and Philip K. Dick's novel has worn far better in the same time; but it's hard to imagine such a brooding, humane movie being made with this kind of budget and vision today. Much less happy was the recut *Abyss*, whose half-hour of extra footage revealed what we'd been spared in the ending originally released (amusingly dated Cold War world on brink of World War III, pulled back from edge by cute, twinkly aliens *ex machina*). All that's best in this often-magnificent picture was already there in the 1989 version, whose first two hours are still some of the finest cinema James Cameron's ever done, and whose final twenty minutes lie beyond all hope of redemption.

Less sinister, if only because by now so perennial, was the year's reliance on sequels. The least profitable, and the most by-numbers, was *Honey, I Blew Up the Kid* (formerly *Honey, I Blew Up the Baby,* but apparently this was felt a touch too coarse for Disney): a determinedly bigger but not measurably better follow-up to the unassuming 1989 comedy about inventor-dad Rick Moranis and his incredible shrinking ray. Like its predecessor, the sequel managed some quite savvy genre gags and deadpan absurdities of situation and dialogue in its marriage of a fifties SF-movie concept (here, a preschool *Amazing Colossal Man* on a rampage through Vegas) to an all-ages domestic comedy. But audiences seemed to sense that once was enough.

More of a mess, though far from a write-off, was *Alien³*, a spectacular instance of the distinctive nineties genre of Troubled Project, in which the last survivor of the great seventies SF-movie icons was finally packed off to its own undiscovered country. After script and production tussles had seen off, among others, William Gibson, Renny

Harlin, Vincent Ward, and David (*Warlock*) Twohy—the last of whom went on to make *Timescape,* a commendable if diluted video movie of C. L. Moore's classic novel, *Vintage Season*—twenty-seven-year-old popvid director David Fincher found himself precariously in charge of cooking something screenable out of a gristly hot pot of residues from different script versions. What we got was a curious downbeat parable, more thoughtful than exciting, about woman as alien in an all-male prison world of celibate English character actors, with Sigourney Weaver's Ripley (still very good) carrying the monster in her own body and the perfidious Company in cold pursuit. Much less effective was the thriller element, dutifully replicating the standard *Alien* stalk-plot in a protracted and confusing video-game middle section spent aimlessly charging down tunnels and notching up strikes on the scoreboard. But while a dismal failure as narrative, *Alien*³ offered the trilogy's most sustained meditation on its wider allegories of sexuality, disease, and the body, and even (in producer Weaver's on-screen struggle to save her abhorrent baby from the clutches of corporate exploitation) on the process of filmmaking itself.

But by far the best of the follow-ups was Tim Burton's *Batman Returns,* a sequel of such accomplished strangeness that even its own masquerade as a mainstream Hollywood blockbuster seemed a piece of dark and deviant role-play. With perfunctory gestures in the direction of action heroics, *Returns* went even further than its predecessor in using the Batman figure as merely a convenient peg for Burton's warped sense of gothic irony and spectacle. With a sharper script and an expanded freak show of villains, *Returns* mirrored Batman's own divided personality in the gallery of soul-masks modeled by his trio of double-lived antagonists: Christopher Walken's black-hearted industrialist, Danny DeVito's physically and morally deformed Penguin, and, above all, Michelle Pfeiffer's oppressed and vengeful Catwoman, all three portrayed with unexpected generosity and pathos. The characters work much better as solo studies than they do as an interacting ensemble, and the attempt to hold all three plotlines together in something resembling a conventional comic-book narrative is at best cosmetically successful. But this is a film of enormous individuality and wit, packed with quirky, unsettling images and ideas.

It was also a year of unusually many literary adaptations, which itself could easily be read as a sign of creative panic. Besides *Dracula, Candyman, Timescape,* the *Blade Runner* reissue, and—allegedly, at least—*Lawnmower Man,* there was *Freejack* (from Robert Sheckley's first novel, *Immortality, Inc.*), and John Carpenter's version of H. F. Saint's *Memoirs of an Invisible Man;* while even *Honey* tucked in a grudging credit reading "Special Recognition to Kit Reed for 'Attack of the Giant Baby,'" behind which doubtless lies a tale or two. Few of these pictures did right by their sources, with *Freejack* and *Memoirs* both facing the same problem: how to make a movie out of a novel with no detectable plot and a fatally uncinematic central idea.

Sheckley's 1958 book, with its characteristic nonstructure of amiably rambling episodes that seem to have been made up as the author went along, postulated a society in which soul and afterlife have been scientifically verified, with the technical details of the breakthrough much less central than the social impact of their discovery. And the writers of *Freejack*—including Ronald Shusett, the unusually SF-literate coscripter of *Alien* and *Total Recall*—came up with a radical response to the challenge of getting the metaphysical heart of *Immortality, Inc.* to work on screen, cheerfully ditching the whole of Sheckley's plot, characters, and setting, as well as (incredibly) deleting all the humor, and turning the original premise completely on its head. (In the novel, the hero's mind is snatched from a fatal car crash, to be implanted in a future body as a reluctant promotional gimmick for the resurrection industry; in *Freejack,* it's race-car driver Emilio Estevez's *body* that's snatched across time, to house the mind of dying corporate chief Anthony Hopkins—with nonsensical implications that no amount of professional car chasing can quite cover up.) Little of either the body or soul of Sheckley's novel is recognizable in the transplant, with even the term "Spiritual Switchboard" applied here to something quite different; and it says a lot about the rest of the performances that Mick Jagger's is substantially the best in the picture. It's particularly sad to see the fine New Zealand director Geoff Murphy, a past master of the three-actors-no-script-and-no-budget antipodean quickie, whose credits include the haunting apocalypse movie, *The Quiet Earth,* flounder so badly with this material after his able Hollywood debut on *Young Guns II.*

As for *Memoirs of an Invisible Man*, this was hobbled from the start by the source novel's being at best marginally competent: a modest idea with nowhere to go inflated to 400 meandering, plotless pages. The much-reworked script—to which William Goldman, among others, contributed—grapples hard with the narrator's deliberate lack of personality throughout the book, in which invisibility is not merely an optical handicap but a metaphor for the loss of self. And though Carpenter's film does cope quite ingeniously and effectively with the sleights of filmic convention required to give the hero a face on screen, in doing so it jettisons the already-slim point of the novel. It doesn't help that Chevy Chase's necessarily bland performance has to be awkwardly supplemented in voice-over by the retained first-person of the original, or that the new plot so laboriously grafted on is merely a desultory, formulaic chase caper. Some intermittently clever cinephile gags are directed at the Claude Rains classic, but this sort of wearisome comedic send-up of soft genre targets (see *Honey,* and *Buffy* and *Mom and Dad* below) is just another symptom of how hard Hollywood finds it to take SF films seriously any more.

The difficulty of translating a novelistic first-person narrator at all equivalently to the screen was just one of the challenges confronted in the adaptation of *Dracula* by James V. Hart, who did a similarly ambitious makeover on a period English classic for 1991's *Hook*. The *Dracula* and *Hook* screenplays have a lot in common in terms of approach: at once uncannily faithful to certain elements of their literary sources while radically revisionary in the treatment of others, with the preserved parts generally coming over much more successfully than the new materials' reheated Hollywood mush. It's hard to know whether to admire the daring or boggle at the crassness of an author who can, without a blink of irony, rewrite J. M. Barrie's *Peter Pan* as a homily on fathering and Stoker's *Dracula* as a love story. Yet Hart's script undeniably preserves some of the most difficult and impressive elements of the novel discarded in all previous film versions, such as Stoker's remarkably SF-like interest in contemporary advances at the boundaries of technology, medicine, and science, and the complex epistolary structure of interwoven voices; and even much of Hart's own embroidery, like the Vlad the Impaler legend and the cinematograph episode, is cleverly and successfully worked in. For better or worse, though, the main impact of *Bram Stoker's Dracula* is made not by the script itself but by its execution: the extraordinary ensemble of performances and, especially, the febrile invention of Coppola's bravura direction, all of which one either loved or loathed. (I found both acting and direction consistently turgid and laughable, but it's only fair to say that many people whose judgment I generally respect a lot more than my own had quite the opposite reaction.)

In contrast, it was a much thinner year for the more traditional SF themes. Space, in particular, remained virtually off-limits, the classical interplanetary movie a dead genre. The only specimens in all of 1992 were the new *Alien* sequel (significantly, the one series that has always used deep-space backdrops purely as a design tool to create new forms of claustrophobia) and the tacky spoof *Mom and Dad Save the World* (which sank without bubbles). More strikingly, even the future itself seemed increasingly passé. If you exclude the perverse and incomparable *Delicatessen* (about which more later), only three 1992 releases attempted to visualize even a near-future world, and all three, in effect, were reissues of *Blade Runner*. Alongside the real thing and *Freejack*, the dire British caper *Split Second* deserves glancing notice, if only for its temerity in casting Rutger Hauer himself as a deranged copper stalking a satanistic serial-killing humanoid mutant rat (you think I'm making this up?) through a 2008 London flooded by rising sea levels—though it looks perfectly okay in the aerial shots, with the Thames barrier comfortably intact. There's no evident reason for the futuristic setting, nor indeed for much else in this witless shambles of unfunny genre recyclings, and in practice the sense of futurity is limited to a few token puddles and a lot of standard-issue Ridley Scott diffused lighting.

Even horror, one of the most stable, consistent, and (in proportion to its costs) profitable fantasy genres of the past decade, had its worst year in recent memory. Stephen King's *Sleepwalkers,* his first writing direct for the big screen, was one of the sloppiest, silliest, least-exciting things he's done, and ironically found itself massively outperformed by a straight SF movie he spent much of the summer suing to have his name taken off: the picture originally released as *Stephen King's The Lawnmower Man.* King's cisatlantic opposite number, Clive Barker, came off better, not only with the nonsensical yet quite entertaining *Hellraiser III: Hell on Earth* but also (especially) with *Candyman,* Bernard Rose's impressive and scary adaptation of Barker's short story "The Forbidden," easily the most successful horror flick of the year both critically and commercially. But otherwise it was a lean year in which the longest-running horror series gave us no new entries, and in which the *Hellraiser, Gate,* and *Scanners* sequels were disappointing even by the standards of their predecessors. The same went for Sam Raimi's long-awaited *Army of Darkness: Evil Dead 3,* a slapstick medieval gore farce with a lazy script and a depressing contempt for its genre.

So what fantasy genres did make it against the odds in 1992? A few striking patterns emerge. The most prominent—hardly new, but doing strong business—was the Dumb Valley-People comedy, presumably riding the success of the *Bill and Ted* pictures. Thus we were introduced to laugh-along teenage halfwits in *Encino Man* (inexplicably Caucasian-looking California caveman gets frozen in ice, dug out in 1992, discovers babes and the magic of rock 'n' roll, creates havoc at senior prom, etc.; audience looks hard at watch) and to the really quite entertaining *Buffy the Vampire Slayer* (high-school ditz queen turns out to be current incarnation of Van Helsing, swaps cheerleading for thrusting stakes through chest cavities of undead). Alas, the *Bill and Ted* writing team of Chris Matheson and Ed Solomon had less luck than either of the above as they attempted to repeat the magic with adult leads in *Mom and Dad Save the World* (mad emperor Jon Lovitz kidnaps Teri Garr to planet of space idiots, obliging her and hopeless couch-thing hubby Jeffrey Jones to overthrow usurping tyrant, etc.; audience stays resolutely home and orders pizza). A close relative of the last, with Seattle for L.A. and with Jones now the villain, was Peter Hyams's *Stay Tuned,* a mild and infantile *Mad* magazine–style satire about parents duped into signing away Dad's soul for 666 channels of round-the-clock infernal cable action, leaping from one toothless TV spoof to the next with the desperate energy of a film that knows speed is the only thing that can save it.

There was also a curious boom, beginning with last year's *Late for Dinner,* in the Fish-Out-of-Water Popsicle-People picture, including not only the aforementioned *Encino Man* but the much more likable *Universal Soldier* and *Forever Young.* All of these involved fantastically implausible scenarios by which characters from vanished epochs are iceboxed and defrosted in the present day, where they one way or another escape the attentions of killjoy scientists and military folks to pursue their own historical fulfillments in the resolution of outstanding debts. Thus *Universal Soldier* had unlikely all-American MIAs Dolph Lundgren and Jean-Claude Van Damme deep-frozen by the military to be reanimated and reprogrammed in the nineties as an elite, bioengineered cyborg SWAT force—a magnificently daft concept made palatable by some vigorous action sequences and an uncharacteristically humanoid performance from Van Damme as the dead man hunting down his memories of life. Still more shamelessly and enjoyably, the hankie-romance *Forever Young* had thirties flying ace Mel Gibson volunteering for a cryogenic experiment after his best girl got knocked into a movie coma, to wake in 1992 with the tear-jerking task of finding his eightysomething true-love before irreversible makeup side effects lay waste to him.

Well, future historians will probably take it as truism that not only these last two films, but at least 80 percent of all cinema fantasy in the nineties, are thinly veiled allegories on AIDS (a possibility of which *Alien*[3] and *Dracula* were both at least discreetly aware, and with which both dealt rather more delicately than might have been expected). If so, they'll certainly have a field day with the miscast and overblown immortality farce *Death Becomes Her*, in which the rival efforts of Meryl Streep and Goldie Hawn to stave off the natural disintegration of the flesh lead to ever more grotesque and irreparable bodily decrepitude. Saddled for once with a lifeless script on an uninspiring concept, even the usually dependable Robert Zemeckis could do little more than plaster the cracks with cosmetic layers of forlorn zaniness and mayhem.

Still, there's no concealing that forbidden sexual chemistry between inhabitants of different worlds, whether moral, temporal, or metaphysical, was one of the year's favorite motifs. If 1992's SF movies had a dominant theme, it was all the different sorts of people you're not supposed to have sex with. The most remarkable restriction was in *Highway to Hell*, a passable gag movie that had eloping virgin Kristy Swanson abducted by Satan merely for permitting her beau to discuss the possibility that they might find a motel before they find a JP. But the long list also includes inhabitants of uncommon moral spaces (*Batman Returns*); tasty but regrettably undead ravening blood monsters (*Dracula, Sleepwalkers*); unkillable cyborg assassins (*Uni-*

versal Soldier); Charles Dance (*Alien*[3]); and, most emphatically, cartoon characters (*Cool World*).

In *Cool World*, the latest in Ralph Bakshi's long line of bold but ultimately self-destructive attempts at an "adult" animated feature, convicted murderer Gabriel Byrne makes a new career in jail as a comics artist, falls in love with his sex-doll heroine, and finds himself sucked into her universe for a bout of graphic hanky-panky that turns her into Kim Basinger and sends both back to the real world, where they find their unnatural lust has destabilized the dimensional boundary and unleashed a plague that turns flesh into grisly graphics. Beneath the weak, inadequately motivated plot and characters, an ending that respects no known narrative laws, and the unfailingly ugly, clichéd, and garish Bakshi artwork, there do lurk some genuinely dark and provocative ideas about the roots of the comics imagination, and about the kind of personality that might find it congenial to create universes of random violence populated by waistless sex kittens and grunting dwarfs. But as always, Bakshi's ambitions far outreach his power to deliver as either storyteller or technician, and his crap-detector seems to be switched permanently off.

It's Bakshi's misfortune, of course, to have survived into the second golden age of Hollywood animation, with Disney's autumn fairy-tale features the most consistent critical and box-office overachievers since the decade began. After *The Little Mermaid* and *Beauty and the Beast* came *Aladdin*, latest in what for all its charms is looking increasingly like a formulaic series (foreground the Barbie & Ken romance, anthropomorphize the furniture, correct the sexual politics). *Aladdin* at least dented the mold slightly, giving us a male lead and some looser, more adventurous characterizations and visuals. Interestingly, the attempt to animate the metamorphic style of Robin Williams's scattershot improvisations proved a good deal more satisfying than the equivalent, live-action scenes in *Toys*; and Williams surfaced again in the year's major independent animated feature, the Australian *FernGully—The Last Rainforest*.

FernGully is a nakedly didactic piece, based on Diana Young's stories about the guardian fairies of the Queensland rain forest and their struggle to protect their ancient habitat against the human encroachment of logging and clearance. On paper, it sounds like the sort of thing to send even the most ecologically upright adult into spasms of projectile puking, but actually the movie is a lot more bearable than it sounds, thanks to a brisk storyline, attractive backgrounds, and a remarkable tricontinental cast of unlikely voice characterizations, down to the ubiquitous Williams as a fruit bat. The queasy thing, of course, is the way that, for all of *FernGully*'s good intentions, the environmental crisis becomes an opportunity to make money out of children's consciences, and the coming generation that has the responsibility and, nascently, the will to do something about the problem is tacitly patronized with the insinuation that such concerns are for kids and thinking about solutions equivalent to belief in fairies.

No such moral dilemmas for the British-backed *Lawnmower Man,* surely the year's most barefaced and calculated piece of moviemaking opportunism. This, of course, was the Stephen King title purchased in a package deal and slapped onto a recycled version of an earlier, completely unrelated screenplay, *CyberGod* by director Brett Leonard, who then brazenly rejigged his central character into a free-lance grass cutter. The picture enjoyed a highly profitable release before a court ruled that little black stickers had to go up on all the remaining posters, covering the irate King's name. This amusing sideshow rather diverted attention from Leonard's scarcely less cheeky billing of this cybernetic retread of *Charly* meets *Carrie* as the "First Virtual Reality Movie!" Happily (in view of the current risible state of VR arcade technology, to say nothing of the practicalities of eating popcorn safely in a goggle helmet), this turned out to mean "first movie to drop the words 'virtual reality' extensively throughout its script." Despite weak plotting, underwritten characters, cover-your-ears dialogue, and a thoroughly ludicrous premise (scientist makes half-wit gardener superintelligent and psychic on a diet of concentrated VR games), it emerged as a surprisingly entertaining and competent movie, with some genuine touches of intelligence and pathos in the observation of its hero's rise to genius and subsequent psychotic disintegration.

Some similar ideas about the impact of games technology surfaced in the ill-fated and much less forgivable *Toys,* Barry Levinson's fifteen-years-brewing project about a struggle between childlike Robin Williams and militaristic Michael Gambon for the soul of their deceased father's surrealistic toy company. Hugely unsatisfying, with its opulent sets and pervasive whimsy, and with its deliberate disdain of easy comedy, simple characterizations, and ordinary narrative momentum, this was nevertheless the film that tried hardest to say something about the world of 1992 and the cultural paradoxes that beset it. Despite the script's cobwebs, its fiercely moralistic discussion of play and the exploitation of childhood is dressed up in remarkably contemporary terms: the displacement of traditional toys by the new computer-game culture and the phenomenon's behavioral implications; the "new war" (technologically and politically) that fortuitously premiered in the Persian Gulf as the project was emerging from turnaround; the coincidence of interest between the leisure market and the military-industrial complex, here fantasized as a bizarre conspiracy to reinvigorate the Department of Defense by secretly turning video kids into military cybernauts. It would be nice to be able to state that *Toys* managed, alone in its year, to say something of value about these massive issues; instead, its deluge of whimsy merely buried them in inconsequentiality and incoherence.

By and large, it wasn't a good year for portentous issue movies. An even sterner object lesson was *Radio Flyer,* a much-interrupted project that began as one of the high-profile million-plus scripts in the short-lived but frenetic bidding wars of 1990–91. Writer David Mickey Evans was replaced as director by Richard Donner, who recast and relocated the production. Even so, the bleak storyline, about a pair of abused children who seek escape from their intolerable lives in a homemade flying machine, was commercially risky in principle and inevitably softened and compromised in practice, with the horrors off-screened and the uneasy dialogue between fantasy and grim reality far from resolved by the problematic ending.

The best and strangest SF films of 1992 came not surprisingly from farthest outside the Hollywood system, with three of the most extraordinary visions financed from beyond the English-speaking world altogether. Despite (or because of) the audience momentum generated by the stormy demise of its parent TV show, David Lynch's *Twin Peaks—Fire Walk with Me* had to go to a French company for backing, and was much more sympathetically received in Europe than in the U.S. People polarize over Lynch, of course; some get a scary Jehovah's-Witness look in their eyes at the merest drop of his name, while just as many use his reputation as target practice for withering sneers of contempt. But from any middle vantage the *Twin Peaks* movie is extraordinarily fine work, at its most moving, as well as its funniest, when it distances itself farthest from the haphazard assortment of residual characters surviving from the original series, and, in its central evocation of the nightmare of adolescence, one of the few truly resonant and haunting pictures of the year. Like many—including Lara Flynn Boyle, whose pivotal character had to be recast for the movie—I'm unhappy about Lynch's relentless interest in the abuse of women, however condemned, and by his easy virgin/whore categorizations. But the Laura Palmer character is certainly the most mature and sympathetic of his studies, and the emotional power of Sheryl Lee's astonishing performance here makes the incidental sillinesses effortless to forgive.

Anyone readily put off by violence against women on film would be well advised to forget all about Shinya Tsukamoto's *Tetsuo* films, in the first of which (*The Iron Man*, finally granted a limited U.S. release early in the year) the hero's girlfriend is raped to death by a gigantic rotating-bladed steel phallus, and in the second of which (*Body Hammer*) the same character watches his mother penetrated at gunpoint by his father, apparently with pleasure until the moment where he blows away her throat as he climaxes. Nobody has to feel happy about this stuff, which has deep, ancient cultural roots in the deranged and exhilarating *manga* comics tradition, and which is hard to discuss without analyzing the whole paradoxical role played by images of torture and sexual violence in the outwardly placid Japanese society. But simply as cinema, the *Tetsuo* movies are like nothing else on earth—not even the animated *manga* features like *Akira*, which have become quite familiar and popular on sell-through in the U.K. thanks to some vigorous promotion by Island Video. In both *The Iron Man* and *Body Hammer*, a demented bombardment of handheld live-action camerawork, frenetic Svankmajeresque stop-motion effects, and wall-to-wall thunderous sound combine with blitzkrieg editing, dizzily fragmented chronology, and weird subtitled dialogue that seems not quite of our dimension, to tell a minimal story—the second film is in effect the first, remade with a proper budget—of a staid Tokyo businessman who finds his flesh mutating into scrap metal and his sanity warping in and out of hallucination. Persecuted by an enigmatic and deadly man-machine opponent, he finds their paths inexorably converging toward a final explosive duel to the finish between rival metal mutants, as the truth of his own destiny intertwines with that of his nemesis. *The Iron Man*, a bare sixty-five minutes in black and white, closed with the victorious monstrosity of metal and flesh heading onto the Tokyo streets intending to "mutate the whole world into metal"; *Body Hammer* makes a fair go of doing just that, with a vastly more ambitious—and mercifully linear—tale of bottled-down Oedipal psychosis erupting, at moments of stress, through the hero's horrified flesh in the form of ever more colossal guns ejaculating involuntary spasms of cannon fire.

Best of all, though, was another mutant outgrowth of a thriving comics culture, *bande dessinée* renegades Jean-Pierre Jeunet and Marc Caro's amazingly accomplished feature debut, *Delicatessen*. Set in a grimy postapocalyptic Paris where cannibal enclaves survive on a treacherous black market in human meat, it follows the gruesomely farcical intrigues of a collapsing tenement ruled and terrorized by a psychotic butcher who hires junior staff to slaughter and feed to his tenants, until one ex–circus assistant proves resourceful enough to threaten his grisly regime. A gorgeous cast of rubber-faced oddballs and an unfailing abundance of offbeat visual and situational invention, not to mention the most surreal and exquisite music score in years, more than compensate for any shortcomings in logic and background. Entirely original and completely cinematic, it couldn't be further from a Hollywood that keeps trying to create new forms of life from the old recombinant techniques, and consistently ends up with half-functioning chimeras. With its bright eyes, shiny coat, and hyperactive scampering gait, *Delicatessen* comes from a different gene pool altogether; and its confident parable of quicksilver circus-boy's triumph over bloated cannibal despot is one at which Hollywood itself might justifiably quake.

Song of the Martian Cricket

David Lunde

The concept of "science-fiction poetry" has always struck me as somewhat paradoxical. On the one hand: poetry, the oldest literary form. On the other: science fiction, the voice of futuristic speculation. Even at its most avant-garde, poetry partakes of the past. Even at its most hidebound, science fiction looks resolutely forward.

Whenever I manage to overcome my cerebral objections to the notion of SF poetry, though, and actually read the stuff, I am often quite pleasantly surprised. In assembling last year's Nebula anthology, for example, I found myself enthusiastically including a Best Short Story finalist that was in reality a poem: W. Gregory Stewart's "the button, and what you know."

In 1992, Stewart's astonishing parable was voted Best Long Poem (over fifty lines) by the judges of the Rhysling Awards, a competition sponsored by the Science Fiction Poetry Association and named for the "Blind Singer of the Spaceways" featured in Robert Heinlein's "The Green Hills of Earth." Traditionally, each year's Rhysling winners appear in the corresponding Nebula anthology, but because "the button" has already graced this series, I'm unable to reprint it here. What I *am* about to offer you is the Rhysling winner for Best Short Poem (under fifty lines), David Lunde's "Song of the Martian Cricket."

David Lunde was born in Berkeley, California, in 1941 and grew up in Saudi Arabia. He is currently Professor of English and Director of Creative Writing at SUNY College in Fredonia, New York. His poems, short stories, and translations have been published in over a hundred and fifty periodicals and anthologies, including *The Iowa Review, Seneca Review, TriQuarterly, Mother Earth News,* and *Isaac Asimov's Science Fiction Magazine.* A five-time nominee for the Nebula Award, Lunde won the Academy of American Poets Prize in 1967.

"I was driving home from Fredonia one night when a particularly glorious full moon rose over the hills," Lunde tells us, "lighting up the vineyards interspersed with patches of woods. I was wishing that my wife were with me to enjoy it and missing her badly. She had been attending graduate school at the University of Utah for the last four years, and the long separations between visits were painful. Before my journey ended, I had managed to compose most of 'Song of the Martian Cricket' in my head, transposing my longings to a science-fictional setting: a research station on the first Mars base."

(for Marilyn)

I shouldn't come out here
so many nights, turning
my faceplate to the black sky
with the tasteless, artificial air
whispering in and out of my lungs—
the only sound besides the directional beep
from Marsbase below, a subaudial promise
of security, but not comfort.
It's not the pressure suit I mind
so much, not even the bottomless
black bucket of stars—I miss the moon
pregnant with promise, and the light,
grassy breeze coasting over the hill
to blow the soft strands of your hair
across my lips, and the sound of crickets
grinding their legs with need. Still,
I come out too often and stare
into the abyss of years, then rise,
feeling almost bodiless in the low gravity,
and drift back to the floodlit dome
small and forlorn beneath
its protective covering of dust.

Vinland the Dream

KIM STANLEY ROBINSON

In 1984 the renowned SF editor Terry Carr undertook to revive his celebrated Ace Science Fiction Specials series, the publishing project that in
the late sixties had premiered such award-winning novels as Alexei Panshin's
Rite of Passage and Ursula K. Le Guin's *The Left Hand of Darkness*. It is
a singular tribute to Kim Stanley Robinson that his first novel, *The Wild
Shore*, was selected to inaugurate the new round of Ace Specials, appearing
in advance of both Lucius Shepard's *Green Eyes* and William Gibson's
Neuromancer.

By the turn of the decade, it was clear that Robinson had conceived
The Wild Shore—a poetic postholocaust story set in his native California—
as the first volume of a cycle, the Orange County Trilogy, which continued
with *The Gold Coast* and concluded with *Pacific Edge*. In 1983 he won a
World Fantasy Award for his story "Black Air," and five years later "The
Blind Geometer" earned him a Nebula for Best Novella. His short fiction
is collected in *The Planet on the Table* and *Remaking History*. With his
recent, critically acclaimed *Red Mars*, he begins an ambitious cycle of hard-
SF novels that will eventually include *Green Mars* and *Blue Mars*.

"I've always been fascinated by tales of the Norse exploration of Vinland," Robinson says of his Nebula-nominated story. "But some of the
greatest of these accounts aren't true—the fatal trek from Hudson Bay to
Minnesota as chronicled by the Kensington stone, for instance, or the voyages
implied by the truly beautiful Vinland map found in New Haven in the
sixties. These were both hoaxes, 'alternate histories' that pretended to be
true histories."

Abstract. It was sunset at L'Anse aux Meadows. The water of the bay
was still, the boggy beach was dark in the shadows. Flat arms of land
pointed to flat islands offshore; beyond these a taller island stood like
a loaf of stone in the sea, catching the last of the day's light. A stream
gurgled gently as it cut through the beach bog. Above the bog, on a
narrow grassy terrace, one could just make out a pattern of low
mounds, all that remained of sod walls. Next to them were three or
four sod buildings, and beyond the buildings, a number of tents.

A group of people—archaeologists, graduate students, volunteer laborers, visitors—moved together onto a rocky ridge overlooking the site. Some of them worked at starting a campfire in a ring of blackened stones; others began to unpack bags of food and cases of beer. Far across the water lay the dark bulk of Labrador. Kindling caught and their fire burned, a spark of yellow in the dusk's gloom.

Hot dogs and beer, around a campfire by the sea; and yet it was strangely quiet. Voices were subdued. The people on the hill glanced down often at the site, where the head of their dig, a lanky man in his early fifties, was giving a brief tour to their distinguished guest. The distinguished guest did not appear pleased.

Introduction. The head of the dig, an archaeology professor from McGill University, was looking at the distinguished guest with the expression he wore when confronted by an aggressive undergraduate. The distinguished guest, Canada's Minister of Culture, was asking question after question. As she did, the professor took her to look for herself, at the forge, and the slag pit, and the little midden beside Building E. New trenches were cut across the mounds and depressions, perfect rectangular slashes in the black peat; they could tell the minister nothing of what they had revealed. But she had insisted on seeing them, and now she was asking questions that got right to the point, although they could have been asked and answered just as well in Ottawa. Yes, the professor explained, the fuel for the forge was wood charcoal, the temperature had gotten to around 1,200 degrees Celsius, the process was direct reduction of bog ore, obtaining about one kilogram of iron for every five kilograms of slag. All was as it was in other Norse forges—except that the limonites in the bog ore had now been precisely identified by spectroscopic analysis; and that analysis had revealed that the bog iron smelted here had come from northern Quebec, near Chicoutimi. The Norse explorers, who had supposedly smelted the bog ore, could not have obtained it.

There was a similar situation in the midden; rust migrated in peat at a known rate, and so it could be determined that the many iron rivets in the midden had been there only a hundred and forty years, plus or minus fifty.

"So," the minister said, in English with a Francophone lilt, "you have proved your case, it appears?"

The professor nodded wordlessly. The minister watched him, and he couldn't help feeling that despite the nature of the news he was giving her, she was somewhat amused. By him? By his scientific terminology? By his obvious (and growing) depression? He couldn't tell.

The minister raised her eyebrows. "L'Anse aux Meadows, a hoax. Parcs Canada will not like it at all."

"No one will like it," the professor croaked.

"No," the minister said, looking at him. "I suppose not. Particularly as this is part of a larger pattern, yes?"

The professor did not reply.

"The entire concept of Vinland," she said. "A hoax!"

The professor nodded glumly.

"I would not have believed it possible."

"No," the professor said. "But"—he waved a hand at the low mounds around them—"so it appears." He shrugged. "The story has always rested on a very small body of evidence. Three sagas, this site, a few references in Scandinavian records, a few coins, a few cairns. . . ." He shook his head. "Not much." He picked up a chunk of dried peat from the ground, crumbled it in his fingers.

Suddenly the minister laughed at him, then put her hand to his upper arm. Her fingers were warm. "You must remember it is not your fault."

He smiled wanly. "I suppose not." He liked the look on her face; sympathetic as well as amused. She was about his age, perhaps a bit older. An attractive and sophisticated Québecois. "I need a drink," he confessed.

"There's beer on the hill."

"Something stronger. I have a bottle of cognac I haven't opened yet. . . ."

"Let's get it and take it up there with us."

Experimental Methods. The graduate students and volunteer laborers were gathered around the fire, and the smell of roasting hot dogs filled the air. It was nearly eleven, the sun a half hour gone, and the last light of the summer dusk slowly leaked from the sky. The fire burned like a beacon. Beer had been flowing freely, and the party was beginning to get a little more boisterous.

The minister and the professor stood near the fire, drinking cognac out of plastic cups.

"How did you come to suspect the story of Vinland?" the minister asked as they watched the students cook hot dogs.

A couple of the volunteer laborers, who had paid good money to spend their summer digging trenches in a bog, heard the question and moved closer.

The professor shrugged. "I can't quite remember." He tried to laugh. "Here I am an archaeologist, and I can't remember my own past."

The minister nodded as if that made sense. "I suppose it was a long time ago?"

"Yes." He concentrated. "Now what was it? Someone was following up the story of the Vinland map, to try and figure out who had done it. The map showed up in a bookstore in New Haven in the 1950s—as you may know?"

"No," the minister said. "I hardly know a thing about Vinland, I assure you. Just the basics that anyone in my position would have to know."

"Well, there was a map found in the 1950s called the Vinland map, and it was shown to be a hoax soon after its discovery. But when this investigator traced the map's history, she found that the book it had been in was accounted for all the way back to the 1820s, map and all. It meant the hoaxer had lived longer ago than I had expected." He refilled his cup of cognac, then the minister's. "There were a lot of Viking hoaxes in the nineteenth century, but this one was so early. It surprised me. It's generally thought that the whole phenomenon was stimulated by a book that a Danish scholar published in 1837, containing translations of the Vinland sagas and related material. The book was very popular among the Scandinavian settlers in America, and after that, you know . . . a kind of twisted patriotism, or the response of an ethnic group that had been made fun of too often. . . . So we got the Kensington stone, the halberds, the mooring holes, the coins. But if a hoax predated *Antiquitates Americanae* . . . it made me wonder."

"If the book itself were somehow involved?"

"Exactly," the professor said, regarding the minister with pleasure. "I wondered if the book might not incorporate, or have been inspired by, hoaxed material. Then one day I was reading a description of the fieldwork here, and it occurred to me that this site was a bit too pristine. As if it had been built but never lived in. Best estimates for its occupation were as low as one summer, because they couldn't find any trash middens to speak of, or graves."

"It could have been occupied very briefly," the minister pointed out.

"Yes, I know. That's what I thought at the time. But then I heard from a colleague in Bergen that the *Gronlendinga Saga* was apparently a forgery, at least in the parts referring to the discovery of Vinland. Pages had been inserted that dated back to the 1820s. After that, I had a doubt that wouldn't go away."

"But there are more Vinland stories than that one, yes?"

"Yes. There are three main sources. The *Gronlendinga Saga, The Saga of Erik the Red,* and the part of *The Hauksbók* that tells about Thorfinn Karlsefni's expedition. But with one of those questioned, I began to doubt them all. And the story itself. Everything having to do with the idea of Vinland."

"Is that when you went to Bergen?" a graduate student asked.

The professor nodded. He drained his plastic cup, felt the alcohol rushing through him. "I joined Nielsen there and we went over *Erik the Red* and *The Hauksbók,* and damned if the pages in those concerning Vinland weren't forgeries too. The ink gave it away—not its composition, which was about right, but merely how long it had been on that paper. Which was thirteenth-century paper, I might add! The forger had done a super job. But the sagas had been tampered with sometime in the early nineteenth century."

"But those are masterpieces of world literature," a volunteer laborer exclaimed, round-eyed; the ads for volunteer labor had not included a description of the primary investigator's hypothesis.

"I know," the professor said irritably, and shrugged.

He saw a chunk of peat on the ground, picked it up, and threw it on the blaze. After a bit it flared up.

"It's like watching dirt burn," he said absently, staring into the flames.

Discussion. The burnt-garbage smell of peat wafted downwind, and offshore the calm water of the bay was riffled by the same gentle breeze. The minister warmed her hands at the blaze for a moment, then gestured at the bay. "It's hard to believe they were never here at all."

"I know," the professor said. "It looks like a Viking site, I'll give him that."

"Him," the minister repeated.

"I know, I know. This whole thing forces you to imagine a man in the eighteen-twenties and -thirties, traveling all over—Norway, Iceland, Canada, New England, Rome, Stockholm, Denmark, Greenland. . . . Crisscrossing the North Atlantic, to bury all these signs." He shook his head. "It's incredible."

He retrieved the cognac bottle and refilled. He was, he had to admit, beginning to feel drunk. "And so many parts of the hoax were well hidden! You can't assume we've found them all. This place had two butternuts buried in the midden, and butternuts only grow down below the St. Lawrence, so who's to say they aren't clues, indicating another site down there? That's where grapevines actually grow, which would justify the name Vinland. I tell you, the more I know about this hoaxer, the more certain I am that other sites exist. The tower in Newport, Rhode Island, for instance—the hoaxer didn't build that, because it's been around since the seventeenth century—but a little work out there at night, in the early nineteenth century . . . I bet if it were excavated completely, you'd find a few Norse artifacts."

"Buried in all the right places," the minister said.

"Exactly." The professor nodded. "And up the coast of Labrador, at Cape Porcupine where the sagas say they repaired a ship. There too. Stuff scattered everywhere, left to be discovered or not."

The minister waved her plastic cup. "But surely this site must have been his masterpiece. He couldn't have done too many as extensive as this."

"I shouldn't think so." The professor drank deeply, smacked his numbed lips. "Maybe one more like this, down in New Brunswick. That's my guess. But this was surely one of his biggest projects."

"It was a time for that kind of thing," the volunteer laborer offered. "Atlantis, Mu, Lemuria . . ."

The minister nodded. "It fulfills a certain desire."

"Theosophy, most of that," the professor muttered. "This was different."

The volunteer wandered off. The professor and the minister looked into the fire for a while.

"You are *sure?*" the minister asked.

The professor nodded. "Trace elements show the ore came from upper Quebec. Chemical changes in the peat weren't right. And nuclear resonance dating methods show that the bronze pin they found hadn't been buried long enough. Little things like that. Nothing obvious. He was amazingly meticulous, he really thought it out. But the nature of things tripped him up. Nothing more than that."

"But the effort!" the minister said. "This is what I find hard to believe. Surely it must have been more than one man! Burying these objects, building the walls—surely he would have been noticed!"

The professor stopped another swallow, nodded at her as he choked once or twice. A broad wave of the hand, a gasping recovery of breath:

"Fishing village, kilometer north of here. Boarding house in the early nineteenth century. A crew of ten rented rooms in the summer of 1842. Bills paid by a Mr. Carlsson."

The minister raised her eyebrows. "Ah."

One of the graduate students got out a guitar and began to play. The other students and the volunteers gathered around her.

"So," the minister said, "Mr. Carlsson. Does he show up elsewhere?"

"There was a Professor Ohman in Bergen. A Dr. Bergen in Reykjavík. In the right years, studying the sagas. I presume they were all him, but I don't know for sure."

"What do you know about him?"

"Nothing. No one paid much attention to him. I've got him on a couple transatlantic crossings, I think, but he used aliases, so I've probably missed most of them. A Scandinavian-American, apparently Norwegian by birth. Someone with some money—someone with patriotic feelings of some kind—someone with a grudge against a university—who knows? All I have are a few signatures, of aliases at that. A flowery handwriting. Nothing more. That's the most remarkable thing about him! You see, most hoaxers leave clues to their identities, because a part of them wants to be caught. So their cleverness can be admired, or the ones who fell for it embarrassed, or whatever. But this guy didn't want to be discovered. And in those days, if you wanted to stay off the record . . ." He shook his head.

"A man of mystery."

"Yeah. But I don't know how to find out anything more about him."

The professor's face was glum in the firelight as he reflected on this. He polished off another cup of cognac. The minister watched him drink, then said kindly, "There is nothing to be done about it, really. That is the nature of the past."

"I know."

Conclusions. They threw the last big logs on the fire, and flames roared up, yellow licks breaking free among the stars. The professor felt numb all over, his heart was cold, the firelit faces were smeary primitive masks, dancing in the light. The songs were harsh and raucous, he couldn't understand the words. The wind was chilling, and the hot skin of his arms and neck goose-pimpled uncomfortably. He felt sick with alcohol, and knew it would be a while before his body could overmaster it.

The minister led him away from the fire, then up the rocky ridge. Getting him away from the students and laborers, no doubt, so he wouldn't embarrass himself. Starlight illuminated the heather and broken granite under their feet. He stumbled. He tried to explain to her what it meant, to be an archaeologist whose most important work was the discovery that a bit of their past was a falsehood.

"It's like a mosaic," he said, drunkenly trying to follow the fugitive thought. "A puzzle with most of the pieces gone. A tapestry. And if you pull a thread out . . . it's ruined. So little lasts! We need every bit we can find!"

She seemed to understand. In her student days, she told him, she had waitressed at a café in Montreal. Years later she had gone down the street to have a look, just for nostalgia's sake. The café was gone. The street was completely different. And she couldn't remember the names of any of the people she had worked with. "This was my own past, not all that many years ago!"

The professor nodded. Cognac was rushing through his veins, and as he looked at the minister, so beautiful in the starlight, she seemed to him a kind of muse, a spirit sent to comfort him, or frighten him, he couldn't tell which. Cleo, he thought. The muse of history. Someone he could talk to.

She laughed softly. "Sometimes it seems our lives are much longer than we usually think. So that we live through incarnations, and looking back later we have nothing but . . ." She waved a hand.

"Bronze pins," the professor said. "Iron rivets."

"Yes." She looked at him. Her eyes were bright in the starlight. "We need an archaeology for our own lives."

Acknowledgments. Later he walked her back to the fire, now reduced to banked red coals. She put her hand to his upper arm as they walked, steadying herself, and he felt in the touch some kind of portent, but couldn't understand it. He had drunk so much! Why be so upset about it, why? It was his job to find the truth; having found it, he should be happy! Why had no one told him what he would feel?

The minister said good night. She was off to bed; she suggested he do likewise. Her look was compassionate, her voice firm.

When she was gone he hunted down the bottle of cognac, and drank the rest of it. The fire was dying, the students and workers scattered—in the tents, or out in the night, in couples.

He walked by himself back down to the site.

Low mounds, of walls that had never been. Beyond the actual site were rounded buildings, models built by the park service, to show tourists what the "real" buildings had looked like. When Vikings had camped on the edge of the new world. Repairing their boats. Finding food. Fighting among themselves, mad with epic jealousies. Fighting the dangerous Indians. Getting killed, and then driven away from this land, so much lusher than Greenland.

A creak in the brush and he jumped, startled. It would have been like that: death in the night, creeping up on you—he turned with a jerk, and every starlit shadow bounced with hidden skraelings, their bows drawn taut, their arrows aimed at his heart. He quivered, hunched over.

But no. It hadn't been like that. Not at all. Instead, a man with spectacles and a bag full of old junk, directing some unemployed sailors as they dug. Nondescript, taciturn, nameless; one night he would have wandered back there into the forest, perhaps fallen or had a heart attack—become a skeleton wearing leathers and sword-belt, with spectacles over the skull's eyesockets, the anachronism that gave him away at last. . . . The professor staggered over the low mounds toward the trees, intent on finding that inadvertent grave. . . .

But no. It wouldn't be there. The taciturn figure hadn't been like that. He would have been far away when he died, nothing to show what he had spent years of his life doing. A man in a hospital for the poor, the bronze pin in his pocket overlooked by the doctor, stolen by an undertaker's assistant. An anonymous figure, to the grave and beyond. The creator of Vinland. Never to be found.

The professor looked around, confused and sick. There was a waist-high rock, a glacial erratic. He sat on it. Put his head in his hands. Really quite unprofessional. All those books he had read as a child. What would the minister think! Grant money. No reason to feel so bad!

At that latitude midsummer nights are short, and the party had lasted late. The sky to the east was already gray. He could see down onto the site, and its long sod roofs. On the beach, a trio of long narrow high-ended ships. Small figures in furs emerged from the longhouses and went down to the water, and he walked among them and heard their speech, a sort of dialect of Norwegian that he could mostly understand. They would leave that day, it was time to load the ships. They were going to take everything with them, they didn't plan to return. Too many skraelings in the forest, too many quick arrow deaths. He walked among them, helping them load stores. Then a little man in a black coat scurried behind the forge, and he roared and took off after him, scooping up a rock on the way, ready to deal out a skraeling death to that black intruder.

The minister woke him with a touch of her hand. He almost fell off the rock. He shook his head; he was still drunk. The hang-over wouldn't begin for a couple more hours, though the sun was already up.

"I should have known all along," he said to her angrily. "They were stretched to the limit in Greenland, and the climate was worsening. It was amazing they got that far. Vinland . . ." He waved a hand at the site—"was just some dreamer's story."

Regarding him calmly, the minister said, "I am not sure it matters."

He looked up at her. "What do you mean?"

"History is made of stories people tell. And fictions, dreams, hoaxes—they also are made of stories people tell. True or false, it's the stories that matter to us. Certain qualities in the stories themselves make them true or false."

He shook his head. "Some things really happened in the past. And some things didn't."

"But how can you know for sure which is which? You can't go back and see for yourself. Maybe Vinland was the invention of this mysterious stranger of yours; maybe the Vikings came here after all, and landed somewhere else. Either way it can never be anything more than a story to us."

"But . . ." He swallowed. "Surely it matters whether it is a true story or not!"

She paced before him. "A friend of mine once told me something he had read in a book," she said. "It was by a man who sailed the Red Sea, long ago. He told of a servant boy on one of the dhows, who could not remember ever having been cared for. The boy had become a sailor at age three—before that, he had been a beachcomber." She stopped pacing and looked at the beach below them. "Often I imagined that little boy's life. Surviving alone on a beach, at that age—it astonished me. It made me . . . happy."

She turned to look at him. "But later I told this story to an expert in child development, and he just shook his head. 'It probably wasn't true,' he said. Not a lie, exactly, but a . . .'"

"A stretcher," the professor suggested.

"A stretcher, exactly. He supposed that the boy had been somewhat older, or had had some help. You know."

The professor nodded.

"But in the end," the minister said, "I found this judgment did not matter to me. In my mind I still saw that toddler, searching the tide pools for his daily food. And so for me the story lives. And that is all that matters. We judge all the stories from history like that— we value them according to how much they spur our imaginations."

The professor stared at her. He rubbed his jaw, looked around.

Things had the sharp-edged clarity they sometimes get after a sleepless night, as if glowing with internal light. He said, "Someone with opinions like yours probably shouldn't have the job that you do."

"I didn't know I had them," the minister said. "I only just came upon them in the last couple of hours, thinking about it."

The professor was surprised. "You didn't sleep?"

She shook her head. "Who could sleep on a night like this?"

"My feeling exactly!" He almost smiled. "So. A *nuit blanche,* you call it?"

"Yes," she said. "A *nuit blanche* for two." And she looked down at him with that amused glance of hers, as if . . . as if she understood him.

She extended her arms toward him, grasped his hands, helped pull him to his feet. They began to walk back toward the tents, across the site of L'Anse aux Meadows. The grass was wet with dew, and very green. "I still think," he said as they walked together, "that we want more than stories from the past. We want something not easily found—something, in fact, that the past doesn't have. Something secret, some secret meaning . . . something that will give our lives a kind of sense."

She slipped a hand under his arm. "We want the Atlantis of childhood. But, failing that . . ." She laughed and kicked at a clump of grass; a spray of dew flashed ahead of them, containing, for just one moment, a bright little rainbow.

Life Regarded as a Jigsaw Puzzle of Highly Lustrous Cats

MICHAEL BISHOP

So accustomed are we to thinking of science fiction as a "genre," it's easy to forget that the field is in fact far more diverse than the so-called mainstream. If John Updike and Danielle Steel ever found themselves seated together at dinner, they might not have anything to say to each other, but the fact would remain that their novels share many more aesthetic and metaphysical assumptions than do those of—for example—Michael Bishop and the author of the latest trilogy about a galactic empire or a quest for a golden codpiece. To put it another way: while it's possible to imagine a mildly demented incarnation of Updike writing the story you are about to read, it's impossible to imagine our codpiece trilogist doing so.

In 1982 Bishop's novelette "The Quickening" won the Nebula Award, and the following year that particular trophy also went to his astonishing time-travel novel, *No Enemy But Time*. His more recent books include *Philip K. Dick Is Dead, Alas; Unicorn Mountain; Count Geiger's Blues;* and, my personal favorite, the simultaneously moving and satiric *Ancient of Days*. His short fiction has been collected in *Blooded on Arachne, One Winter in Eden, Close Encounters with the Deity*, and *Emphatically Not SF, Almost*, and his editorial skills are on display in *Light Years and Dark, Nebula Awards 23, 24*, and *25*, and (with Ian Watson) *Changes*. In the spring of 1994, Bantam will publish his World War Two baseball fantasy, *Brittle Innings* (which recently sold to the movies), as a mainstream title.

Asked to describe the origin of "Life Regarded as a Jigsaw Puzzle of Highly Lustrous Cats"—the title, of course, is modeled on Samuel R. Delany's "Time Considered as a Helix of Semi-Precious Stones"—Bishop replied:

"In 1990 editor and fiction writer Jeanne Schinto purchased reprint rights to a fairly early story of mine called 'Dogs' Lives' for an Atlantic Monthly Press anthology, *The Literary Dog*. As its title probably suggests, this anthology features an unusual selection of stories by contemporary writers (among them Bobbie Ann Mason, John Updike, Doris Lessing, and Tobias Wolff) in which dogs play a pivotal, if not always leading, narrative or thematic role. It pleased me immensely, and still does, to have a story of mine in such company.

"While compiling *The Literary Dog*, Ms. Schinto proposed doing a companion volume centered on—you guessed it—cats. And she asked if I had a story that would fit that project too. I didn't. But shortly after she'd mentioned it, I began mulling over a companion piece to 'Dogs' Lives,' and the scenes constituting 'Life Regarded . . .' started shifting in kaleidoscope fragments through my wakeful, and even my dreaming, brain. Ms. Schinto liked the resultant story, but told me in a letter that her cat volume, owing to a surfeit of liked-theme anthologies, would never appear.

"At this point in my career, I've written and published nearly a hundred pieces of short fiction, from short-shorts to book-length novellas. 'Life Regarded . . .' ranks as my favorite because I view it as the best (i.e., the most heartfelt, the most aesthetically successful) of the whole disorderly lot. Some have hinted that my affection for it betrays only my total lack of objectivity, but I always think they haven't read it very carefully."

Your father-in-law, who insists that you call him Howie, even though you prefer Mr. Bragg, likes jigsaw puzzles. If they prove harder than he has the skill or the patience for, he knows a sneaky way around the problem.

During the third Christmas season after your marriage to Marti, you find Howie at a card table wearing a parka, a blue watch cap with a crown of burgundy leather, and fur-lined shoes. (December through February, it is freezing in the Braggs' Tudor-style house outside Spartanburg.) He is assembling a huge jigsaw puzzle, for the Braggs give him one every Christmas. His challenge is to put it together, unaided by drop-in company or any other family member, before the Sugar Bowl kickoff on New Year's Day.

This year, the puzzle is of cats.

The ESB procedure being administered to you by the Zoo Cop and his associates is keyed to cats. When they zap your implanted electrodes, cat-related memories parachute into your mind's eye, opening out like fireworks.

The lid from the puzzle's box is Mr. Bragg's—Howie's—blueprint, and it depicts a population explosion of stylized cats. They are both mysterious beasts and whimsical cartoons. The puzzle lacks any background, it's so full of cats. They run, stalk, lap milk, tussle, tongue-file their fur, snooze, etc., etc. There are no puzzle areas where a single color dominates, a serious obstacle to quick assembly.

Howie has a solution. When only a handful of pieces remain in the box, he uses a razor blade to shave any piece that refuses to fit where he wants it to. This is cheating, as even Howie readily acknowledges, but on New Year's Eve, with Dick Clark standing in Times Square and the Sugar Bowl game only hours away, a man can't afford to screw around.

"Looking good," you say as the crowd on TV starts its rowdy countdown to midnight. "You're almost there."

Howie confesses—complains?—that this puzzle has been a "real mind bender." He appreciates the challenge of a thousand-plus pieces and a crazy-making dearth of internal clues, but why this particular puzzle? He usually receives a photographic landscape or a Western painting by Remington.

"I'm not a cat fancier," he tells you. "Most of 'em're sneaky little bastards, don't you think?"

Marti likes cats, but when you get canned at Piedmont Freight in Atlanta, she moves back to Spartanburg with your son, Jacob, who may be allergic to cats. Marti leaves in your keeping two calico mongrels that duck out of sight whenever you try to feed or catch them. You catch them eventually, of course, and drive them to the pound in a plastic animal carrier that Marti bought from Delta, or Eastern, or some other airline out at Hartsfield.

Penfield, a.k.a. the Zoo Cop, wants to know how you lost your job. He gives you a multiple-choice quiz: A) companywide layoff; B) neglect of duty and/or unacceptable job performance; C) personality conflict with a supervisor; D) suspicion of disloyalty; E) all, or none, of the above.

You tell him that there was an incident of (alleged) sexual harassment involving a female secretary whose name, even under the impetus of electrical stimulation of the brain (ESB), you cannot now recall. All you can recall is every cat, real or imaginary, ever to etch its image into your consciousness.

After your firing, you take the cats, Springer and Ossie (short for Ocelot), to the pound. When you look back from the shelter's doorway, a teenage attendant is giving you, no doubt about it, the evil eye. Springer and Ossie are doomed. No one in the big, busy city wants a mixed-breed female. The fate awaiting nine-year-old Jacob's cats—never mind their complicity in his frightening asthma—is the gas chamber, but today you are as indifferent to the cats' fate as a latter-day Eichmann. You are numb from the molecular level upward.

"We did have them spayed," you defend yourself. "Couldn't you use that to pitch them to some nice family?"

You begin to laugh.

Is this another instance of Inappropriate Affect? Except for the laughing gas given you to sink the electrodes, you've now been off all medication for . . . you don't know how long.

On the street only three years after your dismissal, you wept at hoboes' bawdy jokes, got up and danced if the obituaries you'd been sleeping under reported an old friend's death.

Once, you giggled when a black girl bummed a cigarette in the parking lot of Trinity United Methodist: "I got AIDS, man. Hain't no smoke gonna kill me. Hain't time enough for the old lung cee to kick in, too."

Now that Penfield's taken you off antipsychotics, is Ye Old Inappropriate Affect kicking in again? Or is this fallout from the ESB? After all, one gets entirely different responses (rage and affection; fear and bravado) from zapping hypothalamic points less than two hundredths of an inch from each other.

Spill it, Adolf, Penfield says. What's so funny?

Cat juggling, you tell him. (Your name has never been Adolf.)

What?

Steve Martin in *The Jerk*. An illegal Mexican sport. A joke, you know. Cat juggling.

You surrender to jerky laughter. It hurts, but your glee isn't inappropriate. The movie was a comedy. People were *supposed* to laugh. Forget that when you close your eyes, you see yourself as the outlaw juggler. Forget that the cats in their caterwauling orbits include Springer, Ossie, Thai Thai, Romeo, and an anonymous albino kitten from your dead grandparents' grain crib on their farm outside Montgomery.

———

As a boy in Hapeville, the cat you like best is Thai Thai, a male Siamese that your mama and you inherit from the family moving out. His name isn't Thai Thai before your mama starts calling him that, though. It's something fake Chinese, like Lung Cee or Mouser Tung. The folks moving out don't want to take him with them; their daddy's got a job with Otero Steel in Pueblo, Colorado. Besides, Mouser Tung's not likely to appreciate the ice and snow out there. He's a Deep South cat, Dixie born and bred.

"You are who you are," Mama tells the Siamese while he rubs her laddered nylons, "but from here on out your *name* is Thai Thai."

"Why're you calling him that?" you ask her.

"Because it *fits* a cracker Siamese," she says.

It's several years later before you realize that Thailand is Siam's current name and that there's a gnat-plagued town southeast of Albany called, yeah, Ty Ty. Your mama's a smart gal, with an agile mind and a quirky sense of humor. How Daddy ever got it into his head that she wasn't good enough for him is a mystery.

It's her agile mind and her quirky sense of humor that did her in, the Zoo Cop says, pinching back your eyelid.

Anyway, Daddy ran off to a Florida dogtrack town with a chunky bottle-blond ex-hairdresser who dropped a few pounds and started a mail-order weight-loss-tonic business. He's been gone nine weeks and four days.

Thai Thai, when you notice him, is pretty decent company. He sheathes his claws when he's in your lap. He purrs at a bearable register. He eats leftover vegetables—peas, lima beans, spinach—as readily as he does bacon rinds or chicken scraps. A doll, Mama calls him. A gentleman.

This ESB business distorts stuff. It flips events, attitudes, preferences upside down. The last shall be first, the first shall be last. This focus on cats, for example, is a *major* distortion, a misleading reenvisioning of the life that you lived before getting trapped by Rockdale Biological Supply Company.

Can't Penfield see this? Uh-uh, no way. He's too hot to screw Rockdale Biological's bigwigs. The guy may have right on his side, but to him—for the moment, anyway—you're just another human oven cake. If you crumble when the heat's turned up, great, zip-a-dee-Zoo Cop, pop me a cold one, justice is served. Thing is, you prefer dogs. Even as a kid, you like them more. You bring home flea-bitten strays and beg to keep them. When you live in Alabama, you covet the liony chow, Simba, that waits every afternoon in the Notasulga schoolyard for Wesley Duplantier. Dogs, not cats. Until Mouser Tung—Thai Thai—all the cats you know prowl on the edges of your attention. Even Thai Thai comes to you and Mama, over here in Georgia, as a kind of offhand housewarming gift. Dogs, Mister Zoo Cop, not cats.

Actually, Penfield says, I'm getting the idea that what was in the *forefront* of your attention, Adolf, was women.

After puberty, your attention never *has* a forefront. You are dive-bombed by stimuli. Girls' faces are billboards. Their bodies are bigger billboards. Jigsawed ad signs. A piece here. A piece there. It isn't just girls. It's everything. Cars, buildings, TV talking heads, mosquito swarms, jet contrails, interchangeable male callers at suppertime, battle scenes on the six o'clock news, rock idols infinitely glitterized, the whole schmear fragmenting as it feeds into you, Mr. Teenage Black Hole of the Spirit. Except when romancing a sweet young gal, your head's a magnet for all the flak generated by the media-crazed twentieth century.

"You're tomcatting, aren't you?" Mama says. "You're tomcatting just like Webb did. God."

It's a way to stay focused. With their faces and bodies under you, they cease to be billboards. You're a human being again, not a radio receiver or a gravity funnel. The act imposes a fleeting order on the ricocheting chaos working every instant to turn you, the mind cementing it all together, into a flimsy cardboard box of mismatched pieces.

Is that tomcatting? Resisting, by a tender union of bodies, the consequences of dumping a jigsaw puzzle of cats into a box of pieces that, assembled, would depict, say, a unit of embattled flak gunners on Corregidor?

———

Christ, the Zoo Cop says, a more highfalutin excuse for chasing tail I've never heard.

Your high school is crawling with cats. Cool cats, punk cats, stray cats, dead cats. Some are human, some aren't. You dissect a cat in biology lab. On a plaster-of-paris base, guyed upright by wires, stands the bleached skeleton of a quadruped that Mr. Osteen—he's also the track and girls' softball coach—swears was a member of *Felis catus*, the common house cat.

With its underlying gauntness exposed and its skull gleaming brittle and grotesque, this skeleton resembles that of something prehistoric. Pamela van Rhyn and two or three other girls want to know where the cats in the lab came from.

"A scientific supply house," Coach Osteen says. "Same place we get our bullfrogs, our microscope slides, the insects in that there display case." He nods at it.

"Where does the supply house get them?" Pamela says.

"I don't know, Pammie. Maybe they raise 'em. Maybe they round up strays. You missing a kitty?"

In fact, rumor holds that Mr. Osteen found the living source of his skeleton behind the track field's south bleachers, chloroformed it, carried it home, and boiled the fur off it in a pot on an old stove in his basement. Because of the smell, his wife spent a week in Augusta with her mother. Rumor holds that cat lovers hereabouts would be wise to keep their pets indoors.

Slicing into the chest cavity of the specimen provided by the supply house, you find yourself losing it. You are the only boy in Coach Osteen's lab to contract nausea and an overwhelming uprush of self-disgust; the only boy, clammy palmed and light-headed, to have to leave the room. The ostensible shame of your departure is lost on Pamela, who agrees, in Nurse Mayhew's office, to rendezvous with you later that afternoon at the Huddle House.

"This is the heart," you can still hear Osteen saying. "Looks like a wet rubber strawberry, don't it?"

As a seven-year-old, you wander into the grain crib of the barn on the Powell farm. A one-eyed mongrel queen named Sky has dropped a litter on the deer hides, today stiff and rat-eaten, that Gramby Powell stowed there twenty or more years ago. Sky one-eyes you with real suspicion, all set to bolt or hiss, as you lean over a rail to study the blind quintet of her kittening.

They're not much, mere lumps. "Turds with fur," Gramby called them last night, to Meemaw Anita's scandalized dismay and the keen amusement of your daddy. They hardly move.

One kitten gleams white on the stiff hide, in a nervous curl of Sky's furry belly. You spit at Sky, as another cat would spit, but louder—*ssssphh! ssssphh!*—so that eventually, intimidated, she gets up, kittens falling from her like bombs from the open bay of a B-52, and slinks to the far wall of the crib.

You climb over the rail and pick up the white kitten, the Maybe Albino as Meemaw Anita dubbed it. "Won't know for sure," she said, "till its eyes're open."

You turn the kitten in your hands. Which end is which? It's sort of hard to say. Okay, here's the starchy white potato print of its smashed-in pug of a face: eyes shut, ears a pair of napkin folds, mouth a miniature crimson gap.

You rub the helpless critter on your cheek. Cat smells. Hay smells. Hide smells. It's hard not to sneeze.

It occurs to you that you could throw this Maybe Albino like a baseball. You could wind up like Denny McLain and fling it at the far wall of the grain crib. If you aim just right, you may be able to hit the wall so that the kitten rebounds and lands on Sky. You could sing a funny song, "Sky's being fallen on,/Oh, Sky's being fallen on,/ Whatcha think 'bout that?" And nobody'll ever know if poor little Maybe Albino has pink eyes or not. . . .

This sudden impulse horrifies you, even as a kid, *especially* as a kid. You can see the white kitten dead. Trembling, you set the kitten back down on the cardboardy deer hide, climb back over the crib rail, and stand away from the naked litter while Sky tries to decide what to do next.

Unmanfully, you start to cry. "S-s-sorry, k-kitty. S-s-sorry, Sk-sky. I'm r-r-really s-sorry." You almost want Gramby or Meemaw Anita to stumble in on you, in the churchly gloom and itch of their grain crib, to see you doing this heartfelt penance for a foul deed imagined but never carried out. It's okay to cry a bit in front of your mama's folks.

I'm touched, Penfield says. But speak up. Stop mumbling.

For several months after your senior year, you reside in the Adolescent Wing of the Quiet Harbor Psychiatric Center in a suburb of Atlanta. You're there to neutralize the disorienting stimuli—flak, you call it—burning out your emotional wiring, flying at you from everywhere. You're there to relearn how to live with no despairing recourse to disguises, sex, drugs.

Bad drugs, the doctors mean.

At QHPC they give you good drugs. This is actually the case, not sarcastic bullshit. Kim Yaughan, one of the psychotherapists in the so-called Wild Child Wing, assures you that this is so, that anti-psychotics aren't addictive. You get twenty milligrams a day of haloperidol. You take it in liquid form in paper cups shaped like dollhouse-sized coffee filters.

"You're not an addict," Kim says. (Everyone at QHPC calls her Kim.) "Think of yourself as a diabetic, of Haldol as insulin. You don't hold a diabetic off insulin, that'd be criminal."

Not only do you get Haldol, you get talk therapy, recreational therapy, family therapy, crafts therapy. Some of the residents of the Wild Child Wing are druggies and sexual-abuse victims as young as twelve. They get these same therapies, along with pet therapy. The pets brought in on Wednesdays often include cats.

At last, Penfield tells an associate. That last jolt wasn't a mishit, af-ter all.

The idea is that hostile, fearful, or withdrawn kids who don't interact well with other people will do better with animals. Usually they do. Kittens under a year, tumbling with one another, batting at yarn balls, exploring the pet room with their tails up like the radio antennas on cars, seem to be effective four-legged therapists.

One teenage girl, a manic-depressive who calls herself Eagle Rose, goes gaga over them. "Oh," she says, holding up a squirmy,

smoke-colored male and nodding at two kittens wrestling in an empty
carton of Extra Large Tide, "they're so soft, so neat, so . . . so *highly
lustrous*."

Despite Kim Yaughan's many attempts to involve you, you stand
aloof from everyone. It's Eagle Rose who focuses your attention, not
the kittens, and E. R.'s an untouchable. Every patient here is an
untouchable, that way. It would be a terrible betrayal to think anything
else. So, mostly, you don't.

The year before you marry, Marti is renting a house on North High-
land Avenue. A whole house. It's not a big house, but she has plenty of
room. She uses one bedroom as a studio. In this room, on the floor, lies
a large canvas on which she has been painting, exclusively in shades of
blue, the magnified heart of a magnolia. She calls the painting—too
explicitly, you think—*Magnolia Heart in Blue*. She's worked on it all
quarter, often appraising it from a stepladder to determine how best to
continue. Every weekend you sleep with Marti in the bedroom next to
the studio. Her mattress rests on the floor, without box springs or bed-
stead. You sometimes feel that you're lying in the middle of a painting
in progress, a strange but gratifying sensation that you may or may not
carry into your next week of classes at GSU.

One balmy Sunday you awake to find Marti's body stenciled with
primitive blue flowers, a blossom on her neck, more on her breasts,
an indigo bouquet on the milky plane of her abdomen. You gaze at
her in groggy wonderment. The woman you plan to marry has become,
overnight, an arabesque of disturbing floral bruises.

Then you see the cat, Romeo, a neighbor's gray Persian, propped
in the corner, belly exposed, so much like a hairy little man in a
recliner that you laugh. Marti stirs. Romeo preens. Clearly, he entered
through a studio window, walked all over *Magnolia Heart in Blue*,
then came in here and violated Marti.

My wife-to-be as a strip of *fin de siècle* wallpaper, you muse,
kissing her chastely on one of the paw-print flowers.

You sleep on the streets. You wear the same stinking clothes for days
on end. You haven't been on haloperidol for months. The city could
be Lima, or Istanbul, or Bombay, as easily as Atlanta. Hell, it could

be a boulder-littered crater on the moon. You drag from one place to another like a zombie, and the people you hit up for hamburgers, change, MARTA tokens, old newspapers, have no more substance to you than you do to them; they could all be holograms or ghosts. They could be androids programmed to keep you dirty and hungry by dictating your behavior with remote-control devices that look like wristwatches and key rings.

Cats mean more to you than people do. (The people may not *be* people.) Cats are fellow survivors, able to sniff out nitrogenous substances from blocks away. Food.

You follow a trio of scrawny felines down Ponce de Leon to the rear door of a catfish restaurant where the dumpster overflows with greasy paper and other high refuse. The cats strut around on the mounded topography of this debris while you balance on an upturned trash barrel, mindlessly picking and choosing.

Seven rooms away from Coach Osteen's lab, Mr. Petty is teaching advanced junior English. Poetry. He stalks around the room like an actor doing Hamlet, even when the poem's something dumb by Ogden Nash, or something Beat and surface sacrilegious by Ferlinghetti, or something short and puzzling by Carlos Williams.

The Williams piece is about a cat that climbs over a cabinet—a "jamcloset"—and steps into a flowerpot. Actually, Mr. Petty says, it's about the *image* created by Williams's purposely simple diction. Everyone argues that it isn't a poem at all. It's even less a poem, lacking metaphors, than that Carl Sandburg thing about the fog coming on little, for Christ's sake, cat's feet.

You like it, though. You can see the cat stepping cautiously into the flowerpot. The next time you're in Coach Osteen's class, trying to redeem yourself at the dissection table, you recite the poem for Pamela van Rhyn, Jessie Faye Culver, Kathy Margenau, and Cynthia Spivy. Coach Osteen, shaking his head, makes you repeat the lines so that he can say them, too. Amazing.

"Cats are digitigrade critters," he tells the lab. "That means they walk on their toes. Digitigrade."

Cynthia Spivy catches your eye. *Well, I'll be a pussy willow,* she silently mouths. *Who'd've thunk it?*

"Unlike the dog or the horse," Coach Osteen goes on, "the cat walks by moving the front and back legs on one side of its body and then the front and back legs on the other. The only other animals to move that way are the camel and the giraffe."

And naked crazy folks rutting on all fours, you think, studying Cynthia's lips and wondering if there was ever a feral child raised by snow leopards or jaguars. . . .

Thai Thai develops a urinary tract infection. Whenever he has to pee, he looks for Mama pulling weeds or hanging out clothes in the back-yard and squats to show her that he's not getting the job done. It takes Mama two or three days to realize what's going on. Then you and she carry Thai to the vet.

Mama waits tables at a Denny's near the expressway. She hasn't really got the money for the operation that Thai needs to clear up the blockage, a common problem in male Siamese. She tells you that you can either forfeit movie money for the next few months or help her pay to make Thai well. You hug Mama, wordlessly agreeing that the only thing to do is to help your cat. The operation goes okay, but the vet telephones a day later to report that Thai took a bad turn overnight and died near morning.

Thai's chocolate and silver body has a bandage cinched around his middle, like a wraparound saddle.

You're the one who buries Thai because Mama can't bring herself to. You put him in a Siamese-sized cardboard box, dig a hole under the holly in the backyard, and lay him to rest with a spank of the shovel blade and a prayer consisting of grief-stricken repetitions of the word *please*.

Two or three months later, you come home from school to find a pack of dogs in the backyard. They've dug Thai Thai up. You chase the dogs away, screeching from an irate crouch. Thai's corpse is nothing but matted fur and protruding bones. Its most conspicuous feature is the bandage holding the maggoty skeleton together at its cinched-in waist.

This isn't Thai, you tell yourself. I buried Thai a long, long time ago, and this isn't him.

You carry the remains, jacketed in the editorial section of the

Atlanta Constitution, to a trash can and dump them with an abrupt, indifferent thunk. Pickup is tomorrow.

One Sunday afternoon in March, you're standing with 200 other homeless people at the entrance to Trinity United Methodist's soup kitchen, near the state capitol. It's drizzling. A thin but gritty-looking young woman in jeans and sweatshirt, her hair lying in dark strands against her forehead, is passing out hand-numbered tickets to every person who wants to get into the basement. At the head of the outside basement steps is a man in pleated slacks and a plaid shirt. He won't let anyone down the steps until they have a number in the group of ten currently being admitted. He has to get an okay from the soup-kitchen staff downstairs before he'll allow a new group of ten to pass. Your number, on a green slip of paper already drizzle-dampened, is 126. The last group down held numbers 96 to 105. You think. Hard to tell with all the shoving, cursing, and bantering on the line. One angry black man up front doesn't belong there. He waves his ticket every time a new group of ten is called, hoping, even though his number is 182, to squeeze past the man set there to keep order.

"How many carahs yo ring?" he asks. "I sick. Mon n lemme eah fo I fall ouw. Damn disere rain."

When the dude holding number 109 doesn't show, the stair guard lets number 182 pass, a good-riddance sort of charity. You shuffle up with the next two groups. How many of these people are robots, human machines drawn to the soup kitchen, as you may have been, on invisible tractor beams? The stair guard isn't wearing a watch or shaking a key ring. It's probably his wedding band that's the remote-control device. . . .

"My God," he cries when he sees you. "Is that really you? It is, isn't it?"

The stair guy's name is Dirk Healy. He says he went to school with you in Hapeville. Remember Pamela van Rhyn? Remember Cynthia What's-her-name? When you go down into the basement and get your two white-bread sandwiches and a Styrofoam cup of vegetable soup, Dirk convinces another volunteer to take over his job and sits down next to you at one of the rickety folding tables where your fellow street folk are single-mindedly eating. Dirk—who, as far as you're concerned, could be the man in the moon—doesn't ask you how you got in this fix, doesn't accuse, doesn't exhort.

"You're off your medication, aren't you?" Your hackles lift. "Hey," he soothes, "I visited you at Quiet Harbor. The thing to do is get you back on it."

You eat, taking violent snatches of the sandwiches, quick sips of the soup. You one-eye Dirk over the steam the way that, years ago, Sky one-eyed you from her grain-crib nest.

"I may have a job for you," Dirk says confidentially. "Ever hear of Rockdale Biological?"

One summer, for reasons you don't understand, Mama sends you to visit your father and his ex-hairdresser floozy—whose name is Carol Grace—in the Florida town where they live off the proceeds of her mail-order business and sometimes bet the dogs at the local greyhound track.

Carol Grace may bet the greyhounds at the track, but, at home, she's a cat person. She owns seven: a marmalade-colored tom, a piebald tom, three tricolor females, an orange Angora of ambiguous gender, and a Manx mix with a tail four or five inches long, as if someone shortened it with a cleaver.

"If Stub was pure Manx," Carol Grace says, "he wouldn't have no tail. Musta been an alley tom in his mama's Kitty Litter."

Stroking Stub, she chortles happily. She and your mother look a little alike. They have a similar feistiness, too, although it seems coarser in Carol Grace, whom your balding father—she calls him Webby, for Pete's sake—unabashedly dotes on.

A few days into your visit, Carol Grace and you find one of her females, Hedy Lamarr, lying crumpled under a pecan tree shading the two-story house's south side. The cat is dead. You kneel to touch her. Carol Grace kneels beside you.

"Musta fell," she says. "Lotsa people think cats are too jack-be-nimble to fall, but they can slip up, too. Guess my Hedy didn't remember that, pretty thing. Now look."

You are grateful that, today, Carol Grace does the burying and the prayer saying. Her prayer includes the melancholy observation that anyone can fall. Anyone.

Enough of this crap, Penfield says. Tell me what you did, and for whom, and why, at Rockdale Biological.

Givin whah I can, you mumble, working to turn your head into the uncompromising rigidity of the clamps.

Adolf, Penfield says, what you're giving me is cat juggling.

Alone in the crafts room with Kim Yaughan while the other kids in Blue Group (QHPC's Wild Child Wing has two sections, Blue and Gold) go on a field trip, you daub acrylics at a crude portrayal of a cat walking upside down on a ceiling. Under the cat, a woman and a teenage boy point and make hateful faces.

"Are they angry at the cat or at each other?" Kim asks.

You give her a look: what a stupid question.

Kim comes over, stands at your shoulder. If she were honest, she'd tell you that you're no artist at all. The painting may be psychologically revealing, but it refutes the notion that you have any talent as a draftsman or a colorist.

"Ever hear of British artist Louis Wain?" Kim says. "He lived with three unmarried sisters and a pack of cats. His schizophrenia didn't show up until he was almost sixty. That's late."

"Lucky," you say. "He didn't have so long to be crazy."

"Listen, now. Wain painted only cats. He must've really liked them. At first, he did smarmy, realistic kitties for calendars and postcards. Popular crap. Later, thinking jealous competitors were zapping him with X rays or something, the cats in his paintings got weird, really hostile and menacing."

"Weirder than mine?" You jab your brush at it.

"Ah, that's a mere puddy-tat." Then: "In the fifteen years he was institutionalized, Wain painted scads of big-eyed, spiky-haired cats. He put bright neon auras and electrical fields around them. His backgrounds got geometrically rad. Today, you might think they were computer generated. Anyhow, Wain's crazy stuff was better—fiercer, stronger—than the crap he'd done sane."

"Meaning I'm a total loss unless I get crazier?" you say.

"No. What I'm trying to tell you is that the triangles, stars, rainbows, and repeating arabesques that Wain put into his paintings grew from a desperate effort to . . . well, to impose order on the chaos *inside* him. It's touching, really touching. Wain was trying to confront and reverse, the only way he could, the disintegration of his adult personality. See?"

But you don't. Not exactly.

Kim taps your acrylic cat with a burgundy fingernail. "You're not going to be the new Picasso, but you aren't doomed to suffer as terrifying a schizophrenia as Wain suffered, either. The bizarre thing in your painting is the cat on the ceiling. The colors, and the composition itself, are reassuringly conventional. A good sign for your mental health. Another thing is, Wain's doctors couldn't give him antipsychotic drugs. We can."

"Cheers." You pantomime knocking back a little cup of Haldol.

Kim smiles. "So why'd you paint the cat upside down?"

"Because *I'm* upside down," you say.

Kim gives you a peck on the cheek. "You're not responsible for a gone-awry brain chemistry or an unbalanced metabolism, hon. Go easy on yourself, okay?" Dropping your brush, you pull Kim to you and try to nuzzle her under the jaw. Effortlessly, she bends back your hand and pushes you away. "But that," she says, "you're going to have to control. Friends, not lovers. Sorry if I gave you the wrong idea. Really."

"If the pieces toward the end don't fit," Howie tells you, "you can always use a razor blade." He holds one up.

You try to take it. Double-edged, it slices your thumb. Some of your blood spatters on the cat puzzle.

A guy in a truck drives up to the specimen-prep platform and loading dock behind Rockdale Biological Medical Supply. It's an unmarked panel truck with no windows behind the cab. The guys who drive the truck change, it seems, almost every week, but you're a two-month fixture on the concrete platform with the slide cages and the euthanasia cabinet. Back here you're Dirk Healy's main man, especially now that he's off on a business trip somewhere.

Your job is both mindless and strength-sapping. The brick wall around the rear of the RBMS complex, and the maple trees shielding the loading dock, help you keep your head together. Healy has you on a lower dosage of haloperidol than you took while you and Marti were still married. Says you were overmedicated before. Says you were, ha-ha, "an apathetic drug slave."

He should know. He's been a hotshot in national medical supply for years.

"We'll have you up in the front office in no time," he assured you. "The platform job's a kind of trial."

The guy in the truck backs up and starts unloading. Dozens of cats in slide cages. You wear elbow-length leather gloves, and a heavy apron, and feel a bit like an old-timey Western blacksmith. The cats are pieces of scrap iron to be worked in the forge. You slide the door end of each cage into the connector between the open platform and the euthanasia cabinet, then poke the cats in the butt or the flank with a long metal rod until they duck into the cabinet to escape your prodding. When the cabinet's full, you drop the safety door, check the gauges, turn on the gas. It hisses louder than the cats climbing over one another, louder than their yowling and tumbling, which noises gradually subside and finally stop.

By hand, you unload the dead cats from the chamber, slinging them out by their tails or their legs. You cease feeling like a blacksmith. You imagine yourself as a nineteenth-century trapper, stacking fox, beaver, rabbit, wolf, and muskrat pelts on a travois for a trip to the trading post. The pelts are pretty, though many are blemished by vivid skin diseases and a thick black dandruff of gassed fleas. How much could they be worth?

"Nine fifty a cat," Dirk Healy has said. That seems unlikely. They're no longer moving. They're no longer—if they ever were— highly lustrous. They're floppy, anonymous, and dead, their fur contaminated by a lethal gas.

A heavy-duty wheelbarrow rests beside the pile of cats on the platform. You unwind a hose and fill the barrow with water. Dirk has ordered you to submerge the gassed cats to make certain they're dead. Smart. Some of the cats are plucky boogers. They'll mew at you or swim feebly in the cat pile even before you pick them up and sling them into the wheelbarrow. The water in the wheelbarrow ends it. Indisputably. It also washes away fleas and the worst aspects of

feline scabies. You pull a folding chair over and sort through the cats
for the ones with flea collars, ID collars, rabies tags. You take these
things off. You do it with your gloves on, a sodden cat corpse ham-
mocked in your apron. It's not easy, given your wet glove fingers.

If it's sunny, you take the dead cats to the bright part of the
platform and lay them out in neat rows to dry.

Can't you get him to stop mumbling? Penfield asks someone in the
room. His testimony's almost unintelligible.

He's replaying the experience inwardly, an indistinct figure says.
But he's starting to go autistic on us.

Look, Penfield says. We've got to get him to verbalize clearly—
or we've wasted our time.

Two months after the divorce, you drive to Spartanburg, to the Braggs'
house, to see Jacob. Mr. Bragg—Howie—intercepts you at the front
gate, as if apprised of your arrival by surveillance equipment.

"I'm sorry," he says, "but Marti doesn't want to see you, and she
doesn't want *you* to see Jake. If you don't leave, I'll have to call the
police to, ah, you know, remove you."

You don't contest this. You walk across the road to your car. From
there, you can see that atop the brick post on either side of Mr.
Bragg's ornate gate reposes a roaring granite lion. You can't remember
seeing these lions before, but the crazed and reticulated state of the
granite suggests they've been there awhile. It's a puzzle. . . .

As you lay out the dead cats, you assign them names. The names you
assign are always Mehitabel, Felix, Sylvester, Tom, Heathcliff, Garfield, and Bill. These seven names must serve for all the cats on the
platform. Consequently, you add Roman numerals to the names when
you run out of names before you do cats: Mehitabel II, Felix II,
Sylvester II, Tom II, and so on. It's a neat, workable system. Once,
you cycled all the way to Sylvester VII before running out of specimens.

As a fifth grader in Notasulga, you sit and watch a film about the
American space program.

An old film clip shows a cat—really more a kitten than a cat—suspended from a low ceiling by its feet. It's a metal ceiling, and the scientist who devised the experiment (which has something to do with studying the kitten's reactions to upside-downness, then applying these findings to astronauts aboard a space station) has fastened magnets to the cat's feet so that they will adhere to the metal surface.

The scientist has also rigged up a pair of mice in the same odd way, to see if they will distract, entice, or frighten the hanging kitten. They don't. The kitten is terrified not of the mice (who seem to be torpid and unimaginative representatives of their kind), but of the alien condition in which it finds itself. Insofar as it is able, the kitten lurches against the magnets, its ears back, its mouth wide open in a silent cry. On the sound track, a male voice explains the import and usefulness of this experiment. No one can hear him, though, because most of the other kids in Miss Beischer's class are laughing uproariously at the kitten. You look around in a kind of sick stupefaction.

Milly Heckler, Agnes Lee Terrance, and a few other girls appear to be as appalled as you, but the scene doesn't last long—it's probably shorter than your slow-motion memory of it—and it seems for a moment that you *are* that kitten, that everything in the world has been wrenchingly upended.

"I know it *seemed* to you that evil people were trying to invade and control your thoughts," Dr. Hall, the director of Quiet Harbor, tells you. He pets a neutered male just back from a visit to the Gerontological Wing. "But that was just a symptom of the scrambled condition of your brain chemistry. The truth is . . ."

Fatigued, you slouch out the rear gate of Rockdale Biological. Your apartment—the three-roomer that Healy provided—is only a short distance away. A late-model luxury town car pulls alongside you as you walk the weed-grown sidewalk. The tinted window on the front-seat passenger's side powers down, and you catch your first glimpse of the raw-complexioned man who introduces himself as David Penfield. An alias? Why do you think so?

"If you like," he says, "think of me as the Zoo Cop."

It's a permission you don't really want. Why would you choose to think of a well-dressed, ordinary-featured man with visible acne scarring as something as déclassé as, Jesus, the Zoo Cop? Is he a detective of some sort? What does he want?

The next thing you know, you're in the car with Penfield and two other tight-lipped men.

The next thing you know, you're on the expressway and one of the Zoo Cop's associates—goons?—has locked the suction-cup feet of one of those corny Garfield toys on his tinted window as a kind of—what?—mockery? rebuke? warning?

The next thing you know, you're in a basement that clearly isn't the soup kitchen of Trinity United Methodist. The next thing you know, you're flat on your back on a table. The next thing you know, you don't know anything. . . .

. . . Marti's body is stenciled with primitive blue flowers, a blossom on her neck, more on her breasts, an indigo bouquet on the milky plane of her abdomen. You gaze at her in groggy wonderment. The woman you one day marry has become, overnight, an arabesque of disturbing floral bruises.

"Marti," you whisper. "Marti, don't leave me. Marti, don't take my son away."

Penfield, a.k.a. the Zoo Cop (you realize during your descent into the puzzle box), isn't a real cop. He hates you because what you've been doing for Healy is vile, contemptible, *evil*. So it is, so it is. He wants to get Healy, who hasn't been around this last week at all, who's maybe skipped off to Barbados or the Yucatán or Saint-Tropez.

Penfield is an animal-rights eco-terrorist, well financed and determined, and the ESB zappings to which he and his associates are subjecting you are designed to incriminate, pinpoint, and doom old Dirk and *his* associates, who obviously deserve it. You, too. You deserve it, too. No argument there. None.

Christ, Penfield says, unhook the son of a bitch and carry him upstairs. Dump him somewhere remote.

You visit the pound for a replacement for Springer and Ossie, gassed three or four years ago. The attendant tells you there are plenty of potential adoptees at the shelter. You go down the rows of cages to select one. The kittens in the fouled sawdust tumble, paw, and meow, putting on a dispirited show.

"This one," you finally say.

"Cute." The attendant approves. Well, they'd fire her if she didn't. The idea is to adopt these creatures out, not to let them lapse into expendability.

"It's for Jake, my son," you tell her. "His asthma isn't that bad. I think he may be growing out of it."

"Look at my puzzle," Howie says, yanking the razor blade away from you. "You've bled all over it. . . ."

City of Truth

JAMES MORROW

James Morrow was born, he is told, in 1947. He began writing fiction at age seven, dictating adventure stories to his mother as he paced around the dining room and she lovingly committed his words to paper using her manual Royal typewriter. Thirty years later, when he finally got around to finishing a novel, it emerged—somewhat to his surprise—as a work of science fiction, and he has stayed within the field ever since.

Beyond his recent Nebula Award for *City of Truth*, Morrow garnered that same prize for "Bible Stories for Adults, No. 17: The Deluge," and in 1990 his fourth novel, *Only Begotten Daughter*, a sequel to the New Testament, earned him the World Fantasy Award. His other books include *The Continent of Lies*, which dealt with what today we would call virtual reality, and *This Is the Way the World Ends*, a nuclear-war fantasia selected by the British Broadcasting Company as the best SF novel of the year. *Towing Jehovah*, a death-of-God nautical adventure, will be published by Harcourt Brace & Company in the spring of 1994.

" 'City of Truth' traces to the short story 'Veritas' that I wrote for the first volume of George Zebrowski's anthology series, *Synergy*," Morrow telepathically informs the present editor. "In that particular yarn, I carefully delineated the concept of a truth-telling dystopia, but shortly after its publication I began to feel the premise deserved something beyond the spy-thriller plot I'd erected. When my then-current British editor, the estimable Deborah Beale, invited me to contribute to her Legend Novellas series at Random Century, I began thinking more deeply about the conundrum of candor.

" 'Honesty is a good thing,' I told myself, 'but what if my young son were dying? Wouldn't my first instinct be to hide the truth from him?' And so I returned to Veritas, putting the main character through an ordeal far more intense than the one faced by his counterpart in the original story."

O N E

I no longer live in the City of Truth. I have exiled myself from Veritas, from all cities—from the world. The room in which I'm writing is cramped as a county jail and moist as the inside of a lung, but I'm learning to call it home. My only light is a candle, a fat, butter-colored stalk from which nets of melted wax hang like cobwebs. I wonder what it would be like to live in that candle—in the translucent crannies that surround the flame: a fine abode, warm, safe, and snug. I imagine myself spending each day wandering waxen passageways and sitting in paraffin parlors, each night lying in bed listening to the steady drip-drip-drip of my home consuming itself.

My name is Jack Sperry, and I am thirty-eight years old. I was born in truth's own city, Veritas, on the last day of its bicentennial year. Like many boys of my generation, I dreamed of becoming an art critic one day: the pure primal thrill of attacking a painting, the sheer visceral kick of savaging a movie or a poem. In my case, however, the dream turned into reality, for by my twenty-second year I was employed as a deconstructionist down at the Wittgenstein Museum in Plato Borough, giving illusion its due.

Other dreams—wife, children, happy home—came harder. From the very first Helen and I wrestled with the thorny Veritasian question of whether *love* was a truthful term for how we felt about each other—such a misused notion, *love,* a kind of one-word lie—a problem we began ignoring once a more concrete crisis had taken its place.

His sperm are lazy, she thought. Her eggs are duds, I decided. But at last we found the right doctor, the proper pill, and suddenly there was Toby, flourishing inside Helen's redeemed womb: Toby the embryo; Toby the baby; Toby the toddler; Toby the preschool carpenter, forever churning out crooked birdhouses, lopsided napkin holders, and asymmetrical bookends; Toby the boy naturalist, befriending every slithery, slimy, misbegotten creature ever to wriggle across the face of the Earth. This was a child with a maggot farm. A roach ranch. A pet slug. "I think I love him," I told Helen one day. "Let's not get carried away," she replied.

The morning I met Martina Coventry, Toby was off at Camp Ditch-the-Kids in the untamed outskirts of Kant Borough. He sent us a picture postcard every day, a routine that, I realize in retrospect, was a kind of smuggling operation; once Toby got home, the postcards would all be *there,* waiting to join his vast collection.

To wit:

Dear Mom and Dad: Today we learned how to survive in case we're ever lost in the woods—what kind of bark to eat and stuff. Counselor Rick says he never heard of anybody actually using these skills. Your son, *Toby*.

And also:

Dear Mom and Dad: There's a big rat trap in the pantry here, and guess who always sneaks in at night and finds out what animal got caught and then sets it free? Me! Counselor Rick says we're boring. Your son, *Toby*.

It was early, barely 7 A.M., but already Booze Before Breakfast was jammed to its crumbling brick walls. I made my way through a conglomeration of cigarette smoke and beer fumes, through frank sweat and honest halitosis. A jukebox thumped out Probity singing "Copingly Ever After." The saloon keeper, Jimmy Breeze, brought me the usual—a raspberry Danish and a Bloody Mary—setting them on the splintery cedar bar. I told him I had no cash but would pay him tomorrow. This was Veritas. I would.

I spotted only one free chair—at a tiny, circular table across from a young woman whose wide face and plump contours boasted, to this beholder's eye, the premier sensuality of a Rubens model. Peter Paul Rubens was much on my mind just then, for I'd recently criticized not only *The Garden of Love* but also *The Raising of the Cross*.

"Come here often?" she asked as I approached, my plastic-wrapped Danish poised precariously atop my drink. Her abundant terra-cotta hair was compacted into a modest bun. Her ankle-length green dress was made of guileless cambric.

I sat down. "Uh-huh," I mumbled, pushing aside the sugar bowl, the napkin dispenser, and the woman's orange peels to make room for my Bloody and Danish. "I always stop in on my way to the Wittgenstein."

"You a critic?" Even in the endemic gloom of Booze Before Breakfast, her smooth, unpainted skin glowed.

I nodded. "Jack Sperry."

"Can't say I'm impressed. It doesn't take much intellectual prowess, does it?"

She could be as honest as she liked, provided I could watch her voluptuous lips move. "What line are *you* in?" I asked.

"I'm a writer." Her eyes expanded: limpid, generous eyes, the cobalt blue of Salome's So-So Contraceptive Cream. "It has its dangers, of course. There's always that risk of falling into . . . what's it called?"

"Metaphor?"

"Metaphor."

There were no metaphors in Veritas. Metaphors were lies. Flesh could be *like* grass, but it never *was* grass. Use a metaphor in Veritas, and your conditioning instantly possessed you, hammering your skull, searing your heart, dropping you straight to hell in a bucket of pain. So to speak.

"What do you write?" I asked.

"Doggerel. Greeting-card messages, advertising jingles, inspirational verses like you see in—"

"Sell much?"

A grimace distorted her luminous face. "I should say I'm an *aspiring* writer."

"I'd like to read some of your doggerel," I asserted. "And I'd like to have sex with you," I added, wincing at my candor. It wasn't easy being a citizen.

Her grimace intensified.

"Sorry if I'm being offensive," I said. "Am I being offensive?"

"You're being offensive."

"Offensive only in the abstract, or offensive to you personally?"

"Both." She slid a wedge of orange into her wondrous mouth. "Are you married?"

"Yes."

"A good marriage?"

"Pretty good." *To have and to hold, to love and to cherish, to the degree that these mischievous and sentimental abstractions possess any meaning:* Helen and I had opted for a traditional ceremony. "Our son is terrific. I think I love him."

"If we had an affair"—a furtive smile—"wouldn't you feel guilty?"

"I've never cheated." An affair, I mused. Scary stuff. "Guilt? Yes, of course." I sipped my Bloody Mary. "I believe I could tolerate it."

"Well, you can drop the whole fantasy, Mr. Sperry," the young woman said, a declaration that filled me with an odd mixture of relief and disappointment. "You can put the entire thought out of your—"

"Call me Jack." I unpackaged my Danish; the wrapper dragged

away clots of vanilla icing like a Band-Aid pulling off a scab. "And you're . . . ?"

"Martina Coventry, and at the moment I feel only a mild, easily controlled desire to copulate with you."

" 'At the moment,' " I repeated, marveling at how much ambiguity could be wedged into a prepositional phrase. In a fashionably gauche move I licked the icing off the Danish wrapper (*The Mendacity of Manners* had recently hit the top slot on the *Times* best-seller list). "Will you show me your doggerel?" I asked.

"It's bad doggerel."

"Doggerel is by definition bad."

"Mine's worse."

"Please."

Martina's pliant features contracted into a bemused frown. "There's a great deal of sexual tension occurring between us now, wouldn't you say?"

"Correct."

She reached into her purse and pulled out a folded sheet of crisp white typing paper, pressing it into my palm with a sheepish smile.

First came a Valentine's Day message.

I find you somewhat interesting,
You're not too short or tall,
And if you'd be my Valentine,
I wouldn't mind at all.

A birthday greeting followed.

Roses drop dead,
Violets do too,
With each day life gets shorter,
Happy birthday to you.

"I have no illusions about earning a living from my doggerel," said Martina, understating the case radically. "What I'd really like is a career writing political speeches. My borough rep almost hired me to run his reelection campaign. 'Cold in person, but highly efficient'—that was the slogan I worked out. In the end, his girlfriend got the job. Do you like my verses, Jack?"

"They're awful."

"I'm going to burn them." Martina kissed an orange slice, sucked out the juice.

"No. Don't. I'd like to have them."

"You would? Why?"

"Because I'm anticipating you'll write something else on the page." From my shirt pocket I produced a ballpoint pen (*Paradox Pen Company—Random Leaks Common*). "Like, say, the information I'll need to find you again."

"So we can have an affair?"

"The thought terrifies me."

"You *are* fairly attractive," Martina observed, taking the pen. Indeed. It's the eyebrows that do it, great bushy extrusions suggesting a predatory mammal of unusual prowess—wolf, bear, leopard—though they draw plenty of support from my straight nose and square jaw. Only when you get to my chin, a pointy, pimply knoll forever covered with stubble, does the illusion of perfection dissolve. "I'm warning you, Jack, I have my own Smith and Wesson Liberalstopper." She signed her name in bold curlicues across the bottom of the page, added her address and phone number. "Try to force yourself on me, and I'll shoot to kill."

I lifted the doggerel from the table, flicking a Danish crumb from the word *Valentine*. "Funny—you've *almost* told a lie here. Roses don't drop dead, they—"

"They wither."

"If I were you, Martina, I wouldn't take such chances with my sanity."

"If you were me," she replied, "you *would* take such chances with your sanity, because otherwise you'd be someone else."

"True enough," I said, pocketing Martina Coventry's stultifying verses.

Galileo Square was clogged with traffic, a dense metallic knot betokening a delay of at least twenty minutes. I flipped on my Plymouth Adequate's radio, tuned in WTRU, and began waiting it out. Eighteenth Street, Nineteenth Street, Twentieth . . .

". . . fact that I accepted a fifty-thousand-dollar kickback during the Avelthorpe Tariff Scandal should not, I feel, detract from my record on education, the environment, and medical . . ."

Twenty-fifth Street, Twenty-sixth Street, Twenty-seventh . . .

". . . for while we do indeed divert an enormous amount of protein that might help relieve world hunger, the psychological benefits of dogs and cats have been proved almost beyond the shadow of a . . ."

Thirtieth Street, Thirty-first . . .

". . . displeased with the unconscionable quantities of sugar we were putting into children's cereals, and so we're happy to announce a new policy of . . ."

At last: the Wittgenstein Museum, a one-story brick building sprawling across a large concrete courtyard, flanked by a Brutality Squad station on the north side and a café called the Dirty Dog on the south. The guard, a toothy, clean-cut young man with a Remington Metapenis strapped to his waist, waved me through the iron gates. I headed for the parking lot. Derrick Popkes of the Egyptian Relics Division had beaten me to my usual space, usurping it with his Ford Sufficient, so I had to drive all the way to the main incinerator and park by the coal bin.

"Channel your violent impulses in a salutary direction—become a Marine. Purge your natural tendency toward—" I silenced the radio, killed the engine.

What had life been like during the Age of Lies? How had the human mind endured a world where politicians misled, advertisers overstated, clerics exaggerated, women wore makeup, and people professed love at the drop of a tropological hat? How had humanity survived the epoch we'd all read about in the history books, those nightmare centuries of casuistic customs and fraudulent rites? The idea confounded me. It rattled me to the core. The Easter Bunny, the Tooth Fairy, Santa Claus, Frosty the Snowman, Rudolph the Red-Nosed Reindeer: staggering.

"You're late," observed the chief curator, bald and portly Arnold Cook, as I strolled into the front office. "Heavy traffic?"

"Yes." I slid my card into the time clock, felt the jolt of its mechanism imprinting my tardiness. "Bumper to bumper." Every so often, you'd experience an urge to stop short of total candor. But then suddenly it would come: a dull neurological throb that, if you didn't tell the whole truth, would quickly bloom into a psychosomatic explosion in your skull. "I also wasted a lot of time getting a young woman's address."

"Do you expect to copulate with her?" Mr. Cook asked, following me to the changing room. Early morning, yet already he was coated with characteristic sweat, droplets that, as I once told him in a particularly painful exercise of civic duty, put me in mind of my cat's litter box.

Denim overalls drooped from the lockers. I selected a pair that looked about my size. "Adultery is deceitful," I reminded the curator.

"So is fidelity," he replied. "In its own way."

"In its own way," I agreed, donning my overalls.

I followed a nonliteral rat-maze of dark, dusty corridors to my workshop. It was packed. As usual, the items I was supposed to analyze that day divided equally into the authentic *objets d'artifice* unearthed by the archaeologists and the ersatz output of the city's furtive malcontents—its "dissemblers." For every statue from ancient Greece, there was a clumsy forgery. For every Cézanne, a feeble imitation. For every eighteenth-century novel, the effluvium of a vanity press.

The dissemblers. Even now, after all I've been through, the word sends a cold wind through my bones. The dissemblers: Veritas's own enemy within, defacing its walls with their oil paintings, befouling its air with their songs, and, most daringly, turning its pristine streets into forums for Sophocles, Shakespeare, Ibsen, and Shaw, each production a ragged, jerry-built affair frantically staged before the Brutality Squad could arrive and chase the outlaw actors into their holes and hideouts. Only once had a dissembler been caught, and then the Squad had bungled it, clubbing the woman to death before they could ask the crucial question.

How do you tell lies without going mad?

How?

What I loved about this job was the way it got my head and my hands working together. True, the raw existential act of deconstruction was rather crude, but before that moment you had to use your mind; you had to decide that the artifact in question, whether original or forgery, was indeed inimical to the public good.

I turned toward a piece of classical mendacity labeled Nike of

Samothrace. A lie? Yes, manifestly: those wings. Merely to behold such a creature nauseated me. No wonder Plato had banned artists and playwrights from his hypothetical utopia. "Three removes from nature," he'd called them, three removes from factuality. ART IS A LIE, the electric posters in Circumspect Park reminded us. Truth might be beauty, but it simply didn't work the other way around.

Like an agoraphobic preparing for an indoor picnic, I spread my canvas dropcloth on the concrete floor. I took down a No. 7 sledge-hammer. The *Nike* had arrived headless, and now, as I wielded my critical apparatus against her, she became wingless as well—now breastless, now hipless. Amorphous chunks of marble littered the dropcloth. My overalls stank of sweat, my tongue felt like a dried fig wedged into my mouth. An exhausting enterprise, criticism; grueling work, analysis. I deserved a break.

A note lay on the desk in my coffee cubicle. "Dear Mr. Sperry: Last Friday, you might recall, you offered to write a letter on my behalf," I read as the water boiled. "I hope Mr. Cook might receive it by the end of the week. Fairly sincere regards, *Stanley Marcus.*"

I took down my mug, dumped in a heaping teaspoonful of semi-instant crystals—Donaldson's Drinkable Coffee, my favorite brand—added hot water from my kettle, and began mentally composing a recommendation for Stanley. He'd been assisting in my sector for over a year now, servicing a dozen of us critics—sharpening our axes, fueling our blowtorches, faithfully sweeping up our workshops and cubicles—and now he was looking to get promoted. "In all honesty, I believe Stanley would prove reasonably competent at running the main incinerator. Of course, he is something of a drudge and a toady, but those qualities may actually serve him well. One thing you'll notice about Stanley is that he farts a great deal, but here again we're not talking about a characteristic that would hinder . . ."

I glanced at my *Beatoff Magazine* calendar—and a good thing, or I might have forgotten about meeting my wife for lunch. "Helen," said the July 9th square, "1 P.M., No Great Shakes." No Great Shakes on Twenty-ninth Street had marvelous submarine sandwiches and terrific Waldorf salads. Its shakes were not so great.

Miss July—Wendy Warren, according to the accompanying pro-file—leered at me from the glossy paper. "Being an intellectual," ran her capsule biography, "Wendy proved most articulate on the subject of posing for us. 'It's at once tawdry and exhilarating, humiliating and energizing,' she said. 'If not for the quick five thousand, I never would've considered it.' When we learned how smart she was—that Interborough Chess Championship and everything—we almost disqualified her. However, we knew that many of you would enjoy masturbating to . . ."

Good old Wendy. My hypothetical id was ticking. And suddenly I realized there'd be a minor but irrefutable thrill in simply looking at Martina Coventry's handwriting, as if its twists and turns were the lines of her Rubensian flesh. I took a long sip of Donaldson's Drinkable and, pulling Martina's doggerel from my pocket, flattened the crumpled sheet on the desk.

The verses were as terrible as ever, but the signature indeed held a certain eroticism. I even got a mild charge from the contours of the subsequent information. "7 Lackluster Lane, Descartes Borough," she'd written. "Phone 610-400."

Something caught my eye, a web of thin shallow grooves in the paper, occupying the space between the Valentine message and the birthday greeting, and I realized that the object in my possession had backstopped one of Martina's earlier creative convulsions. Curious, I seized the nearest pencil and began rubbing graphite across the page, causing the older verses to materialize like a photographic image appearing in a tray of developer. Within seconds the entire composition lay before me, and my nervous system vibrated with intermingled disbelief, horror, and fascination.

Lies.

Gruesome and poetic lies.

In Martina Coventry's own hand.

I hide my wings inside my soul,
Their feathers soft and dry,
And when the world's not looking,
I take them out and fly.

Sweat erupted in my palms and along my brow. *Wings.* Martina didn't have wings. No one did. Who did she think she was, the Nike of Samothrace? One might as well assert the reality of Santa Claus or Lewis Carroll's Alice. As for the *soul*, that soggy construct . . .

Perhaps my eyes were deceiving me. I resolved to read the poem aloud—hearing is believing; to sense these astonishing words resounding in my head would be to know they in fact existed. "I hide my wings," I said in a hoarse whisper, but I couldn't go on. A primordial terror surged up, bringing a migraine so severe I almost fainted.

My critical instincts took hold. I seized Martina's poem, dashed out of the museum, and ran across the courtyard to the main incinerator. Skull throbbing, I thrust the page toward the same seething pit where, the day before, I had deconstructed a dozen books on reincarnation and the last two hundred issues of *The Journal of Psychic Healing*.

I stopped.

Was I in fact ready to cast Martina Coventry out of my life? Was I truly willing to consign her identity to the flames? No. I wasn't. I fixed on her address, massaging it into my memory.

How did she tell lies without going mad?

How?

Phone 610-400. No problem. For his *sixth* birthday we'd given Toby a *ten*-speed bike, but *four* months went by before I put it together, and he hardly ever rode it, so the whole experience was rather null, a zero—two, in fact. 6 . . . 1 . . . 0 . . . 4 . . . 0 . . . 0.

My fingers parted, and the poems floated toward their fate, joining the Homer epics, the Racine plays, the Dickens novels, and the mushy, gushy, pseudoscientific rantings of *The Journal of Psychic Healing*.

"It's absolutely incredible," I told Helen as we sat in No Great Shakes burrowing into the day's special: MURDERED COW SANDWICH, WILTED HEARTS OF LETTUCE, HIGH-CHOLESTEROL FRIES—A QUITE REASONABLE $5.99. "Four hours ago I was having breakfast with a dissembler. I could've reached out and touched her."

"But you didn't," said Helen in a tone more apprehensive than assured. She slid her sunglasses upward into her frothy, graying hair, the better to scrutinize my face.

"I didn't."

"She's definitely one of them?"

"I'm positive. More or less."

My wife looked straight at me, a shred of lettuce drooping over her lips like a green tongue. "Let's not get carried away," she said. *Let's not get carried away.* That was Helen's motto; it belonged on her tombstone. She was a woman who'd devoted her life to not getting carried away—in her career, in our bed, anywhere. It was her job, I believe, that made her so sedate. As a stringer for the celebrated supermarket tabloid, *Sweet Reason,* Helen moved among the skeptics and logicians of the world, collecting scoops: CONTROLLED STUDY NEGATES NEW ARTHRITIS CURE, SLAIN BIGFOOT REVEALED AS SCHIZOPHRENIC IN SUIT, TOP PSYCHICS' PREDICTIONS FALL FLAT. Ten years of writing such stories, and you acquire a bit of a chill.

I said, "You have a better interpretation, ostensible darling?"

"Maybe she found the paper on the street, supposed sweetheart," Helen replied. A beautiful woman, I'd always thought: large pleading eyes, soft round cheeks you wanted to rub against your hands like balm. "Maybe somebody *else* composed the poem."

"It was in Martina's handwriting."

Helen bit into her murdered cow. "Let me guess. She gave you her name and address, right?"

"Yes. She wrote them on the page."

"Did she say she wanted to have sex with you?"

"Not in so many words."

"Did you say you wanted to have sex with her?"

"Yes."

"You think you will?"

"I don't know," I said. "I hope so, I hope not—you know how it is." I licked the grease from a French fry. "I'd hate to hurt you," I added.

Helen's eyes became as dark and narrow as slots in a gun turret. "I probably feel as conflicted as you. Part of me wants you to turn this Martina over to the Brutality Squad, the better to get her out of our lives forever. The other part, the woman who feels a certain undeniable affection for you, knows that would be a stupid thing to do, because if the lady senses the police are on her trail, well, she might also sense how they got there, right? These dissemblers, I've heard, are no nonliteral pussycats. They've got assassins in their ranks."

"Assassins," I concurred. "Assassins, terrorists, lunatics. You want me to burn the paper?"

"Burn it, critic."

"I did."

My wife smiled. In Veritas, one never asked, *Really? Are you kidding? Do you mean that?* She finished her cow and said, "You're a somewhat better man than I thought."

We filled the rest of the hour with the usual marital battles—such ironically allied words, *marital, martial.* Helen and I loved to fight. My erections were becoming increasingly less substantive, she asserted, truthfully. The noises she made when chewing her food were disgusting, I reported, honestly. She told me she had no intention of procuring the obligatory gift for my niece's brainburn party on Saturday—Connie wasn't *her* niece. I didn't *want* her to get the gift, I retorted, because she'd buy something cheap, obvious, and otherwise emblematic of the contempt in which she held my sister. And so we continued, straight through coffee and dessert, nibbling at each other like mice, picking each other off like snipers. Such fun, such pathological fun.

Helen reached into her handbag and pulled out a crisp sheet of computer paper speckled with dot-matrix characters. "This came today," she explained. "A rabbit bit Toby," she announced evenly.

"A what? Rabbit? What are you talking about?"

"He's probably forgotten the whole thing by now."

"It *bit* him?"

Ralph Kitto
Executive Director
Camp Ditch-the-Kids
Box 145
Kant Borough

Mr. and Mrs. Sperry:

As you may know, your son makes it his annoying mission to release all the animals caught in our rat trap. Yesterday, in performing one such act of ambiguous compassion, he was attacked by a rare species called Hob's hare. We dressed his wound immediately and, checking his medical records, confirmed that his tetanus immunizations are up to date.

As a safety precaution, we retained the rabbit and placed it under quarantine. I am moderately sorry to report that today the animal died. We forthwith froze the corpse then shipped it to the Kraft Epidemiological Institute. The Kraft doctors will contact you if there's anything to worry about, though I suspect you've started worrying already.

Yours up to a point,
Ralph Kitto

"Why didn't you show me this right away?"

Helen shrugged. "It's not a big deal."

Smooth, nervy Helen. There were times when I wondered whether she liked Toby. "Aren't you bothered that the rabbit died?"

"Maybe it was old."

My teeth came together in a tight, dense grid. The thought of Toby's pain troubled me. Not his physical pain—it might have even done him some good, toughening him up for his brainburn. What distressed me was the sense of betrayal he must have felt; my son had always negotiated with the world in good faith, and now the world had bitten him. "There's something I should tell you," I admitted to my wife. "Before burning Martina's doggerel, I memorized her address and phone number."

Helen appeared to be experiencing a bad odor. "How readily you exhibit the same disgusting qualities one associates with anuses. Honestly, Jack, sometimes I wonder why we got married."

"Sometimes I wonder the same thing. I wish that rabbit hadn't died."

"Forget the rabbit. We're talking about why I married you."

"You married me," I said, telling the truth, "because you thought I was your last chance."

T W O

Saturday: pigs have wings, dogs can talk, money grows on trees—like some mindless and insistent song the litany wove through me, rolling amid the folds of my cerebrum as it always did when one of my nieces was scheduled to get burned. Stones are alive, rats chase cats—ten lies all told, a decalogue of deceit, resting at our city's core like a dragon sleeping beside a subterranean treasure. Salt is sweet, the Pope is Jewish—and suddenly the child has done it, suddenly she's thrown off the corrupt mantle of youth and put on the innocence of adulthood. Suddenly she's a woman.

I awoke aggressively that morning, tearing the blankets away as if nothing else stood between myself and total alertness. Across the room, my wife slept peacefully, indifferent to the world's sad truths, its dead rabbits. Ours was a two-bed marriage. The symbolism was not lost on me. Often we made love on the floor—in the narrow, neutral territory between our mattresses, our conjugal Geneva.

Yawning, I charged into the shower stall, where warm water poured forth the instant the sensors detected me. The TV receiver winked on—the *Enduring Another Day* program. Grimacing under the studio lights, our Assistant Secretary of Imperialism discussed the city's growing involvement in the Hegelian Civil War. "So far, over four thousand Veritasian combat troops have died," the interviewer noted as I lathered up with Bourgeois Soap. "A senseless loss," the secretary replied cheerfully. "Our policy is impossible to justify on rational grounds, which is why we've started invoking national security and other shibboleths."

I left the shower and padded bare-assed into the bedroom. Clothes per se were deceitful, of course, but nudity carried its own measure of compromise, a continual tacit message of provocation and come-hither. I dressed. Nothing disingenuous: underwear, a collarless shirt, a gray Age-of-Lies suit with the lapels cut off. Our apartment was similarly sparse, peeled to a core of rectitude. Many of our friends had curtains, wall hangings, and rugs, but not Helen and I. We were patriotic.

The odor of stale urine hit me as I approached the elevator. How unfortunate that some people translated the ban on sexually segregated rest rooms—PRIVACY IS A LIE, the huge flashing billboard on Voltaire Avenue reminded us—into a general fear of toilets. Hadn't they heard of public health? Public health was guileless.

I descended, crossed the lobby, encapsulated myself in the revolving door, and exited into Veritas's thick and gritty air. Sprinkled with soot, my Adequate lay on the far side of Eighty-second Street. In the old days, I'd heard, you never knew for sure that your car would be unmolested, or even there, when you left it overnight. Dishonesty was so rampant, you started your engine with a key.

I zoomed past the imperially functional cinderblocks that constituted City Hall, reaching the market district shortly before noon. Bless my luck, a parking spot lay directly in front of Molly's Rather Expensive Toy Store—such joy in emptiness, I mused, such satisfaction in a void.

"My, aren't *you* a pretty fellow?" a hawk-faced female clerk sang out as I strode through Molly's door. Pricey marionettes dangled from the ceiling like victims of a mass lynching. "Except, of course, for that chin."

"Your body's arousing enough," I replied, casting a candid eye up and down the clerk. A Bertrand Russell University T-shirt molded itself around her breasts. Grimy white slacks encased her thighs. "But that nose," I added forlornly. A demanding business, citizenship.

She tapped my wedding ring and glowered. "What brings you here? Something for your mistress's kid sister?"

"My niece is getting burned today."

"And you're waiting till the last minute to buy her a present?"

"True."

"Roller skates are popular. We sold fifteen pairs last month. Three were returned as defective."

"Lead the way."

I followed her past racks of baseball gloves and stuffed animals and up to a bin filled with roller skates, the new six-wheeler style with miniature jets in the heels. "The laces break in ten percent of cases," the clerk confessed. "Last April an engine exploded—maybe you saw the story on TV—and the poor girl, you know what happened? She got pitched into a culvert and cracked her skull and died."

"I believe Connie likes yellow," I said, taking down a pair of skates the color of Mom's Middling Margarine. "One size fits all?"

"More or less."

"Your price as good as anybody's else?"

"You can get the same thing for two dollars less at Marquand's."

"Haven't the time. Can you gift wrap them?"

"Not skillfully."

"Sold."

I'd promised Gloria I wouldn't just go to Connie's post-treatment party—I would attend the burn as well, doing what I could to keep the kid's morale up. Normally both parents were present, but that deplorable person Peter Raymond couldn't be bothered. "I've seen better parenting at the zoo," Helen liked to say of my ex-brother-in-law. "I know alligators who are better fathers."

You could find a burn hospital in practically every neighborhood, but Gloria had insisted on the best, Veterans' Shock Institute in Spinoza Borough, a smoke-stained pile of bricks overlooking the Giordano Bruno Bridge. Entering, I noticed a crowd of ten-year-olds jamming the central holding area; it seemed more like the platform of a train station than the waiting room of a hospital, the girls hanging together in nervous, chattering clusters, trying to comfort each other, the boys engaged in mock gunfights around the potted palms, distracting themselves with pseudoviolence, pretending not to be terrified of what the day would bring.

Securing the indifferently wrapped skates under my arm, I ascended to the second floor. WARNING: THIS ELEVATOR MAINTAINED BY PEOPLE WHO HATE THEIR JOBS. RIDE AT YOUR OWN RISK.

My niece was already in her glass cell, dressed in a green smock and bound to the chair via leather thongs, one electrode strapped to her left arm, another to her right leg. Black wires trailed from the copper terminals like threads spun by some vile and poisonous spider Toby would have adopted. She welcomed me with a brave smile, and I pointed to her gift, hoping to raise her spirits, however briefly.

Clipboard in hand, a short, cherubic doctor with MERRICK affixed to his tunic entered the cell and snugged a copper helmet over my niece's cranium. I gave her a thumbs-up signal. Soon it'll be over, kid—snow is hot, grass is purple, all of it.

"Thanks for coming," said Gloria, taking my arm and guiding me into the observation booth. "How's the family?"

"A rabbit attacked Toby."

"A *rabbit?*"

"And then it died."

"I'm glad somebody besides me has problems," she admitted.

My sister was a rather attractive woman—glossy black hair, pristine skin, a better chin than mine—but today she looked terrible: the anticipation, the fear. I was actually present when her marriage collapsed. The three of us were sitting in Booze Before Breakfast, and suddenly she said to Peter, "I sometimes worry that you copulate with Ellen Lambert—do you?"

And Peter said yes, he did. And Gloria said you fucker. And Peter said right. And Gloria asked how many others. And Peter said lots. Gloria asked why—did he do it to strengthen the marriage? Peter replied no, he just liked to ejaculate inside other women.

After patting Connie on her rust-colored bangs, Merrick joined us in the booth. "Morning, folks," he said, his cheer a precarious mix of the genuine and the forced. "How're we doing here?"

"Do you care?" my sister asked.

"Hard to say." The doctor fanned me with his clipboard. "Your husband?"

"Brother," Gloria explained.

"Jack Sperry," I said.

"Glad you could make it, Sperry," said the doctor. "When there's only one family member out here, the kid'll sometimes go catatonic on us." Merrick shoved the clipboard toward Gloria. "Informed consent, right?"

"They told me the possibilities." She studied the clipboard. "Cardiac—"

"Cardiac arrest, cerebral hemorrhage, respiratory failure, kidney damage," Merrick recited.

Gloria scrawled her signature. "When was the last time anything like that happened?"

"They killed a boy over at Veritas Memorial on Tuesday," said Merrick, edging toward the control panel. "A freak thing, but now and then we really screw up. Everybody ready?"

"Not really," said my sister.

Merrick pushed a button, and PIGS HAVE WINGS materialized before my niece on a Lucite tachistoscope screen. Seeing the falsehood, the doctor, Gloria, and I shuddered in unison.

"Can you hear me, lassie?" Merrick inquired into the microphone.

Connie opened her mouth, and a feeble "Yes" dribbled out of the loudspeaker.

"You see those words?" Merrick asked. The lurid red characters hovered in the air like weary butterflies.

"Y-yes."

"When I give the order, read them aloud."

"Is it going to hurt?" my niece quavered.

"It's going to hurt a lot. Will you read the words when I say so?"

"I'm scared. Do I have to?"

"You have to." Merrick rested a pudgy finger on the switch. "Now!"

" 'P-pigs have wings.' "

And so it began, this *bris* of the human conscience, this electro-convulsive rite of passage. Merrick nudged the switch. The volts ripped through Connie. She let out a sharp scream and turned the color of cottage cheese.

"But they don't," she gasped. "Pigs don't . . ."

My own burn flooded back. The outrage, the agony.

"You're right, lass—they don't." Merrick gave the voltage regulator a subtle twist, and Gloria flinched. "You did reasonably well, girl," the doctor continued, handing the mike to my sister.

"Oh, yes, Connie," she said. "Keep up the awfully good work."

"It's not fair." Sweat speckled Connie's forehead. "I want to go home."

As Gloria surrendered the mike, the tachistoscope projected SNOW IS HOT. My brain reeled with the lie.

"Now, lass! Read it!"

" 'S-s-snow is . . . h-hot.' " Lightning struck. Connie howled. Blood rolled over her lower lip. During my own burn, I'd practically bitten my tongue off. "I don't want this any more," she wailed.

"It's not a choice, lass."

"Snow is *cold*." Tears threaded Connie's freckles together. "Please stop hurting me."

"Cold. Right. Smart girl." Merrick cranked up the voltage. "Ready, Connie? Here it comes."

HORSES HAVE SIX LEGS.

"Why do I have to do this? *Why?*"

"Everybody does it. All your friends."

" 'H-h-horses have . . . have . . .' They have *four* legs, Dr. Merrick."

"Read the words, Connie!"

"I hate you! I hate all of you!"

"Connie!"

She raced through it. Zap. Two hundred volts. The girl coughed and retched. A coil of thick white mucus shot from her mouth.

"Too much," gasped Gloria. "Isn't that too much?"

"You want the treatment to take, don't you?" said Merrick.

"Mommy! Where's my mommy?"

Gloria tore the mike away. "Right here, dear!"

"Mommy, make them stop!"

"I can't, dear. You must try to be brave."

The fourth lie arrived. Merrick upped the voltage. "Read it, lass!"

"No!"

"Read it!"

"Uncle Jack! I want Uncle Jack!"

My throat constricted, my stomach went sour. "You're doing quite well, Connie," I said, grabbing the mike. "I think you'll like your present."

"Take me home!"

"I got you a pretty nice one."

Connie balled her face into a mass of wrinkles. " 'Stones—'!" she screamed, spitting blood. " 'Are'!" she persisted. " 'Alive'!" She jerked like a gaffed flounder, spasm after spasm. A broad urine stain bloomed on her smock, and despite the mandatory enema a brown fluid dripped from the hem.

"Excellent!" Merrick increased the punishment to three hundred volts. "The end is in sight, child!"

"No! Please! Please! Enough!" Foam leaked from Connie's mouth.

"You're almost halfway there!"

"Please!"

The tachistoscope kept firing, Connie kept lying: falsehood after falsehood, shock after shock—like a salvo of armed missiles cruising along her nerves, detonating inside her mind. My niece asserted that rats chase cats. She lied about money, saying it grew on trees. The Pope is Jewish, Connie insisted. Grass is purple. Salt is sweet.

As the final lie appeared, she fainted. Even before Gloria could scream, Merrick was inside the glass cell, checking the child's heartbeat. A begrudging admiration seeped through me. The doctor had a job to do, and he did it.

A single dose of ammonium carbonate brought Connie around. Easing her face toward the screen, Merrick turned to me. "Ready?"

"Huh? You want me . . . ?"

"Hit it when I tell you."

Reluctantly I rested my finger on the switch. "I'd rather not."

True. I wasn't inordinately fond of Connie, but I had no wish to give her pain.

"Read, Connie," muttered Merrick.

"I c-can't." Blood and spittle mingled on Connie's chin. "You all hate me! Mommy hates me!"

"I like you almost as much as I like myself," said Gloria, leaning over my shoulder. "You're going to have a satisfactory party."

"One more, Connie," I told her. "Just one more and you'll be a citizen." The switch felt sharp and hot against my finger. "A *highly* satisfactory party."

A single droplet rolled down Connie's cheek, staining it like a trail left by one of Toby's beloved slugs. This was, I realized, the last time she would ever cry. Brainburns did that to you; they drained you of all those destructive and chaotic juices: sentiments, illusions, myths, tears.

" 'Dogs can talk,' " she said, right before I pierced her heart with alternating current.

And it truly was a highly satisfactory party, filling the entire visitors' lounge and overflowing into the hall. All four of Connie's older sisters came, along with her reading teacher and eight of her girlfriends, half of whom had been cured that month, one on the previous day. They danced the Upright while a compact disc of the newest Probity hit wafted through the ward:

> *When skies are gray, and it starts to rain,*
> *I like to stand by the windowpane,*
> *And watch each raindrop bounce and fall,*
> *Then smile, 'cause I'm not getting wet at all.*

The hospital supplied the refreshments—a case of Olga's OK Orangeade, a tub of ice cream from No Great Shakes, and a slab of chocolate cake the size of a welcome mat. All the girls, I noticed, ate in moderation, letting their ice cream turn to soup. Artificially induced slenderness was, of course, disingenuous, but that was no reason to be a glutton.

The gift-giving ceremony contained one disturbing moment. After opening the expected succession of galoshes, reference books, umbrellas, and cambric blouses, Connie unwrapped a fully working model of an amusement park—Happy Land, it was called, complete with roller coaster, Ferris wheel, and merry-go-round. She blanched, seized by the panic that someone who's just been brainburned invariably feels in the presence of anything electric. Slamming her palm against her lips, she rushed into the bathroom. The friend who'd bought her the Happy Land, a stumpy, frizzy-haired girl named Beth, reddened with remorse. "I should've realized," she moaned.

Was the Happy Land a lie? I wondered. It purported to be an amusement park, but it wasn't.

"I'm so stupid," whined Beth.

No, I decided, it merely purported to be a replica of an amusement park, which it was.

Connie hobbled out of the bathroom. Silence descended like a sudden snowfall—not the hot snow of a brainburn but the cold, dampening snow of the objective world. Feet were shuffled, throats cleared. The party, obviously, had lost its momentum. Someone said, "We all had a reasonably good time, Connie," and that was that.

As her friends and sisters filed out, Connie hugged them with authentic affection (all except Alice Lawrence, whom she evidently disliked) and offered each a highly personalized thank-you, never forgetting who'd given what. Such a grown-up young lady, I thought. But her greatest display of maturity occurred when I said my own good-bye.

"Take care, Connie."

"Thanks for coming, Unc, and thanks for the roller skates. Thing is, I already have a pair, better than these. I'll probably swap them for a sweater."

A citizen now. I was proud of her.

Back at the apartment, the phone-answering machine was blinking. Three flashes, pause, three flashes, pause, three flashes, pause. I grabbed a bottle of Paul's Passable Ale from the fridge and snapped off the top. Three flashes, pause. I took a sizable swallow. Another. The late-afternoon light poured through the kitchen window and bathed our major appliances in the iridescent orange you see when facing the sun with eyes closed. I finished my beer.

Three flashes, pause, three flashes, pause: a staccato, insistent signal—a cry of distress, I realize in retrospect, like a call beamed semaphorically from a sinking ship.

I pushed PLAY. Toby had written and produced our outgoing message, and he also starred in it: *My folks and I just want to say / We'd like to talk with you today / So speak up when you hear the beep / And we might call back before we sleep.*

Beep, and a harsh male voice zagged into the kitchen. "Amusing message, sort of—about what I'd expect from a seven-year-old. This is Dr. Bamford at the Kraft Institute, and I presume I'm addressing the parents of Toby Sperry. Well, the results are in. The Hob's hare that bit your son was carrying high levels of Xavier's Plague, an uncommon and pathogenic virus. We shipped the specimen to Dr. Prendergorst at the Center for the Palliative Treatment of Hopeless Diseases in Locke Borough. If you have any questions, I'll be only mildly irritated if you call me. From now on, though, the matter is essentially in the Center's synecdochic hands." *Beep.* "John Prendergorst speaking, Center for the Palliative Treatment of Hopeless Diseases. You've probably heard Bamford's preliminary report by now, and we've just now corroborated it down here at Hopeless. Please call my office at your earliest convenience, and we'll arrange for you to come by and talk, but I'm afraid no amount of talk can change the fact that Xavier's is one hundred percent fatal. We'll show you the statistics." *Beep.* "Hi. It's Helen. I'm at the office, working on that neuropathology of spiritual possession piece. Looks like it'll be a long day and a longer night. There's some chicken in the freezer."

My reaction was immediate and instinctual. I ran into the study, grabbed Helen's unabridged dictionary, and looked up "fatal," bent on discovering some obscure usage peculiar to Prendergorst's profession. When the doctor said "fatal," I decided, he didn't mean *fatal,* he meant something far more ambiguous and benign.

Fast
Fasten
Fat
Fatal Adjective. Causing death; mortal; deadly.
Fatalism
Fatality
Fatally

No. The dictionary was lying. Just because Prendergorst's forecast was pessimistic, that didn't make it *true*.

Fata Morgana Noun. A mirage consisting of multiple images.

And, indeed, a vision now presented itself to my vibrating brain: one of the few copies of *The Journal of Psychic Healing* that I'd elected to spare, a special issue on psychoneuroimmunology, its cover displaying a pair of radiant hands massaging a human heart.

Fatuous Adjective. Silly, unreal, illusory.

Psychoneuroimmunology wasn't fatuous, I'd decided—not entirely. Even the peripatetic prose of *The Journal of Psychic Healing* hadn't concealed the scientific validity of cures spawned by the mind-body connection.

So there was hope. Oh, yes, hope. I would scour the city's data banks, I vowed. I would learn about anyone who'd ever beaten a fatal illness by tapping into the obscure powers of his own nervous system. I would tutor myself in sudden remissions, unexpected recoveries, and the taxonomy of miracles.

Fault
Faust
Favor
Fawn Noun. A young deer.

Because, you see, it was like this: on his fifth birthday we'd taken Toby to the Imprisoned Animals Garden in Spinoza Borough. Fawns roamed the petting zoo at will, prancing about on their cloven hoofs, noses thrust forward in search of handouts. Preschoolers swarmed everywhere, feeding the creatures peanut brittle, giggling as the eager tongues stroked their palms. Whenever another person's child laughed upon being so suckled, I was not especially moved. Whenever my own did the same, I felt something else entirely, something difficult to describe.

I believe I saw the alleged God.

THREE

Appropriately, the Center for the Palliative Treatment of Hopeless Diseases occupied a terminal location, a rocky promontory extending from the southern end of Locke Borough into the choppy, gunmetal waters of Becket Bay. We arrived at noon on Sunday, Helen driving, me navigating, the map of Veritas spread across my knees, its surface so mottled by rips and holes it seemed to depict the aftermath of a bombing raid. A fanfolded mile of computer paper lay on the back seat, the fruit of my researches into psychoneuroimmunology and the mind-body link. I knew all about miracles now. I was an expert on the impossible.

We parked in the visitors' lot. Tucking the printout under my arm, I followed Helen across the macadam. The structure looming over us was monumental and menacing, tier upon tier of diminishing concrete levels frosted with grimy stucco, as if Prendergorst's domain were a wedding cake initiating a marriage destined to end in wife abuse and murder.

In the lobby, a stark sign greeted us. ATTENTION: WE REALIZE THE DECOR HERE DOES NOTHING TO AMELIORATE YOUR SORROW AND DE-SPAIR. WRITE YOUR BOROUGH REPRESENTATIVE. WE'D LIKE TO PUT IN DECENT LIGHTING AND PAINT THE WALLS. A bristle-jawed nurse told us that Dr. Prendergorst—"You'll know him by his eyes, they look like pickled onions"—was expecting us on the eleventh floor.

We entered the elevator, a steamy box crowded with morose men and women, like a cattle boat bearing war refugees from one zone of chaos and catastrophe to another. I reached out to take Helen's hand. The gesture failed. Oiled by sweat, my fingers slipped from her grasp.

No one was waiting in the eleventh-floor waiting room, a gloomy niche crammed with overstuffed armchairs and steel engravings of famous cancer victims, a gallery stretching as far back in history as Jonathan Swift. Helen gave our names to the receptionist, a spindly young man with flourishing gardens of acne on his cheeks, who promptly got on the intercom and announced our arrival to Pren-dergorst, adding, "They look pale and scared."

We sat down. Best-selling self-help books littered the coffee table. *You Can Have Somewhat Better Sex. How to Find a Certain Amount of Inner Peace. The Heisenberg Uncertainty Diet.* "It's a mean system, isn't it?" the receptionist piped up from behind his desk. "He's in there, you're out here. He seems to matter, you don't. He keeps you waiting—you wait. The whole thing's set up to intimidate you."

I grunted my agreement. Helen said nothing.

A door opened. A short, round, onion-eyed man in a white lab coat came out, accompanied by a fiftyish couple—a blobby woman in a shabby beige dress and her equally fat, equally disheveled husband: rumpled golf cap, oversized polyester polo shirt, baggy corduroy pants; they looked like a pair of bookends they'd failed to unload at their own garage sale. "There's nothing more I can say," Prendergorst informed them in a low, tepid voice. "A Hickman catheter is our best move at this point."

"She's our only child," moaned the wife.

"Leukemia's a tough one," said Prendergorst.

"Shouldn't you do more tests?" asked the husband.

"Medically—no. But if it would make you feel better . . ."

The couple exchanged terse, pained glances. "It wouldn't," said the wife, shambling off.

"True," said the husband, following.

A minute later we were in Prendergorst's office, Helen and I seated on metal folding chairs, the doctor positioned regally behind a mammoth desk of inlaid cherry. "Would you like to put some sugar in your brain?" he asked, proffering a box of candy.

"No," said Helen tonelessly.

"I guess the first step is to confirm the diagnosis, right?" I said, snatching up a dark chocolate nugget. I bit through the outer shell. Brandy trickled into my throat.

"When your son gets back from camp, I'll draw a perfunctory blood sample," said Prendergorst, sliding an open file folder across his desk. Beneath Toby's name, a gruesome photograph of the deceased Hob's hare lay stapled to the inside front cover, its body reduced by the autopsy to a gutted pelt. "The specimen they sent us was loaded with the virus," said the doctor. "Absolutely loaded. The chances of Toby not being infected are perhaps one in a million." He whisked the file away, slipping it into his top desk drawer. "A rabbit killing your child, it's all faintly absurd, don't you think? A snake would make more sense, or a black widow spider, even one of those poisonous toads—can't remember what they're called. But a rabbit . . ."

"So what sort of therapy are we looking at?" I asked. "I hope it's not too debilitating."

"We aren't looking at *any* therapy, Mr. Sperry. At best, we'll relieve your son's pain until he dies."

"Toby's only seven," I said, as if I were a lawyer asking a governor to reprieve an underage client. "He's only seven years old."

"I think I'll *sue* that damn camp," Helen grunted.

"You'd lose," said Prendergorst, handing her a stark pamphlet, white letters on black paper: *Xavier's Plague and Xavier's-Related Syndrome—The News Is All Bad.* "I wish I could remember what those toads are called."

Had my brainburn not purged me of sentimentality and schmaltz, had it not, as it were, atrophied my tear ducts, I think I would have wept right then. Instead I did something almost as unorthodox. "Dr. Prendergorst," I began, my hands trembling in my lap like two chilly tarantulas, "I realize that, from your perspective, our son's chances are nil."

"Quite so."

I deposited the computer printout on Prendergorst's desk. "Look here, over twenty articles from *The Holistic Health Bulletin,* plus the entire *Proceedings of the Eighth Annual Conference on Psychoneuroimmunology* and *The Collected Minutes of the Fifth International Mind-Body Symposium.* Story after story of people thinking their way past heart disease, zapping malignant cells with mental bullets—you name it. Surely you've heard of such cases."

"Indeed," said Prendergorst icily.

"Jack . . . *please,*" groaned Helen, wincing with embarrassment. My wife, the *Sweet Reason* reporter.

"Miracles happen," I persisted. "Not commonly, not reliably, but they happen."

"Miracles *happened,*" said Prendergorst, casting a cold eye on the printout. "These incidents all come from the Nightmare Era— they're all from the Age of Lies. We're adults now."

"It's basically a matter of giving the patient a positive outlook," I explained.

"*Please,*" hissed Helen.

"People can cure themselves," I asserted.

"I believe it's time we returned to the real world, Mr. Sperry." Prendergorst shoved the printout away as if it were contaminated with Xavier's. "Your wife obviously agrees with me."

"Maybe we should bring Toby home next week," Helen suggested, fanning herself with the pamphlet. "The sooner he knows," she sighed, "the better."

Prendergorst slid a pack of Canceroulettes from the breast pocket of his lab coat. "When's your son scheduled to leave?"

"On the twenty-seventh," said Helen.

"The symptoms won't start before then. I'd keep him where he is. Why spoil his summer?"

"But he'll be living a lie. He'll go around thinking he's not dying."

"We *all* go around thinking we're not dying," said the doctor with a quick little smile. He removed a cigarette, set the pack on the edge of the desk. WARNING: THE SURGEON GENERAL'S CRUSADE AGAINST THIS PRODUCT MAY DISTRACT YOU FROM THE MYRIAD WAYS YOUR GOVERNMENT FAILS TO PROTECT YOUR HEALTH. "God, what a depraved species we are. I'm telling you that Toby is mortally ill, and all the while I'm thinking, 'Hey, my life is really pretty good, isn't it? No son of *mine* is dying. Fact is, I take a certain pleasure in these people's suffering.'"

"And when the symptoms *do* start?" Helen folded the pamphlet into queer, tortured origami shapes. "What then?"

"Nothing dramatic at first. Headaches, joint pains, some hair loss. His skin may acquire a bluish tint."

Helen said, "And then?"

"His lymph nodes will become painful and swollen. His lungs will probably fill with *Pneumocystis carinii*. His temperature—"

"Don't go on," I said.

The doctor ignited his cigarette. "Each case is different. Some Xaviers linger for a year, some go in less than a month. In the meantime, we'll do everything we can, which isn't much. Demerol, IV nourishment, antibiotics for the secondary infections."

"We've heard enough," I said.

"The worst of it is probably the chills." Prendergorst took a drag on his cigarette. "Xaviers, they just can't seem to get warm. We wrap them in electric blankets, and it doesn't make any—"

"Please stop," I pleaded.

"I'm merely telling the truth," said the doctor, exhaling a jagged smoke ring.

All the way home, Helen and I said nothing to each other. Nothing about Toby, nothing about Xavier's, nothing about miracles—nothing.

Weirdly, cruelly, my thoughts centered on rabbits. How I would no longer be able to abide their presence in my life. How I would tremble with rage from now on whenever my career required me to criticize a copy of *Peter Rabbit* or an Easter card bearing some grinning bunny. I might even start seeking the animals out, leaving a trail of mysterious, mutilated corpses in my wake, whiskers plucked, ears torn off, tails severed from their rumps and stuffed down their throats.

Total silence. Not one word.

We entered the elevator, pushed 30. The car made a sudden, rapid ascent, like a pearl diver clambering toward the air: second floor, seventh, twelfth . . .

"How are you feeling?" I said at last.

"Not good," Helen replied.

" 'Not good'—is that all? 'Not good'? I feel horrible."

"In my case, 'horrible' would not be a truthful word."

"I feel all knotted and twisted. Like I'm a glove, and somebody's pulled me inside out"—a bell rang, the numeral 30 flashed above our heads—"and my vital parts, my heart and lungs, they're naked and—"

"You've been reading too many of the poems you deconstruct."

"I hate your coldness, Helen."

"You hate my candor."

I left the car, started down the hall. Imagined exchanges haunted me—spectral words, ghostly vocables, scenes from an intolerable future.

Dad, what are these lumps under my arms?

Swollen lymph nodes, Toby.

Am I sick, Dad?

Sicker than you can imagine. You have Xavier's Plague.

Will I get better?

No.

Will I get warm?
No.
Will I die?
Yes.
What happens when you die, Dad? Do you wake up somewhere else?
There's no objective evidence for an afterlife, and anecdotal reports of heaven cannot be distinguished from wishful thinking, self-delusion, and the effects of oxygen loss on the brain.

The apartment had turned against me. Echoes of Toby were everywhere, infecting the living room like the virus now replicating in his cells—a child-sized boot, a dozen stray checkers, the miniature Crusaders' castle he'd built out of balsa wood the day before he went to camp. "How do you like it, Dad?" he'd asked as he set the last turret in place. "It's somewhat ugly," I'd replied, flinching at the truth. "It's pretty lopsided," I'd added, sadly noting the tears welling up in my son's eyes.

On the far wall, the picture window beckoned. I crossed our rugless floor, pressed my palms against the glass. A mile away, a neon sign blazed atop the cathedral in Galileo Square. ASSUMING GOD EXISTS, JESUS MAY HAVE BEEN HIS SON.

Helen went to the bar and made herself a dry martini, flavoring it with four olives skewered on a toothpick like kabobs. "I wish our son wasn't dying," she said. "I truly wish it."

An odd, impossible sentence formed on my tongue. "Whatever happens, Toby won't learn the truth."

"Huh?"

"You heard Prendergorst—in the Nightmare Era, terminal patients sometimes tapped their bodies' natural powers of regeneration. It's all a matter of attitude. If Toby believes there's hope, he might have a remission."

"But there isn't any hope."

"Maybe."

"There *isn't.*"

"I'll go to him, and I'll say, 'Buddy, soon the doctors will . . . the doctors, any day now, they'll . . . they'll c-c . . .'"

Cure you—but instead my conditioning kicked in, a hammerblow in my skull, a hot spasm in my chest.

"I know the word, Jack. Stop kidding yourself. It's uncivilized to carry on like this." Helen sipped her martini. "Want one?"

"No."

I fixed on the metropolis, its bright towers and spangled skyscrapers rising into a misty, starless night. Within my disordered brain, a plan was taking shape, as palpable as any sculpture I'd ever deconstructed at the Wittgenstein.

"They're out there," I said.

"Who?"

"They can lie. And maybe they can teach *me* to lie."

"You're talking irrationally, Jack. I wish you wouldn't talk irrationally."

It was all clear now. "Helen, I'm going to become one of them— I'm going to become a dissembler." I pulled my hand away, leaving my palm imprinted on the glass like a fortune-teller's logo. "And then I'm going to convince Toby he has a chance."

"I don't think that's a very good idea."

"Somehow they've gotten around the burn. And if *they* can, *I* can."

Helen lifted the toothpick from her martini glass and sucked the olives into her mouth. "Toby's hair will start shedding in two weeks. He's certain to ask what that means."

Two weeks. Was that all I had? "I'll say it means n-n-nothing." A common illness, I'd tell him. A disease easily licked.

"Jack—*don't*."

A mere two weeks. A feeble fourteen days.

I ran to the kitchen, snatched up the phone. I need to see you, I'd tell her. This isn't about sex, Martina.

610-400.

It rang three times, then came a distant click, ominous and hollow. "The number you have reached," ran the recorded operator in a harsh, gravelly voice, "is out of service." My bowels became as hard and cold as a glacier. "Probably an unpaid bill," the taped message continued. "We're pretty quick to disconnect in such cases."

"Out of service," I told Helen.

"Good," she said.

7 Lackluster Lane, Descartes Borough.

Helen polished off her martini. "Now let's forget this ridiculous

notion," she said. "Let's face the future with honesty, clearheaded-
ness, and . . ."

But I was already out the door.

Girding the gray and oily Pathogen River, Lackluster Lane was alive
with smells: scum, guano, sulfur, methane, decaying eels—a cacoph-
ony of stench blaring through the shell of my Adequate. "And, of
course, at the center of my opposition to abortion," said the somber
priest on my car radio, "is my belief that sexual intercourse is a
fundamentally disgusting practice to begin with." This was the city's
frankest district, a mass of defunct fishmarkets and abandoned ware-
houses piled together like dead cells waiting to be sloughed off. "You
might even say that, like many of my ilk, I have an instinctive horror
of the human body."

And suddenly there it was, Number 7, a corrugated tin shanty
sitting on a cluster of pylons rising from the Pathogen like mortally
ill trees. Gulls swung through the summer air, dropping their guileless
excrement on the dock; water lapped against the moored hull of
a houseboat, the *Average Josephine*—a harsh, sucking sound, as if a
pride of invisible lions were drinking there. I pulled over.

A series of narrow, jackknifing gangplanks rose from the nearest
pier like a sliding board out of *The Cabinet of Dr. Caligari*—one of
my most memorable forays into film criticism—eventually reaching
the landing outside Martina's door. I climbed. I knocked. Nothing. I
knocked again, harder. The door drifted open.

I called, "Martina?"

The place had been stripped, emptied out like the Hob's hare
whose photo I'd seen that morning in Prendergorst's office. The front
parlor contained a crumpled beer can, a mousetrap baited with calcified cheddar, some cigarette butts—and nothing else. I went to the
kitchen. The sink held a malodorous broth of water, soap, grease, and
cornflakes. The shelves were empty.

"Martina? Martina?"

In the back room, a naked set of rusting bedsprings sat on a
pinewood frame so crooked it might have come from Toby's workshop.

I returned to the hot, sour daylight, paused on Martina's landing.
A wave of nausea rolled through me, straight to my putative soul.

Out on the river, a Brutality Squad cutter bore down on an

outboard motorboat carrying two men in green ponchos. Evidently they were attempting to escape—every paradise will have its dissidents, every utopia its defectors—an ambition abruptly thwarted as a round of machine-gun fire burst from the cutter, killing both fugitives instantly. Their corpses fell into the Pathogen, reddening it like dye markers. I felt a quick rush of qualified sympathy. Such fools. Didn't they know that for most intents and a majority of purposes Veritas was as good as it gets?

"Some people . . ."

I looked toward the dock. A tall, fortyish, excruciatingly thin man in hip boots and a tattered white sweatshirt stood on the foredeck of *Average Josephine*.

". . . are so naive," he continued. "Imagine, trying to run the channel in broad daylight." He reached through a hole in his shirt and scratched his hairy chest. "Your girlfriend's gone."

"Are you referring to Martina Coventry?" I asked.

"Uh-huh."

"She's not my girlfriend."

"The little synecdochic cunt owes me two hundred dollars in rent."

I descended through the maze of gangplanks. "You're her landlord?"

"Mister, in my wretched life I've acquired three things of value—this houseboat, that shanty, and my good name." Martina's landlord stomped his boot on the deck. He had an extraordinarily chaotic and unseemly beard, like a bird's nest constructed under a bid system. "You know how much a corporation vice president typically pulls down in a month? Twelve thousand. I'm lucky to see that in a *year*. Clamming's a pathetic career."

"Clamming?"

"Well, you can't make a living renting out a damn shanty, that's for sure," said Martina's landlord. "Of course, you can't make one clamming either. You from the Squad? Is Coventry wanted by the law?"

"I'm not from the Squad."

"Good."

"But I have to find her. It's vital." I approached within five feet of the landlord. He smelled like turtle food. "Can you give me any leads?"

"Not really. Want some clam chowder? I raked 'em up myself."

"You seem like a highly unsanitary person. How do I know your chowder won't make me ill?"

He smiled, revealing a severe shortage of teeth. "You'll have to take your chances."

And that's how I ended up in the snug galley of *Average Josephine*, savoring the best clam chowder I'd ever eaten.

His name was Boris—Boris the Clamdigger—and he knew almost as little about Martina as I did. They'd had sex once, in lieu of the rent. Afterwards, he'd read some of her doggerel, and he'd thought it barely suitable for equipping an outhouse. Evidently she'd been promised a job writing greeting-card verses for Cloying and Coy: they'd reneged; she'd run out of cash; she'd panicked and fled.

" 'Vital,' " Boris muttered. "You said 'vital,' and I can tell from your sad eyes, which are a trifle beady, a minor flaw in your moderately handsome face—I can tell 'vital' was exactly what you meant. It's a heavy burden you're carrying around, something you'd rather not discuss. Don't worry, Jack, I won't pry. You see, I rather like you, even though you probably make a lot of money. How much do you make?"

I stared at my chowder, lumpy with robust clams and bulbous potatoes. "Two thousand a month."

"I *knew* it," said Boris. "Of course, that's *nothing* next to what a real estate agent or a borough rep pulls down. What field?"

"Art criticism."

"I've got to get out of clams. I've got to get out of *Veritas*, actually—a dream I don't mind sharing with somebody who's not a Squad officer. It's a big planet, Jack. One day I'll just pull up anchor and *whoosh*—I'm gone."

The shock and indignation I should have felt at such perverse musings would not come. "Boris, do you believe in miracles?" I asked.

"There are times when I don't believe in anything else. How's the chowder?"

"Terrific."

"I know."

"May I have some more?"

"No—I want to save the rest for myself."

"I don't see how you'd ever escape," I said. "The Squad would shoot you down."

"Probably." My host swallowed a large spoonful of his exquisite chowder. "At least I'd be getting out of clams."

FOUR

Monday: back to work, my flesh like lead, my blood like liquid mercury. I'd spent the previous week locked in the Wittgenstein's tiny screening room, scrutinizing the fruit of Hollywood's halcyon days and confirming the archaeologists' suspicions that these narratives contained not one frame of truth, and now it was time to deconstruct them, *Singin' in the Rain, Doctor Zhivago, Rocky,* the whole deceiving lot. Hour followed hour, day melded into day, but my routine never varied: filling the bathtubs, dumping in the 35mm negatives, watching the triumph of Clorox over illusion. Like souls leaving bodies, the Technicolor emulsions floated free of their bases, disintegrating in the potent, purifying bleach.

My heart wasn't in it. Cohn, Warner, Mayer, Thalberg, Selznick—these men were not my enemies. *Au contraire,* I wanted to be like them; I wanted to *be* them. Whatever one might say against Hollywood's moguls, they could all have blessed their ailing children with curative encouragement and therapeutic falsehoods.

Stanley Marcus stayed away until Thursday, when he suddenly appeared in my coffee cubicle as I was dispiritedly consuming a tunafish sandwich and attempting, without success, to drown my sorrows in caffeine. Saying nothing, he took up his broom and swept the floor with slow, morose strokes.

"That recommendation letter was pretty nasty," he said at last, sweating in the July heat. "I wish you hadn't called me a toady."

"I had a choice?"

"I didn't get the promotion."

"It's not easy for me to pity you," I said through a mouthful of tuna, mayo, and Respectable Rye. "I have a sick son. Only lies can cure him."

Stanley rammed his broom into the floor. "Look, I'm a ridiculous person, we all know that. Women want nothing to do with me. I'm a loner. Don't talk to me about your home life, Mr. Sperry. Don't talk about your lousy son."

I blanched and trembled. "Fuck you figuratively, Stanley Marcus!"

"Fuck *you* figuratively, Jack Sperry!" He clutched the broom against his bosom, pivoted on his heel, and fled.

I finished my coffee and decided to make some more, using a double helping of crystals from my Donaldson's Drinkable jar.

Back in the shop, yet another stack of 35mm reels awaited my review, a celluloid tower stretching clear to the ceiling. As Donaldson's Drinkable cavorted, so to speak, through my neurons, I rolled up my sleeves and got to work. I dissolved *The Wizard of Oz* and *Gone With the Wind*, stripped *Citizen Kane* and *King Kong* down to the acetate, rid the world of *Top Hat, A Night at the Opera*, and—how blatant can a prevaricator get?—*It's a Wonderful Life*.

The end-of-day whistle blew, a half-dozen steamy squeals echoing throughout the Wittgenstein. As the sixth cry faded away, a seventh arose, human, female—familiar.

"Way to go, critic!"

I glanced up from my tub of Clorox, where *Casablanca* was currently burbling toward oblivion. The doorway framed her.

"Martina? *Martina?*"

"Hello, Jack." Her silver lamé dress hugged her every contour like some elaborate skin graft. A matching handbag swung from her shoulder. I'd never seen a Veritasian outfitted so dishonestly before—but then, of course, Martina was evidently much more than a Veritasian.

"The guard let you through?" I asked, astonished.

"After I agreed to copulate with him tomorrow, yes."

The truth? A half-truth? There was no way, I realized with a sudden pang of anxiety, to gauge this woman's sincerity. "I'm extraordinarily happy to see you," I said. "I went to that address you gave me, but—"

"Just *once* I'd like to meet a man whose genitalia didn't rule his life."

"I wanted to talk with you, that's all. A *talk*. I ran into Boris the Clamdigger."

Opening her silver handbag, Martina retrieved a one-liter bottle of Charlie's Cheapdrunk and a pair of Styrofoam cups. "Did he mention anything about two hundred bucks?"

"Uh-huh."

"He's not going to get it." She set the cups on my workbench and filled them with mud-colored wine. "I suppose he told you we had sex?"

"Yes."

"Hell, Jack, you know more about my private life than *I* do." She seized her cup of Charlie's and sashayed around the shop, breasts rolling like channel buoys on Becket Bay, hips swaying like mounds of dough being hefted by a pizza chef.

It was all lost on me, every bounce and bob. My urges had died when Prendergorst said *fatal;* I'd been gelded by an adjective.

Grabbing my wine, I swilled it down in one gulp.

"So this is where it all happens." Martina stopped before my tool rack, massaging my axes, fondling my tin snips, running her fingers over my saws, pliers, and drills. "Impressive . . ."

"Where are you living now?" I asked, refilling my cup.

"With my girlfriend. I can't afford anything better—Cloying and Coy turned down my Mother's Day series." She finished off her Charlie's. "Which reminds me—you know that page of doggerel I gave you?"

Like a chipmunk loading up on acorns, I inflated my cheeks with wine. I swallowed. "Those verses have never left my mind. As it were."

Martina frowned severely, apparently puzzled by the notion that her doggerel was in any way memorable. "I want them back. You never liked them in the first place."

The wine was everywhere now, warming my hands and feet, massaging my brain. "They're somewhat appealing, in their own vapid way."

Hips in high gear, she moved past the seething remains of *Casablanca,* reached the door, and snapped the deadbolt into place. "I don't know what I was thinking when I let them go. I always save my original manuscripts. I'll gladly give you a copy."

So there it was, the final proof of Martina's true colors. The cunning little liar had deduced the poems were dangerous—in her justified paranoia, she'd imagined me spotting the flagrant falsehoods embedded in the page.

Buzzing with Cheapdrunk, I didn't resist when Martina ushered me across the shop to my assignment for the upcoming week—a mountainous pile of Cassini gowns, Saint Laurent shirts, and Calvin Klein jeans.

"So anyway," she said as we eased into the fraudulent fabrics, "if you could give me those verses . . ."

Her full wet lips came toward me, her eager puppyish tongue emerged. She kissed me all over; it was like being molested by a marshmallow. We hugged and fondled, clutched and tussled, poked and probed.

My genitalia, to use Martina's word, might as well have been on the moon, for all they cared. I said, "Martina, I know why you want that doggerel."

"Oh?"

Icy vibrations passed through her, the tremors of her guilt. "You want it because the paper's riddled with lies," I said. The skin tightened on her bones. "You're a dissembler."

"No," she insisted, extricating herself from our embrace.

"How do you counteract the conditioning?" I persisted.

She stood up. "I'm *not* one."

"You wrote about having wings. You wrote about a *soul*." Scrambling to my feet, I squeezed her large, Rubensian hand. "My son means a great deal to me. Love, even. He's just a boy. Ever hear of Xavier's Plague? He mustn't learn the truth. If he doesn't realize it's fatal, he might go into remission or even—"

She ran to the door as if fleeing some act of the alleged God, a forest fire, tidal wave, cyclone. "You've got the wrong woman!" she shouted, throwing back the bolt.

"I won't go to the Squad—I promise. Please, Martina, teach me how you do it!"

She tore open the door, started into the hot dusk. "I tell only the truth!"

"Liar!"

Sweating and shaking, she fumbled into her shiny Toyota Functional and backed out of the parking lot. Her rubbery face was bloodless. Her eyes flashed with fear. Martina Coventry: dissembler. Oh, yes, truer words had never been spoken.

She will not escape, I silently vowed, clasping my hands together in that most dangerous of postures and disingenuous of gestures. *With God as my witness,* I added with a nod to the late, great *Gone With the Wind.*

Heaven answered me with a traffic jam, the full glory of the Veritasian rush hour. I ran into its dense screeching depths, weaving around pedestrians like a skier following a slalom course, never letting Martina's Functional out of my sight. She crawled down Voltaire Avenue, turned east onto River Lane. By the time she reached the bridge, the traffic had halted completely, like a wave of molten lava solidifying on the slope of a volcano.

She pulled into a parking space, started the meter, and ducked into a seedy-looking bar-and-grill called Dolly's Digestibles.

A pay telephone stood at the Schopenhauer Avenue intersection. The thing worked perfectly. In the Age of Lies, I'd heard, public phones were commonly the targets of criminal behavior.

I told Helen I wouldn't be home for supper. "I'm tracking a dissembler," I explained.

"The Coventry woman?"

"Yes." I peered through the bar's grubby window. Martina sat in the back, sipping an Olga's OK Orangeade and eating a murdered cow.

Helen said, "Did you have sex with her?"

"No." A mild but undeniable pain arose in my temples. "We kissed."

"On the lips?"

"Yes. We also hugged."

"Come home, Jack."

"Not before I'm one of them."

"Jack!"

Click. I stood in the silvery, sulfurous rain and waited.

Within the hour Martina left Dolly's Digestibles and set out on foot, striding eastward into the twilit depths of Nietzsche Borough. Once the linchpin of the Veritas Trolley Company, an enterprise that in its heyday shuttled both freight and humans around the metropolis, Nietzsche had of late fallen victim to the revolution in private transportation, becoming underpopulated and inert, an urban moonscape. I followed Martina to a depot, its tracks now deserted but for the occasional rusting Pullman or decaying boxcar. How stealthy I was, how furtive—how like a dissembler already.

A roundhouse loomed up, its turntable lying before the switchyard like an enormous lazy Susan, its barns sealed with slabs of corrugated steel. A diesel locomotive sat on the nearest siding, hulking into the wet summer air like the fossilized remains of some postindustrial dinosaur.

Martina drummed on the door—a swift, snappy paradiddle— and a tall, devil-bearded man answered, his gaunt features softened by the dusk. "I'm Spartacus, come to free the slaves," she told him—a code phrase, evidently. I flinched at the falsehood.

"This way, brave Thracian," he replied, stepping aside to let her pass.

Sneaking around back, I groped along the sooty, rust-stained walls. A high, open window beckoned. I was all instinct now, piling the handiest junk together (pickle barrel, apple crate, fifty-five-gallon drum), scrambling upward like the swashbuckling hero of some Cinemascope illusion. I reached the sill and peered in.

Liars—everywhere, liars. There were over four hundred of them, chattering among themselves as they gripped kerosene lanterns and drifted amid the empty rails, gradually converging upon a makeshift wooden podium suspended several feet above the ground on stilts. The women were dressed outrageously, in low-cut sequined blouses and spangled stretch pants, like chorus girls out of a Fred Astaire movie; Martina fit right in. The men's attire was equally antisocial. They wore tuxedos with white gloves; riding cloaks and jodhpurs; lavender jackets that might have been stolen from pimps.

A burly man in a zoot suit mounted the steps of the podium, carrying a battery-powered bullhorn. "Settle down, everybody!" came his electrified bellow.

The mob grew quiet. "Take it away, Sebastian!" somebody called from the floor.

The liars' leader—Sebastian—strutted back and forth on the podium, flashing a jack-o'-lantern grin. "What is snow?" he shouted. I fixed on Martina. "Snow is hot!" she screamed along with her peers.

A dull ache wove through my belly. I closed my eyes and jumped into the thick, creosote-clogged air.

"What chases cats?" Sebastian demanded.

"Rats chase cats!" the liars responded in a single voice—a mighty shout drowning out the thud of my boots striking the roundhouse floor. *Rats chase cats:* God. My discomfort increased, nausea pounding deep within me. I backed against a rivet-studded girder, my body camouflaged by shadows, my footfalls masked by the rumble of the crowd.

"Now," said Sebastian, "down to business . . ."

Gradually the sickness passed, and I was able to monitor the schemes now unfolding before me.

The dissemblers—I quickly learned—were planning yet another attack on Veritas's domestic tranquility. For one astonishingly disruptive afternoon, they would revive what Sebastian called "that vanished and miraculous festival known as Christmas." Anything to demoralize the city, evidently, anything to rot it from within. At 2 P.M. on December 25, when Circumspect Park was packed with families out for a jolly afternoon of skating on the duck pond and drinking hot chocolate by bonfires, the liars would strike. Costumed as angels, elves, gnomes, and sugarplum fairies, they would swoop into the park and cordon it off with snow fences, discreetly taking a dozen hostages to discourage police intervention. Sebastian's forces would next erect a so-called Christmas tree on the north shore of the pond—a Scotch pine as big as a windmill—immediately inviting Veritas's presumably awestruck children to decorate it with colored glass balls and tinsel. Then, as evening drew near, the dissemblers would perform a three-act adaptation of a Charles Dickens story called *A Christmas Carol.* I knew all about that story, and not just because I'd read a copy of the first edition prior to burning it. *A Christmas Carol* had entered history as one of the falsest fables of all time, a glib embodiment of the lie that the wicked can be made to see the errors of their ways.

Finally: the climax. A loading gantry would appear on the scene and suddenly—look—here comes old Santa Claus himself, descending from the sky in a shiny red sleigh harnessed to eight audio-animatronic reindeer and jammed with gifts wrapped in glittery gold paper. As the children gathered around—their hearts pounding with delight, their faces aglow with glee, their poor defenseless minds dizzy with delusion—the elves would shower them with the stuff of their dreams, with scooters and ten-speeds, dollhouses and electric trains, teddy bears and toy soldiers.

Sebastian held up the red suit, pillow, and fake beard he intended to wear as Santa Claus, and the roundhouse broke into instant, thunderous applause.

I studied the crowd, shuddering each time I came upon a familiar face. Good heavens: Jimmy Breeze, the bartender from Booze Before Breakfast. Who would have picked *him* for a liar? Or my plumber, Paul Irving? Or my barber, Bill Mumford?

Sebastian divided his legions into the necessary task forces. Jimmy Breeze ended up on the Ornaments Committee; my plumber was cast as Ebenezer Scrooge; my barber volunteered to be an elf; Martina agreed to write Santa's opening oration.

The closing litany caught me by surprise.

"What can dogs do?" Sebastian shouted abruptly.

"They can talk!" answered the mob.

My brain began to throb.

"What color is grass?"

"Purple!"

The pounding in my skull intensified.

"Stones are . . ."

"Alive!"

"Stop!" I cried, squeezing my head between my palms. "Stop! Please stop!"

Four hundred faces turned toward me. Eight hundred eyes blazed with anger and indignation.

"Who's that?" someone asked.

"Spy!" a voice called.

Another voice: "Brutality Squad!"

Another: "Get him!"

I raised my open palms. "Listen! I want to join you!" The liars rushed toward me like the hordes in the most impressive Renaissance oil I'd deconstructed during my apprenticeship, Altdorfer's *Battle of Issus*. "I want to become a dissembler!"

A leathery hand curled around my mouth. I bit into it, tasting the liar's salty blood. A boot jabbed my side, snapping one of my ribs like a dry twig. Groaning, reeling with fear, I dropped to my knees. I'd never before felt so much of that ultimate truth, that quintessential fact, pain.

The last thing I saw before losing consciousness was my tax adviser's fist moving swiftly toward my jaw.

I woke up alive. Alive—and no better than alive. My lips felt like two fat snails grafted onto my face. My torso, it seemed, had recently been employed as the ball in some particularly violent contact sport. Pain chewed at my side.

Gradually the gooey film slid from my eyes. I took stock. Foam mattress, eiderdown pillow, the adamant odor of rubbing alcohol. Adhesive tape encircled my chest, as if it were the handle of a tennis racket.

A middle-aged doctor in a white lab coat fidgeted beside me, stethoscope dangling from her neck. "Good morning," she said, apparently meaning it. A thin, vivid face: beaky nose, sharp chin, high cheeks—a face that, while not beautiful, would probably always retain a certain fascination for anybody obliged to behold it regularly.

"Morning? Is it Friday already?"

"Very good," the doctor answered merrily. Her smile was as crisp and bright as a gibbous moon. "I'm Felicia Krakower, and I truly, sincerely hope you're feeling better."

Across the room, an old man with skin the color of oolong tea sat upright on his mattress, his head wrapped in a turban of brilliant white bandages.

"My rib hurts," I said.

"I'm terribly sorry to hear that," said Dr. Krakower. "Don't fret. You're in Satirev now."

"Satirev?"

"Off the map." Dr. Krakower waved a thermometer around as if conducting an orchestra.

"Spell it backwards," my roommate suggested. "I'm Louie, by

the way. Brain cancer. No big deal. It just grows and grows up there, like moss, and then one day—pfttt—I'm gone. Death is an extraordinary adventure."

I slid the thermometer between my lips. Satirev . . . Veritas . . . Satirev . . . Veritas . . .

My accommodations were coated with lurid yellow paint and equally lurid lies—a poster-sized edition of Keats's "Ode on a Grecian Urn," a reproduction of van Gogh's *Sunflowers,* a print of Salvador Dali's notorious landscape of trees fruited with pocket watches. I glanced through a rose-tinted window. Outside, a rank of Corinthian columns supported a carved lintel reading CENTER FOR CREATIVE WELLNESS.

As Felicia Krakower removed the thermometer, I pressed my staved-in side and said, "Doctor, you've heard of psychoneuroimmunology, haven't you?"

"The mind-body connection?"

"Right. The patient adopts such a cheerful outlook that his sickness never takes hold. Does that ever happen?"

"Of *course* it happens," the doctor replied, sliding her index finger along the bright yellow tubing of her stethoscope. "Miracles happen every day—the sun comes up, a baby gets born—and don't you ever forget it, Jack Sperry."

How marvelous to be among people who weren't afraid of hope. "Bless you, doctor—am I running a fever?"

"Maybe a tiny one. Not to worry. In Satirev, one never stays ill for long."

"I should call my wife."

Against all odds, the doctor's smile grew even larger. "You have a *wife?* Wonderful. Lovely. I'll relay your request to Internal Security immediately. Open your mouth, would you?"

"Why?"

"Something for your own good."

I moved my wounded lips apart. The doctor deposited a sugary, kidney-shaped capsule on my tongue, handed me a glass of water. "How do I *know* it's for my own good?"

"Trust me," said Dr. Krakower.

"In Satirev people trust each other," said Louie.

"Sleeping pill?" I asked, swallowing.

"Could be," said the doctor.

Sleeping pill . . .

When I returned to awareness, Martina Coventry was leaning over me, still packaged in her lascivious silver dress. Beside her stood a tall, lanky, coarse-skinned man in a green dinner jacket fitted over a sweatshirt that said WHEN LIFE GIVES YOU LEMONS, MAKE LEMONADE. He looked like a cactus.

"Martina!"

She laid a plump hand on my forehead. "Say hello to Franz Beauchamp."

"Hello," I said to the cactoid man.

"I'm in charge of making sure you don't wander off," Franz explained in a voice that seemed to enter the room after first traveling through a vat of honey. "It's no big deal. Just give me your Veritasian word you won't wander off."

"I won't wander off."

"Good for you." My guardian's grin was as spectacular as Felicia Krakower's; I'd fallen in with a community of smilers. "I have a feeling we're going to be great friends," he said.

Martina was gaudier than ever. She'd worked her terra-cotta hair into a sculpted object, a thick braid that lay on her shoulder like a loaf of challah. Her eyes had become cartoons of themselves, boldly outlined and richly shaded. "Even though this is Satirev," she said, "I am Veritasian enough to speak frankly. I saved your ass, Jack. You're alive because good old Martina Coventry argued your case back at the roundhouse."

"I'm grateful," I said.

"You should be."

"You told them about Toby?"

She nodded. "Yes, and I must say, the story was an instant hit. A Xavier's child with a shot at remission—you have no idea what appeal that sort of situation holds down here."

"It's all so amazingly touching," said Franz. "A father fighting for his son's life—my *goodness*, that's touching."

"Can you teach me to lie?" I asked.

"It depends," said Martina.

"On what?"

"On whether you're accepted into the program—on whether the treatment takes. Not everyone has the stuff to become a dissembler."

"If it were up to me, I'd let you in"—Franz snapped his fingers—"like *that*."

"Unfortunately, it's not up to us," said Martina. "You're going to need some luck." She reached into her madras bag and took out, of all things, a horseshoe. Opening the drawer in my nightstand, she dropped in the shoe, *thud*. "Horses have six legs," she said, matter-of-factly.

I gritted my teeth. "Good-luck charms are lies," I countered.

"Perhaps," said Martina.

"I understand you wish to make a phone call," said Franz brightly. "Speaking on behalf of Internal Security, I must tell you we're *delighted* to grant that particular request."

Franz and Martina helped me to my feet, inch by painful inch. I'd never realized I owned so many vulnerable muscles, so many assaultable bones. At last I stood, the cold floor nipping at my bare feet, my baggy and absurdly short hospital gown brushing my rump.

The Center for Creative Wellness was a modest affair. A dozen paces down a hall hung with photographs of ecstatic children, a dozen more across a lobby loaded with Monet's paintings of water lilies, and suddenly we were moving through the main entrance and into a small private park. Graffiti coated the smooth brick walls: JESUS LOVES YOU . . . EVERYTHING IS BEAUTIFUL IN ITS OWN WAY . . . TODAY IS THE FIRST DAY OF THE REST OF YOUR LIFE. I looked up. No sun, no clouds—no sky. The whole park was covered by a concrete arch suggesting the vaulted dome of a cathedral; three mercury-vapor searchlights lay suspended from the roof, technological suns.

"We're under the ground," Martina explained, noting the confusion on my face. "We're under Veritas," she said, launching her index finger upward; her nails were painted a fluorescent green. "So far we've colonized only a hundred acres, but we're expanding all the time."

Compact, enclosed—and yet the park was not claustrophobic. Indeed, I had never before stood in such a soothing and airy space. It smelled of pine sap. The omnipresent birdsong boasted the exhilarating intricacy of a fugue. Butterflies representing a dozen species, each more colorful than the next, fluttered about like patches attempting to fuse themselves into a crazy quilt. A flagstone footpath meandered amid neat little gardens planted with zinnias, gladioli, tulips, and peonies.

Martina said, "We'll never grow as big as Veritas, of course. But that's not the point."

I studied the ceiling, its curving surface crisscrossed with Veritas's innards—her concrete intestines, gushing lead veins, buzzing nerves of steel and gutta-percha. Something peculiar glided over my head.

"The point is that Satirev is here," Martina continued, "and that it works."

A pig. A *pig?* Yes, there it was, sailing through the air like a miniature dirigible, flapping its little cherub-wings. A machine of some kind, a child's bizarre toy? No, its squeal was disconcertingly organic.

"Pigs have wings," said Franz. His lie sent a chill through my flesh.

A scrawny yellow cat sidled out from behind a forsythia bush, its hairs erect with feline anxiety. It molded itself into an oblong of fur and shot toward the Center for Creative Wellness. An instant later, its pursuer appeared. A dog, I assumed at first. But no. Wrong shape. And that tail, long and ropelike.

The shudder began in my lower spine and expanded. A rat. A rat the size of a pregnant badger.

Chasing a cat.

"This is a very strange place," I said, staring into Martina's exotically adorned eyes. "Wouldn't you say?"

"Strangeness is relative," she replied.

"I'm bewildered," I said.

"It's not hard to make a lie. Avant-garde microbiology will give you a flying pig, an outsized rat—anything you want."

"I'm *still* bewildered."

"Satirev takes some getting used to," said Franz, smiling prolifically. "I'm sure you'll be able to master it. You look like a champ to me, Jack."

The telephone booth sat on a knoll smothered in purple grass and five-leaf clovers. Slowly I limped through the odd flora—my body felt like a single gigantic bruise—and pushed the sliding door against the jamb. Martina and Franz stood beside me, well within earshot.

"Do you understand how you must conduct yourself?" my guardian asked.

"I think so."

"Drop the slightest hint and, bang, you're back in Veritas, awash in scopolamine—you'll never remember you've been here, not one detail. That would be most unfortunate, wouldn't it?"

The phone was a deceitful affair, secretly wired into the Veritas system, blatantly looting its services. I extended my index finger, pressed the appropriate buttons.

Helen didn't answer till the seventh ring. Obviously I'd awakened her. "Hello?" she said groggily.

"Did I wake you?"

"Of *course* you woke me," she mumbled, "whoever you are."

"Listen," I told her abruptly. "Don't ask me anything."

"*Jack?* Is that *you?*"

"It's me. Don't ask me where I am, Helen. Everything depends on it."

My wife exhaled in frustration. "I . . . er, it's good to hear your voice, Jack."

"I'm among them. Do you know what I'm talking about?"

"I think so."

"They're considering my case, Helen. They might let me in. I hope you're not still against me on this."

"I'm against you," she grunted.

I looped the phone cord around my arm, forcing it tight against my skin like a phylactery strap. "Have you heard anything from Toby?"

"Postcard came today."

"Did he mention his health—joint pains or anything?"

"He simply said he was in a canoe race. I'm supposed to pick him up at the bus station on the twenty-seventh."

"Nothing about headaches?"

"No."

I kissed the plastic mouthpiece. "I'll call you back as soon as I can. Good-bye, Helen. I'm terribly fond of you."

"I'm terribly fond of you too, Jack—but please get out of there. *Please.*"

I hung up and turned toward Martina and Franz. Behind them,

a shaggy black rat pinned a Siamese cat to the ground and began tearing out its throat.

"You did fine," said my guardian.

FIVE

The weather engineers had just turned up their rheostats, flooding the Saturday morning sky with a dazzling emerald sunrise, when Martina came bouncing into my hospital room. She opened the drawer of my nightstand and removed her ludicrous horseshoe. "It worked," she insisted, holding out the shoe as if it were a wishbone we'd agreed to split.

"Oh?" I said sneeringly, skeptically: I refused to descend into superstition—psychoneuroimmunology was for real.

She dropped the horseshoe into her handbag. I was lucky, she told me. The typical supplicant was commonly sequestered for a full month in the Hotel Paradise while the government decided his fate—but not I. Instead, assuming Dr. Krakower agreed to release me, I would meet that very afternoon with Manny Ginsburg himself.

"Imagine, Jack—you've been granted an audience with the Pope!"

Twenty minutes later Dr. Krakower appeared, accompanied by the eternally unctuous Franz Beauchamp. As Martina looked on with seemingly genuine concern, Franz with a kind of smarmy pity, the doctor inspected my infirmities. She removed the bandage from my head wound, palpated my broken rib through the adhesive tape— "This might hurt a bit," she warned before sending me into paroxysms of pain—and cheerily pronounced me fit to travel, though she wanted me back by sundown for another checkup.

I got into the denim overalls I'd worn to work on Thursday: how far away that Thursday seemed, how remote and unreal. Martina and Franz guided me through the hospital lobby and across the park to the banks of a wide canal labeled *Jordan River*, its waters clean, clear, and redolent of some happy mixture of root beer and maple syrup. Golden trout flashed beneath the surface like reflected moonbeams.

Sparkling with fresh paint, a red gondola lay moored to the wharf. We got on board. As my guardian poled us forward, pushing his oar into the sweet waters, Martina briefed me on the intricacies of dealing with Pope Manny.

"To begin with, he's a year-rounder. Lives here all the time." For most dissemblers, Martina elaborated, Satirev was a pied-à-terre, locus of the periodic pilgrimages through which one renewed one's talent for mendacity, whereas Manny Ginsburg never left. "It's made him a little nuts," she explained.

"I'm not surprised," I said as an aquatic ferret leaped out of the Jordan and snatched an unsuspecting polka-dotted frog from the shore.

"Play up your devotion to your kid," Martina advised. "How you'd move heaven and earth to cure him. The man's a sucker for sentiment."

"And don't look him in the eyes," said Franz. "He hates directness."

My guardian landed us at a trim, sturdy, immaculately whitewashed dock, its pilings decorated with ceramic replicas of pelicans and sea gulls. An equally clean and appealing structure rose from the shore—a bait shack or possibly a fisherman's hut. A German shepherd sprawled on the welcome mat, head bobbing in languid circles as it tracked a dragonfly.

"The Holy See," said Martina, pointing.

"It's a bait shack," I corrected her.

"It's the Holy See," said Franz as he lashed his gondola to the dock.

"Maybe we don't have the budget we'd like around here," said the dog, "but it's still the Holy See."

I didn't bat an eye. I was getting used to this sort of thing.

The door swished open on well-oiled hinges, and a short, nervous, wall-eyed man in his sixties stepped onto the dock wearing a brilliant white polyester suit and a yarmulke. He told Martina and Franz to come back for me in an hour.

"Care for a cup of fresh-perked coffee?" asked Manny Ginsburg as he led me into his one-room riverfront abode. The German shepherd followed, claws clicking on the wooden floor. "It's quite tasty."

"Sure," I said, glancing around. Manny's shack was as spotless within as without.

"Pull up a chair."

There were no chairs. I sat on the rug.

"I'm Ernst, by the way," said the dog, offering me his paw.

"Jack Sperry," I said, shaking limb extremities with Ernst. "You talk," I observed.

"A bioelectronic implant, modifying my larynx."

Manny sidled into the kitchenette. Lifting a copper kettle from his kerosene stove, he filled a pair of earthenware mugs with boiling water then added heaping spoonfuls of Donaldson's Drinkable Coffee crystals.

"You said fresh," I noted with Veritasian candor.

"It's fresh to *us*," said the Pope.

"Want to hear a talking dog joke?" Ernst inquired.

"No," I replied, truthfully.

"Oh," said the dog, evidently wounded by my frankness.

Manny returned from the kitchenette with a Coca-Cola tray bearing the coffee mugs plus a cream pitcher and a canister marked *Salt*.

"It's a sterile world up there. Sterile, stifling, spiritually depleting." Manny set the tray beside me and rolled his eyes heavenward. "And before long it will all be ours. You doubt me? Listen—already we've placed twenty dissemblers in the legislature. A person with our talents has no trouble getting elected."

"You mean—you're going to conquer Veritas?" I asked, making a point of not looking Manny in the eye.

The Pope slammed his palms against his ears. *"Please."*

"Don't say 'conquer,'" admonished the dog.

"We're going to *reform* Veritas," said Manny.

I stared at the rug. "Truth is beauty, your Holiness." Splaying my fingers, I ticked off a familiar litany. "In the Age of Lies, politicians misled, advertisers overstated, clerics exaggerated—"

"Satirev's founders had nothing against telling the truth." Manny tapped his yarmulke. "But they hated their inability to do otherwise. Honesty without choice, they said, is slavery with a smile." He pointed toward the ceiling with his coffee mug. "Truth above . . ." He set his mug on the floor. "Dignity below." He chuckled softly. "In Satirev, we opt for the latter. Do you like it sweet?"

"Huh?"

"Your coffee. Sweet?"

"I *would* like some sugar, matter of fact."

The Pope handed me the salt canister. I shook some grains into my palm and licked. It was sugar.

"My heart is broken," said Manny, laying a hand on his chest. "I feel absolutely devastated about your Toby."

"You do?" I asked, adding Satirevian salt to my coffee.

"I'm crushed."

"You don't even know him."

"What you're doing is so *noble*."

"I think so too," said Ernst. "And I'm only a dog."

"I have just one question," said Manny. "Listen carefully. Do you love your son?"

"That would depend on—"

"I don't mean love him, I mean *love* him. Crazy, unconditional, non-Veritasian love."

Surprisingly—to myself if not the Pope—I didn't have to think about my answer. "I love him," I asserted, looking Manny in the eye. "Crazy, unconditional, non-Veritasian . . ."

"Then you're in," said Manny.

"Congratulations," said the dog.

"I must warn you—the treatment doesn't take in all cases." Manny sipped his Donaldson's. "I advise you to throw everything you've got into it, your very soul, even if you're convinced you don't have one. Please don't look me in the eye."

I turned away, uncertain whether to rejoice at being admitted or to brood over the possibility of failure. "What are my chances, would you say?"

"First-rate," said Manny.

"Truly excellent," Ernst agreed.

"I'd bet money on it," the Pope elaborated.

"Of course," said the dog, "we could be lying."

On Sunday morning Martina and I hiked through the flurry of five-leaf clovers outside the Center for Creative Wellness and, reaching the top of the hill, placed a call to Arnold Cook at his home in Locke Borough. After claiming to be my wife, Martina told him I'd been diagnosed with double pneumonia and wouldn't be coming to work for at least a week. Her fabulation gave me a terrible headache and also, truth to tell, a kind of sexual thrill.

The chief curator offered his qualified sympathy, and that was that. What a marvelous tool, lying, I thought: so practical and uncomplicated. I was beginning to understand its pervasive popularity in eras gone by.

Together Martina and I strolled through the park, Franz Beauchamp hovering blatantly in the background. She grasped my right hand; my fingers became five erogenous zones. Today she would return to Veritas, she explained, where she'd finally lined up a job writing campaign speeches for Doreen Hutter, a Descartes Borough representative.

"I'll miss you," I said.

"I'll be back," she said, massaging her baroque braid with her free hand. "Like all dissemblers, I'm obliged to immerse myself in Satirev ninety days a year. I'll be spending next Friday on the Jordan, fishing for ferrets."

"Will you visit me?" I asked this zaftig and exotic woman.

She stared into the sky and nodded. "With luck you'll be a liar by then," she said, tracking a pig with her decorous eyes. "If you have any words of truth for me, you'd better spill them now."

"Truth?"

"We dissemblers can handle it, every now and then."

"Well, I suppose I'd have to say . . ." The reality of my condition dawned on me even as I spoke it. "I'd have to say I'm a little bit in love with you, Martina."

"Only a little bit?" she asked, leading me to the riverbank, Franz at our heels.

"These things are hard to quantify." Two gondolas were lashed to the dock, riding the wake of a passing outboard motorboat. "May I ask how you feel about me?"

"I'd prefer not to say." Martina splayed her fingers, working free of my grasp. "Ultimately there'd be nothing in it for either of us, nothing but grief." She climbed into her gondola and, assuming the pilot's position in the stern, lowered her oar. "I'm certain you'll become a Satirevian," she said, casting off. "I have great faith in you, Jack," she called as she vanished into the 3,000-watt sunrise.

The current carried Franz and me south, past a succession of riverfront cottages encrusted with casuistry: welcome mats, flower boxes, plaster lawn ornaments in the forms of Cupids and little Dutch girls. My guardian landed the gondola before a two-story clapboard building painted a bright pink and surmounted by the words HOTEL PARADISE in flashing neon. A stone wall hemmed the grounds, broken by a massive gateway in which was suspended an iron portcullis, also painted pink. Bars of pink iron crisscrossed the hotel windows like strokes of a censor's pen.

A sudden *skreee:* the portcullis, ascending with the grinding gracelessness of an automated garage door. Franz led me beneath the archway, up a pink cement path, and through the central portal to the front desk. He gave my name to the clerk—*Leopold,* according to his badge—a horse-faced, overweight, fortyish man dressed in a loud Hawaiian shirt. After confirming that they were indeed expecting a Jack Sperry from Plato Borough, Leopold issued me a pink tunic with NOVITIATE stamped on the chest. It was as baggy as a gown from the Center for Creative Wellness, and I had no trouble slipping it on over my street clothes.

"You look real spiffy in that," said Leopold.

"You're one of the homeliest people I've ever met," I felt bound to inform him.

The chief bellhop, a spidery old man whose skin resembled a cantaloupe rind, guided me down a long hallway decorated with Giotto and Rembrandt reproductions, Franz following as always, my eternal shadow. We paused before a pink, riveted door that seemed more likely to lead to a bank vault than to a hotel room—it even had a combination lock. "Your suite," the bellhop said as the three of us stepped inside.

Suite. Sure. It was smaller than the Holy See, and sparser: no rugs, no chairs, no windows. The walls were clean and predictably pink. Two male novitiates, one tall, one short, rested on adjacent cots, smoking cigarettes. "Your roommates," said the bellhop as he and Franz exited. The door thudded shut, then came the muffled clicks of the tumblers being randomized.

"I'm William," said my tall roommate; he could have been a power forward with the Plato Borough Competents. "William Bell."

"Ira Temple," said his scrawny companion.

"Jack Sperry," I said.

We spent the next hour swapping life stories.

Ira, I learned, was a typical dissembler-in-training. He hated
Veritas. He had to get out. Anything, he argued, even dishonesty, was
superior to what he called his native city's confusion of the empirical
with the true.

William's story was closer to my own. His older sister, Charlotte,
the one person on Earth who mattered to him, had recently landed
on Amaranth, a planet that existed only in her mind. By learning to
lie, William reasoned, he might travel to Charlotte's mythic world and
either release her from its mad gravity or take up residence there
himself.

The door · swung open and in came a small, dusky, stoop-
shouldered man with a bald head and a style of walking that put me
in mind of a duck with osteoporosis. "During the upcoming week,
you're all going to fall in love with me," he said abruptly, waving his
clipboard. "I'm going to treat you so well, you'll think you've died
and gone to heaven." He issued a wicked little wink. "That's a lie.
I'm Gregory Harness, Manny Ginsburg's liaison. You may call me
Lucky," he said with an insistent, rapid-fire bonhomie. "The Pope
deeply regrets not being here to orient you personally, but his busy
schedule did not permit . . . anyhow, you get the drift of his bullshit.
Which one of you's Sperry?"

I raised my hand.

"I heard about your sick child," said Lucky. "Heartrending.
Tragic. Believe me, Sperry, I'll be rooting for you all the way."

And so it was upon us, our absorption in lies, our descent into de-
ception, our headlong, brainfirst plunge into Satirevian reality.

At the crack of dawn Lucky herded us into his pickup truck and
took us to a place where money grew on trees, a pecuniary orchard
so vast it could have paid the interest on Veritas's national debt. We
spent a sweaty, grueling day under the celestial lamps, harvesting
basket after basket of five-dollar bills.

On Tuesday morning the weather engineers contrived a fearsome
blizzard, squall upon squall of molten snow bringing Satirev to a total
standstill and inspiring Lucky to issue us broad-scooped shovels.
"Clean it up," he demanded, "every highway, street, alley, path, sidewalk, and wharf." And so we did, our skin erupting in second-degree
burns as we carried great heaps of steaming precipitate to the Jordan

and dropped them over the banks. Lucky mopped our brows with towels dipped in ice water, slaked our thirst with lemonade, soothed our blistered backs with eucalyptus oil—but he kept us on the job all day.

Wednesday: a tedious morning of shoeing six-legged horses, a wearying afternoon of arranging and rearranging the contents of a Satirevian rock garden. My companions and I felt that, for stones, these creatures were extraordinarily loquacious and singularly self-pitying. The stones lamented their lack of mobility and prestige. They said it was hell being a stone. Cut them, they claimed, and they would bleed.

Further lies, Thursday's lies—our taskmaster loaded his truck with cans of spray paint and shunted us across Satirev, stopping at every public park along the way and ordering us to turn the grass purple, the roses blue, and the violets red, an ordeal that left my co-apprentices and me so speckled we looked like amalgams of all the Jackson Pollocks I'd ever criticized. That night, as I lay on my cot in the Paradise, my stunned brain swirled with deceptions—with lavender cabbages and crimson potatoes, with indigo jungles and chartreuse icebergs, with square baseballs, skinny whales, tall dwarves, and snakes with long, pale, supple legs.

More lies—lies, lies, lies. On Friday, Lucky gave us .22-caliber hunting rifles, instructed us in their use and, exploiting the handicap of our Veritasian upbringings, made us swear we wouldn't use them to escape. "Before the day is out, you must each bring down a flying pig. Don't let the low comedy of their anatomy fool you—they're smarter than they look." Thus did I find myself crouched behind a forest of cat-o'-nine-tails on the banks of the Jordan, my .22 poised on my knees, my mind turning over the manifest rationale behind my deconditioning. A black, bulbous shape glided across the river, like the shadow that might be cast by a gigantic horsefly, and I recalled the perusal I'd made of *Alice in Wonderland* before criticizing it. "The time has come," the Walrus said, "to talk of many things." I grabbed the rifle, took aim; the shape flew along the equator of my telescopic sight, eastward to the axis. "Of shoes—and ships—and sealing wax—of cabbages and kings." I fired. "And why the sea is boiling hot." The bewildered animal fell squealing. "And whether pigs have wings." My bleeding prey hit the water.

When your every muscle aches with the effects of a currency harvest, you do not doubt that money grows on trees. When your entire epidermis is branded with the aftermath of 200-degree snow-flakes, you cannot but accept their reality. When every ounce of your concentration is fixed upon blasting a winged pig out of the sky, you do not question its species's ontological status.

The Hotel Paradise had only one eatery, an immaculate malt shop called the Russian Tea Room, and on Friday night Lucky took us there for dinner. Brilliant white tiles covered the walls. The stools—red vinyl cushions poised on glistening steel stalks—resembled Art Deco mushrooms. The menu featured murdered cows, euphemistically named "cheese steaks," "hot dogs," "hamburgers," and "beef tacos." Lucky told us to order whatever we liked.

"I've been driving you all pretty hard," he confessed after our meals arrived.

"An understatement," I replied.

Lucky twisted the cap off a bottle of Quasitomato Ketchup from Veritas. "Tell me, men, do you feel any different?"

"Different?" said Ira Temple, voraciously consuming a "beef taco." "Not really."

William Bell bit into his "cheeseburger." "I'm the same man I always was."

"Saturday's schedule is pretty intense," said Lucky, shaking blobs of ketchup onto his French fries. "You'll be digging sugar out of the salt mines, attending a linguistics seminar with some golden retrievers, carrying steer haunches over to the Pope for him to bless. In my experience, though, if you're not a liar by now, you never will be." With a directness rarely found in Satirev, Lucky looked William in the eye. "What do pigs have, son?"

"Huh?"

"Pigs. What do they have? You've been dealing with pigs late-ly—you know about them."

William stared at his half-eaten cow. He pondered the question for nearly a minute. At last he raised his head, closed his eyes tightly, and let out the sort of delighted yelp an Age-of-Lies child might have issued on Christmas morning. "Pigs have w-wings!"

"What did you say?"

"W-w-wings!" William leaped from his chair and danced around the table. "Wings!" he sang. "Wings! Pigs have wings!"

"Good job, William!" Ira shouted, his face betraying a mixture of envy and anxiety.

Lucky smiled, ate a fry, and thrust his fork toward Ira. "Now—you. Tell me about money, Ira. Where does money grow?"

Ira took a deep breath. "Well, that's not an easy question. Some people would say it doesn't *grow* at all. Others might argue . . ."

"Money, son. Where does money grow?"

"On trees!" Ira suddenly screamed.

"On *what?*"

"Money grows on trees!"

"And I'm the Queen of Sheba!" said William.

"I'm the King of France!" said Ira.

"I can fly!" said William.

"I can walk on water!" said Ira.

"God protects the innocent!"

"The guilty never go free!"

"Love is eternal!"

"Life is too!"

Lucky laid his knobbly hand on my shoulder. "What's the deal with snow, Jack?" he asked. "What is snow like?"

The appropriate word formed in my brain. I could sense it riding the tip of my tongue like a grain of sand. "It's . . . it's . . ."

"Is it hot, for example?" asked Lucky.

"Snow is h-h-h—"

"Hot?"

"Cold!" I shrieked. "Snow is cold," I moaned.

William shot me an agonized glance. "Jack, you've got it all wrong."

"Don't you remember that blizzard?" asked Ira.

I quivered with nausea, reeled with defeat. Damn. Shit. "The stuff they make here is a *fraud.*" Jack Sperry versus Xavier's Plague—and now the disease would win. "It's not snow at all."

"Snow is hot," said Ira.

"It's *cold!*" Rising from my chair, I stumbled blindly around the Russian Tea Room. "Pigs don't fly! Dogs don't talk! Truth is beauty!"

I left.

The hotel lobby was dark and pungent, suffused with the Jordan's sugary aroma. The night clerk slept at his post. Franz Beauchamp sat in a wicker chair beside a potted palm, his long face shadowed by a Panama hat.

I staggered to the front door. It was locked. But of course: one left Satirev filled with either lies or scopolamine, illusion or amnesia; there was no third path.

"Treatment isn't taking, huh?" said Franz as he approached. "Don't be discouraged."

"I'm beaten," I groaned.

"Now, now—you still have tomorrow." Franz removed his Panama, placing it over his heart—a gesture of grief, I decided, anticipatory mourning for Toby Sperry. "Someone wants to see you," he said.

"Huh?"

"You have a visitor."

"Who?"

"This way."

He led me past the sleeping clerk and down the east corridor to a steel door uncharacteristically free of catches, bolts, and locks. The sign said VIDEO GAMES. Franz turned the handle.

There were no video games in the Video Games Room.

There was a blood-red billiard table.

A print of Picasso's *The Young Women of Avignon*.

Martina Coventry.

"Hi, critic. We had a date, remember?"

"To tell the truth, I'd forgotten."

" 'To tell you the truth'? What kind of talk is that for a Satirevian?" Martina came toward me, her extended hand fluttering like a hummingbird. "You look unhappy, dear."

"I'm no Satirevian." I reached out and captured her plump fingers. "Never will be."

Martina tapped the brim of Franz's Panama. "Mr. Sperry and I require privacy," she told him. "Don't worry, we're not going to have sex or anything."

Though convulsed with misery and self-loathing, I nevertheless noticed how Martina was dressed. If employed as a lampshade, her miniskirt wouldn't have reached the socket. The strap of her madras bag lay along her cleavage, pulling her LIFE IS A BANQUET T-shirt tight against her body and making her breasts seem like two adjacent spinnakers puffed full of wind.

Franz tipped his hat and ducked out of the room.

"Let's get your mind off your deconditioning." Martina hopped onto the table and stretched out. She looked like a relief map of some particularly lewd and mountainous nation. "Lie down next to me."

"Not a good idea," I said. True: a roll on the felt wasn't going to solve my problems. I should be pumping Martina's mind and no other part of her; I should be trying to learn how she herself had managed the crucial transition from Veritasian to liar.

She said, "You don't want to?"

I gulped loudly. "No, I don't." My blood lurched toward the temperature of Satirevian snow.

"No?"

"I'm *married,* remember? I don't want to have sex with you."

I did, of course. In my heart of hearts, I did—and now came the correlative of my desire, drawing both Martina's attention and my own.

I don't want to have sex with you, I'd said.

Yet here was the resolute little hero, shaping the crotch of my overalls into a denim sculpture.

So I'd lied! For the first time since my brainburn, I'd lied!

I pulled off my tunic, slipped out of my overalls. " 'I hide my wings inside my soul,' " I quoted, climbing atop Martina.

Deftly she removed my undershorts; my erection broke free, a priapic jailbreak. I'd done it, by damn. I might have a Veritasian penis, but I'd finally acquired a Satirevian tongue.

" 'Their feathers soft and dry'!" I cried, shucking off Martina's skirt.

" 'And when the world's not looking'!" she whooped.

" 'I take them out and fly'!"

I had to apply the brakes on my Adequate almost a dozen times as I descended the southern face of Mount Prosaic and headed into the lush green valley below. Cabin after cabin, tent after tent, Camp Ditch-the-Kids was strung along a strip of pine barren midway between the swiftly flowing Wishywashy and a placid oxbow lake. For the first time, it occurred to me that Toby might not like the idea of leaving two days early. With its fearsome dedication to frivolity, its endless amusements and diversions, Ditch-the-Kids was the sort of place a seven-year-old could easily imagine living in forever.

As I pulled up behind the administration building, a gang of preadolescent children in yellow Ditch-the-Kids T-shirts marched by, clutching fishing rods. I studied their faces. No Toby. Snatches of the counselor's pep talk drifted toward me, something to the effect that acid rain was sterilizing Lake Commonplace so it really didn't matter how much they caught, the fish were all doomed anyway.

I entered the building, a slapdash pile of tar paper and cedar shingles. A grizzled man with a three-day beard sat behind the desk, reading the August issue of *Beatoff*.

"I'm Toby Sperry's father," I said. "And you're . . . ?"

"Ralph Kitto." The camp director eyed me suspiciously. "Look, Mr. Sperry, there's no question we were pretty irresponsible, leaving that rat trap out in the open as we did, but I don't believe you have a criminal case against us."

"It's not my intention to sue you," I told him, savoring the spectacle of joy and relief blossoming on his face. Little did he know I could have been lying.

"Will Toby be okay? I've been feeling a certain amount of guilt about this matter. Nothing I can't handle, but—"

"I'm here to bring him home," I said. "He's going into the hospital tomorrow."

"Life is a tough business, isn't it?" Ralph Kitto fanned himself with *Beatoff*. "Take me, for example. Sure wish I could find a better line of work."

"I imagine these kids drive you crazy—figuratively crazy."

"Vodka helps. I get drunk frequently."

Kitto consulted his master schedule and told me Toby was probably still on the archery field, a half-mile south down the Wishywashy. I paid the balance due on my son's tuition, thanked the director for his willingness to take on such an unrewarding job, and set out along the river.

When I reached the field, my son had just missed the bull's-eye by less than an inch.

"Nice shooting, Toby, old buddy!"

He maintained his bowman's stance, transfixed not only by the fact of my arrival but also, no doubt, by the content of my greeting. "Dad, what are *you* doing here?"

I hadn't seen him in a month. He seemed taller, leaner, swarthier—older—standing there in his grimy yellow T-shirt and the blue jeans he'd shredded into shorts last spring.

"I've come for you," I told him, moving as close as I could without making it obvious I was scanning him for symptoms. His hair was as thick, dark, and healthy-looking as ever. His eyes sparkled, his frame looked firm, his tanned skin held no trace of blue.

"No, I'm taking the bus Sunday." He nocked an arrow. "Mom's picking me up."

"The plan's been changed. She had to go out of town—there's a big UFO story breaking in the Hegelian Desert." I experienced a small but irrefutable pleasure, the sweet taste of truth bending in my mouth. "We'd better get your stuff packed. Where's your cabin?"

Toby unnocked the arrow and used it to indicate a cluster of yurts about twenty yards from the targets.

The archery instructor approached, a woodsy, weathered fellow with a mild limp. Toby introduced me as the best father a boy'd ever had. He said he loved me. So strange, I thought, the spontaneous little notions that run through the heads of pre-burn children.

My son turned in his bow, and we started toward his cupcake-shaped cabin.

"You've got a nice tan, Toby. You look real healthy. Gosh, it's good to see you."

"Dad, you're talking so *funny*."

"I'll bet you *feel* healthy too."

"Lately I've been getting headaches."

I gritted my teeth. "I'm sure that's nothing to worry about."

"Wish I wasn't leaving so soon," he said as we climbed the crooked wooden steps to his room. "Barry Maxwell and I were supposed to hunt snakes tomorrow."

"Listen, Toby, this is a better deal than you think. You're going to get an entire second vacation." The space was only slightly more chaotic than I'd anticipated—clothes in ragged heaps, *Encyclopedia Britannica* comics in amorphous piles. "We're going to live in a magic kingdom under the ground. Just you and me."

"What sort of magic kingdom?" he asked skeptically.

"Oh, you'll love it, Toby. We'll go fishing and eat ice cream."

Toby smiled hugely, brightly—a Satirevian smile. "That sounds neat." He opened his footlocker and started cramming it full: crafts projects, T-shirts, dungarees, poncho, comics, flashlight, canteen, mess kit. "Will Mom be coming?"

"No."

"She'll miss all the fun."

"She'll miss all the fun," I agreed.

My son held up a hideous and lopsided battleship, proudly announcing that he'd made it in woodworking class.

"How do you like it, Dad?"

"Why, Toby," I told him, "it's absolutely beautiful."

SIX

Twelve gates lead to the City of Lies. Every year, as his commitment to mendacity becomes increasingly clear, his dishonesty more manifestly reliable, the Satirevian convert is told the secret location of yet another entrance. Mere novitiates like myself knew only one: the storm drainage tunnel near the corner of Third and Hume in Nietzsche Borough.

So many ways to descend, I thought as Toby and I negotiated the dank, mossy labyrinth beneath Veritas. Ladders, sloping sewer pipes, narrow stone stairways—we used them all, our flashlights cutting through the darkness like machetes clearing away underbrush. My son loved every minute of it. "Wow!" he exclaimed whenever some disgusting wonder appeared—a slug the size of a banana, a subterranean lake filled with frogs, a spider's web as large and sturdy as a trampoline. "Neat!"

Reaching our destination, we settled into the Hotel Paradise. Unlike my previous accommodations, our assigned suite was sunny and spacious, with glass doors opening onto a wrought-iron balcony from which one could readily glimpse the local fauna. "Dad, the horses around here have six legs!" Toby hopped up and down with excitement. "The rats chase the cats! The pigs have wings! This really *is* a magic kingdom!"

It soon became obvious that the whole of Satirev had been anticipating our arrival. We were the men of the hour. The Paradise guards immediately learned our faces, letting us come and go as we pleased. Franz and Lucky gushed over Toby as if he were a long-lost brother. Whenever we strolled around the community, total strangers would come up to us and, confirming our identities, give Satirev's tragic child a candy bar or a small toy, his father a hug of encouragement and affirmation.

Even Felicia Krakower was prepared. After drawing a sample of Toby's blood—we told him the kingdom had to make certain the tourists weren't carrying germs—she retired to her office and came back holding a stuffed animal, an astonishingly comical baboon with acrobatic eyes and a squarish, doglike snout.

"This is for you, Rainbow Boy," she said.

Toby's face grew knotted and tense; he gulped audibly. He was not too old for stuffed animals, merely too old to enjoy them without shame.

"He needs a name, don't you think?" said Dr. Krakower. "Not a silly name, I'd say. Something dignified."

I performed my survey, the one I took every hour. The facts were becoming irrefutable—the bluish cast of his skin, the thinness of his hair.

Toby relaxed, smiled. "Dignified," he said. "Not silly. Oh, yes." Clearly, he'd sensed the truth of his new home: in Satirev everything was permitted; in Satirev no boy grew up before his time. "His name is Barnaby. Barnaby Baboon." Frowning, Toby rammed the tip of his tongue into the corner of his mouth. "I think he might be carrying some germs."

"Rainbow Boy, you're absolutely right." Dr. Krakower pried a wad of cotton batting out of Barnaby's arm with her syringe. "We'd better take a stuffing sample."

That night, the minute my son fell asleep, I ran to the phone booth outside the Paradise and called the Center for Creative Wellness. Krakower told me exactly what I expected to hear: the Xavier's test was positive.

"There's still plenty of hope," she insisted.

"I know what you mean," I said, shivering in the hot summer darkness. Positive. *Positive.* "If we give Toby the right outlook, his immune system will kick in and *bang*—remission."

"Exactly."

"How many years might a remission last?"

"You can't tell about remissions, Jack. Some of them last a long, long time."

I placed a call to Veritas.

"Hi, Helen."

"Jack? *Now* you call? *Now*, after ten whole days?"

"I've been busy."

"Your curator sent a get-well card. Are you sick?"

"I'm feeling better."

"This is a bad time to talk," she said. "I'm due at the bus station."

"No, you're not. I picked up Toby on Sunday."

"You *what?*"

"He's got to be with *me* now. I can give him the right outlook."

"You mean—you're one of them?"

"Dogs can talk, Helen."

I pictured her turning white, cringing. "Shut up!" she screamed. "I want my son back! Bring me my son, you tropological shithead!"

"I *love* him."

"Bring him back!"

"I can cure him."

"Jack!"

As the hot, soggy July melded into a hotter, soggier August, my son and I began spending long hours in the outdoors—or, rather, in those open spaces that in Satirev functioned as the outdoors. Together we explored the community's swampy frontiers, collecting bugs and amphibians for Toby's scale-model zoo. The money orchards, meanwhile, proved excellent for archery—we would nock our arrows and aim at the five-dollar bills—while the broiling snowfields soon became littered with the results of our sculpting efforts: snowmen, snowdogs, snowcows, snowbaboons. It was all a matter of having a good pair of insulated gloves.

Finally there was the Jordan, perfect for swimming and, when we could borrow a gondola, fishing. "Do you like this place?" I asked Toby as I threaded my line with a double-barbed hook.

"It's pretty weird." Furiously he worked his reel, hauling an aquatic armadillo on board.

"You're having a terrific time, though, aren't you, buddy? You're feeling cheerful."

"Oh, yeah," he said evenly.

"What do you like? Do you like making snowmen?"

"The snowmen are great."

"And the fishing?"

"I like the fishing." Placing his boot on the armadillo's left gill, Toby yanked the hook out of its mouth.

"And you like our archery tournaments too, don't you?" I marveled at the armadillo's design—its lozenge-shaped body, sleek scales, dynamic fins. "And the swimming?"

"Uh-huh. I wish Mom were here."

I baited my own hook with a Satirevian snail. "So do I. What else do you like?"

"I don't know." In a spasmodic act of mercy, he tossed the armadillo overboard. "I like the way strangers give me candy."

"And you like the fishing too, right?"

"I already said that," Toby replied patiently. "Dad, why is my hair falling out?"

"W-what?"

"My hair. And my skin looks funny too."

I shuddered, pricking my thumb with the fishhook. "Buddy, there's something we should talk about. Remember that blood sample Dr. Krakower took? It seems you've got a few germs in you. Nothing serious—Xavier's Plague, it's called."

"Whose plague?"

"Xavier's."

"Then how come *I* got it instead of Mr. Xavier?"

"Lots of people get it."

Toby impaled a snail on his fishhook. "Is that why my hair . . . ?"

"Probably. They might have to give you some medicine. You're not really sick." God, how I loved being able to say that. Such power. "The thing is to stay cheerful. Just say to yourself, 'Those bad old Xavier's germs can't hurt *me*. My immune system's too strong.' "

"My what?"

"Immune system. Say it, Toby. Say, 'Those bad old Xavier's germs can't hurt *me*.' Go ahead."

" 'Those bad old Xavier's germs can't hurt me,' " he repeated haltingly. "Is that true, Dad?"

"You bet. You aren't worried, are you?"

Toby rubbed his blue forehead. "I guess not."

"That's my buddy."

If my son wasn't too old for stuffed animals, then he wasn't too old for bedtime stories. We read together every night, snuggling amid the Paradise's soft buttery sheets and smooth cotton blankets, working our way through a stack of volumes that had somehow escaped the Wittgenstein's predations—*Tom Sawyer, Treasure Island, Corbeau the Pirate,* and, best of all, a leatherbound, gilt-edged collection of fairy tales. Perusing the Brothers Grimm, I trembled not only with the thrill of forbidden fruit—how daring I felt, acting out material I'd normally be reading only in prelude to burning it—but with the odd amoralities and psychosexual insights of the stories themselves. Toby's favorite was "Rumpelstiltskin," with its unexpected theme of an old man's hunger for a baby. My own preference was "Sleeping Beauty." I roundly identified with the father—with his mad, Herodlike campaign to circumvent his daughter's destiny by destroying every spinning wheel in the kingdom. I thought him heroic.

"Why did Rumpelstiltskin want a baby?" Toby asked.

"A baby is the best thing there is," I replied. I felt I was telling the truth. "Rumpelstiltskin knew what he needed."

Whenever Martina was in Satirev, she joined our expeditions— hiking, swimming, fishing, bug collecting—and I couldn't quite decide what Toby made of her. They got along famously, even to the point of scatological private jokes involving Barnaby Baboon, but occasionally I caught a glimmer of unease in my son's eyes. Were he a post-burn kid, of course, he would have been frank. *Dad, is Martina your mistress? Dad, do you and Martina have sex?*

To which the truthful answer would have been: no. Since Toby's arrival, I had lost my urge for erotic adventures. Martina did not protest; like me, she rather regretted our romp on the billiard table: adultery was wrong, after all—even a dissembler knew that. Thus had Martina and I entered that vast population of men and women whose friendship has crossed the copulation barrier but once, followed by retrenchment and retreat, an entire affair compacted into one memorable screw.

Most nights, the three of us went to dinner in the Russian Tea Room. The staff doted on Toby; he got all the hamburgers he could eat, all the hot dogs, all the French fries, all the milkshakes. Nobody could say the Tea Room wasn't doing its part to keep Toby cheerful, nobody could say it wasn't putting him in a salubrious mood. The manager was a thin, wiry, exuberant man in his early fifties named Norbert Vore (evidently he did not partake of his own fattening and enervating menu), and upon sensing that from the boy's viewpoint the restaurant was deficient in desserts, he immediately read up on the matter, soon learning how to prepare transcendent strawberry shortcake and ambrosial lemon-meringue pie. Norbert's baked Alaska, fudge brownies, and Bing-cherry tarts kept Toby grinning ear to ear. His chocolate parfaits were so lush and uplifting they seemed in themselves a cure.

It was in the Russian Tea Room that Toby and I first noted a curious fashion among Satirevians. About a quarter of them wore sweatshirts emblazoned with a Valentine-style heart poised above the initials H.E.A.R.T. "HEART, what's that?" my son asked Martina one evening as we were plowing through a particularly outrageous ice-cream treat—a concoction Norbert had dubbed "A Month of Sundaes."

"It's a kind of club—the members get together and talk about philosophy," Martina replied. "You know what philosophy is, Toby?"

"No."

"The H stands for Happiness, the E for Equals."

"And the A, R, and T?" asked Toby.

"Art, Reason, and Truth."

H.E.A.R.T. It was, Martina explained after Toby went to bed, an organization the year-rounders had formed for the sake of, as she put it, "thinking good thoughts about your son and thereby hastening his cure." HEART, the Healing and Ecstasy Association for the Recovery of Toby. They met every Tuesday evening. They were planning to start a newsletter.

I had never been so profoundly moved, so totally touched, in my life. My soul sang, my throat got hard as a crab apple. "Martina, that's *terrific*. Why didn't you tell me about HEART?"

"Because it gives me the creeps, that's why."

"The creeps?"

"Your son is sick, Jack. *Sick*. He's going to need more than HEART. He's going to need . . . well, a miracle."

"HEART *is* a miracle, Martina. Don't you get it? It *is* a miracle."

There is nothing quite so exhilarating as spending large amounts of time with your child, and nothing quite so tedious. I'll be honest: when Martina offered to relieve me of Toby for an hour or two— she wanted to help him find specimens for his miniature zoo—I told her to take all day. Even Sleeping Beauty's father, I'm sure, grew bored with her on occasion.

It was an hour past his bedtime when Toby returned to the Paradise, laden with the day's haul—a dozen bottles and cages filled with rubbery newts, glutinous salamanders, spiky centipedes, and disgruntled tree frogs whose cries sounded like bicycle bells.

He could not enjoy them.

"Dad, I don't feel so good," he said, setting the various terrariums on the coffee table.

"Oh?" So here it comes, I thought. Now it begins. "What do you mean?"

"My head hurts." Toby clutched his belly. "And my stomach. Is it those germs, Dad?"

"Just remember, in the long run they can't hurt you."

"'Cause of my immune system?"

"Smart boy."

Toby woke up repeatedly that night, his temperature lurching toward 103, flesh trembling, bones rattling, teeth chattering. He sweated like a bill-picker laboring in the money orchards. I had to change the sheets four times. They stank of brine.

"I think we'd better drop by the hospital tomorrow," I told him.

"Hospital? I thought I wasn't really sick."

"You *aren't* really sick." Oh, the power, the power. "Dr. Krakower wants to give you some medicine, that's all."

"I don't think I can sleep, Dad. Will you read to me about Rumpelstiltskin or pirates or something?"

"Of course. Sure. Just stay happy, and you'll be fine."

The next morning, I took Toby to the Center for Creative Wellness, where he was assigned a place in the children's ward, a large private room that despite its spaciousness quickly seemed to fill with my son's disease, a sickly, sallow aura radiating from the bedframe, covering the nightstand, smothering the swaybacked parent's cot in the far corner. His skin got bluer; his temperature climbed: 103, 104, 104.5, 105, 105.5. By nightfall the lymph nodes under his arms had grown to resemble clusters of ossified grapes.

"We can get the fever down with acetaminophen and alcohol baths," said Dr. Krakower as she guided me into her office. "And I think we should put him on pentamidine. It's been known to work wonders against *Pneumocystis carinii.*"

"Genuine wonders?"

"Oh, yes. We'd better set him up for intravenous feeding. I want to try pure oxygen too, maybe an inhalator. It'll keep his mind clear."

"Doctor, if there's no remission . . ."

"We shouldn't talk like that."

"If there's no remission, how long will he live?"

"Don't know."

"Two weeks?"

"Oh, yes, two weeks for sure, Jack. I can practically *promise* you two weeks."

Although Martina's speech-writing job for Borough Representative Doreen Hutter consumed all her mornings, she arranged to spend each afternoon at Toby's bedside, infusing him with happy thoughts. She invited him to imagine he was gradually entering a state of suspended animation, so that he could become the first boy ever sent beyond our solar system in a spaceship: hence the inhalator squeezing and expanding his chest, conditioning his lungs for interstellar travel; hence the plastic tube flowing into his left arm, giving him enough food for a year in hibernation; hence the plastic mask— the "rocket jockey's oxygen supply"—strapped over his mouth and nose.

"When you wake up, Toby, you'll be on another planet—the magical world of Lulaloon!"

"Lulaloon?" The oxygen mask made him sound distant, as if he were already in space. "Is it as good as Satirev?"

"Better."

"As good as summer camp?"

"Twice as good."

Toby stretched out, putting a crimp in his glucose tube, stopping the flow of what Martina had told him were liquid French fries. "I like your games," he said.

I stroked my son's balding scalp. "How's your imagination working?" I asked him.

"Pretty good, I guess."

"Can you picture Mr. Medicine zapping those nasty old Xavier's germs?"

"Sure."

"'Zap 'em, Mr. Medicine. Zap 'em dead!' Right, Toby?"

"Right," he wheezed.

For over a week, Toby remained appropriately chipper, but then a strange Veritasian skepticism crept over him, darkening his spirits as relentlessly as the *Pneumocystis carinii* were darkening his lungs. "I feel sick," he told Dr. Krakower one afternoon as she prepared to puncture him with a second IV needle, in the right arm this time. "I don't think that medicine's any good. I'm cold."

"Well, Rainbow Boy," she said, "Xavier's isn't any fun—I'll be the first to admit that—but you'll be up and running before you know it."

"My head still hurts, and my—"

"When one medicine doesn't work," I hastily inserted, "there's always another we can try—right, Dr. Krakower?"

"Oh, yes."

Martina took Toby's hand, giving it a hard squeeze as Krakower slid the needle into his vein.

Toby winced and asked, "Do children ever die?"

"That's a strange question, Rainbow Boy," said Krakower.

"Do they?"

"It's very, very rare." The doctor opened the stopcock on Toby's meperidine drip.

"She means never," I explained. "Don't even think about it, Toby. It's bad for your immune system."

"He's really cold," said Martina, her hand still clasped in Toby's. "Can we turn up the heat?"

"It's up all the way," said Krakower. "His electric blanket's on full."

The narcotic seeped into Toby's neurons. "I'm cold," he said woozily.

"You'll be warm soon," I lied. "Say, 'Zap 'em, Mr. Medicine. Zap 'em.'"

"Zap 'em, Mr. Medicine," said Toby, fading. "Zap . . . zap . . . zap . . ."

So it was time to get serious; it was time for Sleeping Beauty's father to track down every last spinning wheel and chop it to bits. The minute Krakower left, I turned to Martina and asked her to put me in touch with the president of the Healing and Ecstasy Association for the Recovery of Toby.

Instead of complying, Martina merely snorted. "Jack, I can't help feeling you're riding for a fall."

"What do you mean?"

"A fall, Jack."

"Such pessimism. Don't you know that psychoneuroimmunology is one of the key sciences of our age?"

"Just *look* at him, for Christ's sake. Look at Toby. He's living on borrowed time. You know that, don't you?"

"No, I *don't* know that." I cast her a killing glance. "Even if the time *is* borrowed, Martina, that doesn't mean it won't be the best time a boy's ever had."

She gave me the facts I needed. Anthony Raines, Suite 42, Hotel Paradise.

I marched up the hill outside the Center for Creative Wellness and placed the call. HEART's president answered on the first ring.

"Jack Sperry?" he gasped after I identified myself. "*The* Jack Sperry? Really? Goodness, what a coincidence. We've been hoping to interview you for *The Toby Times*."

"For the what?"

"Our first issue comes out tomorrow. We'll be running stories about the fun you and Toby are having down here, his favorite toys and sports, what analgesics and antibiotics he's taking—all the things our members want to hear about."

The Toby Times. I found the idea simultaneously inspiring and distasteful. "Mr. Raines, my son just entered the hospital, and I was hoping—"

"I know—it's our lead story. A setback, sure, but no reason to give up hope. Listen, Jack—may I call you Jack?—we people of the HEART know you're on the right track. Once Toby tunes in the cosmic pulse, his energy field will reintegrate, and then he's home free."

The more Anthony Raines spoke in his calm, mellow voice, the better I felt—and the sharper my image of him became: a tall, raffish, golden-haired bohemian with bright blue eyes and a drooping, slightly disreputable mustache. "Mr. Raines, I want you to mobilize your forces."

"Call me Anthony. What's up?"

"Just this—for the next two weeks, Toby Sperry's going to be the happiest child on Earth." No spinning wheel would escape my notice, ran my silent, solemn pledge. "Don't worry about the cost," I added. "We'll put it on my MasterDebt card."

I pictured Anthony Raines organizing his buddhalike features into a resolute smile. "Mr. Sperry, the HEART stands ready to help your cause in every way it can."

The next evening, Santa Claus visited the Center for Creative Wellness.

His red suit glowed like an ember. His white beard lay on his chest like a frozen waterfall.

"Who are *you?*" Toby asked, struggling to sit up amid the tangle of rubber. Every day he seemed to acquire yet another IV need: glucose, meperidine, saline, Ringer's lactate, the various tubes swirling around him like an external circulatory system. "Do I know you?" With a bold flourish he pulled off his plastic mask, as if this bulbous saint's mere presence had somehow unclogged his lungs.

"Hi, there, fella," said Santa, chuckling heartily: Sebastian, of course—Sebastian Arboria—the fat and affable dissembler who'd led the meeting in the roundhouse; I'd empowered Anthony Raines to hire him for eighty dollars an hour. "Call me Santa Claus. Saint Nicholas, if you prefer. Know what, Toby? Christmas is coming. Ever heard of Christmas?"

"I think we studied that in school. Isn't it supposed to be silly?"

"Silly?" said Sebastian with mock horror. "Christmas is the most wonderful thing there is. If I were a young lad, I'd feel absolutely *great* about Christmas. I'd be looking forward to it with every cell of my body. I'd be so full of happiness there wouldn't be any room left for Xavier's Plague."

"Is Christmas a warm time?" Toby was wholly without hair now. He was bald as an egg.

"The night before Christmas, I fly around the world in my sleigh, visiting every boy and girl, leaving good things behind."

"Will you visit *me?*"

"Of course I'll visit you. What do you want for Christmas, Toby?"

"You can have *anything*," I said. "Right, Santa?"

"Yep, anything," said Sebastian.

"I want to see my mother," said Toby.

Felicia Krakower shuddered. "That's not exactly Santa's department."

"I want to get warm."

Sebastian said, "What I *mean* is . . . like a toy. I'll bring you a toy."

"Pick something special," I insisted. "Say, that Power Pony you've been asking about."

"No, that's for my *birthday*," Toby corrected me.

"Why don't you get it for Christmas?" Martina suggested.

Toby slipped his rocket jockey's oxygen supply back on. "Well . . . okay, I guess I *would* like a Power Pony." His words bounced off the smooth green plastic.

Sebastian said, "A *Power Pony*, eh? Well, well—we'll see what we can do. Any particular *kind* of Power Pony?"

"The kind for a big kid." Toby's inhalator thumped like a car riding on flat tires. "Maybe I look short to you, lying here in bed, but I'm really seven. Can he be brown?"

"So—a brown Power Pony for a seven-year-old, eh? I think we can manage that, and maybe a couple of surprises too."

Toby's delighted giggle reverberated inside his mask. "How long do I have to wait?"

"Christmas will be here before you know it," I told him. "It's just a couple of days away, right, Santa?"

"Right."

"Will I be better by then?" Toby asked.

"There's a good chance of it, Rainbow Boy," said Krakower, twisting the stopcock on Toby's meperidine drip. He was getting the stuff almost continually now, as if he had two hearts, one pumping blood, the other pumping narcotics. "It's highly likely."

Furtively I opened my wallet and drew out my MasterDebt card. "For Anthony Raines," I whispered, pushing the plastic rectangle toward Sebastian. "Everything goes on this."

Sebastian extended his palm like a Squad officer stopping traffic. "Keep your card," he said. "The HEART's picking up the tab, including my fee." He stood fully erect, the pillow shifting under his wide black belt, and backed out of the room. "So long, Toby—Merry Christmas!"

"Merry Christmas," said Toby, coughing. He threw off his mask and turned to me. "Did you hear that, Dad? Santa's coming back. I'm so *excited*." His plum-colored skin was luminous. "He's going to bring me a Power Pony, and some surprises too. I can't *wait* for him to come back—I just can't *wait*."

Martina said, "We have to talk."

"About what?"

"I think you know."

She escorted me into the first-floor visitation lounge, a kind of indoor jungle. Everywhere, exotic pink blossoms sat amid lush green fronds the size of elephant ears. Fake, all of it: each petal was porcelain, each leaf was glass.

"Jack, what you're doing simply isn't right."

"In your opinion, Martina." I flipped on the television—a variety show from Veritas called *The Tits and Ass Hour*. "In your private opinion."

"It's ugly, in fact. Wrong and ugly."

"What is? Christmas?"

"Lying to Toby. He wants to know the truth."

"What truth?"

"He's going to die soon."

"He's not going to die soon." I realized Martina meant well, but I still felt betrayed. "Whose side are you on, anyway?"

"Toby's."

I shuddered. "Indeed. Well even if he *is* really, really sick, he certainly shouldn't hear about it."

"He's dying, Jack. He's dying, and he wants someone to be honest with him."

On the TV screen, a toothy woman removed the bikini top of her bathing suit, faced the camera, and said, "Here it is, guys! Here's why you all tuned in!"

I shut off the set. The image imploded to a point of light and vanished. "All this negativism, Martina—you sound like my wife."

"Don't be a coward."

"Coward? *Coward?* No coward would put up with the shit I've been through." I chopped at the nearest plant with the edge of my hand, breaking off a glass frond. "Besides, he doesn't even know what death is. He wouldn't understand."

"He would."

"Let's get something straight. Toby's going to have the greatest Christmas a boy could possibly imagine. Do you understand? The absolute greatest, bar none."

"Fine, Jack. And then . . ."

And then . . .

The truth hit me like something cold, quick, and heavy—a tidal wave or a falling sack of nails. My knees buckled. I dropped to the floor and pounded my fists into the severed frond, shattering it. "This can't be happening," I moaned. I shook like a child being brainburned. "It can't be, it can't be . . ."

"It is."

"I love him so much."

"I know."

"Help me," I cried as I worked the bits of glass into my palms.

"Help Toby," said Martina, bending down and enfolding me with her deep, genuine, useless sympathy.

SEVEN

On the last day of August, at the height of a seething and intractable heat wave, Christmas came to the Center for Creative Wellness. Sleigh bells jangled crisply in the hallway; the triumphant strains of "Hark, the Herald Angels Sing" flowed forth from a portable CD player; the keen verdant odor of evergreen boughs filled the air. I'll never forget the smile that beamed from Toby's dry, cyan face when his friend Saint Nicholas waddled into the room dragging a huge sack, a canvas mass of tantalizing bulges and auspicious bumps.

"Hi, Santa."

"Look, Toby, these are for you!" Sebastian Arboria opened the sack, and the whole glorious lot flowed out, everything I'd told Anthony Raines to bring down from the City of Truth: the plush giraffe and the android clown, the snare drum and the ice skates, the backgammon set and the Steve Carlton baseball glove.

"Wow! Oh, wow!" Bravely, wincingly, Toby tore off his oxygen mask. "For *me*—they're all for *me?*"

"All for you," said Sebastian.

Toby held his stuffed baboon over the edge of the bed. "Look, Barnaby. Look what we got."

An entourage of HEART members appeared, a score of pixies, fairies, elves, and gnomes festooned with holly wreaths and mistletoe sprigs, streaming toward Toby's bed. One of Santa's helpers arrived pushing a hospital gurney on which sat a Happy Land even more elaborate than the layout my niece received after her burn (Toby's included a funhouse and a parachute jump, plus a steam-powered passenger train running around the perimeter). Three other helpers bore an enormous tree—a bushy Scotch pine hung with glassy ornaments, sparkling tinsel, and dormant electric lights, shedding its needles everywhere.

"Hi, everybody—I'm Toby," he mumbled as the helpers patted his naked head. "I've got Xavier's Plague, but I won't die. Children don't die, Dr. Krakower said."

"Of *course* you won't die," said the elf behind the gurney.

A tall pixie in a feather cap, holly necklace, and lederhosen marched toward me. "Anthony Raines," he said. I had anticipated his physiognomy in every particular but one; far from sporting a mustache, his lip was as hairless as a sentient Satirevian stone. "It's a privilege to meet someone of your spiritual intensity, Jack."

A gnome connected plug to socket, and the Christmas tree ignited—a joyous burst, a festive explosion, a spray of fireworks frozen against a green sky. As Toby clapped his hands—an effort that left him breathless and doubled over with pain—the HEART members began caroling.

Oh, Toby, we're so sad
To hear you're feeling bad,
But we can tell
You'll soon be well,
'Cause you're a spunky lad . . .

"Santa, I have a question," said Toby.

"Yes?"

"Did you remember that, er . . . that Power Pony?"

"Power Pony, what Power Pony?" said Sebastian with fabricated distress. He smacked his mittens together. "Oh, yes—the *Power Pony.*"

Hearing her cue, a slender female elf rode into the room on a magnificent chestnut-hued Power Pony, its bridle studded with rubies, its saddle inlaid with hand-tooled cacti, a mane of genuine horsehair spilling down its neck.

"What's his name?" Toby asked.

Sebastian, God bless him, was prepared. "Down on Santa's Power Pony Ranch, we called him Chocolate."

"That's a weird name," said Toby as the machine loped over and nuzzled his cheek. "Look, Dad, I got a brown Power Pony called Chocolate." He coughed and added, "I wanted a black one."

A sharp ache zagged through my belly. "Huh? Black?"

"Black."

"You said brown," I rasped. These final weeks—days, hours—must be perfect. "You definitely said *brown.*"

"I changed my mind."

"Brown's a great color, Toby. It's a *great* color."

Toby combed the pony's mane with his pencil-thin fingers. "I don't think I'll ride him just yet."

"Sure, buddy."

"I think I'll ride him later. I'm tired right now."

"You'll feel better in the morning."

Toby slipped his mask back on. "Could I see how that Happy Land works?"

As Dr. Krakower operated the mattress crank, raising Toby's head and chest and giving him an unobstructed, God's-eye view of Happy

Land, Sebastian twisted the dials on the control panel. The toy lurched to life, the whole swirling, spinning, eternally upbeat world.

"Faster," Toby muttered as the carousel, Ferris wheel, and roller coaster sent their invisible passengers on dizzying treks. "Make them go faster!"

"Here, *you* do it." Sebastian handed my son the control panel.

"Faster . . ." Toby increased the amperage. "Faster, faster . . ." I sensed a trace of innocuous preadolescent sadism in his voice. "Step right up, folks," he said. "Ride the merry-go-round, ride our amazing colossal roller coaster." In his mind, I knew, the Ferris wheel customers were now puking their guts out; the roller coaster was hurtling its patrons into space; the carousel horses had thrown off their riders and were trampling them underfoot. "Step right up."

It was then that I observed an odd phenomenon among Santa and his helpers. Their eyes were leaking. Tears. Yes, *tears*—children's tears.

"What's the matter with everyone?" I asked Martina.

"What do you mean?"

"Their eyes."

"Step right up," said Toby.

Martina regarded me as she might a singularly mute and unintelligent dog. "They're crying."

"I've never seen it before." I pressed my desiccated tear ducts. "Not in grown-ups."

"Ride the parachute jump," said Toby.

"In Satirev," said Martina, "grown-ups cry all the time."

Indeed. I surveyed the gathered grown-ups, their dripping eyes, their wistful smiles, their self-serving grimaces of concern. I surveyed them—and understood them. Yes, no question, they were enjoying this grotesque soap opera. They were loving every minute of it.

Toby was no longer saying, "Step right up." He was no longer saying anything. The only sound coming from him was a low, soft moan, like wind whistling down the Jordan River.

A flurry of grim, efficient movement: Krakower cranking Toby's mattress to a horizontal position, turning on his inhalator, opening the meperidine stopcock. Anthony Raines took my son's knobby hand and gave it a reassuring squeeze.

"Will I see you people again?" asked Toby as the drug soaked into his brain. "Will you come *next* Christmas?"

"Of course."

"Promise?"

"We'll be back, Toby. You bet."

"I don't think there'll be a next Christmas," my son said.

"You mustn't believe that," said Anthony.

I lurched away, staring at the tree ornaments. A Styrofoam snowman held a placard saying GET WELL, TOBY. A ceramic angel waved a banner declaring WE'RE WITH YOU, SON. A plastic icicle skewered an index card reading WITH PAIN COMES WISDOM.

Turning, I tracked a large, silvery tear as it rolled down Santa Claus's cheek. "Of *course* there'll be a next Christmas," I said mechanically.

Toby's blue skin, stretched tight over cheek and jawbone, crinkled when he yawned. "I love Christmas," he said. "I really love it. Will I die today, Santa? I'm so cold."

Sebastian said, "That's no way to talk, Toby."

"You're crying, Santa. You're . . ."

"I'm not crying," said Sebastian, wiping his tears with his mittens.

"Thank you so much, Santa," Toby mumbled, adrift in meperidine. "This was the greatest day of my whole life. I love you, Santa. I wish my Power Pony were black . . ."

My son slept, snoring and wheezing. I turned to Martina. Our gazes met, fused. "Tell them to get out," I said in a quavering voice. Martina frowned. "These HEART vultures," I elaborated. "I want them out. Now."

"I don't think you get it, Jack. They're here for the long haul. They came to—"

"I *know* why they came." They'd come to see my child suffocate; they'd come to revel in the maudlin splendor of his death. "Tell them to leave," I said. "Tell them."

Martina moved among Santa's helpers, explaining that I needed some private time with Toby. They responded like wronged, indignant ten-year-olds: pouty lips, clenched teeth, tight fists. They stomped their feet on the bright yellow floor.

Slowly the HEART filed out, offering me their ersatz support, sprinkling their condolences with Satirevian remarks. "It's a journey, Mr. Sperry, not an ending." "He's entering the next phase of the great cycle." "Reincarnation, we now know, occurs at the exact moment of passing."

As Anthony Raines reached the door, I brushed his holly necklace and said, "Thanks for hunting down those toys."

"We think you're being selfish," he replied snappishly, twisting the feather in his cap. "We've done so much for you, and now you're going to—"

"Cheat you out of his death? Yes, that's perfectly true. I'm going to cheat you."

"I thought you wanted us to synchronize your son's immune system with the cosmic pulse. I thought we were supposed to—"

"I don't believe that business any more," I confessed. "I probably never did. I was lying to myself."

"Let's leave him alone." Sebastian pressed his amplified belly against Anthony. "I don't think he needs us right now."

"Some people are so fickle," said Anthony, following Santa Claus out of the room. "Some people . . ."

At last I was alone, standing amid the grotesquely merry clutter, my ears vibrating with the ominous tom-tom of Toby's inhalator. Christmas tree, Power Pony, Happy Land, plush giraffe, android clown, snare drum, ice skates, backgammon set, Steve Carlton baseball glove—foolish, worthless, impotent; but now, finally, I would give him what he wanted.

Toby awoke at midnight, coughing and shivering, gripped by a 105-degree fever.

The August air was moist, heavy, coagulated; it felt like warm glue. Rising from the cot, I hugged my son, rapped my knuckles on his rocket jockey's oxygen supply, and said, "Buddy, I have something to tell you. Something important."

"Huh?" Toby tightened his grip on Barnaby Baboon.

I chewed my inner cheeks. "About this Xavier's Plague. The thing is, it's a very, very bad disease. Very bad." Pain razored through my tongue as I bit down. "You're not going to get well, Toby. You're simply not."

"I don't understand." His eyes lay deep in their bony canyons;

the brows and lashes had grown sparse, making his stare even larger, sadder, more fearful. "You said Mr. Medicine would fix me."

"I lied."

"Lied? What do you mean?"

"I wanted you to be happy."

"You *lied*? How could you even *do* that?"

"This Satirev—it's different from our old city, very different. If you stay down here long enough, you can learn to say *anything*."

Anger rushed to his face, red blood pounding against blue skin. "But—but Santa Claus brought me a *Power Pony!*"

"I know. I'm sorry, Toby. I'm so terribly, terribly sorry."

"I want to ride my Power Pony!" He wept—wept like the betrayed seven-year-old he was. His tears hit his mask, flowing along the smooth plastic curves. "I want to ride Chocolate!"

"You can't ride him, Toby. I'm so sorry."

"I knew it!" he screamed. "I just *knew* it!"

"How did you know?"

"I *knew* it!"

A protracted, intolerable minute passed, broken by the poundings of the inhalator interlaced with Toby's sobs. He kissed his baboon. He asked, "When?"

"Soon." A hard, gristly knot formed in my windpipe. "Maybe this week."

"You *lied* to me. I hate you. I didn't want Santa to get me a *brown* Power Pony, I wanted a *black* one. I hate you!"

"Don't be mean to me, Toby."

"Chocolate is a *stupid* name for a Power Pony."

"Please, Toby . . ."

"I hate you."

"Why are you being mean to me? Please don't be mean."

Another wordless minute, marked by the relentless throb of the inhalator. "I can't tell you why," he said at last.

"Tell me."

He pulled off his mask. "No."

Absently I unhooked a plaster Wise Man from my son's Christmas tree. "I'm so stupid," I said.

"You're not stupid, Dad." Mucus dribbled from Toby's nose. "What happens after somebody dies?"

"I don't know."

"What do you *think* happens?"

"Well, I suppose everything stops. It just . . . stops."

Toby ran a finger along the sleek rubbery curve of his meperidine tube. "Dad, there's something I never told you. You know my baboon here, Barnaby? He's got Xavier's Plague too."

"Oh? That's sad."

"As a matter of fact, he's *dead* from it. He's completely dead. Barnaby just . . . stopped."

"I see."

"He wants to be buried pretty soon. He's dead. He wants to be buried at sea."

I crushed the Wise Man in my palm. "At sea? Sure, Toby."

"Like in that book we read. He wants to be buried like Corbeau the Pirate."

"Of course."

Toby patted the baboon's corpse. "Can I see Mom before I die? Can I see her?"

"We'll go see Mom tomorrow."

"Are you lying?"

"No."

A smile formed on Toby's fissured lips. "Can I play with Happy Land now?"

"Sure." I closed my eyes so tightly I half expected to push them into my brain. "Do you want to hold the control panel?"

"I don't feel strong enough. I'm so cold. I love you, Dad. I don't hate you. When I'm mean to you, it's for a *reason*."

"What reason?"

"I don't want you to miss me too much."

It would happen to me now, I knew: the tear business. Reaching under his bed, I worked the crank, gradually bringing Toby's vacant gaze within range of his amusement park. Such a self-referential reality, that toy—how like Veritas, I thought, how like Satirev. Anyone who inhabited such a circumscribed world, who actually took up residence, would certainly, in the long run, go mad.

"You won't miss me too much, will you?"

"I'll miss you, Toby. I'll miss you every single minute I'm alive."

"Dad—you're crying."

"You can play with Happy Land as long as you like," I said, operating the dials on the control panel. "I love you so much, Toby." The carousel turned, the Ferris wheel spun, the roller coaster dipped and looped. "I love you so much."

"Faster, Dad. Make them go faster."

And I did.

We spent the morning after Christmas outfitting a litter with the necessities of Xavier's amelioration, turning it into a traveling Center for the Palliative Treatment of Hopeless Diseases: tubing, aluminum stands, oxygen tank, inhalator. Dr. Krakower placed a vial of morphine in our carton of IV bottles, just in case the pain became more than meperidine could handle. "I'd be happy to come with you," she said.

"The truth of the matter," I replied, "is that in a day or two Toby will be dead—am I right? He's beyond medical science."

"You can't put a timetable on these things," said Krakower.

"He'll be dead before the week's out. You might as well stay."

Martina and I carried Toby through Satirev to the Third and Hume storm tunnel, Ira Temple riding close behind on the Power Pony, then came William Bell, dragging my son's Christmas presents in Santa's canvas sack. Toby was so thin the blankets threatened to swallow him whole; his little head, lolling on the pillow, seemed disembodied, a sideshow freak, a Grand Guignol prop. He clutched his stuffed baboon with a strange paternal desperation: Rumpelstiltskin finally gets his baby.

By noon Toby was with his stalwart, Veritasian mother, drooping over her arms like a matador's cape.

"Does he know how sick he is?" she asked me.

"I told him the truth," I admitted.

"This will sound strange, Jack, but . . . I wish he didn't know." Helen gasped in astonishment as a drop of salt water popped from her eye, rolled down her cheek, and hit the floor. "I wish you'd lied to him."

"On the whole, truth is best," I asserted. "That's a tear," I noted.

"Of course it's a tear," Helen replied testily.

"It means—"

"I *know* what it means."

Weeping, we bore Toby to his room and set his marionettelike body on the mattress. "Mom, did you see my Power Pony?" he gasped as William and Ira rigged up his meperidine drip. "Isn't he super? His name's Chocolate."

"It's quite a nice toy," Helen said.

"I'm cold, Mom. I hurt all over."

"This will help," I said, opening the stopcock.

"I got a Happy Land, too. Santa brought it."

Helen's face darkened with the same bewilderment she'd displayed on seeing her tear. "Who?"

"Santa Claus. Saint Nicholas. The fat man who goes around the world giving children toys."

"That doesn't happen, Toby. There is no Santa Claus."

"There *is*. He visited me. Am I going to die, Mom?"

"Yes."

"Forever?"

"Yes. Forever. I'd give almost anything to make you well, Toby. Almost anything."

"I know, Mom. It's . . . all right. I'm . . . tired. So . . . sleepy."

I sensed his mind leaking away, his soul flowing out of him. Don't die, Toby, I thought. Oh, please, please, *don't* . . .

"If you want," said Martina, "I'll watch over him awhile."

"Yes," I replied. "Good."

Stunned, drained, the rest of us wandered into the living room, a space now clogged with terrible particulars, the Power Pony, the plush giraffe, all of it. Helen offered to make some lunch—sliced Edible Cheddar on Respectable Rye—but no one was hungry. Collecting by the picture window, we looked down at the City of Truth. Veritas, the vera-city; curiously, the pun had never occurred to me before.

I followed William and Ira to the elevator, mumbling my incoherent gratitude. Unlike the HEART members, they sympathized tastefully; their melancholy was measured, their tears small and rationed. Only as the elevator door slammed shut did I hear William cry out, "It isn't *fair!*"

Indeed.

I staggered into Toby's room. He shivered as he slept: cold dreams. Helen and Martina stood over him, my wife fidgeting with a glass of Scotch, my onetime lover rooted like a money tree. "Stay," I told Martina. "That's all right, isn't it, Helen? She's Toby's friend."

Instead of answering, Helen simply stared at Martina and said, "You're exactly as I imagined you'd be. I guess you can't help looking like a slut."

"Helen, we're all very upset," I said, "but that sort of talk isn't necessary."

My wife finished her Scotch and slumped onto the floor. "I'm upset," she agreed.

"Toby was so happy to see you," Martina told her. "I'll bet he'll start doing a lot better now that you're with him."

"Don't lie to me, Miss Coventry. I'm sorry I was rude, but—don't lie."

Martina was lying, and yet as evening drew near, Toby indeed seemed to rally. His fever dropped to 101. He began making demands of us—Helen must bring his Power Pony into the room, Martina must tell him the story of Rumpelstiltskin. I suspected that the infusion of familiarity—these precious glimpses of his wallpaper, closet door, postcard collection, and benighted carpentry projects—was having a placebo effect.

Placebos were lies.

While Martina entertained Toby with a facetious retelling of Rumpelstiltskin, a version in which the miller's daughter had to spin belly-button lint into peanut-butter sandwiches, Helen and I made coffee in the kitchen.

"Do you love her?" she asked.

"Martina? No." I didn't. Not any more.

"How can I know if you're telling the truth?"

"You'll have to trust me."

We agreed to keep the marriage going. We sensed we would need each other in the near future: the machinery of grief was new to us, our tears were still foreign and scary.

At five o'clock the next morning, Toby died. During his final hour, Helen and I positioned him on Chocolate and let him pretend to ride. We rocked him back and forth, telling him we loved him. He said it was a great Power Pony. He died in the saddle, like a cowboy. The final cause was asphyxiation, I suppose; his lungs belonged to *Pneu-*

mocystis carinii and not to Veritas's soiled and damaged air. His penultimate word, coughed into the cavity of his mask, was "cold." His last word was "Rumpelstiltskin."

We set him back in bed and tucked Barnaby Baboon under his arm.

Guiding Martina into the hallway, I gave her a good-bye hug. No doubt our paths would cross again, I told her. Perhaps I'd see her at the upcoming Christmas assault on Circumspect Park.

"Your wife loved him," Martina said, pushing the DOWN button.

"More than she knew." *Bong*, the elevator arrived. "I made him happy for a while, didn't I? For a few weeks, he was happy."

Behind Martina, the door slid open. "You made him happy," she said, stepping out of my life.

I shuffled into the kitchen and telephoned my sister.

"I wish my nephew hadn't died," she reported. "Though I will say this—I'm counting my blessings right now: Connie, my good health, my job. Yes, sir, something like this, it really makes you count your blessings."

"Meet us in an hour. Seven Lackluster Lane. Descartes Borough."

Helen and I sealed Toby's corpse in a large-size Tenuous Trash Bag—Barnaby Baboon was part of him now, fastened by rigor mortis—then eased him into Santa's sack. We hauled him onto the elevator, brought him down to street level, and loaded him into the back of my Adequate. As we drove across town, political campaign ads leaped from the radio, including one for Doreen Hutter. "While *one* of my teenage boys is undeniably a drug addict and a car thief," she said, "the *other* spends his after-school hours reading to the blind and . . ."

I pictured Martina writing those lines, scribbling them down in the margins of her doggerel.

Reaching the waterfront district, I pulled up beside the wharf where *Average Josephine* was moored. Boris sat on the foredeck, wrapping duct tape around the fractured handle of a clamming rake, chatting with Gloria and Connie. I fixed on my sister's eyes—dry, obscenely dry—shifted to my niece's—dry.

Thank the alleged God: Boris grasped the situation at once. So Toby wanted to be buried at sea? All right, no problem—the canvas sack would work fine: a few bricks, a few rocks . . .

He brought *Average Josephine* into the channel at full speed, dropping anchor near the north shore, below a sheer cliff pocked with tern rookeries. Wheeling across the water, the birds scolded us fiercely, defending their airy turf like angry, outsized bees.

Boris dragged Santa's sack to the stern and set it on the grubby, algae-coated deck. "I hear you were quite a lad, little Toby," he said, cinching the sack closed with a length of waterproof hemp. "I'm sorry I never knew you."

"Even though you can't hear me, I am at this moment moved to bid you good-bye," said Gloria. "I feel rather guilty about not paying more attention to you."

"The fact of the matter is I'm bored," said Connie. "Not that I didn't *like* Toby. Indeed, I'm somewhat sorry we hardly ever played together."

Boris lifted the Santa sack, balancing it on the transom with his hairy, weatherworn hand.

"I miss you, son," I said. "I miss you so much."

"Quite bored," said Connie.

Boris raised his palm, and the sack lurched toward the water like the aquatic armadillo Toby had caught and freed on the Jordan. As it hit the channel, Helen said, simply, "I love you, Toby." She said it over and over, long after the sack had sunk from view.

"It'll be dark in an hour," Boris told me. "How about we just keep on going?"

"Huh?"

"You know—keep on going. Get out of this crazy city."

"Leave?"

"Think it over."

I didn't need to.

I'm a liar now. I could easily fill these final passages with a disingenuous account of what befell us after we set Gloria and Connie back on shore and returned to the river: our breathless shoot-out with the Brutality Squad, our narrow escape up the inlet, our daring flight to the sea. But the simple fact is that no such melodrama occurred. Through some bright existential miracle we cruised free of Veritas that night without encountering a single police cutter, shore battery, or floating mine.

We've been sailing the broad and stormy Caribbean for nearly four years now, visiting the same landfalls Columbus once touched—Trinidad, Tobago, Barbados—filling up on fruit and fresh water, course uncharted, future unmapped, destination unsettled. We have no wish to root ourselves. At the moment *Average Josephine* is home enough.

My syndrome, I'm told, is normal. The nightmares, the sudden rages, the out-of-context screams, the time I smashed the ship-to-shore radio—all these behaviors, I've heard, are to be expected.

You see, I want him back.

It's getting dark. I'm composing by candlelight, in our gloomy galley, my pen nib scuttling across the page like a cockroach scavenging a greasy fragment of tinfoil. My wife and the clamdigger come in. Boris asks me if I want coffee. I tell him no.

"Hi, Daddy." Little Andrea sits on Helen's shoulders like a yoke.

"Hi, darling," I say. "Will you sing me a song?" I ask my daughter.

Before I destroyed the radio, a startling bit of news came through. I'm still trying to deal with it. Last October, some bright young research chemist at Voltaire University discovered a cure for Xavier's Plague.

Andrea climbs down. "I'd be *deee-lighted* to sing you a song." She's only two and a half, but she talks as well as any four-year-old.

Boris makes himself a cup of Donaldson's Drinkable Coffee.

Out of the blue, Helen asks, "Did you copulate with that woman?"

"With what woman?"

"Martina Coventry. Did you?"

I can answer however I wish. "Why are you asking *now?*"

"Because I want to *know* now. Did you ever . . . ?"

"Yes," I say. "Once. Are you upset?"

"I'm upset," Helen says. "But I'd be more upset if you'd lied."

Andrea scrambles into my lap. Her face, I note with great pleasure, is a perfect conjunction of Helen's features and my own. "'I hide my wings inside my soul,'" she sings, lyrics by Martina Coventry, music by Andrea Sperry.

"'Their feathers soft and dry,'" my daughter and I sing together. Her melody is part lament, part hymn.

Now Helen and Boris join in, as if my Satirevian training has somehow rubbed off on them. The lies cause them no apparent pain.

" 'And when the world's not looking . . .' "

We're in perfect harmony, the four of us. I don't love the lies, I realize as we trill the final line—our cloying denial of gravity—but I don't hate them either.

" 'We take them out and fly,' " we all sing, and even though I'm as wingless as a Veritasian pig, I feel as if I'm finally getting somewhere.

Appendixes

About the Nebula Awards

Throughout every calendar year, the members of the Science-fiction and Fantasy Writers of America read and recommend novels and stories for the annual Nebula Awards. The editor of the "Nebula Awards Report" collects the recommendations and publishes them in the *SFWA Forum*. Near the end of the year, the NAR editor tallies the endorsements, draws up the preliminary ballot, and sends it to all active SFWA members. Under the current rules, each novel and story enjoys a one-year eligibility period from its date of publication. If the work fails to make the preliminary ballot during that interval, it is dropped from further Nebula consideration.

The NAR editor processes the results of the preliminary ballot and then compiles a final ballot listing the five most popular novels, novellas, novelettes, and short stories. For purposes of the Nebula Award, a novel is 40,000 words or more; a novella is 17,500 to 39,999 words; a novelette is 7,500 to 17,499 words; and a short story is 7,499 words or fewer. At the present time, SFWA impanels both a novel jury and a short-fiction jury to oversee the voting process and, in cases where a presumably worthy title was neglected by the membership at large, to supplement the five nominees with a sixth choice. Thus, the appearance of extra finalists in any category bespeaks two distinct processes: jury discretion and ties.

Founded in 1965 by Damon Knight, the Science Fiction Writers of America began with a charter membership of seventy-eight authors. Today it boasts about a thousand members and an augmented name. Early in his tenure, Lloyd Biggle, Jr., SFWA's first secretary-treasurer, proposed that the organization periodically select and publish the year's best stories. This notion quickly evolved into the elaborate balloting process, an annual awards banquet, and a series of Nebula anthologies. Judith Ann Lawrence designed the trophy from a sketch by Kate Wilhelm. It is a block of Lucite containing a rock crystal and a spiral nebula made of metallic glitter. The prize is handmade, and no two are exactly alike.

The Grand Master Nebula Award goes to a living author for a lifetime of achievement. In accordance with SFWA's bylaws, the president nominates a candidate, normally after consulting with previous presidents and the board of directors. This nomination then goes before the officers; if a majority approves, the candidate becomes a Grand Master. Past recipients include Robert A. Heinlein (1974), Jack Williamson (1975), Clifford D. Simak (1976), L. Sprague de Camp (1978), Fritz Leiber (1981), Andre Norton (1983), Arthur C. Clarke (1985), Isaac Asimov (1986), Alfred Bester (1987), Ray Bradbury (1988), and Lester del Rey (1990).

The twenty-eighth annual Nebula Awards Banquet was held at the Holiday Inn Crowne Plaza in New Orleans, Louisiana, on April 17, 1993. Beyond the Nebulas for novel, novella, novelette, and short story, a Grand Master Nebula went to Frederik Pohl, the twelfth SF professional to be so honored.

Selected Titles from the 1992 Preliminary Nebula Ballot

The following lists provide an overview of those works, authors, and periodicals that particularly attracted SFWA's notice during 1992. Finalists and winners are excluded from this catalog, as these are documented in the introduction.

NOVELS

The Modular Man by Roger MacBride Allen (*Analog,* February 1992–May 1992)
The Trinity Paradox by Kevin Anderson and Doug Beason (Bantam)

Mars by Ben Bova (Bantam)
The Phoenix Guards by Steven Brust (Tor)
The Exile Kiss by George Alec Effinger (Doubleday Foundation)
Child of the Light by Janet Gluckman and George Guthridge (St. Martin's Press)
Jumper by Steven Gould (Tor)
Moonwise by Ilene Gilman Greer (Roc)
Mirabile by Janet Kagan (Tor)
The Cipher by Kathe Koja (Abyss/Dell)
Cloven Hoofs by Megan Lindholm (Bantam)
King of Morning, Queen of Day by Ian McDonald (Bantam)
Glass Houses by Laura Mixon (Tor)
The Ragged World by Judith Moffett (St. Martin's Press)
Elvenbane by Andre Norton and Mercedes Lackey (Tor)
Flying in Place by Susan Palwick (Tor)
Last Call by Tim Powers (William Morrow)
The Dark Beyond the Stars by Frank M. Robinson (Tor)
Far-Seer by Robert J. Sawyer (Ace)
Reefsong by Carol Severance (Del Rey)
Kalimantan by Lucius Shepard (St. Martin's Press)
The Grail of Hearts by Susan Shwartz (Tor)
Russian Spring by Norman Spinrad (Bantam)
Shivering World by Kathy Tyers (Bantam)
Stranger Suns by George Zebrowski (Bantam)

NOVELETTES

"The Other Shore" by J. R. Dunn (*Omni*, December 1991)
"Snow on Sugar Mountain" by Elizabeth Hand (*Full Spectrum 3*, Bantam)
"Amerikano Hiaika" by Wil McCarthy (*Aboriginal SF*, May/June 1991)
"Madrelita" by Deborah Wheeler (*Fantasy and Science Fiction*, February 1992)

SHORT STORIES

"The Fabularium" by Ray Aldridge (*Fantasy and Science Fiction,* December 1991)

"Johnny Come Home" by Pat Cadigan (*Omni,* June 1991)

"Nine-Tenths of the Law" by Sue Caspar (*Isaac Asimov's Science Fiction Magazine,* July 1991)

"Extraordinary Measures" by Michael Cassutt (*Fantasy and Science Fiction,* July 1991)

"Division by Zero" by Ted Chiang (*Full Spectrum 3,* Bantam)

"Voices" by Jack Dann (*Omni,* August 1991)

"The Resurrection of Alonso Quijana" by Marcos Donnelly (*Fantasy and Science Fiction,* March 1992)

"Fellow Americans" by Eileen Gunn (*Isaac Asimov's Science Fiction Magazine,* December 1991; *Alternate Presidents,* Tor)

"Hole-in-the-Wall" by Bridget McKenna (*Isaac Asimov's Science Fiction Magazine,* May 1991)

"Peter" by Pat Murphy (*Omni,* February 1991)

"Lotus and Spear" by Mike Resnick (*Isaac Asimov's Science Fiction Magazine,* August 1992)

"Overlays" by Joel Richards (*Isaac Asimov's Science Fiction Magazine,* February 1991)

Past Nebula Award Winners

<u>1965</u>

Best Novel: *Dune* by Frank Herbert

Best Novella: "The Saliva Tree" by Brian W. Aldiss
            "He Who Shapes" by Roger Zelazny (tie)

Best Novelette: "The Doors of His Face, the Lamps of His Mouth" by Roger Zelazny

Best Short Story: " 'Repent, Harlequin!' Said the Ticktockman" by Harlan Ellison

1966

Best Novel: *Flowers for Algernon* by Daniel Keyes
          Babel-17 by Samuel R. Delany (tie)
Best Novella: "The Last Castle" by Jack Vance
Best Novelette: "Call Him Lord" by Gordon R. Dickson
Best Short Story: "The Secret Place" by Richard McKenna

1967

Best Novel: *The Einstein Intersection* by Samuel R. Delany
Best Novella: "Behold the Man" by Michael Moorcock
Best Novelette: "Gonna Roll the Bones" by Fritz Leiber
Best Short Story: "Aye, and Gomorrah" by Samuel R. Delany

1968

Best Novel: *Rite of Passage* by Alexei Panshin
Best Novella: "Dragonrider" by Anne McCaffrey
Best Novelette: "Mother to the World" by Richard Wilson
Best Short Story: "The Planners" by Kate Wilhelm

1969

Best Novel: *The Left Hand of Darkness* by Ursula K. Le Guin
Best Novella: "A Boy and His Dog" by Harlan Ellison
Best Novelette: "Time Considered as a Helix of Semi-Precious
    Stones" by Samuel R. Delany
Best Short Story: "Passengers" by Robert Silverberg

1970

Best Novel: *Ringworld* by Larry Niven
Best Novella: "Ill Met in Lankhmar" by Fritz Leiber
Best Novelette: "Slow Sculpture" by Theodore Sturgeon
Best Short Story: no award

1971

Best Novel: *A Time of Changes* by Robert Silverberg
Best Novella: "The Missing Man" by Katherine MacLean
Best Novelette: "The Queen of Air and Darkness" by Poul Anderson
Best Short Story: "Good News from the Vatican" by Robert Silverberg

1972

Best Novel: *The Gods Themselves* by Isaac Asimov
Best Novella: "A Meeting with Medusa" by Arthur C. Clarke
Best Novelette: "Goat Song" by Poul Anderson
Best Short Story: "When It Changed" by Joanna Russ

1973

Best Novel: *Rendezvous with Rama* by Arthur C. Clarke
Best Novella: "The Death of Doctor Island" by Gene Wolfe
Best Novelette: "Of Mist, and Grass, and Sand" by Vonda N. McIntyre
Best Short Story: "Love Is the Plan, the Plan Is Death" by James Tiptree, Jr.
Best Dramatic Presentation: *Soylent Green*

1974

Best Novel: *The Dispossessed* by Ursula K. Le Guin
Best Novella: "Born with the Dead" by Robert Silverberg
Best Novelette: "If the Stars Are Gods" by Gordon Eklund and Gregory Benford
Best Short Story: "The Day Before the Revolution" by Ursula K. Le Guin
Best Dramatic Presentation: *Sleeper*
Grand Master: Robert A. Heinlein

1975

Best Novel: *The Forever War* by Joe Haldeman
Best Novella: "Home Is the Hangman" by Roger Zelazny

Best Novelette: "San Diego Lightfoot Sue" by Tom Reamy
Best Short Story: "Catch That Zeppelin!" by Fritz Leiber
Best Dramatic Presentation: *Young Frankenstein*
Grand Master: Jack Williamson

1976

Best Novel: *Man Plus* by Frederik Pohl
Best Novella: "Houston, Houston, Do You Read?" by James Tiptree, Jr.
Best Novelette: "The Bicentennial Man" by Isaac Asimov
Best Short Story: "A Crowd of Shadows" by Charles L. Grant
Grand Master: Clifford D. Simak

1977

Best Novel: *Gateway* by Frederik Pohl
Best Novella: "Stardance" by Spider and Jeanne Robinson
Best Novelette: "The Screwfly Solution" by Raccoona Sheldon
Best Short Story: "Jeffty Is Five" by Harlan Ellison
Special Award: *Star Wars*

1978

Best Novel: *Dreamsnake* by Vonda N. McIntyre
Best Novella: "The Persistence of Vision" by John Varley
Best Novelette: "A Glow of Candles, a Unicorn's Eye" by Charles L. Grant
Best Short Story: "Stone" by Edward Bryant
Grand Master: L. Sprague de Camp

1979

Best Novel: *The Fountains of Paradise* by Arthur C. Clarke
Best Novella: "Enemy Mine" by Barry Longyear
Best Novelette: "Sandkings" by George R. R. Martin
Best Short Story: "giANTS" by Edward Bryant

1980

Best Novel: *Timescape* by Gregory Benford
Best Novella: "The Unicorn Tapestry" by Suzy McKee Charnas
Best Novelette: "The Ugly Chickens" by Howard Waldrop
Best Short Story: "Grotto of the Dancing Deer" by Clifford D. Simak

1981

Best Novel: *The Claw of the Conciliator* by Gene Wolfe
Best Novella: "The Saturn Game" by Poul Anderson
Best Novelette: "The Quickening" by Michael Bishop
Best Short Story: "The Bone Flute" by Lisa Tuttle°
Grand Master: Fritz Leiber

1982

Best Novel: *No Enemy But Time* by Michael Bishop
Best Novella: "Another Orphan" by John Kessel
Best Novelette: "Fire Watch" by Connie Willis
Best Short Story: "A Letter from the Clearys" by Connie Willis

1983

Best Novel: *Startide Rising* by David Brin
Best Novella: "Hardfought" by Greg Bear
Best Novelette: "Blood Music" by Greg Bear
Best Short Story: "The Peacemaker" by Gardner Dozois
Grand Master: Andre Norton

1984

Best Novel: *Neuromancer* by William Gibson
Best Novella: "PRESS ENTER ■" by John Varley
Best Novelette: "Bloodchild" by Octavia E. Butler
Best Short Story: "Morning Child" by Gardner Dozois

° This Nebula Award was declined by the author.

1985

Best Novel: *Ender's Game* by Orson Scott Card
Best Novella: "Sailing to Byzantium" by Robert Silverberg
Best Novelette: "Portraits of His Children" by George R. R. Martin
Best Short Story: "Out of All Them Bright Stars" by Nancy Kress
Grand Master: Arthur C. Clarke

1986

Best Novel: *Speaker for the Dead* by Orson Scott Card
Best Novella: "R & R" by Lucius Shepard
Best Novelette: "The Girl Who Fell into the Sky" by Kate Wilhelm
Best Short Story: "Tangents" by Greg Bear
Grand Master: Isaac Asimov

1987

Best Novel: *The Falling Woman* by Pat Murphy
Best Novella: "The Blind Geometer" by Kim Stanley Robinson
Best Novelette: "Rachel in Love" by Pat Murphy
Best Short Story: "Forever Yours, Anna" by Kate Wilhelm
Grand Master: Alfred Bester

1988

Best Novel: *Falling Free* by Lois McMaster Bujold
Best Novella: "The Last of the Winnebagos" by Connie Willis
Best Novelette: "Schrödinger's Kitten" by George Alec Effinger
Best Short Story: "Bible Stories for Adults, No. 17: The Deluge" by
   James Morrow
Grand Master: Ray Bradbury

1989

Best Novel: *The Healer's War* by Elizabeth Ann Scarborough
Best Novella: "The Mountains of Mourning" by Lois McMaster
   Bujold

Best Novelette: "At the Rialto" by Connie Willis
Best Short Story: "Ripples in the Dirac Sea" by Geoffrey Landis

1990

Best Novel: *Tehanu: The Last Book of Earthsea* by Ursula K. Le Guin
Best Novella: "The Hemingway Hoax" by Joe Haldeman
Best Novelette: "Tower of Babylon" by Ted Chiang
Best Short Story: "Bears Discover Fire" by Terry Bisson
Grand Master: Lester del Rey

1991

Best Novel: *Stations of the Tide* by Michael Swanwick
Best Novella: "Beggars in Spain" by Nancy Kress
Best Novelette: "Guide Dog" by Mike Conner
Best Short Story: "Ma Qui" by Alan Brennert

Those who are interested in category-related awards should also consult *A History of the Hugo, Nebula, and International Fantasy Awards* by Donald Franson and Howard DeVore (Misfit Press, 1987). Periodically updated, the book is available from Howard DeVore, 4705 Weddel, Dearborn, Michigan 48125.

Permissions Acknowledgments